VI KEELAND

The Spark
Edited by: Jessica Royer Ocken
Proofreading by: Elaine York, Julia Griffis
Cover Model: Alessandro Dellisola
Photographer: Jakub Koziel
Cover designer: Sommer Stein, Perfect Pear Creative
Formatting, Elaine York, Allusion Publishing,
www.allusionpublishing.com

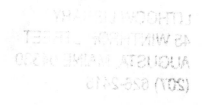

THE
SPARK

1

Autumn

I'm definitely getting too old for this.

I tossed a pile of mail on the couch and plopped down beside it. It was barely six o'clock, and I wouldn't have minded climbing into bed and calling it a day. I needed a vacation from my four-day mini vacation. Thank goodness I'd scheduled myself a weekend to recover. My girls' trip/ early bachelorette party in Vegas for my friend Anna—the one where we were all going to relax by the pool and get spa treatments—had turned into all-night clubbing and almost missing my flight home earlier today because I'd overslept. It had definitely been a while since I drank more than two glasses of wine in the span of a week, and I was feeling my ripe old age of twenty-eight before the sun had even set this Friday night. Thank God I didn't have to work tomorrow.

I briefly considered going the hair-of-the-dog route and sucking back a vodka cran while zoning out on Netflix, but then my phone rang, crashing me back to reality.

Ugh...

1

Dad flashed on the screen. I should've just gotten it over with and spoken to him, but I didn't have the energy. Nonetheless, allowing myself to avoid the stress speaking to my father would inevitably cause reminded me of the other thing I needed to do that I'd been avoiding all afternoon. *Laundry.* One of my least-favorite tasks—mostly because it required me to sit downstairs in my building's dingy basement laundry room. Up until a few months ago, I would start my laundry and come back forty-five minutes later to make the switch to the dryer. But that practice had come to a halt after one of my loads went missing—an entire load of wet bras and underwear. Who the hell stole wet clothes? At least nab dry ones. Nevertheless, it was an expensive lesson, and now I didn't leave the basement until my clothes were washed and dried.

Sighing, I begrudgingly went to the bedroom, where my suitcase still sat on the bed, and unzipped it. I'd packed a linen skirt on top that I hadn't wound up wearing, and I figured I'd hang it in the bathroom and hope the wrinkles worked themselves out over the course of a couple of steamy showers. I hated ironing almost as much as I hated doing laundry downstairs.

But when I flipped open the top of the suitcase, my linen skirt wasn't on top. At first I thought my bag must've been selected for search, and things hadn't been put back in order... Though the wingtip shoe I lifted was most definitely not mine.

Shit.

I rummaged through the suitcase in a panic.

Slacks, running clothes, a men's dress shirt... A sickening feeling washed over me, and I scrambled to look at the luggage tag. I'd never filled out the identification card inside, but the leather had my initials embossed on the outside.

2

And this one...had no initials.

Crap. Crap. Crap.

I'd grabbed the wrong bag off the luggage carousel. I started to sweat. All of my makeup was in that bag! Not to mention a week's worth of my best outfits and shoes. I needed to get it back. Rushing to the kitchen, I grabbed my cell from the charger on the counter and Googled the number for the airline. After wading through a half-dozen prompts, I reached a recording.

"Thank you for calling American Airlines. Due to unprecedented call volume, your estimated wait time is approximately forty-one minutes."

Forty-one minutes! I blew out a rush of air. *Great. Just great.*

In the meantime, while I waited on hold on speakerphone, listening to staticky music, it hit me that whoever's luggage I had might very well have mine. I hadn't even checked the luggage tag to see if, unlike mine, the identification information was filled in.

I zipped back down the hall to my bedroom.

Bingo!

Donovan Decker—kind of a cool name. And he lived here in the city! Thankfully, Donovan even had his phone number listed. *It couldn't be that easy, could it?* I doubted it, but considering I still had forty minutes before I could speak to someone at the airline, I wasn't losing much for trying. So I swiped to end my call. I started to punch in the numbers on the tag, and then decided to hit *67 first to make my number private. With my luck, the guy wouldn't have my luggage, but he'd be a total creeper.

I was caught off guard when a man's deep voice answered on the first ring. I hadn't yet figured out what I was going to say.

"Uhhh. Hi. My name is Autumn, and I think I might have your luggage."

"That was quick. I just hung up with you guys two minutes ago."

He must've thought I was calling from the airline. "Oh, no. I don't work for American. I traveled home this morning and must've grabbed the wrong bag at JFK."

"What are your initials?"

"My initials?"

"Yeah, you know, the first letter of your first name and the first letter of your last name."

I rolled my eyes. "I know what initials are. I just don't understand why you would ask—*Oh!* Does that mean you have my luggage? I have my initials embossed on the luggage tag."

"That depends on what your initials are, Autumn. The first letter matches."

"My initials are AW."

"Well, then it seems you are indeed the thief who clipped my luggage."

Sure, I hadn't checked my luggage tag, but it offended me that he was calling me a thief. "Wouldn't we both be thieves? Since you're in possession of *my* luggage?"

"I only took yours because it was the last one left rotating around the carousel. You see, unlike you, *I* checked the luggage tag the first time it passed, and when I saw it wasn't mine, I left it for the rightful owner to claim. But the line at baggage customer service was twenty deep, and I had a meeting I was already late for. So I took the one I have hostage until the airline could sort it out."

My shoulders slumped. "Oh. Sorry."

"It's fine. Are you here in the City?"

"I am. Could we possibly meet to swap bags?"

"Sure. When and where? I'm out now, but I'll be back in an hour or two."

The tag had an address on the Upper East Side, but I lived on the West Side, farther downtown. "Could we meet at the Starbucks on 80th and Lex?" That was closer to him, but at least I'd only have to drag the suitcase onto one subway.

"I can't think of any *excuse* not to. What time?"

That was sort of a weird way to phrase a yes, and the way he emphasized the word *excuse* seemed odd. But hey, I was getting my bag back. So what if he turned out to be a little strange? At least I'd hidden my phone number, and we were meeting in a public place.

"How about eight?"

"I'll see you then."

It sounded like he was about to hang up. "Wait..." I said. "How will I know it's you?"

"I'll be the one holding your luggage, Autumn W."

I chuckled. "Oh, yeah. Sorry...long week in Vegas."

I bent and lifted the shoe from the top of the bag. Ferragamo. *Expensive.* And big, too. A quick peek revealed it was a size thirteen. The inner teenager in me couldn't help but think *big feet, big....* Plus, the guy had a deep, sexy voice. I would definitely be exploring more of the dude's luggage after we hung up.

"I'll meet you at eight," he said.

"See you then." I was just about to swipe my phone off when something hit me. *Oh God!* "Hello? *Wait*...are you still there?"

It took a heartbeat or two, but the sexy voice came back on the line. "What's up?"

"Ummm... Did you...open my bag?"

"I unzipped it at the airport to make sure it wasn't mine when I noticed the luggage tag initials."

"Did you...see anything?"

"There was a pink thong on top, so that pretty much sealed the deal that it didn't belong to me. But I didn't rummage through, if that's what you're asking."

I forgot I'd shoved that thong in at the last minute. It had been at the back of a drawer when I'd checked the hotel room one last time on my way out. But I'd take him seeing my underwear over *the other* stuff inside my bag. I blew out a sigh of relief. "Okay, that's great. Thank you. I'll see you at eight at Starbucks."

"Whoa. Hang on a second—not so fast. You sounded pretty nervous that I might've gone through your bag. Are you hiding something sinister in there? I'm not going to be walking around with a suitcase full of drugs or something, am I?"

I cracked a smile. "No, definitely not. I just...I'd prefer if you didn't go through it."

"Did you rummage through mine?"

I glanced at the shoe in my hand. Taking out one measly piece of footwear wouldn't be considered rummaging, right? *Nah.* "No, I didn't."

"Are you planning on it?" he asked.

I had no idea what the man looked like, yet I could tell by his voice that he was smiling now.

"Nope," I lied.

"Alright. Then we have a deal. I won't go through your bag, and you won't go through mine."

"Okay. Thank you."

"Do I have your word on that, Autumn W? I might have some things I'd prefer you didn't see in there."

"Like what?"

He chuckled. "See you at eight."

After we hung up, I tossed the shoe back into the suitcase and bent to close it. But as I reached for the zipper, my curiosity got the best of me. Was he just screwing with me, or did he really have something in here he didn't want me to see? Of course, I knew what I had in mine, which made me extra curious.

I shook my head and started to pull the zipper closed. About halfway, I laughed out loud. Who was I kidding? Now that I didn't have laundry to do, I had almost a full two hours to kill before I met Mr. Bigfoot. This suitcase would taunt me all that time. I'd most certainly give in eventually, so why not put myself out of that misery and just take a little look-see inside now? Then I'd be able to relax. He'd never know I hadn't lived up to my end of the bargain. Not to mention, for all I knew, he was elbow deep in *my* suitcase right now. In that case, it would only be fair that I got to go through his, right?

I nibbled my lip for a few seconds as a wave of guilt washed over me. But I quickly forced that out of my mind. *Of course I'm right.*

Feeling justified now, I unzipped the suitcase and took a minute to mentally note how everything was packed: a white dress shirt was folded on top, and two shoes were set on either side, heels facing up. I carefully unpacked those and placed them on the bed next to the suitcase in the same order. The next layer had more folded clothes: two expensive dress shirts, a pair of sweats, boxer briefs, and a few T-shirts, one of which had something emblazoned on the front—familiar lettering that began HA—so I unfolded it to see what it said. *Harvard Law.*

Ugh. *One of those.* No wonder he could afford Ferragamo shoes.

Underneath the pile of clothes was a white laundry bag—the kind a hotel gives you to put your dry cleaning in, but most people used it to separate their dirty clothes. With no desire to sort through smelly socks, I started to fold the clothes back into the suitcase, feeling a twinge of disappointment. But when I smoothed out the layers of the pile, I felt something lumpy and hard underneath in the plastic laundry bag. So I took the clothes back out and looked inside, hoping to find...I'm not sure what. Though what I found was definitely not what I expected.

The bag was filled with at least twenty or thirty of those little shampoo bottles hotels give out. Actually, a closer inspection revealed some were conditioner and a few were moisturizer. Buried on the very bottom were also three little sewing kits and half-a-dozen toothbrushes wrapped in plastic—the kind you could get at the front desk of a hotel when you forgot yours.

What the heck had Mr. Bigfoot done? Rob a housekeeping cart? This kind of stuff, though a lesser quantity, is what you'd usually find in my suitcase since I was broke all the time. But it wasn't the type of thing you'd expect in the suitcase of a man who had gone to Harvard and wore seven-hundred-dollar dress shoes.

Now I was even more curious to meet Donovan Decker.

I arrived at Starbucks almost twenty minutes early, so I went online to treat myself to a flat white with honey almond milk. Even ordering it had me salivating, thinking about the sweet, creamy drink. Expensive coffee was my indulgence, but it didn't happen too often with the five-dollar price tag and my skimpy budget.

I stood at the end of the counter, waiting for my drink and mindlessly scrolling on my phone, when a man walking through the front door caught my attention.

Oh, wow.

Now that was one good-looking man. Describing him as merely tall, dark, and handsome didn't cut it, not by a mile. Jet-black hair framed a magnificent face with a chiseled, masculine bone structure, full lips, and a

Romanesque nose. I wasn't the only one to notice, either. I watched as the Adonis took a step back outside to hold the door open for a woman exiting the store, and the poor lady caught one glimpse of him and literally tripped over her own feet.

Seemingly oblivious that he'd caused the incident, he extended a hand to help her up, flashed a killer smile, and strolled inside. His bright blue eyes scanned the room, stopping right on my ogling ones. Embarrassed at being caught, I quickly diverted my attention back to my phone. A few seconds later, I was still pretending to be enraptured by my screen when footsteps came to a halt in front of me. I glanced up and blinked a few times. The guy from the door flashed a crooked smile.

"Were you able to control yourself?"

My forehead wrinkled. "Excuse me?"

His eyes danced with mirth, and his voice lowered. "I bet you couldn't."

I stared at him for an awkward moment before finally shaking my head. "What on Earth are you talking about?"

The man's brows furrowed. "We made a deal, remember? I wouldn't go through yours, if you didn't touch mine?"

I'd watched the man walk in, stood right in front of him staring for at least a solid minute, and it took until *now* for me to notice he had something in his hand.

"Oh my God. You have my suitcase!"

He laughed but still looked perplexed. "What did you think I was talking about?"

"I...I don't know. I was thoroughly confused."

"I thought you saw me walk in."

I did. But I hadn't made it past your face. "No, I hadn't noticed. Sorry. I guess I was just zoning out."

The barista behind the counter yelled my name. I was glad for an excuse to put some distance between this guy

9

and me. I needed a moment to gather my wits. Though when I returned, I still felt a little off-kilter.

"Thank you for meeting me to swap suitcases," I said. "I'm really sorry I took the wrong one."

"No problem."

I rolled his case forward and released the handle. But the Adonis didn't do the same. In fact, he pulled my bag closer to his side.

"Before we switch..." He tilted his head and studied my face. "I'm curious to know if you kept your word."

I mimicked his pose and tilted my head. "What if I say I didn't?"

"Well, then you'd have to pay a penalty for violating the terms of our deal."

I raised a brow, intrigued. "A penalty?"

He nodded. "That's right. There's a penalty."

I laughed as I lifted my coffee for a sip. "I just got back from a girls' weekend in Vegas. Pretty sure this overpriced drink just used up the last five dollars in my bank account."

"I wasn't referring to a monetary penalty."

"What kind of a penalty, then?"

He stroked the stubble on his chin for a moment. "You'd have to have coffee with me."

Did this guy really think that would be a hardship? I debated how to answer. If I told the truth, it would be embarrassing. I mean, I went through the man's personal belongings. But the flipside was I'd get to check him out some more over coffee. Then again, I'd be agreeing to spend time with a complete stranger. Though...whenever I met a guy online, I usually met him at a coffeehouse, and I probably knew more about this guy after going through his suitcase than I would from an online chat. Not to mention, none of my online dates had looked like Donovan Decker lately. In fact, none had made it further than coffee in a while.

Adonis had been watching my face as I debated my answer. His smirk made me think he already knew I'd checked out his bag. So, what the hell?

I stood tall and met his stare. "Was the lady from housekeeping harmed in the robbery?"

His eyes narrowed for a heartbeat, but then a giant smile spread across his face. He held his hand out toward the seating area. "After you, Autumn W."

2

Donovan

Almost 10 months later

"This is ludicrous. They searched my home—turned it upside down and didn't even clean up before they left. And they took my property with them. What are you doing about it?"

"I warned you I thought this was imminent," I said. "Did you do what I instructed you to do last week?"

"Yes."

My client's right eyelid twitched. This fucker would never be able to take the stand. I'd met him three times before today, for the sum total of maybe six hours, and I already knew his right eyelid had a tic when he lied. Not to mention, he was about thirty seconds away from taking a dirty hanky out of his pocket and wiping the sweat beading up on his ruddy forehead.

I sighed and looked over at the woman sitting next to him. She smiled with a twinkle in her eye. What a joke. I bet I could tell Warren Alfred Bentley's twenty-five-year-old fiancée that I needed to discuss my strategy with her in private and bend her over my desk. Not that I had any interest in that shit. Gold-diggers were definitely not my thing.

"Warren..." I glanced between the spoiled, sixty-year-old money manager and his platinum-haired princess once more and nodded toward the door. "Perhaps you and I should speak privately."

"Anything you have to say to me, you can say in front of Ginger."

"Actually, that's not exactly the way it works. Ginger isn't your wife, and—"

He interrupted me. "She's my fiancée. What's the difference?"

Didn't he at least watch *Law & Order*, for fuck's sake? "A fiancée can be compelled to testify; a wife cannot."

He shook his head. "Ginger would never do that."

Sure she wouldn't. It would take the prosecutor ten minutes of threatening to charge her as an accomplice before she rolled on your saggy old ass. But I had to play along with the game—at least in front of this woman.

"I'm sure she wouldn't. But attorney-client privilege not only protects you, it also protects Ginger. You want to make sure the DA can't come sniffing around the future Mrs. Bentley, don't you?"

"Of course."

"Then why don't I have my assistant make Ginger a cappuccino from the new machine we just put in the guest lounge. Everyone's been raving about it." *For the dumb twenty-grand price tag I heard they paid for a machine that makes coffee with some frothed milk, the thing better make a decent cup of Joe.*

Warren looked to Ginger, who nodded, and he grumbled, "Fine."

"I'll just be a minute." I stood and walked around my desk, extending my hand for Ginger to go ahead of me. "Right this way."

My assistant wasn't at her desk, so I showed the trophy fiancée to the lounge and promised to send Amelia in as soon as she returned. As I turned away, Ginger grabbed my elbow. She wrapped her arms around my neck and moved in for a hug before I could stop her.

"Thank you very much, Mr. Decker. I'm so worried about Warren."

Her hard tits pressed against my chest. They must've been a new purchase and hadn't had time to soften.

I politely disentangled myself and backed away. "No thank you needed. I'm just doing what I'm paid to do."

Back in my office, I figured it was time to get real with my client. I took off my suit jacket and tossed it on the guest chair next to Warren before settling back in at my desk and rolling up my shirtsleeves—something I rarely did because it exposed more ink on my forearms than most of my rich, hobnob clients were comfortable with.

"So...Mr. Bentley. We don't know each other that well yet, but there are two things you should know about me. One, when you ask me for advice, you're going to get it. Often that means you won't like what I have to say, but I'm not paid to tell you what you want to hear. I'm not your friend or your lackey. I'm your lawyer—and the best one you're going to find. Since you're sitting on the other side of my desk and not somewhere else, I'm going to assume you already know that because you've asked around. So don't ask me a question and expect a tiptoe answer. You pay me by the hour. Therefore, I won't be wasting any of your time blowing smoke up your ass. You'll get the answer you need—but like I said, it won't always be the answer you want."

I took a breath. I could see he was about to interrupt me, so I put my hand up. "Please excuse me, but I'm going to keep going here, so we can get on the same page. The second thing you need to know about me is that I'm very good at reading people. In fact, that's the biggest reason I'm able to charge twelve-hundred dollars an hour. Often this skill I have works to your advantage. I know when a prosecutor is bluffing and when a jury is or isn't working in my favor and it's time to cut a deal. But often that same skill can be a disadvantage for you—because I also will usually know when you're lying. And I won't work with a client who isn't truthful with me. If I can't trust you, how do you expect me to get a jury to trust you? So if I catch you lying to me on a frequent basis, I will fire you as a client."

Warren's face bloomed crimson. "Now wait a minute. I'll have you know—"

I cut him off. "I'm aware you're a member of the same country club as one of the senior partners. This isn't the first time I've had a client who runs in the same social circle as members of this firm. And it also wouldn't be the first time I've fired a client who has those types of connections. Yes, Dale or Rupert will be unhappy with me, but at the end of the day, I make them millions a year, and you don't. So they'll get over it. You, on the other hand, will not. Because the government's case against you is all but airtight. And when you have to go down the street to another firm and another attorney, you'll be doing twenty-five years, because I'm the only shot you have at beating this, Mr. Bentley. Some may call me arrogant for saying that, but I don't really give a flying fuck. Because while I may be that...it's also the God's honest truth."

I sat back in my chair and had a little staring contest with Mr. Bentley. He was pissed—I'm sure it had been decades since anyone spoke to him that way. And right this moment, he was currently mulling over firing me. But in the end, the people who find themselves sitting on the other side of my desk, the people who get involved in complicated, crooked schemes that get them in hot water? They aren't dumb. They're intelligent. Very much so. And they love their freedom. So most have done their homework before they step one foot through my door, and they know I'm their best shot at keeping said freedom.

From here, now that I'd given my little speech, we'd play a game of chicken. The first man who spoke lost.

Three or four minutes ticked by—which is a long-ass time to sit and stare at a man in silence—but eventually Warren caved.

He leaned forward and rested his hands on his knees. "Fine. What's our next move?"

I spent the next forty-five minutes going over strategy. He wasn't happy when I told him he likely wouldn't be able to post bail once the feds froze his assets. But we were still early in the game, so he was at least partially in denial—thinking his friends and business associates would come to the rescue.

Maybe they'd show for fifty-grand bail, but his was going to be seven figures.

When we were done and had a game plan, my client blew out a deep breath.

"How long do I have before they arrest me?"

"A day—two, tops."

"What do I do until then?"

I held his eyes. "You sure you want my advice on that?"

He frowned, but nodded.

"Go home, Mr. Bentley. Call in a private chef to make your favorite meal and then fuck your hot fiancée. Because your assets will be frozen by morning, and once that happens? She'll be hocking that rock on her finger to pay for a first-class ticket back to wherever she came from."

"May I see your ID, please?"

I leaned back in my chair and smirked at my friend across the table.

"Fuck off," Trent grumbled while pulling his license out of his wallet. He hadn't even looked up to see my face, yet he knew I was enjoying the moment.

The waitress perused his ID and handed it back to him. This routine was a pretty frequent occurrence. Trent Fuller was thirty but didn't look a day over eighteen. I'd never seen him with facial hair, and we'd gone to bachelor-party benders that lasted four days in New Orleans.

I smiled at our server. "He's late hitting puberty. You want to see mine?"

"It's okay. You look over twenty-one."

"You sure? Not even to take a peek at my address, in case you're in the neighborhood?"

The waitress blushed. I was teasing, though she was pretty, albeit a little young for me.

"I'll be back with your drinks in a minute."

Trent grabbed a breadstick from the middle of the table and crunched into it.

"Who was the hot blonde I saw you walk out to reception with her father this afternoon?"

"The old dude is her fiancé, not her father. But if you're interested, I'm pretty sure she's going to be in the market for another sucker pretty soon. My client is about to lose a bunch of the assets that make him so handsome."

"Damn. We never get women who look like that in the intellectual property division."

"You want to run with the big dogs, you gotta learn to pee in the tall grass."

Trent's face wrinkled. "What the hell does that even mean?"

I chuckled. "No idea. How'd things go with the woman you managed not to scare off a few weeks ago?"

My buddy and I went out for happy hour or dinner once or twice a month. We both worked eighty hours a week at the firm, so free time wasn't something we had in droves.

Trent frowned. "I took her out to dinner at a really nice restaurant. Left her a message the next day to say I had a good time, and she's not returning my calls."

"Did you entertain her during the meal with your usual riveting conversation about copyrights and patents?"

"Fuck off."

I laughed. I was kidding, of course. Trent was actually a pretty funny guy. He was witty and smart. It was totally her loss, but I'd never admit that to him.

"How about you?" he said. "How did things go with the brunette you met? She seemed really nice."

"Gone. Failed test two."

He shook his head. "You and your ridiculous tests. When was the last time someone made it past two?"

The waitress came and delivered Trent's wine and my beer before disappearing again. I knew exactly the last time a woman had made it past my so-called ridiculous tests. Though I didn't need to mention it had been a while, just to help prove my friend's point.

He prodded. "Seriously, how long?"

"I don't know..."

"You do too know. You remember shit you heard in the womb, Decker." He shook his head. "It was the luggage woman, wasn't it? The redhead you spent the weekend with who pulled the disappearing act on Monday morning. What was her name again? Summer?"

I took a long draw from my beer. "Autumn."

It had been ten months since I walked into that coffee shop to swap luggage, and three days less than that since

I'd last seen her. We'd met to exchange luggage and wound up sitting in Starbucks until it closed. After, we went out to dinner, then back to my place later when we shut down the restaurant. *Autumn W.* I'd even blown off a day of work after she ditched me, the first time I'd done that since I started at Kravitz, Polk and Hastings seven years ago.

We'd barely slept the entire weekend, even though we hadn't had actual sex. Another first for me—spending three nights with a woman I wasn't sleeping with. Yet I'd never been so wired about meeting someone in my life, and I'd *thought* the feeling was mutual. Which was why I'd been shocked as shit when I got out of the shower Monday morning and found an empty apartment. No note. No number. I'd never even gotten her last name. The only thing I had to go on was a folded-up piece of paper, an odd list I'd forgotten to stick back into her luggage when I'd rummaged through it. I still had it folded in my wallet at this very moment. Yet another thing I wouldn't be mentioning to Trent.

"You do know why you couldn't find anything wrong with that one, right?" Trent sipped his wine. "Because she blew you off. If she hadn't, you would've found some test for her to fail. Maybe what you need to do is add *not blowing me off* to your list of tests. That way you aren't pining after a woman who ghosted you. What happened with the one you met at McGuire's last week, anyway?"

"We went out to dinner the next night...no red flags. So I asked her if she liked hockey. She said she was a big fan and came over to watch the game the next day. Played with her phone the entire first period. She didn't even know how many *quarters* were in the game."

"You know, you think it's a problem that she stretched the truth a little. But I think her telling you she liked hockey was a good thing. It shows she's willing to compromise and sit around while you watch a game just to spend some time with you. Does she have to love sports and watch every minute?"

"No, not at all. But when I asked her if she liked hockey, her response was, 'I love it. Watch it all the time.' That's a consistency problem right there. If what she says and what she does are inconsistent off the bat, that's a red flag." I sucked back my beer. "Plus, the next day, she sent me a picture of her tits."

Trent shook his head. "Only you would count that as a strike against a woman."

No naked selfies for at least a month. Even if I ask for them. Now, I realize that asking for something and then holding that against a woman who gives it to me might make me an asshole, but it is what it is.

I shook my head. "I like naked selfies as much as the next guy. But if a woman is sending you one when you've known her less than a week—that's a big red flag."

"Whatever. I'll take a naked selfie whenever a woman wants to send it."

I smirked. "The problem with that is the only women you attract are ones who look your age, so it's considered child pornography."

"Dickhead."

As usual, our conversation shifted from our pathetic social life to sports before it eventually landed back on the firm. We could talk shit about that place for days. But lately our focus had been on whether I'd make partner.

"So how's the vote tally going?" Trent asked.

I was up against some stiff competition. Once every five years, our firm opened the partnership doors to two of its best-performing associates. The average time on the partnership track was ten to twelve years. I'd been with Kravitz, Polk and Hastings for just shy of seven when old man Kravitz told me I was up for consideration a few months ago. If I made the cut this year, I'd be the youngest person to make partner in the firm's history—something I really wanted. Being the first to break that record meant more to me than the extra money I'd be pulling in. I already didn't have enough time to spend all the cash I made.

"I think I only need Rotterdam and Dickson to get the two-thirds I need."

"The Dick should be easy to bag. He's in your division."

"I know. But he hasn't presented his bare ass for me to kiss lately. I also just found out that if he votes for me and I make partner, I'd be breaking *his* record. He made partner in eight years."

"Shit. Well, you better hope his ego is smaller than yours, then."

"Don't remind me."

It was almost eleven o'clock by the time we left the restaurant. On our way out, my phone buzzed. I looked at the caller ID and shook my head. "Speak of the devil."

"Who is it?"

"The Dick."

"It's pretty late for him to be calling, isn't it?"

"Yeah, no shit. Guess puckering up doesn't have a quitting time." I swiped to answer. "Donovan Decker."

"Decker. I need a favor."

"Of course. What's up, boss?" I pumped my closed fist up and down in the universal whacking off motion as Trent looked my way.

"I need you to pick up another pro bono case."

Fuck. I'd already done my annual allotment. What I needed was to bill every last hour I could before the partners' vote, not spend hours on an unbillable case. Yet...I needed Dickson, so I sucked it up. "No problem. Send me the file, and I'll look at it first thing in the morning."

"I need you to jump on it right now."

"Now?"

"Can you get down to the seventy-fifth precinct?"

That was the last place I wanted to go at *any* time of the day. I frowned, but answered, "Yeah, sure."

"The kid's name is Storm. He's a minor."

"First or last name?"

"Pretty sure it's his last name. He goes by Storm, so I'm not sure what his first name is. His social worker is on her way and will meet you there."

"Okay. No, problem."

"Thanks, Decker. I owe you one."

I swiped my phone off. The fucker better remember that in two months.

I hadn't stepped foot in this place in more than thirteen years, yet the minute I walked in, I recognized the familiar smell. Trying to ignore the memory, I headed right to the desk sergeant.

"How you doing? Do you have a kid named Storm here? I'm not sure if it's his last name or first."

"Who's asking?"

"I'm his legal counsel."

The old timer looked me up and down. "I'm guessing this is pro bono for some fancy firm."

"Good guess. I take it he's here?"

The cop picked up the phone and punched in a few numbers. "I got a pretty boy out here for Storm. Looks more expensive per hour than my ex-wife's asshole divorce attorney I had to shell out for, so...no rush."

The police weren't exactly fans of defense attorneys. I shook my head. "You should try a more original hobby. Being miserable to all lawyers is pretty cliché. But regardless, I shouldn't have to remind you that all questioning stops now. And I assume you've made the requisite good-faith attempt to contact the kid's parent or guardian before asking him anything."

"Are you sure you're not related to the kid? You have the same winning disposition." He motioned toward the other side of the room and went back to staring at his computer. "Make yourself comfortable on the nice wooden bench. I'll call you whenever we get around to it."

I sighed, but I knew arguing at a police station was generally pointless. So I did as told and parked my ass on the bench. A half hour later, I was engrossed in answering emails when I heard the station door open and close. I didn't bother to look up until I heard the sergeant say *Augustus Storm*. He was talking on the phone again, while a woman stood in front of him at the desk.

Augustus, huh? I smirked. No wonder the kid stuck with Storm. It was hard enough to gain respect in this neighborhood without being saddled with a name like *Augustus*. I straightened my tie and stood, intending to walk over to the woman I assumed was the kid's social worker. But one look at her profile and my step faltered.

I froze.

The side of her face looked awfully familiar...

As I stared, she again spoke to the desk sergeant, so I leaned in and paid close attention.

That voice.

I knew that sweet, feathery sound—the kind that could tell a person to fuck off without them even knowing it.

But it wasn't until the sergeant pointed in my direction, and the woman turned, that I realized this woman *had* told me to fuck off—not in so many words but with her actions. Our eyes met and I smiled, though the sentiment wasn't reciprocated. Instead, the woman's eyes widened as I approached.

"Hello, Autumn."

3

Autumn

O<i>h crap.</i>

The desk sergeant, completely oblivious to our reactions, waved his hand in Donovan's direction. "Kid's lawyer is over there."

"Umm...yeah. Thank you."

I took a few hesitant steps. Lord, he was even better looking than I remembered. *Wow. Just...wow.*

His eyes were a unique blue-gray color to begin with, but the sparkle currently emanating from them made it nearly impossible to look away.

I cleared my throat. "Hello."

He held out his hand. "From the look on your face, I assume you didn't expect to see me either."

I shook my head. "Definitely not."

His hand was still outstretched, and he pointed his eyes down. "It's clean, I swear. Washed them in the men's room a little while ago."

I felt foolish avoiding contact, so I put my hand in his. Just like the first time, it hit with a spark. My pulse raced, and goose bumps dashed up my arm, over my shoulder, and straight to the back of my neck, making all the little hairs stand up. Except now it was even worse than the first time, because I knew what it felt like to have those hands all over my body—best sexual chemistry of my life, *by a landslide,* and we'd never even had actual sex.

It was almost midnight, and Donovan looked like he hadn't yet changed from a long day of work, which meant he probably hadn't sprayed on cologne since this morning, yet he *still* smelled sinfully good. He held my hand in his for longer than an acceptable business handshake, and his eyes stayed fixed on my face. The air around us seemed to crackle with that same electricity as the first time we met, and I had to look away to cool off. But diverting my eyes to our joined hands only made me notice the monogrammed initials on his black dress shirt and the expensive-looking watch wrapped around one very masculine wrist. This was most definitely a no-win situation.

I withdrew my hand and tucked it safely into my pocket. "You're here for Storm?"

He nodded. "I am indeed."

"So that means you work for Kravitz, Polk and Hastings?"

"Correct again."

I mumbled under my breath, at least I'd *meant* to keep it under my breath. "I had no idea."

He tilted his head. "How could you? It's not like you left me a number so we could get to know each other better."

I normally wasn't a person who blushed, but I felt heat travel up my face. I looked away, needing to disentangle from the web I felt caught in. "Umm...did you get to speak to Storm yet?"

"No. They wouldn't even tell me what he was brought in for."

I sighed. "Fighting. *Again*."

"I take it this isn't his first rodeo?"

I shook my head. "Definitely not. He's gotten into quite a few fights, and then one time he was picked up for shoplifting."

Something shifted in the man standing before me. He still had the light in his eyes, it just didn't feel focused on me in the same way anymore. Donovan put his hands on his hips as he slipped into lawyer mode. "How old is he?"

"He's twelve, or he will be in less than a week."

"That's good. Thirteen is a magic number here in the City. So I'm glad he's not there yet."

I nodded. "But the judge threatened to move him last time. He lives at Park House, which is one of the better youth group homes. The judge said if he saw him back in front of him again, he would move him to a juvenile detention center. That can't happen. It'll only make things worse for him."

The door leading to the area where all the cops sat in the back opened. "Storm!" someone yelled.

Donovan put his hand out for me to walk ahead of him.

At the door, the policeman lifted a clipboard. "Name?"

"I'm Autumn Wilde, Storm's social worker."

Donovan spoke from behind me. "Donovan Decker, legal counsel."

We were led through the bullpen and down a long hallway. The officer opened the last door on the right. Inside, we found Storm handcuffed to a bench against the wall.

"Are the cuffs really necessary? My client is not even twelve," Donovan said.

The officer shrugged. "Broke the nose of an adult. He's considered dangerous."

"I'll take the risk. Uncuff him."

The officer shook his head, but did as Donovan asked. Storm rubbed his wrists as soon as the cuffs were off.

"Thanks, *pig*," Storm spat.

Donovan brushed past me and stood in front of his client, looking down. He pointed to the officer and spoke with a stern and steady tone. "Augustus, apologize to the nice officer."

"But he..."

"*Now*."

Storm rolled his eyes. "Fine. Whatever. I'm sorry you're a pig."

"Not like that, Augustus," Donovan warned.

"Fine. *Sorry*."

The officer looked at us on his way out. "Good luck with that."

The minute the door shut, Storm stood and started to say it wasn't his fault. Donovan simply raised his hand and shot him a warning look. Shockingly, Storm closed his mouth.

"Sit down and answer only the questions Autumn and I ask."

Storm sulked, but he also shut up and took a seat at the table. Donovan pulled out a chair and nodded for me to sit in it.

"Thank you."

I spoke to Storm as Donovan dug into his bag and unpacked his lawyerly stuff. "You know what the judge said last time, Storm."

"It wasn't my fault. The dude started it."

Donovan clicked his pen and readied a yellow legal pad. "Let's start there. Does the dude have a name?"

"Sugar."

"How about an actual name?"

Storm shrugged. "I don't know. Everyone around the neighborhood calls him Sugar."

"Fine. Tell me what precipitated you and Sugar getting into it."

Over the next twenty minutes, Storm wove some elaborate tale that started with his bike being stolen and ended with him getting into a fight with an eighteen year old. I'd known him for three years now, so I knew better than to take him at his word when he was scared. And he *was* scared being at the police station, whether he would ever admit it or let me see a glimpse of that vulnerability or not.

Donovan made some calls, asking I have no idea who at midnight about a guy named Sugar, and then he left the room to speak to the police.

When he came back, he said, "I have good news and bad news. The good news is that I got them to keep you here for the night rather than ship you over to central booking. Since you're a minor, you'll stay in a holding cell by yourself. Then in the morning, they'll bring you over to the courthouse for arraignment. But the bad news is they're charging you with felony assault. You cracked the guy's nose and deviated his septum. He's going to need surgery."

I shook my head. "Shoot. Alright, well, I guess we have no choice but to take it one day at a time." I looked over at Storm. "I'm glad you'll get to stay here tonight at least."

A little while later, Donovan and I said goodnight to Storm. I hated to leave him alone, but this wasn't our first time doing this, and it wasn't like I had a choice. We promised to meet him at the courthouse and told him to try to get some sleep.

Outside on the precinct steps, I blew out a deep breath. "Thank you for coming. I don't know what to do with him anymore."

"Does he have any family?"

"His mother is an addict. When they found him, he was living in an abandoned building by himself. He'd been living in a car with her and her newest boyfriend until the boyfriend gave the mother an ultimatum—the kid went or he did. Storm left the next day because the car had heat, and he didn't want his mother to be outside in the cold. He doesn't know of any other family, and the mom says it's just them."

Donovan raked a hand through his hair. "That's tough."

"He's a smart kid, too. Doesn't do any homework or put in any effort and still gets good grades on all his tests. He also speaks Spanish and Russian pretty fluently, and he knows some Polish, too."

"Three languages? Is his mother bilingual?"

"Nope. Mom is German, I think. But she doesn't speak anything other than English. When I asked her about it, she said they bounced around Brooklyn a lot. When they lived in Brighton Beach, he went to school with a lot of Russian kids, and he just picked it up. Polish he learned when they lived near Greenpoint. Spanish he's absorbed from various friends over the years."

"Smart kid. His brain sounds like a sponge."

"It is. Yet I can't seem to get through to him."

"Kids on their own don't easily accept help or listen to people. But I guess I don't need to tell you that."

I nodded "I just hope he doesn't get sent to a juvey detention center. Some of them are as tough on kids as a prison."

Donovan nodded. "I know. I'll do my best."

I suddenly realized how quiet it was outside the police station. It was just the two of us, and that gave me the urge to flee as fast as possible. "Is there anything you need from me for the arraignment?"

"No, it's just a formality."

"Oh. Okay. Well, thanks again. I'll see you in the morning, then." I waved awkwardly and started to walk away.

But Donovan caught my hand.

"Not so fast..."

Shit.

I chanced a look up at him, and he silently raised his brows as if he was expecting me to speak.

"What?" I said.

"Are we just going to pretend that weekend never happened?"

I bit my bottom lip, praying it was a rhetorical question. When the silence stretched, I managed, "That would be great. Thanks."

Donovan smiled. "Nice try, but not a chance."

I sighed.

"I went back to that Starbucks every day for two weeks, hoping to run into you." He paused and searched my eyes. "Since you snuck out of my place and didn't leave me any way to contact you, I didn't even know your last name until you said it to the police officer inside. Wilde..." He smiled. "It suits you."

My heart squeezed a little. Almost a year had passed, and yet I still thought of him every time I passed *any* Starbucks. Only unlike him, I'd avoided going in the one we'd met at after our weekend together.

"Sorry...I, uh..."

His brows drew together. "Are you married?"

"God, no."

"Did you...not have a good time? Because I thought you did." He flashed a dimpled, crooked smile, which made my knees a little weak. "I thought you had *multiple* good times."

I couldn't help but laugh. "Yes, I did have a good time."

"So then why the brush-off?"

"I just... I was looking for what we had. Not more."

He seemed to digest that for a minute before nodding. "You could've just said that. I'm a big boy. I would've liked to have said goodbye. Maybe even made you some breakfast—given you some coffee, at least."

I felt embarrassed and was glad it was so dark out. "Sorry. I, I'm not good at those things."

Donovan rubbed his bottom lip with his thumb. That was one of the things I'd felt drawn to when we first met. He took his time and picked his words, rather than doing what most people do—spewing whatever thoughts immediately came to mind. Well, that and his broad shoulders, mesmerizing eyes, and bone structure that should've made him a candidate to be a fifth head carved on Mt. Rushmore. Screw presidents. *That* I'd go see.

"You're sorry? So that means you feel badly about the way things left off?"

My face wrinkled. "Yes. That's why I apologized."

"Well, since you feel badly, I should let you make it up to me. So that we're even."

I chuckled. "And how exactly would I do that?"

"Have the coffee you skipped out on with me...now." He nodded across the street. "There's a twenty-four-hour diner a block over."

It was tempting, but I knew it was a bad idea. I offered a conciliatory smile. "It's pretty late. I should get home."

Donovan forced a smile, though I could see he was disappointed. Honestly, I was, too. He shoved his hands into his pockets. "I'll see you tomorrow, then?"

I nodded. "Goodnight, Donovan."

I thought that was the end of it, and we both started to walk away, but after a few steps, he yelled. "Hey, Red!"

I stopped and turned around. Even though I had auburn hair, he was the only person who'd ever called me that.

"Court will only take about an hour. So it won't be too late for coffee afterward."

I laughed. "Goodnight, Mr. Decker."

"Oh, it has been a good night." He smiled. "And I'm looking forward to tomorrow."

4
Donovan

"You don't speak unless the judge asks you a question and I give you the okay to answer. Understood?"

"Whatever."

Spending the night locked up in a jail cell hadn't done much for my client's sunny disposition. While attitude from a client would normally have me up in arms, it was an effort to act pissed off with this kid. He reminded me so much of myself at that age that I found it amusing.

I cleared my throat. "Not *whatever*. Tell me you understood what I said and you will follow my rules."

Storm rolled his eyes. "Fine. Speak when spoken to. I get it, alright?"

"That's better."

I pushed up my shirtsleeve to check the time on my watch. We still had a few minutes before the guard would call him for the obligatory lineup and march of criminals upstairs to the courtroom. Only attorneys were allowed downstairs to visit clients before arraignment, so this was the first time I'd been alone with him. I figured I might as well make good use of the opportunity.

"Your social worker—how long have you been working with her?"

He shrugged. "I don't know. A couple of years, I guess."

"Everything good with her?"

Another shrug. "Her ass looks good."

I pointed a finger at him. "Hey, don't be disrespectful, you little shit."

"What, you don't like her ass? It's nice and round."

"First of all, she's a lady, so you don't talk like that. Second of all, I'm guessing she's probably the only good thing you have in your life most of the time, so don't bite the hand that feeds you. And lastly, you're *twelve*." I left off *fourth of all, it isn't nice and round; it's more like an upside-down heart.*

"Whatever. She's cool. She can drive a truck."

My brows furrowed. "Autumn can drive a truck? You mean like a pickup truck?"

Storm shook his head. "Nope. A big eighteen-wheeler."

"How do you know that?"

"Because once we were at one of those dumb retreats Park House makes us go to upstate. A guy parked his rig blocking the entrance to the place. Him and another guy were talking. She got out of our car and asked him to move it, and he told her he was busy and he'd get to it. That pissed her off. So she asked him if the keys were in it. The guy laughed and told her to help herself if she thought she could drive a truck with eighteen speeds. She told us to stay in the car, and then she drove the truck a block away and parked it and came back."

I don't know what type of information I'd been fishing for, but it hadn't been that. Though I'd take it. "What else do you know about Ms. Wilde?"

He shrugged. "She hates fighting. A couple of times she was around when kids got into it. Those are pretty much the only times I've seen her get *really* mad. She also doesn't answer her phone when her dad calls most of the time, and she's got bad taste in music."

"What kind of music does she listen to?"

The kid made a face. "What, are you writing a book?"

Luckily the guard saved the little pain in the ass from any more interrogation. He opened the door and said, "Let's go, Storm. Showtime."

I folded the leather book where I'd jotted down a few things I wanted to remember and stood with my client. "Don't forget, I don't care what the judge says *to you* or *about you*, you don't say a word without my permission."

He frowned, but nodded as he walked out.

Back upstairs, I made a pit stop in the men's room before heading to room 219, where Storm's arraignment would be held in about fifteen minutes. I perked up upon finding a certain redheaded social worker sitting on a bench outside the room. Autumn was scribbling on a pad on her lap, so she didn't see me approach.

"Good morning."

She blinked her big green eyes up at me. "Oh, hi. I'm glad we got to see each other before the hearing."

"You missed me, huh?" I grinned.

She laughed. "Actually, after I got home last night, I thought of a few things you might want to tell the judge about Storm. I was just writing them down."

"Let's see what you got." I took the seat next to her and put my hand out for her to pass me the list.

Perusing the notes, I already knew most of what she'd written after talking to my client and pulling his rap sheet. Autumn had listed his prior arrests, his mother's name, and the name of the shrink he was required to see monthly as part of his last plea deal. She also listed his grades. I lifted the paper closer to make sure I read that last part correctly.

"Is this right? His overall average is a ninety-nine?"

Autumn nodded. "And he's taking all advanced classes, too. The only reason he doesn't have a hundred is because he got a ninety in gym."

My eyebrows shot up. "Gym? Seriously? That's what's weighing him down?" Last night she'd mentioned the kid was a good student, and when I'd asked him how things were going in school earlier today, he'd grumbled *fine*. I assumed that meant he wasn't failing anything, and his grades were probably low seventies.

"He got in trouble twice in gym for pegging kids with a soccer ball, so the teacher lowered his grade. Otherwise he'd have a hundred."

I shook my head. "His grades are actually good information to mention to this judge. His wife is a teacher, so he gives a lot of weight to how kids do in school. I'll use it. Thanks."

As I went to hand Autumn the paper back, something clicked, and I instead pulled it in for closer inspection. *Yep, it was her list.*

The afternoon of the day we'd met to exchange luggage, I'd gone through her bag. She'd been so adamant that I not look; how could I not? Inside, there was some pretty damn intriguing shit—huge vibrators and whatnot, which I'd later learned had been props for the bachelorette party she'd just returned from. But I'd also come across some sort of a list—a list of excuses, with some crossed out. I'd forgotten all about it until I found it under my bed the following week. It must've slipped under there when I was repacking her bag. I had no idea if she'd written the list or what the meaning of it was, but seeing her handwriting made me remember. She had pretty distinct, slanty cursive.

"Are you a lefty?" I asked.

She nodded and held her hand up to show me the back of her wrist. "Was it the ink I always have on the back of my hand or my terrible handwriting that gave it away?"

"The slantiness. My assistant has it, too."

It had been a long time since I'd perused the list she'd written, so I couldn't remember most of what was on it. I knew there were some basic excuses, things like: My phone is about to die. Work is calling on the other line. I'm about to go into a building where the service is terrible. But there were also some pretty strange ones, like *my fish is drowning*.

Autumn tucked the information about Storm back into a folder on her lap and started to say something when her phone rang. *Dad* flashed on the screen. Remembering what Storm had told me—that she rarely answered the phone when her father called—the frown on her face as she read the name made sense. While she debated answering, a court officer opened the door next to us.

He looked down at his clipboard and yelled to no one in particular, "Case 5487723-B, Storm!"

Autumn glanced over at me and took a deep breath. "That's us."

We stood. Her phone was still in her hand and *Dad* started to flash again. I wasn't sure if she noticed, so I pointed my eyes down to it. "Do you need to get that first?"

"No, it's fine. I'll call him back later."

The arraignment went pretty smoothly. I entered a plea on behalf of my client, and Storm was released to the custody of the state as represented by social services. He'd also have to report to a JPO—juvenile probation officer. But we'd have a few months before we needed to build a case. Still, the kid needed to keep out of trouble.

Once we'd collected his things from the property room, I asked Autumn if I could have a few minutes alone with my client.

"Sure. Of course."

I nodded toward the men's room a few doors down. "Step into my office, little man."

"Can I take a piss while you chew my ear off?"

"You can wait until I'm done. Let's go."

Inside the men's room, I waited until the guy washing his hands was done and out the door. Then I leaned against a sink and folded my arms across my chest.

"I talked to some people. Sugar didn't just take your bicycle." I leveled my client with a glare.

He looked away. "Yeah, he did. He stole my bike."

"*Stole* implies he took it without properly compensating you. But that's not what happened, is it, Storm?"

Early this morning I'd reached out to a friend who still lived in the neighborhood Storm hung out in and asked him to do a little digging. Apparently Sugar was a local dealer. I wasn't sure what had gone down, but I had a pretty good hunch.

"The guy's a jerk."

Storm was a big kid for barely twelve, but I was a little over six foot two. I leaned over with my hands on my thighs and spoke to him at eye level. "I already have the truth. So if you try to lie to me, I'll know," I bluffed. "I can't defend you unless you're honest with me. You might be able to take care of yourself on the street, but trust me, you'll be in trouble if they transfer you to a place like Wheatley Juvenile Detention Center. I hear you're a smart kid. Do you know what recidivism is?"

Storm shook his head.

"It's when someone repeats a behavior—usually it's something that was done to them. Eighty percent of the kids over at Wheatley were physically abused or sexually abused as kids. Can you put two plus two together and figure out what I'm telling you happens over at Wheatley?"

The muscle in Storm's jaw flexed, but he held strong.

"Why don't we start from the beginning? How much did you owe Sugar?"

He mulled over his answer for a minute before looking down. "Forty."

I knew it. "He took your bike because you didn't pay him, and you tried to get it back."

"I didn't think he was home. I just wanted my bike back."

"Do you just smoke weed, or do you do other drugs?"

"Just smoke weed."

I stared into his eyes for a solid thirty seconds. Street kids were way harder to read than suit-wearing assholes who stole millions, but I was pretty sure he was telling the truth.

I stood and nodded. "Alright. I'll see what I can do with that information. But you're on thin ice, kid. You can't do anything wrong—not buy weed, get into another fight, nothing. Hell, don't even litter."

He frowned. "Fine."

I tilted my head toward the door. "Let's go. Ms. Wilde is waiting."

As we got to the door to the men's room, Storm stopped and looked at me. "If you're my lawyer, we have attorney-client privilege, right?"

The corner of my mouth twitched. Kid was smarter than Mr. Bentley already. "That's right."

"So you can't tell Ms. Wilde I bought weed, right?"

I'd basically told him the place he might get sent was filled with child molesters, and he was more concerned about letting Autumn down. That was my first glimpse of the child still inside that growing body of his.

I put my hand on his shoulder. "You have my word."

Outside in the hall, Autumn looked between us. "Everything okay?"

I nodded. "All good."

"The clerk said he has twenty-four hours to register with the juvenile-probation department, but the building is right next door. Do you think it's okay if we walk over now?"

"I think that's a good idea."

Autumn looked at Storm, then me. "Okay, well...say thank you to Mr. Decker."

The last thing I needed was to be out of the office all morning, but I wasn't ready to let Autumn walk away again so fast. It wouldn't be the first time I worked through the night to make up for lost billable hours. "I'll walk over with you. I know a few of the JPOs. Maybe I can get you in faster."

"Oh, that would be great, if you don't mind."

———

"I didn't know you did this type of criminal law," Autumn said. "I thought you did more white-collar crime."

Autumn and I were sitting in the hall over at the Probation Department while Storm's new JPO talked to him alone. I had zero reason to be here anymore, now that he was in—well, zero professional reason.

"I do," I told her. "Haven't touched anything but money laundering, insider trading, and embezzlement in at least six years. I was an ADA for a year right out of law school prosecuting Class B felonies. Made the switch to the other side and then a year later traded up from street crimes to Wall Street crimes. But one of the partners at my firm asked me to take Storm's case as part of our pro bono program. He's actually the one who does regular street-criminal work, but I'm up for partner, and he knows I need his vote, so he dumped it on me." I caught Autumn's eye.

"I thought the guy was being his usual asshole self, but I'm thinking I might owe him a thanks now."

She tried to hide her smile by looking down. "What's the partner's name who assigned you?"

"Blake Dickson. We call him The Dick, because he is."

Autumn nodded.

"How was your friend's wedding? It must've happened by now, right? Did the bride do her dance down to the altar?"

Autumn's mouth dropped open. "She did, and the wedding was a blast, but I can't believe you remember that."

"It's pretty hard to forget a story about a bride planning to dance down the aisle to 'Crazy Bitch' by Buckcherry."

She laughed. "I guess so."

"Plus..." I caught her eye. "I remember everything about our weekend together."

I debated saying anything else, but she'd really rocked me when she pulled her disappearing act, and I felt the need to let her know it. So I ignored the fact that I probably sounded like a desperate wuss and cleared my throat. "I remember that you only ever have one earbud in at a time, never two, so you can be aware of your surroundings. But you alternate the right and left one every Sunday—so the other doesn't feel neglected. You also speed when you go over bridges, just in case they collapse. And you know a crapload of random facts because you have an incessant need to do a deep dive on anything you hear about that you feel like you don't have enough knowledge on, which causes you to get lost in Google searches for hours. If I'm not mistaken, it was lottery winners after we watched that movie about a guy who won the lottery and lost all his money. You spent an hour telling me about random things that have better odds than winning the lottery while

I made us dinner. Also, you sleep with the covers over your head, and you're so small, it's hard to tell if you're in the bed or it's just a lump of covers."

Autumn blinked a few times. "How do you know how I sleep? We never slept in the same room except for a few short naps. I slept in your bed, and you slept on the couch."

I smiled. "I checked on you. I might've pulled the covers back and watched you sleep for a minute or two once."

"That's kind of creepy..."

"I wanted to make sure you were okay. And then I couldn't take my eyes off of you. You're beautiful, even when you sleep."

She looked away, and when she turned back, she avoided eye contact. "I'm nervous about what's going to happen to Augustus this time. His last arrest was only a few months ago."

I guessed that was the end of our trip down memory lane... "I might have something I can use to make this go away."

"What do you mean?"

"Prosecutors don't particularly enjoy punishing twelve year olds, especially ones who have potential, like Storm. So if you can bring them something they *do* enjoy prosecuting, and help them see there's also a good path for your client without putting him in a juvey detention center or shipping him someplace where he'll only wind up worse, then usually they'll work something out."

Her nose wrinkled. "I'm not following you. Who would they enjoy prosecuting?"

Even without attorney-client privilege, I wasn't going to break my word to Storm. Kids like him don't trust easily, so if they so much as smell that you might not have honored your word, you lose them for good.

"Leave it to me, okay?"

She looked wary. "Okay…"

This time, when she tried to look away, I made sure I got through to her. "Autumn?"

She lifted her eyes to meet mine. "Trust me, okay? I'm going to do everything I can for him."

With a sigh, she nodded. "Okay. Thank you."

My cell phone buzzed in my pocket. Digging it out, I saw that it was the office. I looked over at Autumn. "Excuse me for a minute."

She nodded, so I swiped to answer and stood, taking a few steps away. "Donovan Decker…"

"Decker, how did the hearing go?"

Yeah, hello to you, too, Mr. Dick.

"Hey, Blake. The hearing went fine. Pretty standard."

"Will you be able to get the kid off?"

"I'll do my best. I might have a little leverage to work."

"You better. There's a lot riding on this for you."

Seriously? Seven damn years of pulling in tens of millions on high-profile cases, and my fate comes down to a pro bono case for a twelve-year-old kid I shouldn't even have while he's deciding how to vote on whether I make partner or not? I wanted to tell him to eat shit, but instead *I* ate shit—though I had to physically swallow in order to force down my thoughts and make room for my ass kissing.

"Absolutely, I won't let you down."

Click. The asshole hung up on me.

I shook my head and grumbled under my breath. *You have a good day, too, Dick.*

However aggravated the short conversation had made me, my anger quickly dissipated as I turned around. Autumn had her thick auburn hair in her hand, and she was tying it up in one of those buns girls could do faster than a ninja. She looked beautiful with it down or up, but seeing it piled on top of her head reminded me of the morning I'd woken up and found her standing in front of my stove, cooking while wearing one of my T-shirts. She'd been humming "Little Boxes," an old song that had made a comeback as the theme song to the show *Weeds*, and I'd secretly snapped a picture of her. Trent still busted my balls about that pic. I'd showed it to him once, enlarging it so he couldn't see her bare legs, but it had been in my favorites folder—the only picture I'd ever hit the little heart on and put in there on my iPhone.

I hadn't realized I'd been staring until Autumn caught me. The corners of her lips turned up ever so slightly, and her head tilted to one side. I walked over, feeling good that she seemed to like me watching her.

"Sorry. That was my office. You must have friends in high places for The Dick to call and check on how things are going. I think that's the third time the guy has called me in seven years, and this is the second call in twenty-four hours about your case."

"Hmm...yeah, I guess so."

"You said your father was a lawyer, right? Is that how you got my firm to take this case? He knows someone? We were closed to accepting any new pro bono cases this year."

"Actually, it wasn't through my dad. I sort of know someone at your firm."

"Sort of know?"

She looked down. "I'm dating one of the attorneys."

My stomach sank. She was involved with another man? Someone I *knew*? But if I thought that news was a kick in the gut, I had another thing coming when she dropped the next bomb.

"Which attorney?" I asked.

She winced through a forced smile. "I believe you call him *The Dick*."

5

Donovan

I sat at my desk with a business card between my fingers, turning it over and over, lost in thought. I didn't even notice that Juliette had walked in until she planted her ass in one of my chairs.

"Tu en fais une tête," she said.

"Nah. I'm not in the mood for a handjob. Thanks anyway."

She laughed. "Why the long face, my friend?"

"Just thinking about a case."

Juliette was originally from France, but we'd started as summer interns at the firm together, along with Trent and twelve others. The three of us had been the only ones hired that fall, and we'd been tight ever since. She and Trent spent a lot of time talking about their love lives, or lack of, usually—analyzing why their relationships never seemed to work out. I'd comment and give my opinions, but it wasn't often that we scrutinized my dating life, because for the most part, I'd been relatively happy with how my non-relationships worked out. Today, though, I thought I could use a woman's opinion...

"Let me ask you something—do you have a type?"

"In men?"

I nodded. "Either in looks or personality?"

"I do. I tend to be attracted to losers."

I grinned. "No, really."

"Unfortunately, I'm not joking. I'm attracted to the artsy type—painters, sculptors, writers—most of whom are unemployed half the time."

"What attracts you to them?"

She shrugged. "I don't know. I guess I love that they wear their heart on their sleeves. Artist types tend to be in touch with their emotions and care about things I care about, like the environment and social justice. I find a man who's passionate about things that don't necessarily make him money very sexy."

"What about physically?"

"You've met guys I've dated. They're usually thin with a hippy kind of earthy look—sort of like you're not quite sure if they might be homeless or not." She looked me up and down. "Basically the opposite of you, pretty boy. But why are you asking me this?"

"I'm trying to figure out how a woman could date me and then a total asshole."

She smirked. "Aren't those the same thing?"

I wadded up a piece of paper from my desk and threw it at her.

She laughed and caught it. "What's going on with you? Spill the beans, Decker."

I sighed. "Do you remember me telling you about Autumn?"

"Sure. The woman you spent an entire celibate weekend with and fell for because she didn't give it up and dumped you before you could dump her?"

I rolled my eyes. She sounded like Trent. "That's not why I liked her. But whatever—I don't have time to debate it. I still need to bill twelve more hours today, and there's only six hours left. Anyway, I ran into her."

"Oh, wow. How'd that go?"

I frowned. "She told me she hadn't left me her number because she wasn't looking for more than we had."

"Ouch."

I shook my head. "But our chemistry is still there."

"Sounds like she's just not into a relationship, then."

"That's the thing. She's seeing someone now."

"Maybe you caught her when she was going through something."

"I don't know." I shrugged. "Maybe."

"Did you get her number anyway?"

I held up the business card still in my hand. "She's the social worker on a pro bono case for a minor who was arrested. So she gave it to me for business, not exactly because she wants me to take her out."

"Okay... I'm still lost on where we started this conversation. Is Autumn the woman who's dating the asshole?"

I nodded.

"You met him? He was with her?"

"No, he wasn't with her. But I've definitely met him." I looked her straight in the eyes. "She's dating Blake Dickson."

Juliette's eyes narrowed. "*The* Blake Dickson? Like, as in one of the partners whose vote you need to make partner?"

I blew out a deep breath. "One and the same."

⌒

That night, I decided to take a detour on my way home from work. I was a little overdressed for the neighborhood

48

I'd be going to, so I removed my tie and shoved it into my pocket—not that it was going to make me stand out any less as I roamed the streets after I got off the subway.

The looks I got as I walked down the sidewalk were pretty amusing—half the people eyed me like they were considering stealing my wallet, and the other half scattered like cockroaches, assuming the guy in the dark suit was probably a narc.

I found Dario exactly where I'd left him eleven years ago: sitting on his stoop four doors down from where I'd once lived. It was almost eleven o'clock at night, but you wouldn't know it from all the people hanging around.

"Oh, shit." He stood and smiled. "What the hell are you wearing? Did you lose a bet?"

We shook hands in a way no one around the office ever did—a series of shakes and bumps ending in a one-shoulder guy hug.

"This is how men who don't live in the same building as their mothers dress, shit for brains."

He shook his head. I was just busting chops, and he knew it. Dario had never left because his mother refused to leave the apartment she'd been in for more than forty years. She was confined to a wheelchair, and he would always stick close to take care of her.

He looked around at his buddies, most of whom I'd never seen before. "Anyone got a hankie? My boy here probably doesn't want to sit on a dirty stoop."

I laughed. "I don't. So whadda you say we take a walk around the block?"

He nodded and told his buddies he'd be back, that he needed to *walk me back to the train so I wouldn't get mugged*.

Once we were out of earshot, I said, "How's Rosanne doing?"

"Mom's doing alright. You remember old man Stimpson?"

"Of course. He decapitated that big snowman we spent hours building after that crazy snowstorm we had when we were seven or eight."

Dario smirked. "That's right. I pretended my mom sent me down to borrow sugar or something and stole his corncob pipe. How can you make a snowman without a pipe?"

I laughed. "What about Stimpson? Something happen to him?"

"Nah. He's still kicking around. But he comes and spends time with my mom a few times a week. His old lady died a few years back. Mom says he's her special friend."

"No shit? Your mom is stooping Stimpson?"

Dario punched me. "You don't want me to mess up that suit, do you?"

I chuckled. "Good for Rosanne. I'm glad she's happy. But listen, I came by to get some information that might help out a client of mine. He's twelve and reminds me a lot of the two of us at his age."

"Poor little bastard..."

"Yeah, no shit." I smiled. "Any chance you know a guy they call Sugar?"

"Sure. He's a pharma over on Lyme Street."

Pharma was short for pharmacist, which meant he was a local drug dealer. I knew that much already since Storm had admitted the truth about their fight.

"Know anything else about him?"

"I know he used to rough up his old lady. She's got three older brothers, and they paid him a little visit. The next day both his arms were in casts from shoulder to wrist."

I was glad he was an asshole and not a friend of Dario's. "Who's he work for?"

"I'm assuming what we're talking about here is between us? I don't mind if you jam him up, but I don't want my name getting out as no snitch."

"Of course not. I might dress like one, but I'm not a total douchebag."

Dario snickered. "Sugar works for Eddie D., who works for the Big Man."

Excellent—a line of assholes. I nodded. "Thanks for the info."

My oldest friend and I walked around the block a few more times. He caught me up on the neighborhood. Back in the day, I couldn't wait to get out of this place, yet there was something comforting about being back. Maybe it was the trust I had in some of my old buddies, and they had in me. Years could pass, but we'd been through too much shit together for that bond to ever break.

When we rounded our way back to Dario's porch for the fourth time, we stopped. "Have you heard from Linda?" he asked.

My jaw tensed at the mention of my mother. "Not in a while. She must've found some other sucker to give her money."

Dario nodded. "I hear you. Gonna come up and hang out for a while?"

"Nah. Another time. I gotta be back at the office at the crack of dawn."

We shook, and my friend punched me lightly on my arm. "Don't take three years before you stop by again."

"I won't. Take care, Dario, and tell your mom I said hello."

The next day I put a call in to the ADA assigned to Storm's case. I learned he was out for the rest of the week, so it would be a while before I'd be able to talk to him and have an excuse to call Autumn. Yet I kept eyeing her business card on my desk. Right before I headed out to lunch, I took the card and tossed it into my drawer. Maybe removing her name from plain sight would help me stop thinking about her so much.

I met Trent and Juliette in a conference room to have lunch. We'd ordered in Chinese from the place down the block.

"So, I have gossip," Juliette said as we dug in.

"If you're going to force us to listen to dumb stories again, this time they'd better be about actual people," I said, opening my food carton.

Last time we'd had lunch, Juliette had told us some elaborate story about a woman dating a dozen guys. I'd been getting into it until I realized the people she was talking about weren't actual friends of hers. She'd been reciting crap from the last few episodes of *The Bachelor*.

"Oh, this is about actual people. Though, I know you secretly want to know what happened to Kayla when she took Jeff home for her hometown visit and had to tell him she has a kid. But I'll save that for after."

"Gee, thanks," I grumbled.

"Be nice, or I won't tell you that I ran into my friend Trina earlier today in the ladies' room."

"Which one is Trina again?" Trent asked.

Juliette grinned and looked in my direction, even though I hadn't asked the question. "She's Blake Dickson's assistant."

Now *that* got my attention. "What did she have to say?"

"I asked her how her grumpy boss was doing. She said he'd been more tolerable lately."

My fork froze with a shrimp halfway to my mouth. "I don't want to know what's making him more tolerable."

She scrunched up her face. "Ewww. I didn't go into that kind of detail. But she said he's been seeing someone new. I thought you might want to know what the deal is between them."

"The deal between who?" Trent asked.

I forgot I hadn't yet told him about my run-in with Autumn. "I'll catch you up in a minute," I said. I lifted my chin to Juliette. "Go on."

"Well, they've only been dating about a month and a half, and they only see each other once a week, that she knows of. Not surprisingly, The Dick makes his assistant make his dinner reservations." Juliette shook her head. "She said Autumn's only ever called the office once, when she was returning Dickson's call. So things don't sound too serious."

Trent's forehead wrinkled. "Autumn? The woman who ghosted you?"

I filled him in on what had transpired since the call I'd gotten when we were out to dinner. He leaned back in his chair.

"Shit. So what are you going to do?"

"Considering I need Dickson's vote?" I shrugged. "Nothing."

Trent and Juliette looked at each other. Some unspoken communication passed between them, and they both cracked up.

"What the hell is so funny?"

"You," Juliette snorted. "You say it as if you actually believe it."

"Believe what?"

"That you can control going after something you want."

6

Donovan

When Saturday night arrived, I was looking forward to doing absolutely damn nothing—maybe watch whatever new action flick was currently streaming, water my plants, kick my feet up on my coffee table, and suck back a cold beer or two. I deserved a reward. I'd managed to catch up on my billable hours, and I hadn't broken down and called a certain woman whose name I would not be thinking about tonight—especially when I climbed into bed later. Over the last few days, I'd managed to talk myself down off the cliff I'd been standing on. I'd worked seven long years to get where I was today, and I was not going to let a woman fuck that up, especially not one who had no interest in me.

Nope. I was not interested in Autumn Wilde.

Not in the least.

I picked up the spray bottle on my kitchen counter and walked over to the first of more than a dozen plants scattered around my apartment.

"She's not my type anyway."

Spray. Spray.

As if to challenge that statement, my brain conjured up a memory of Autumn from our weekend together—long legs, creamy skin, gorgeous, deep red hair, tiny waist, and a pretty full ass for a little thing...

"Fine," I grumbled. "So maybe she's sort of my type—physically, anyway. But she's definitely more work than I could handle."

Spray. Spray.

Though...when I looked back at the weekend we'd spent together, which I'd definitely done on a few hundred occasions, *work* wasn't exactly how I'd describe it. Just the opposite. Autumn and I had been holed up here in my apartment for three full days, and it was probably the most effortless good time I'd had in...maybe forever. We'd talked until the sun came up and spent the days renting movies, fooling around a bit, laughing, and falling asleep snuggled on the couch. I'd even done her damn laundry while she'd slept.

I shook my head and moved on to the next plant.

"*Fine.*"

Spray. Spray.

"But what the hell do you expect me to do? She's not interested. Plus, she's dating my boss. So does it even matter if she's a walking wet dream who could make me smile for an entire weekend *without* having sex? Or that I can still smell her perfume right now even though I haven't been near her in two days? Or that I can remember the taste of her from every kiss we've shared?"

Spray. Spray.

"I'll tell you the answer. *No. It doesn't fucking matter.*"

Even if there were a hundred reasons I couldn't get her out of my mind, she was dating *my boss*. That alone had to tip the scale to the stay-the-hell-away side, clearly outweighing all the reasons to call her. I just needed to get my mind off of her for a while. That's all.

So I finished watering my plants in silence, got a cold beer from the fridge, and sat down on the couch to scroll through the movie choices on Netflix. But as I watched the preview for some movie that seemed like it should've been titled *Ocean's Nine Hundred and Ninety or Whatever*, my cell vibrated in my pocket. I briefly considered ignoring it, but the workaholic in me couldn't let it go to voicemail. So I dug it out and swiped to answer a number I didn't recognize as I brought my beer to my lips. "Donovan Decker."

"Hi, ummm... It's Autumn. I'm sorry to bother you."

I immediately sat up and planted the beer on the coffee table. Something was wrong. I could hear the stress in her voice. "What happened?"

"It's Storm. He ran away."

I raked a hand through my hair. *Shit.* One of the terms of his release was that he had to remain under the direct care and control of Social Services. "How long has he been gone?"

"Since about four o'clock this afternoon. Today is his birthday. The last time he spoke to his mother, she promised she'd visit him on his birthday. She never showed up. Visiting hours ended at 3:30, and when the residence manager went to check on him, she found a broken window and Augustus was gone. They know they're required to call the Probation Department if anything like this happens, but I'm friends with Lita, the manager there, so she called me first. I asked her if I could call it in... But that was five hours ago, and I never did. I didn't know who else to call. Can I get him in more trouble if I continue to hold off on calling?"

"You can get *yourself* in trouble. As his social worker, you have a legal duty to act."

"I don't care about that, but..." She paused, and I heard a knock in the background. "I'm sorry. Can you hang on a second?"

"Yeah."

I listened to muffled voices. The man's voice got loud, and I thought he said, "It's just five damn dollars." The hairs on the back of my neck stood up.

"Autumn?" I yelled into the phone.

She came back on after a few seconds. "Sorry—where was I?"

"Forget where you were with your story. Where are *you* right now?"

"I'm in a parking lot. I think I'm on Delaney Street or maybe it was Delancey. I don't remember what I turned on."

I walked to the closet to get my shoes. "You're in Storm's neighborhood?"

"Yeah. I've been looking for him the last few hours."

"Are you in a car?"

"Yes."

"Did someone just knock on your window and ask for money?"

"Yeah. I pulled into an empty lot to call you, and I didn't notice anyone. I think maybe some homeless people might be living here."

I shook my head as I grabbed my keys and wallet from the counter. "If you're on Delaney, you're about eight blocks from the seventy-fifth precinct, where he was held the other night. It's on the corner of Sutter and Essex. Punch that into your GPS and go. I'll meet you in the parking lot of the station. Don't roll down your window to answer anyone, and keep your doors locked."

"Are we going to ask the police for help finding Storm?"

"Something like that. I'll be there as soon as I can. Once you get to the police station, just sit in your car. Don't go in without me."

"Okay."

—

Autumn jumped when I knocked on her window. She looked relieved when she realized it was me, and she pressed the button to roll it down.

"Do you mind if we take your car?" I said.

"No, that's fine. But where are we going?"

"To find Storm."

"I thought we were going to ask the police for help?"

"No, this was just the safest place I knew of to put you until I could get here."

"Oh..."

I walked around the car and got into the passenger seat. Autumn looked around the parking lot. "Is that your car over there?" She pointed.

"Yep."

"Nice. Are you sure you don't want to take yours?"

I buckled. "Definitely not. This will fit in better. People in this neighborhood don't trust two types of people—police and haves."

"Haves?"

"Yeah. They consider themselves *have nots*, and haves are outsiders. If we're going to drive around, your Hyundai will be less conspicuous than my overpriced Mercedes."

"Okay."

I pointed down the street. "Pull out and make a left, then go straight for about a half mile. We'll start at the closest park."

Autumn did as I asked. As we waited at a red light, she said, "Why did you buy it?"

58

"What?"

"The Mercedes. You said it was overpriced. So why did you buy it?"

"I didn't. The firm leases it. They give us three choices of cars so we look the part when we go see a client. I don't drive it that often since I live and work in the City and prefer trains."

"Oh."

A minute later, she said, "What kind of car would you get if you were buying it?"

"If I was buying it and wasn't planning on pulling up to a client in it?"

She nodded.

"A nineteen seventy Ford Bronco."

"Really? A fifty-year-old car? I don't know what it looks like."

"Did you ever see the movie *Speed*?"

"I'm not sure."

"Well, it's what Keanu Reeves drove. I watched that movie twenty times when it came out, just to check out his character's car."

She smiled. "That's not the type of car I would have expected you to covet."

"I think there's a lot about me you're going to find out tonight that you might not have expected." I pointed up ahead. "Pull over in front of those of stores."

"Near that group of guys?"

"Yeah."

Autumn did as I asked. But when she put the car in park, she went to turn off the ignition.

"Keep it running. I'll just be a minute."

"I want to go with you."

"You're not going with me."

"Why not?"

"Can you just trust me?"

She sighed. "Okay, okay. I'll wait in the car."

I opened my door and turned back before getting out. "Lock the doors behind me."

There were three guys standing in front of a closed neighborhood grocery store. They eyed me as I approached.

"I'm looking for a twelve-year-old kid named Storm. Any chance you've seen him around?"

The taller of the three lifted his chin. "Who's asking?"

"I am. Name's Decker."

He shook his head. "I don't know any Decker."

"I don't live in the neighborhood anymore. I used to hang with Dario over on Cleveland Street and ate my meals with Bud most nights."

The guy rubbed his chin. "Decker, huh? That does sound familiar."

"Look, I'm trying to find the kid to keep him out of more trouble than he's already in." I tilted my head toward the car. "That's his social worker in the car. She's putting her neck on the line right now by not calling in that he disappeared from Park House. If I don't find him, we're going to have to call it in, and then he's in deeper shit than he needs to be."

Two of the guys looked at each other, and one nodded. "I don't know if the kid you're looking for is there, but there's a group around that age that hangs out in the abandoned lot over on Belmont Ave. And check out behind the pizza place off Jerome Street."

"Thanks."

Autumn and I stopped at the park, since it was on the way. I ran out and looked around, but it was empty. Then I gave her directions to the abandoned lot the guys at the store had mentioned.

"You know this neighborhood pretty well. Did you have clients here when you did street crimes?"

"Nope. Used to live here myself."

"Really? I don't think you mentioned that when we... met to exchange luggage."

I looked over and waited until her eyes met mine. "I don't think you mentioned that I only had seventy-two hours to fill you in on my life story because you were going to disappear."

She smiled sadly. "I guess I deserve that."

We both stayed quiet until we pulled up at the abandoned lot. Again, I got out by myself and had a few words with the people I encountered. Unfortunately, Storm wasn't there, but one of the kids knew him and suggested trying some girl named Katrina's block, because Storm "got it bad for the girl."

Over the course of two hours, we went from place to place. It was beginning to feel like a futile attempt when I finally saw a kid about Storm's size walking alone on a block he shouldn't have been walking alone on. We rolled up and sure enough, it was him.

As we pulled close, Autumn asked, "Can I handle this?"

I nodded. "Of course. Just stick close to the car, please. And if he acts like a little punk and takes off running, you get back in the car and let me chase him down on foot. Deal?"

"Deal."

I watched from the car as Autumn and Storm spoke. It looked like she laid into him good, and the kid was smart enough to just take it and not argue back. After about ten minutes, he climbed into the backseat while Autumn got behind the wheel. I turned.

"I'm sure Autumn covered most of what needs to be said, so I'm just going to add two things." I counted off with my finger. "One, you may not give a shit what happens to you, but Autumn here could be arrested for not reporting that you took off. I'm going to take a leap of faith and assume you didn't know that. But now that you do, you need to think twice about how your actions affect others—especially a person who is good to you." Storm was avoiding eye contact, so I spoke with a stern tone. "Look at me."

His eyes flashed as they met mine.

"How many people in your life can you count on? I got a pretty good feeling that number is low. So I'm going to give you some life advice, man to man—not attorney to dumbass client. When you find a person who has your back, you make sure you have theirs. So from now on, before you do something stupid, you act like a man and think about the consequences. Got it?"

Surprisingly, he didn't grumble too much. "Got it."

Autumn was driving, so she couldn't see our interaction, but I nodded in her direction, hoping he'd take a hint.

Storm frowned but after a moment, he spoke. "Sorry, Autumn. I didn't mean to cause trouble for you."

Satisfied, I went on with my lecture. "And number two, you might be a tough kid, but you don't walk around these streets alone at night. You stick with a buddy, or better yet, two or three of them. If you grew up here, you know what you were just doing was dumb. You might have friends and know the blocks to keep off of, but it's not safe out here alone, no matter how tough you are."

He wasn't as receptive to that comment, but at least he didn't argue. Honestly, half the struggle for a kid in his situation was knowing which battles to fight and which to surrender to. Storm was smart and had figured that one out early.

"I don't remember which way the police station was," Autumn said as she drove. "Do I make a right or a left at the light?"

"The police station is to the right, but go left. Let's drop him off at Park House before you take me back to my car."

"It's okay. I can handle it from here. I already have you out so late."

"I'm fine. I'd rather make sure the resident manager didn't jump the gun and call Probation, and also that no one gives you a hard time."

"Oh, alright. Thanks."

Park House was quiet, and luckily no one had called Probation. So once I knew there was no trouble brewing, I waited outside to give Autumn and Storm some time to talk. I sensed she'd wanted to have another heart to heart with him.

I was leaning against her car when she walked out a few minutes later.

"Everything go okay?"

She nodded. "Though I also thought everything was going to be okay the other day when I dropped him off. I just don't get what it's going to take to scare him."

"Unfortunately, not much scares a kid like him."

Autumn's eyes quietly roamed my face. "It sounds like you're saying that from personal experience."

"I am."

She made a face that reminded me why I didn't often talk about how I grew up. I *loathed* pity. That shit should be saved for people who can't help themselves.

I shoved my hand into my pockets. "Every screwed-up kid who manages to pull himself up out of the dirt has one person who made a difference in his life. You're Storm's person. You may need to use that to your advantage at times."

"What do you mean?"

"He doesn't value himself right now. But he does value you. Don't hesitate to do what I did in the car—remind him his consequences could get *you* in trouble or hurt you in some way. He'll do the right thing by you, even if he won't yet do the right thing for himself."

"That feels really manipulative to lay on him."

I smiled. "Trust me, he's manipulating you more."

Autumn sighed. "Thank you. Not just for coming with me, but for giving me some insight into what's going on in Storm's mind. They don't teach that kind of stuff in social work school."

"Anytime."

"I owe you one. I'm not sure I can put on a cape and come to your rescue like you did for me tonight. But keep my IOU in your pocket in case you need some help with social service on a case someday or whatever."

I nodded.

"Come on," she said. "I'll drop you back at your car before it's time for you to be at work already."

"Actually, how about if we go out for a cup of coffee or a drink? I'm not tired."

Autumn nibbled her bottom lip. "I should get going."

It would've been smarter to use her IOU to have her put a good word in for me with her boyfriend, but instead I reached into my pocket and pretended to pull something out. Extending my empty hand to her, I said, "I'd like to cash in this IOU that's been burning a hole in my pocket." I smiled. "Have coffee with me."

7

Autumn

"Is that Latin?" My eyes followed Donavan's arm as he lifted his drink.

"It is."

"What does it mean? If you don't mind me asking."

"Not at all. *Vincit qui se vincit.* It translates to *He conquers who conquers himself.* Someone I'm close to used to say it all the time when I was a kid getting in trouble. It basically means if I can control myself, I can conquer anything."

"That simplifies a lot, doesn't it?"

Donovan smiled, flashing one of his dimples, and it set off a flutter in the pit of my belly. His smile had a sort of devilish quality lurking beneath the surface. It was confident and somehow overtly sexual. *Dangerous.* That's what it was. I trained my eyes away from his face, only to have them land on his forearms. That certainly didn't help my situation much. They were so muscular and tanned, and all of the tattoos made the entire package insanely sexy.

"You know, you look very different in jeans and a T-shirt than you do in a suit and tie."

His eyes moved over my face. "Oh yeah? Which do you like better?"

That was a tough question, like having to decide between Godiva milk chocolate truffles or dark. Both were delicious. Though there was something dangerous to my sanity about a man who looked as good as Donovan did in a custom suit *and* had all those tattoos hidden underneath. But I didn't think it was smart to share those thoughts, so I shrugged and went back to enjoying my fries.

When I looked up, I found Donovan staring at me like I had two heads. "What?" I wiped my chin and looked down at my shirt. "Did I drip or something?"

His face was an odd mix of amused and grossed out. "Did you just dunk your French fry into your chocolate shake and eat it?"

"Oh." I chuckled. "I guess I did."

"That's disgusting."

"Have you ever tried it?"

"No."

"Then how do you know it's disgusting? You might love it."

Donovan smirked as he sipped his chocolate shake. "Never ate dog shit, either. Pretty sure there are some things you don't need to try in order to know they're not going to taste good."

"Whatever." I shrugged. "You don't know what you're missing."

Donovan and I had gone to a twenty-four-hour diner for coffee, not too far from Park House. But I was sort of hungry since I hadn't had dinner, so I decided to get a shake and fries, while he'd opted for just a shake. Coming here with him was probably a dumb thing to do, but how could I say no after he'd spent hours combing the streets to find Storm with me? At least that's why I told myself I'd agreed to come. It had nothing whatsoever to do with how beautiful the man sitting across from me was, or how strongly the magnetic pull toward him gripped me.

"Did you know that French fries are one of the most expensive foods in Venezuela?" I wagged a fry at him. "McDonald's even took them off their menu there for a while."

"I didn't know that. Did you go to Venezuela recently?"

I shook my head. "I read it when I was looking something up once."

He smirked. "Let me guess—someone mentioned that potatoes were the starchiest food, and that sent you down the Google rabbit hole. I've missed your deep dives and random trivia."

I stuck my tongue out because, well, he was right. I had found that on one of my tumbles down the research rabbit hole, so I had no comeback.

Donovan's eyes dropped to my mouth. "You shouldn't stick that thing out, unless you're planning on using it." He winked.

I laughed. But I also sucked down enough of my shake to give me a brain freeze, because I needed to cool off. Stirring what was left in my glass with the straw, I said, "So...I hope I didn't interrupt anything when I called this evening. It is a Saturday night and all."

He smiled. *God, he really needs to stop doing that.*

"Are you asking me if I was out on a date?"

"No," I said defensively. "I was just saying I hope I didn't interrupt anything good."

"You did."

I frowned, feeling an unexpected pang of jealousy. "Oh. Sorry."

Donovan leaned in, his smirky smile widening. "I had a hot date with Bruce Willis planned. How about you? Any plans spoiled for this evening?"

I shook my head. "Just a night of catching up with *The Bachelor*."

Donovan's nose scrunched up. "You like that show?"

"I'm addicted to it—so much so that I can't handle the stress of watching it once a week and waiting to find out what happened. I record them and don't start until I can spend an entire evening bingeing the episodes. My friend Skye and I watch it together."

He chuckled. "I find it amusing when women talk about the people on that show like they're real."

"What do you mean *like they're real*. They *are* real."

"You don't think shows like that are scripted?"

"Don't say that!"

He laughed. "Did I just tell eight-year-old Autumn there's no Santa Claus?"

"Well, even if it is scripted, it's better than—which aging action hero did you say you were going to watch? Bruce Willis or Tom Cruise?"

"Bruce."

"Those movies are faker than *The Bachelor*. Most of the actors don't even do their own stunts."

Donovan's eyes flickered down to my lips a moment. It was less than a second—I could've blinked and missed it—yet that fraction of a second set off a frenzy of butterflies in my belly. *This*. This was the reason I'd done something I'd never done before and spent an entire weekend with a man I barely knew. We just had to look at each other, and sparks flew.

I felt the need to change the subject, but really, what was safer than talking about action movies?

"Anyway..." I said. "I'm glad I didn't interrupt any big plans you had for tonight."

He nodded, and then silence fell while he watched me. I got the distinct feeling he was debating saying something, and when he finally spoke, I realized I was right.

"So...the Dickster. How long has that been going on?"

I stirred my shake again to avoid eye contact. "Not too long. A month or so."

He nodded. "I guess things changed over the last year, then?"

My eyebrows dipped together. "What do you mean?"

"After our luggage exchange, you disappeared because you only wanted what we'd had—a weekend, not a relationship. And now you're in one."

"I'm not in a serious relationship with Blake. We're just dating."

"Yet you gave him your phone number and let him see you more than once..."

"It's different."

"How?"

"Well, Blake and I only really see each other once a week, if that. We keep things simple. He's divorced with kids and not looking for anything complicated."

"I would've kept things simple, if that's what you wanted."

"Really? Because I wouldn't have been able to."

"Why not?"

"I don't know." I shook my head. "But the time we spent together didn't feel like something simple to me. Did it for you?"

He studied me. "No, but that doesn't mean I would have pushed you for more than you were ready to give. I work eighty to ninety hours a week most weeks, anyway."

I sighed. "I just prefer to keep things uncomplicated."

"So things with Dickson...they're uncomplicated?"

"Yes."

"And that means…"

"I don't know. I guess it means I don't have to worry about either of our feelings becoming too much."

Donovan scratched his chin. "Let me see if I understand this. You liked me, and you had a good time that weekend we spent together. But you thought one or both of us might develop feelings. You have no worry about that with Dickson, so you keep seeing him."

"Well…yes."

"So you only date men you don't really like?"

"I, uhh…no… I mean…well." I shook my head. "Stop lawyering me. You're making me confused at what I'm even saying."

Donovan smiled and shook his head. "It really sucks to be on this side."

"What side?"

"The it's-not-you-it's-me bullshit. I'm usually the one deflecting like you are right now."

"I'm not deflecting. I'm trying to be honest with you."

Again, his eyes dropped to my lips. Only this time, they lingered much longer. When they finally lifted to look at my face, it felt like he could see right through me. "So the two of you aren't exclusive, then?"

"It's exclusive for me."

He squinted. "And it's not for him?"

I shrugged. "Maybe it is. I'm not sure. We've never discussed it. But I prefer to only…you know…with one person at a time."

Donovan's jaw flexed, and his tanned skin seemed to grow a shade darker. He gave a curt nod. "Understood."

A few minutes later, the waitress came to check on us. When I said I didn't want anything else, Donovan asked for the check. It was late, but I got the feeling his sudden desire to call it a night had nothing to do with the time.

After we argued over the bill and Donovan paid, we headed to my car. The ride back to the police station was quiet, yet the air felt filled with unspoken words. I pulled into the spot next to his car and put the car in park.

"Well, thanks again for tonight. I really appreciate everything you've done for Storm."

"Not a problem."

Donovan opened the car door and turned back to face me once he was out. The parking lot lights cast a soft, yellowish glow on his handsome face. He looked at me for a moment and then slowly—as if giving me time to stop him—reached out and cupped my cheek, stroking my skin with his thumb. My heart ricocheted in my chest.

"Why does it feel so damn wrong to get out of this car without kissing you goodnight?" His eyes once again fell to my lips, and I couldn't control how fast my chest started to rise and fall.

"I...I don't know."

He leaned in slowly. At first I thought he was actually going to do it, but at the last moment he veered, and his lips went to my ear instead. "Would you stop me if I did?"

In that moment, I absolutely would not have. Worse, part of me *wanted* him to do it. *Really badly.* I'd held my breath, waiting for it even.

But when I said nothing, Donovan pulled back and searched my eyes. He caressed my cheek one last time before he moved away.

"What's between us might not be simple, but it's also not over. Get home safe, Red."

8

Donovan

Being in the old neighborhood over the last week reminded me it had been too long since I'd stopped by to see Bud. Bud—real name Frances Yankowski—was the closest thing to a father I'd ever known. If I'm being real, he was pretty much the closest thing to a mother, too. So the following night, rather than go home after leaving the office, I headed back to Brooklyn and stopped in at a local business to find out where Bud set up shop these days. I walked into a corner deli that had been there since I was a kid, though I'd never seen the woman behind the counter before.

"Hi. Can you tell me how to get to Bud's Flower Shop, please?" That was code for *Where is Bud squatting to feed the community tonight?* All of the local businesses knew the answer and never minded helping spread the word. At least they didn't mind sharing the information with people who seemed like they could use a free meal.

But the cashier looked me up and down and frowned.
Yeah, I know. I didn't change out of my work clothes.
Most people judge you because you wear hand-me-downs

with holes in them, but not in my old stomping ground. Walk in looking like you shop at Brooks Brothers, and you're bound to piss someone off.

"Four sixty-two Carnie Street." She lifted her chin to the aisles behind me. "You look like maybe you can afford to bring some dessert or something."

"Good idea." I smiled and grabbed half a dozen packages of cookies off the shelf and brought them up to the register to pay. "You have a good night."

When I arrived at the address the woman had given me, people were walking in and out of a dilapidated house with boarded-up windows, so I knew it was the right place. Bud served a community dinner seven days a week in whatever abandoned building or parking lot he could find. Sometimes he got to stay at one location for months, other times he'd get kicked out after just a day or two. The people who usually made a stink about him were the landlords who'd let the building get so run down it was no longer rentable, or the bank who'd repossessed the property. Cops looked the other way for Bud. Over the years, I'd even seen them drop off people they'd picked up who needed a meal.

For his day job, Bud owned a Boar's Head provisions route. Every morning he delivered fresh meats to delis, restaurants, and supermarkets, but he also picked up their soon-to-expire food, which he turned into a daily feast to feed the hungry and homeless of the community. But *no one* ate for free more than once. No exceptions. You had to work for Bud in order to continue to be fed, whether you helped tend his garden, loaded and unloaded his truck full of supplies, or pitched in and did lawn work for the restaurants that helped him. Bud was the heart of this community, and he was also the only way I'd eaten a decent meal most of the time when my mom took off.

Entering the rundown house, I walked over to the row of tables where Bud was dishing food out of battery-operated hot plates. He might be close to seventy now, but he was sharp as a tack and never missed a thing. I hadn't thought he'd noticed me come in, until he grumbled without looking up.

"Jesus Christ, you look like a narc." Bud waved the serving spoon in his hand, motioning to my suit.

I chuckled. If I were wearing a French maid outfit, I'd get my balls busted less around here. "Nice to see you, too, Bud."

He nodded toward the empty spot next to him behind the serving table. "Get an apron on, kid. I could use help. But I wouldn't want you to mess up that monkey suit."

Thirteen or thirty, it didn't matter. I did whatever the old man said. So for the next hour, we served dinner side by side, shooting the shit as we dished out pasta primavera, broccoli, and day-or-two-old bread that he'd turned into garlic toast. I asked him about his beloved plants, and he rattled on about some new variegated tomato seeds he was growing that were *developed in Mexico*. The way he said it told me I was supposed to be impressed by that. At seven thirty sharp, we turned off the hot plates, which were dragged in and out every day so no one could steal them, and we took two plates of food outside to the front stoop and sat down to eat ourselves.

"So what's new in the land of movers and shakers? You get off any of those Ponzi-scheme idiots who rob people of their retirement savings lately?"

"Luckily, no." I shoveled a heaping forkful of pasta into my mouth. It was probably the best-tasting thing I'd had in months. Bud didn't screw around when it came to cooking or his plants. I wiped sauce from my mouth. "How's your knee doing?"

"It's holding up. The humidity's been low, so that helps. I have no idea why Florida is the land of old people. Dry heat is so much easier on old bones."

Bud caught me up on all the latest neighborhood gossip—who was feuding with who, and who got caught doing what. I told him I'd stopped down to see Dario the other day, and before I knew it, we were the only two left at the house.

"Welp…" He stood. "Guess we better be going before the druggies get annoyed we're hanging out in their crib."

I smiled. "I'll load your van."

I packed up all of the serving supplies and locked the back of Bud's van with the same rusted chain and padlock he'd been using since I was a kid.

Still holding it, I said, "I think it might be time for a new lock."

"Why? Is that one broken?"

"No, but it's rusted to shit. One day the key isn't going to turn it anymore."

Bud shrugged. "Then that'll be the day I spring for a new lock."

We shook hands next to the van. "If you're not busy this weekend," he said, "I gotta turn over the garden. Could use an extra set of hands."

"Saturday or Sunday?"

"Saturday. Got plans with my lady friend on Sunday."

Shit. I needed to work on Saturday—keep my billing up. I'd have to go in at the crack of dawn, but I'd figure out a way to pull it off. "What time?" I asked.

"Two sounds good to me. When you're done, you can help me prep for the night's dinner service."

I nodded. "Sounds good. See you Saturday."

I started to walk away, but turned back. "Hey, you mind if I bring someone?"

Bud shrugged. "He got arms and know how to use a shovel?"

"He's got arms, and I can teach him how to use a shovel if he doesn't know. It's a twelve-year-old client of mine. Sadly, the kid reminds me a lot of myself at that age."

"Oh Lord." Bud shook his head. "Not sure I can handle two of you. But yeah, fine. Bring 'em."

"Shovel? You just told Mrs. Benson at Park House we were going to your office to talk about strategy."

"Well, that wasn't a total lie. I consider wherever I am to be my office, and I did want to discuss your case for a few minutes at some point today."

"But why are you going to shovel someone's dirt?"

I glanced at Storm and back to the road. "*I'm* not."

"You just said we were going to some guy's house to dig up his old garden so he can get ready to plant a new one. Isn't that digging in dirt?"

"Yes, but you asked why *I* was going to shovel dirt. *I'm* not. *We* are."

Storm looked at me like I had two heads. "I'm not shoveling dirt."

"You wanna bet?"

"What the fuck?"

I pointed at him. "Watch your language. Bud will have you chop a dozen onions, even if he doesn't need them chopped, if you talk like that. Plus, have some respect. I'm older than you, and I'm also your attorney."

"If you're my attorney, you should be getting me off instead of taking me to dig dirt."

I had to stop myself from laughing out loud. This kid was *sooo* me at twelve. Which was why I knew he needed a man like Bud in his life.

"Do you know about the free dinner that's open to people in your old neighborhood?"

"You mean the old man who feeds the crackheads?"

"His name is Bud, and he doesn't just feed people with addiction problems. Anyone who's hungry can go and eat a hot meal from him every night. That's whose garden we're turning over."

Storm shrugged. "Whatever. Why do we have to help?"

"Because if you don't help plant the trees, you don't deserve to sit in the shade."

His face scrunched up. "We're planting trees, too?"

I smiled. "No. I just meant you have to give back to people who give in life."

"Why?"

"A lot of reasons. It helps others who need help. It'll make you feel good about yourself. It teaches you values."

Storm pretty much tuned out. He looked around the front of my car. "Is this real wood?"

I nodded. "It's walnut."

"So you help plant trees and then you make people chop 'em down to put inside your fancy car."

I couldn't hide my smile this time. "You're a wise ass."

Storm pointed his finger at me. "Watch your language, or you'll be chopping onions."

This was going to be one long-ass day.

⌒

"So what's his story?" Bud stood at the back window of his house, watching Storm as he worked in the garden.

I washed my hands at the kitchen sink. "Lives at Park House. Very smart. Useless parents. Uses his fists to get out his anger."

Bud's eyes met mine briefly before he returned to looking outside. "Sounds like a boy I used to know."

Drying off my hands, I filled two glasses with cold water and went to stand next to him at the window. "Yeah." I handed him a glass. "He could definitely use some direction."

Bud chugged his water. "Drugs?"

I shook my head. "Weed. Nothing else that I'm aware of."

"Well, that's good. Any family to speak of?"

"Mother's alive. But she didn't even show to visit on his birthday. She's an addict."

Bud frowned. His daughter had been an addict. He lost her to an overdose the same year I was born. It wasn't something he talked about often, but I knew it was part of how he'd started feeding people. He used to drag her out of the type of buildings he spent his nights in now. Often when he'd gone looking for her, he'd seen hungry kids sitting around while their strung-out parents used what little money they had for more drugs. Him feeding the neighborhood and spending time in the places he did always felt like part punishment and part penance to me—for not being able to save his daughter.

"He has a social worker he seems to trust," I said. "Autumn."

Bud nodded. "It's good he has someone. Though we both know the people down at social services tend to rotate in and out pretty fast. One day they're here, the next they're gone, and then a kid like Storm feels abandoned all over again."

I knew that to be true, so I refrained from mentioning that his social worker had already left *a kid like Storm* feeling abandoned—*me*.

Storm finished up the last of the garden turnover while Bud and I started to prep for his nightly meal service.

Once all three of us were done, I stepped outside to call Park House and let the manager know I was going to take Storm to dinner and I'd have him back after. Of course, she was fine with it since lawyers were on the list of approved visitors who could take kids out of the building. It also left her one less person to worry about.

When I went back inside, I asked Storm to help me start loading Bud's van. "I thought tonight we'd help serve dinner with Bud."

Storm shrugged. "Fine."

He'd never say so, but I was pretty sure he'd actually liked working in the garden this afternoon.

"What's Bud short for?" he asked as we walked back up the path to the house. "Budrick or something?"

"Bud's name is actually Frances. Everyone just calls him Bud because of his garden—bud as in plant buds. The man can grow anything."

Storm shook his head. "Frances is worse than Augustus."

I ruffled Storm's hair as I opened the door. "Go wash up, *Augustus*."

⸺

The day had gone even better than I'd expected. Storm had let down his guard, and I was pretty sure he was shocked to see a few people he knew at dinner service, including one of his buddies from the neighborhood.

I pulled up at Park House and parked the car. "I told the manager I spoke to earlier that I was taking you to dinner," I said. "I didn't mention *where* we were going to eat."

Storm smirked. "Are you telling me to lie?"

"Absolutely not. If anyone asks, you tell them the truth. I was just letting you know that I didn't elaborate on where dinner was, so if it doesn't come up, it doesn't come up."

Storm's smile widened. "So...don't lie, but omit some of the details."

I shoved his shoulder. "Don't be a pain in my ass."

He chuckled. "I'm going to tell Bud you said *ass* so you'll have to chop onions."

We got out of the car and walked toward the entrance. "Be nice. Or you won't have the opportunity to take Bud up on his offer."

Bud had asked Storm if he might be interested in an old bike he had in his garage in exchange for painting his backyard fence.

"Can you take me over there next weekend so I can start painting?"

I nodded. "Let me talk to Autumn and see what she says."

Inside Park House, I checked Storm in at the front desk. He surprised me when he extended his hand. "Thanks," he said.

I smiled as we shook. "No problem."

On my way back to the car, I felt pretty damn good. It had been too long since I'd spent time with Bud. Plus, I'd gotten the feeling that maybe Bud could use a Storm in his life almost as much as Storm could use a Bud.

Then there was the added bonus—I had a reason to call Autumn tomorrow.

9

Autumn

"Everything go okay?" my assistant asked when I finally strolled into the office midafternoon. "I thought you'd be back in a couple of hours."

I sighed. "Yeah, so did I. Judge O'Halloran denied the plaintiff's motion for a continuance, so we wound up starting the trial. I'm lucky my opening argument was ready to go."

"Oh, wow. Yeah, good thing." She pointed toward my office door. "Your messages are on your desk, but a woman called twice. I don't think it was a client because I didn't recognize the name, and when I asked her what it was in reference to, she said it was personal." My assistant winced. "She sounded sort of upset and frustrated, so you might want to call her back first."

My forehead wrinkled. I hadn't pissed any women off lately, at least that I knew of. "What was her name?"

"Autumn Wilde. Her number is on your desk."

Shit. What did Storm get himself into now? And here I thought I'd gotten through to him a little bit yesterday.

I took off my suit jacket and tossed it over the back of my chair. Before I even had time to look at the stack of messages on my desk, my assistant popped her head into my office. "Umm...you have a call on line one."

I shook my head. "Tell them I'll call them back. I need a minute to get organized."

"It's Autumn Wilde again."

I nodded. "I'll take it. Can you shut the door behind you, please?"

Sitting down at my desk, I grabbed the receiver and pushed line one. "Autumn, what's going on?"

"Why haven't you called me back?"

"Because I was in court all morning and afternoon. What happened? Did Storm get in trouble again?"

"No. But I'm sure it's only a matter of time before he does considering you have him hanging out with drug addicts."

My head reared back. "What?"

"Why in the world would you think taking a troubled twelve-year-old kid to an abandoned building filled with drug addicts would be a good idea?"

I held my hand up, even though she obviously couldn't see me. "Hang on a second. I think you only have half the story."

"Really? So you didn't take Storm to an abandoned building last night? One that was boarded up?"

"I did, but—"

"And the building wasn't filled with drug addicts and homeless people? Oh, and one guy calls himself Jesus and offered to have Storm join his disciples?"

I shook my head. "Artemis is harmless. He's a little mentally ill, but he'd never hurt anyone."

"Seriously, Donovan? A *little* mentally ill? *What the hell*?"

82

"Listen, I know it sounds bad. But you're getting everything completely out of context. Did Storm tell you why we were there, or about Bud?"

"*Storm* didn't tell me anything. When I saw him earlier today, I asked him how his weekend was, and he just shrugged and said fine. But apparently he'd been bragging to some kids about hanging out in a crack den, and one of the younger boys was smart enough to come tell me—mostly because he looks up to Storm, and the kid's mother died of a drug overdose, so he was worried."

Shit. I scrubbed my face with my hands. "Okay. It's really not what it sounds like. I took Storm to meet Bud—a local who serves a nightly dinner in the community. I've known him for more than twenty years. He's a good guy, and Storm was never out of my sight. He was never in any danger. I swear."

"If he was never in any danger, and where you took him was such an upstanding place, then why did you lie to the house manager?"

"I didn't lie. I said I was taking him to dinner."

"Don't lawyer me, Donovan. Omitting information is as much a lie as telling an outright lie—because you're not divulging the true story. It may be perfectly acceptable in your line of work, but it isn't in mine, or in life in general."

I dragged a hand through my hair. "Look, I'm sorry. I didn't mean to upset you. I really think Bud can be good for Storm. I'd planned on calling you today, but court ran long. Bud offered Storm a job, and I think—"

"A job? Doing what? Selling drugs?"

I sighed. Autumn had a picture in her head, and I wasn't going to be able to change it unless she saw the real story for herself. I looked at my watch. It was a little after five. "Did you eat dinner yet?"

"No. But what's that—"

I interrupted her this time. "Good. Don't. I'll pick you up in an hour. We can discuss this over a meal."

"I'm not going out to dinner with you!"

"Don't flatter yourself. It's not a date. Bud gets insulted if you visit him and don't eat his cooking. So you'll need to eat in order to check out where I took Storm. You need to see it for yourself. Text me your address."

"And then when he was thirteen, he stole a Cadillac and crashed into a police car."

I held up my hands. "I did *not* steal the car. Jimmy Lutz's brother bought it for a hundred bucks."

Bud shook his head. "He bought a one-year-old Cadillac in pristine condition for a hundred bucks, and he and his dumbass friend thought it was on the up and up, so they took it for a ride. Made it three blocks and crashed right into the back of a police car."

Autumn laughed. She'd pretty much had a smile on her face since the minute we sat down with Bud. I'd forgotten what a charmer the old man could be. And I hoped he kept telling stories—I didn't even give a shit if they made me look like a total idiot—because staring at the smile on Autumn's face trumped my need to look cool by a landslide. Autumn caught me watching her, and her eyes narrowed for a second—as if she was trying to figure out what was going on in my head. I'd happily tell her, but I'd probably get smacked. It was her own fault, though, really. Because how could she expect me to watch her lips curve up in delight and *not* remember how they'd done the same thing when I'd gone down on her the weekend we'd spent together?

Some women make weird-ass faces as they orgasm— eyes squeezed closed, mouth contorted like they've just sucked on a lemon. I'd been with a woman who right before it hit, all the color would drain from her face and her eyes would go wide. Then her mouth opened for a silent scream. The first time I saw it, I thought there might be an axe murderer above me about to chop into my skull. But not Autumn. She *smiled* her way through orgasm. And it was fucking phenomenal.

After Bud told a few more stories about what a rotten kid I was, he excused himself to go talk to someone else.

I nodded toward the long-haired, hippie-looking guy wearing ripped jeans, who could have passed for one of the homeless who came to eat. "That's the pastor at the local Episcopalian church. Bud doesn't allow anyone to come in and preach—whether that be an addiction counselor or a member of the clergy. But he keeps in contact with all the local church leaders. If there's anything going on in this community, that crew knows about it."

Autumn watched Bud greet the pastor, and the two men walked outside together. "He's pretty amazing. I can't believe he's only missed four days of serving dinner in twenty-six years. Doesn't he ever get sick?"

"I honestly can't remember him ever being sick, at least not sick enough to keep him down. Though I'm not sure anything could keep that man down, except maybe a rope and some chains." I scoffed. "Even then, he'd find a way."

"I'm sorry I jumped to conclusions about you bringing Storm here. I had no idea so many lessons could be taught in a place like this."

"It's fine. I should've given you the heads up. But I'd only planned to take him to meet Bud, not bring him to dinner here. I'm not even sure what I expected to happen by bringing him to Bud's place. I guess I just feel like Bud saved me, so maybe some of that might rub off on Storm."

Autumn smiled warmly. "I guess your mom had you volunteer with Bud because you got yourself into trouble as a teenager?"

I pushed the corn on my plate around with my fork. "Volunteer? Not exactly. I started working for Bud because I was hungry."

Autumn's smile wilted. "Oh, I'm sorry. I just assumed..."

"It's fine. You don't have to be sorry. I'm not ashamed of where I came from or the things I had to do to eat. Not anymore, anyway. I just don't talk about them often because once people know your mother was a prostitute and sometimes disappeared for days or weeks at a time, leaving an eight year old to fend for himself, they look at you differently."

Autumn's face softened. I pointed at it with my fork. "Like that. They look at me exactly like that."

She smiled. "Sorry. Do you have any other family?"

"Just Bud. My mother's still alive—at least the last time she made contact to ask for money she was. My father was a John. My mother had no idea which one and didn't seem to think it was important anyway. Both my grandparents died before I was born. They had my mom late in life, and as far as I know, she was an only child. Although, half the stuff that comes out of my mother's mouth is lies, so it's possible I have some blood relatives somewhere. I could be related to the Queen of England, for all I know."

Autumn was quiet for a moment. "It's funny. You're sort of like an onion. The first time we met at that coffee shop, I thought I had you pegged."

"Pegged as what?"

She shrugged. "I assumed you were like most of the men I grew up around in Old Greenwich, Connecticut— smart, educated, well-off, a silver spoon of sorts. You know, with going to Harvard and wearing custom-made shirts and cufflinks. Though the thirty mini bottles of shampoo and conditioner and other stuff that were in your suitcase really confused me."

"That makes two of us, then. I was confused as to why you needed four giant vibrators in your bag."

Autumn's cheeks turned bright pink. She covered her face with her hands. "Oh my God." She laughed. "I can explain that..."

"I sort of figured it out once we had coffee and you mentioned that you'd just come back from a bachelorette party and had some embarrassing decorations in your bag. Unless you just usually carry those around with you." I lifted my chin toward her purse. "Is there one in there right now?"

"No!" She laughed. "God...I'm glad at least we were both snoopers, then."

"I actually hadn't gone through your bag until you were so adamant about me *not* going through it. Then I had to."

"Alright, well..." She shook her head. "You know why I had some odd stuff. So I think it's only fair that you tell me about the stuff in your bag. Did you pass an unattended housekeeping cart on your way out and feel like a rebel or something?"

"Nah. Just an old habit. When I was a kid and my mom didn't come home for a long stretch, I'd run out of most things. So I'd sneak into a hotel, find someone from housekeeping, pretend I was a guest and ask for a few extra of everything." I shrugged. "I travel a decent amount for business, so I haven't paid for shampoo or toothpaste in years. I usually don't ask for extra anymore, unless I happen to see a person from housekeeping in the hall. On that trip, when I passed the room next door, a woman was cleaning. I asked if she could leave an extra or two in my room. She said no problem and told me I looked just like her son. When I came back, she'd left a shitload."

Autumn smiled. "See? You're an onion. I never would've guessed you had all those tattoos hidden under the crisp dress shirt you wore when we met at Starbucks either. When I asked you about them, you said you went through some wild teenage years. So I assumed you'd rebelled against your uptight, wealthy family for a while. Then there were the plants all over your apartment. Those really threw me, for some strange reason. You said you just liked plants, but I assumed there'd been a woman in your life at one point who'd left them behind."

I smiled. "Bud got me into plants. I work too much to have a dog or a hobby, so they're pretty much it."

"I see that now."

"Plus, they don't talk back."

"Talk *back*? As in, you talk to them?"

I shrugged. "Usually I just practice my opening or closing for a case on them, but sometimes they catch the brunt of things when I'm pissed off."

Autumn smiled. I couldn't help but stare at her lips. When she caught me, I pointed down to her plate. "You want more?"

She rubbed her stomach. "No, thanks. But it was really delicious."

I nodded. "So what's your story? You know so much about my life now, yet I don't really know much about you."

"What do you want to know?"

I shrugged. "I don't know. How'd you get into social work? Did you always want to help kids?"

"No, I pretty much took the long road to get here. I went to undergrad school for business and then started law school at Yale. But I did my first year and decided it wasn't what I wanted to do."

"Seriously?"

"Yup. You already know my father is a lawyer. Yale was his alma mater, and he'd always hoped I'd go there."

"*He*'d always hoped, not you?"

"I know this sounds silly, but I don't know if I ever considered what I wanted before I started school. Since I didn't have a passion for anything else, and that was what I was expected to do, I went through the motions."

"What made you change your mind?"

Autumn looked down. "Everything."

I stayed quiet, waiting for more, but she didn't elaborate.

"So how did you get into social work?"

She sighed. "It's sort of a long story. But I met a young girl who'd gone through some tough times, and I wanted to help her in some way, except I didn't know how. That got me thinking, so I audited a class that was part of the masters in social work program to see if that might be what I wanted to do. By the third week in, I decided to enroll in the full program. I'm working on my PhD in counseling psychology now. I take part-time classes. I took the summer off, but I should finish next year."

"Wow. That's impressive. It's not easy to jump off a path once you get on. I give you a lot of credit for backing up and figuring out what you wanted to do. Most people would've just finished law school and been miserable practicing."

"Thanks." She smiled. "What about you? Did you always know you wanted to be a lawyer?"

"I knew I'd either need one or be one. I just wasn't sure which way things would shake out."

She laughed. "Is it a coincidence that you grew up struggling, and you're in a profession that pays well and you deal with wealthy clients? Whereas I grew up in

Old Greenwich, Connecticut, pretty much spoiled and surrounded by wealthy people, and I'm in a profession that pays crappy, and I deal with mostly people in poverty all day?"

I rubbed my chin. "I guess we both learned what we didn't want out of life." I paused. "Do you still keep in touch with her?"

Autumn's brows drew together. "Who?"

"The girl you met who you wanted to help, but didn't know how?"

She smiled. "I do, actually. Skye turns twenty-two next month, and she's become my best friend over the years."

Bud walked over and pointed to his watch. "Time to close up shop." He motioned to two guys standing a few feet behind him. "I got Tweedle Dee and Tweedle Dum to help me break down and load everything in the van. Why don't you two kids get out of here before it gets too late?"

I raised my hand to my ear and cupped it. "What's that? I must've heard you wrong. It sounded like you just offered me a *free meal*." I looked across the table to Autumn. "No one eats for free more than once on Bud's watch."

Bud waved his hand at me. "Watch it, smartass. Or I'll make you sand the rust off some pipes I have in my basement."

I shook my head. "Is it time to do that already? Feels like just yesterday you had me doing that with a piece of sandpaper that had been used so much it barely had any grit left on it."

Bud winked at Autumn. "I had fresh sandpaper in the drawer all along. I don't remember what he'd done that time to piss me off, but I'm sure he deserved it."

Autumn laughed. "I believe you."

"Besides," Bud said, "I got some holes in my walls that can use spackling, if you haven't lost your touch with

VI KEELAND

a Spackle knife. I know manual labor isn't your thing these days. I can tell by your soft-looking hands, pretty boy."

"My hands are not soft, old man."

"Good." He nodded. "Then you can pay me back for dinner when you bring the kid to start earning that bike."

I looked over at Autumn. "Is it okay with you if Storm does some work for Bud?"

She nodded with a smile. "I think that would be really good for him."

We said goodbye to Bud, and I told him I'd see him the following weekend. Autumn was quiet on the drive back to her apartment. So was I, but that was mostly because I spent the time debating kidnapping her and dragging her to my place to remind her how incredible our weekend together had been. A few buildings away from hers, I parked and cut the engine.

"I'm going to walk you up," I announced.

"That's not necessary."

"Maybe not, but I'm going to do it anyway."

I jogged around to her side of the car so I could open the door and offered my hand to help her out. She hesitated, but took it. Way too soon, we were at her door.

She turned to face me. "Thank you for tonight. And again, I'm sorry for jumping down your throat without understanding where you had taken Storm and why."

I shrugged. "It's okay. He needs someone to protect him. I'd rather you get pissed off than no one giving a shit at all."

Autumn nodded but looked down. When she looked back up, I could see hesitation in her face. "Can I ask you something personal?"

"Shoot."

"Was social services ever involved when you were younger? I mean, you found Bud because you needed a place to eat. Didn't they intervene?"

I shrugged. "Sometimes. Mostly when I got in trouble. But I'd call my friends and have them go to my mother's usual places, and they'd pay her twenty bucks to go down to the police station and pretend she gave a shit, like I was just an out-of-control kid. Social services didn't really look deeper since someone had come to pick me up. Guess there's too many kids like Storm who have no one to even pretend."

She sighed. "The system is far from perfect."

"It all worked out in the end."

"I guess."

"Can I ask you something personal now?"

"Of course. It's only fair since I'm so nosy."

"What's the reason you don't want a relationship and only date guys who want the same?"

She frowned. "You really cut to the chase, don't you?"

"Sorry. Occupational hazard, I guess. But I'd like to understand what I'm missing here. I know it's something."

Autumn nodded. She looked away before she started speaking again. "I was in a relationship that...ended. And I'm just not ready for that again."

I could see she was uncomfortable talking about it, but she'd let me in a bit, so I gently pushed. "How long ago did it end?"

"Six years."

Wow. That was a long time to get over things. But it dawned on me that maybe she'd suffered a loss. That could definitely make it take longer than usual to get back on the horse, so to speak.

Before I could ask anything more, she turned to go in.

"Goodnight, Donovan. Thanks again for everything."

10
Autumn

Ten years ago

"That was a nice gift you gave Lena." The deep voice seemed to come out of nowhere.

"Jesus. You scared the crap out of me."

"How long have you been sitting back here?"

"I don't know." I shrugged. "Maybe twenty minutes."

The backyard was pitch dark, but I knew the voice. *Braden Erlich.* The son of my dad's newest partner at work. Correction, the *ridiculously hot* son of my dad's newest partner at work.

"Are the lights broken?" he asked. "The ones that go on when they detect motion?"

"Not that I'm aware of."

Braden was quiet for a moment. "So that means you haven't moved in twenty minutes?"

I smiled in the dark. "It's sort of a hobby of mine. I like to see how long I can stay still before the motion detectors catch me."

"What's your record?"

I detected a hint of amusement in his voice.

"Twenty-six minutes."

He went silent for a while. "Alright. Let's see if we can break it."

I laughed, but I was careful not to move my face too much or let my body shake. "You're going to stand there and not move so I can break my record?"

"That depends."

"On what?"

"If you admit that you re-gifted the present I just saw your dad's fiancée open inside."

"What makes you think I re-gifted it?"

"My mother gave it to you at your high school graduation party three months ago."

Shit. Did she? I closed my eyes. *Oh my God. I think she might've.* "Sorry," I said.

"What are you sorry for? Not wanting a porcelain figurine when you're eighteen?"

"It's a Lladro. It probably cost seven-hundred dollars."

"Didn't cost my mother that much."

"How do you know?"

"Because she got it as a gift from my grandmother two years ago."

My eyes widened. "Are you kidding?"

"Nope."

I chuckled. "Wow. Now I definitely don't feel bad."

"You shouldn't. You're too pretty to feel bad."

Oh wow. I was definitely glad we were still in the dark, so he didn't see me blush. "Thank you."

"You're welcome."

"Did you know there's a limited-edition Lladro that costs forty-seven-thousand dollars? They only made five hundred of them."

"So you checked out the value before deciding to re-gift, huh?"

I laughed. "Actually, no. Sometimes I just read up on really random things."

"Interesting."

I probably sounded like a complete dork. "I don't sit at home doing it or anything. It's just something I do once in a while."

"I like that. You're curious."

A solid minute went by, and neither of us said anything. Eventually, Braden spoke. "Are you still there?"

"I am."

"Weren't you afraid Lena would remember you opening that at your graduation party?"

"Lena wasn't at my graduation party. She and my dad only met on the Fourth of July."

"That was less than two months ago."

"Yep."

"And they're engaged already?"

"He proposed on their one-month anniversary."

"Wow."

"Yeah. That seems to be a thing for him. He proposed to his last wife on their six-month anniversary."

"His last wife? How many has he had?"

"This will be his fourth."

"What number was your mom?"

"She was the first. She died when I was twelve."

"I'm sorry."

"Thank you."

"I feel bad for making you talk about it. I think I know where I can get a nice Lladro to make it up to you."

I laughed. "I'm good. But thanks for the offer."

"Why are you sitting out here in the dark, anyway?"

"It's all people from my dad's work inside and Lena's family. Plus, it's a clear night, and I like looking up at the stars."

"Have you ever gone to Long Wharf Park to see the stars?"

"No. Where is it?"

"New Haven."

I sighed. "My father gives me a hard time about driving on I-95 at night since I only got my license six months ago. Maybe my friend Alley will take me."

He was quiet for a bit. "I've been driving three years."

My heart sped up. Was he saying he wanted to take me to see the stars?

Before I could answer, he spoke again. "I'll tell you what. How about we make a little bet? If you beat your record, I'll give you directions to the best spot to see the stars. But if you don't, you have to let me take you."

Ummm... Who cares about the dumb record?

I immediately started figuring out how I could get the motion detector to go off without looking like I'd done it on purpose.

"So...do we have a deal?" Braden said.

I tried to come off nonchalant. "Sure. Why not?"

Five seconds later, the lights came on. I blinked as my eyes adjusted. Had I moved? I didn't think I had.

I looked over at Braden, who sported an ear-to-ear smile.

"I didn't budge," I said.

His smile grew wider. "I know. I swung my arm in the air. The bet you agreed to didn't specify whose fault it would be that the lights went on, only that they did." He tilted his head and held out his hand. "Come on, let's get out of here."

11

Autumn

"**H**ey!" I smiled at my friend Skye's face flashing on the screen and swiped to answer. I'd never seen the picture before. Her eyes were crossed and her tongue dangled out adorably.

"I'm starting to feel neglected," she said. "You don't call... You don't write..."

I laughed. "When did you change your photo in my phone?"

"Last time I was over. If I remember correctly, you were ignoring me, busy on your laptop researching the origin of some song you'd heard on a commercial."

"Ah...yes. 'Magic' by The Pilots. They're from Scotland, you know."

"Of course I know. You told me that and four hundred other facts you looked up after watching a ten-second commercial."

A taxi on the street next to me blew its horn.

"Where are you?" Skye asked.

"On my way to meet Blake for dinner. I took an Uber, but traffic was at a standstill so I got out to walk the last two blocks."

"Blake? That's the new guy I said sounded boring?"

"He's very nice."

"So is my seventy-eight-year-old neighbor, Wilbur. Remind me to set you up if this doesn't work out."

"Cute."

"Anyway, I just called to find out if we're still on for next week and see if everything turned out alright with the kid of yours who went missing. You were supposed to call me the next day."

"Sorry. Things have been a little...I don't know... weird lately. I've felt so scatterbrained. I should've called. But we did find Storm, and he's doing okay, and we are most definitely on for next week. I'm dying to know what happens with Kayla."

"Alright, great. But is everything okay otherwise, though? Something causing you to feel weird?"

"Do you remember a guy I told you about named Donovan?"

"The luggage guy with all the plants whose bones you wanted to hop, but didn't?"

I smiled. "That's him."

"What about him?"

"Well, we ran into each other again."

"Ooooh—that guy was definitely more interesting than the new one. He had tattoos. I've never met a boring dude with tats. Let me guess, Blake doesn't have any?"

I sighed. "He actually doesn't."

"So are you seeing Green Thumb now, too?"

I shook my head. "Not on a personal level, but he is representing Storm, so I guess I will be seeing him." The restaurant where I was meeting Blake was only a few buildings down. "Listen, I need to run. I'm just about to walk in to dinner. I'll see you next week?"

"Can't wait. Have a good night."

"You, too."

I swiped to end the call just as I reached the door to the restaurant. Before going inside, I stopped and took a deep breath. I could have used a few more minutes to clear my head, but I was already late, and I didn't want to be rude. I'd hoped my mood would improve before I arrived, but instead I'd gone from not feeling like going out to dreading it. But I plastered on my best smile as the hostess showed me to the table. Blake was already seated.

He stood and kissed my cheek. "You look gorgeous."

"Thank you."

He pulled out my chair, and I sat. "Sorry I'm late."

"I was starting to think you were going to stand me up."

"My Uber canceled three times. I should have texted you."

"I would've picked you up from your friend's house."

I'd almost forgotten that I'd lied to Blake and told him I was coming straight from a friend's house to avoid having him pick me up. I'd said it without any thought, really. When he'd told me he'd be at my place at seven, for some reason I panicked and blurted that I'd meet him at the restaurant. Then I'd been stuck making up a reason he couldn't come by my place. The last few days I'd done my best to avoid thinking about why I'd done it, because deep down, I knew the answer. I didn't want Blake in my apartment because I couldn't stop thinking about another man. Which was exactly the reason I had forced myself to come tonight, when I would've preferred to sit at home and stare at the TV.

"She lives all the way on the other side of town, and your office is so close to here."

"You're worth the inconvenience."

I forced a smile. The waitress came over with the wine menu. I knew Blake liked red, so I browsed through and said, "Whatever you want is fine."

"You sure?"

"Positive."

I'd met Blake on Tinder. We'd gone out for coffee, which was my usual go-to first meeting. That way if it was awkward, or the guy turned out to be a creep, I was put out of my misery relatively fast. But Blake and I had never had a minute of awkwardness since we'd started seeing each other. Our conversation always seemed to flow naturally, and we'd never had an uncomfortable silence...until now. I wasn't sure if it was in my head or not, but I suddenly felt clumsy, with nothing to say. So I reached for a breadstick to have a reason not to speak.

"How was work this week?" he asked. "You sounded busy when we spoke the other day."

I nodded. "Our case load is supposed to be eighteen. Yesterday I was assigned my thirty-first active case."

"Your office sounds like mine. Except more cases means more money for me. It just means extra work for you."

I nodded. "I don't even want to think about what I actually make per hour."

"Did you ever think about going to law school? There's good money in it, and you can still help people by taking on some pro bono cases."

I'd never mentioned that I *had* gone to law school for a year, and I had no desire to discuss it now, for some reason. So I shook my head. "Yeah, I don't think that's for me."

"Speaking of pro bono, how are things going with the kid you needed some help with?"

"It's going well." *If you count running away a few days after being arrested and then hanging out at a makeshift homeless shelter as going well, that is.*

"Good. Let me know if the attorney I assigned you isn't giving you the attention you need."

Oh, he's giving me lots of attention.

I remembered Donovan saying he was up for partner and needed Blake's vote, so I figured putting in a good word for him might help. It was the least I could do.

"Donovan's actually been great. This wasn't Storm's first time in trouble, so it's not such an easy case. But he's definitely working harder than any of the other lawyers I've dealt with over the years with my kids." I cleared my throat. "Has he been at your firm long?"

"A little over seven years. I've never been a big fan of his, personally. But he has an impressive track record."

I immediately felt defensive. "He seemed nice enough to me. What don't you like about him?"

"He's got a chip on his shoulder. It's typical of the kind of guys we hire."

"What kind of guys is that?"

Blake shrugged. "Spoiled silver spoons from Ivy League schools."

Clearly he didn't know his employee very well. But the last thing Donovan needed was his boss's suspicions to be raised by me defending him. So I put on a plastic smile. "I know the type, but he seems to be doing a great job for Storm."

The waitress delivered our wine. She poured a sip for Blake, and he tasted it and nodded before she filled both our glasses.

"Decker is up for partner," Blake explained. "We add two every five years. One guy is a lock; he's been with the firm twelve years and is solid. So it's between Decker and half a dozen other candidates for the second spot. But really, it's between him and one other guy."

"Oh? Are you leaning toward one more than the other?" I felt anxious waiting for his answer.

"Not Decker," he said after a moment. "The other guy's been with us ten years. He's put in his time."

My heart sank. "Oh. So it's more based on seniority?"

"Not always. I made partner after eight. Decker bills more hours than anyone, but he doesn't need his ego stroked by making it in record time."

I inwardly sighed. "Well, it sounds like you've made your decision, then."

"There's still time before the vote." He reached across the table and laced his fingers with mine. "I have a bet with one of the other partners that Decker fires a client who did something stupid this afternoon. If he can manage to control himself and not do that *and* he takes good care of you, I might consider swinging my vote."

"My place okay?" Blake buckled his seatbelt and looked over at me for an answer.

"Ummm... I think I'm actually going to just go home. I've had a headache coming on all day, and it's that time of the month, so I could use a good night's sleep."

Blake frowned but tried to cover it up. "Of course."

At my apartment building, he walked me to the door. "Are you free next Saturday afternoon, by any chance?"

"Umm..."

"We have a firm barbecue for the partners. To be honest, it's usually torture. I could use the plus one. Most people bring their families or a date. Having you by my side would make the day more bearable."

He read the hesitancy on my face.

"Plus, my partners would like to meet you."

I was taken aback. "They know about me?"

"I had to mention I was seeing someone in order to get the approval from the other partners to allow me to add a pro bono case after we'd already gone over our allotment for the year. I might've bragged about what a do-gooder the woman I was seeing is."

Damn it. How could I say no to being his plus one when he'd gone out of his way for me? I couldn't, so I forced yet another smile. "Sure. A barbecue sounds fun."

Since we'd gone to dinner at seven, it was only nine thirty when I plopped down on my couch wearing my favorite pair of sweats. It was too late to start binge-watching *The Bachelor*. Plus, I'd promised Skye I'd wait for us to watch it together. So instead I scrolled through social media on my phone.

But my mind was elsewhere. It had been ever since Blake and I spoke about Donovan—even before that, if I was honest with myself. I also wasn't quite sure how to handle the information he'd shared with me at dinner about what Donovan needed to do in order to make partner. On one hand, it would be wrong to share a private conversation I'd had with the guy I was dating. On the other hand, Donovan had gone above and beyond for Storm and me when he'd helped me search for him—not to mention introducing him to Bud and trying to teach him some values. So it felt like I owed Donovan one, and passing along a little inside information as a payback might settle our score.

I sat there for ten minutes, staring at Donovan's phone number in my contacts while I debated it over and over again. At one point, my phone buzzed in my hand, and when I realized who'd texted me, it was the sign I needed to make a decision.

Donovan: Bud needs to push Storm working for him tomorrow until late afternoon. He forgot he has an appointment.

I typed back.

Autumn: Oh, okay. Thanks for letting me know. What time do you think I should bring him over?
Donovan: 3 should be good.
Autumn: Thanks.

I tapped my pointer finger to my lips for a minute, debating one last time how to bring up what I'd learned. Eventually, I decided it would be a better live conversation.

Autumn: Are you busy? Can you talk for a moment?

My phone rang five seconds later. I picked it up with a smile. "Hello."

"Haven't you figured it out yet?" he said. "I'm never too busy for you."

God, I felt that velvety, deep voice down in my belly. The sound of it and his flirting had my smile stretching so wide, I was surprised my face didn't crack. "I bet you say that to all the girls."

"Nope. Just one."

I laughed. "Listen, this is kind of weird to bring up, but I spoke to Blake earlier, and he asked me how everything was going with Storm's case. I said everything was going great, and then he mentioned you were up for partner."

"Okay..."

"He said he was still undecided on his vote, but that there were two things that might sway it in your favor."

"What's that?"

"Doing well on Storm's case and—I don't actually know what case this refers to, but he said you had a client who did something stupid today, and if you could manage to not fire him, that would bode well for you."

Donovan was quiet for so long, I wondered if he might've hung up.

"Are you still there?"

He let out a long groan. "*Fuuuuck!*"

"What's the matter?"

"I fired him twenty minutes ago."

"You fired the client? I didn't even know that was a thing."

From the sound of his voice, I pictured him dragging his hand through his hair. "It's my thing." He paused. "*Damn it!*"

"Sorry."

"It's not your fault. I just...*fuck...fuck...fuck*! I need to get in touch with Bentley."

"Is that the client?"

"Yeah."

"Alright. Well, I'll let you go deal with that."

"Jesus, seven years of working my ass off could've gone out the window if you hadn't told me that."

It felt good to have helped. "Well, now I'm glad I went tonight after all."

"Went?"

"To dinner with Blake."

The line fell silent. When Donovan finally spoke again, his voice was flat. "I gotta run. Thanks for the information."

12

Donovan

"**W**hat the hell?"

I stood at the curb of Bud's house with a bag of garbage in hand, watching a car come down the street. The sound of something scraping along the asphalt grew louder as it approached, and sparks shot out of the driver's side wheel well. When the car pulled up, I realized it was Autumn behind the wheel. Her side quarter panel was completely dented in, and something metal hung from it, which must've been the source of the friction and sparks. I could see she was frazzled, especially after she parked and attempted to get out, but the door wouldn't seem to open.

"Stop," I yelled and put my hand up. She still jammed her shoulder into the door one more time. I walked over next to the car. "Let me try to open it from this side."

The first few tugs on the door opened it slightly, but not enough for her to get out. So I lifted a foot up on the side of the door for leverage and yanked the thing wide. Autumn climbed out grumbling, while Storm walked around from the passenger side of the car looking a little nervous. He hadn't seemed that uneasy the night he was locked up at the police station.

"What happened to your car?" I asked.

"Someone hit me."

"Are you okay?" I looked at Storm. "You good?"

"We're fine," Autumn assured me. "We weren't in the car when it happened. I stopped a few blocks away to pick up a cake to bring Bud. When I came out, someone had smashed into my car." She looked over at the dent, then nodded toward Storm. "Thankfully, this one doesn't think I'm capable of walking into a store without a bodyguard, or he would've been in it."

That made me smile. It's not like she would've been mugged in broad daylight around here—well, at least the chances of it were low—but I wouldn't have let her go in alone either.

I nodded at Storm. "Good looking out."

Autumn rolled her eyes. "When I asked the other driver for his insurance card, he said he didn't have any. Who drives without insurance?"

"Did you get a police report?" I asked.

"I did—even though the guy didn't want me to call them."

Well, that explained why they were an hour late. I'd been beginning to think she wasn't going to show, that maybe she was pissed off because of the attitude I'd given her last night on the phone.

I crouched down next to her tire and took a peek inside the wheel well. "The cop should've called a tow truck. You shouldn't have driven this thing."

"It's just a dent."

I shook my head. "Look at the rim of the tire. It's supposed to be round, Autumn."

She squinted and then frowned. "Oh...I didn't notice that."

"Your rim is bent, part of the body of your car is pushing against the brakes on the tire, and you're dragging metal."

She sighed. "Great."

I nodded toward Bud's house. "Come on. Let's go inside. There's a good body shop a few blocks away—or at least there was a few years ago. I'll check with Bud to see if it's still open. If it is, we can ask them to take a look and see if they can make it safe for driving. Then at least you can get it fixed somewhere closer to home."

"How would we get it there? You just said it wasn't safe for me to drive."

"It's not. That's why I'll be driving your car, and you can follow me in mine. Storm can stay here with Bud."

"Thank you for this," Autumn said.

I opened the passenger door of my car outside Demott's Body Shop.

Autumn looked up at me before she got in. "Listen, about last night on the phone. I'm sorry if I upset you."

"It's fine. I realized something after we hung up that made me feel better."

Her face wrinkled. "What?"

"You were talking to me about Dickson—telling me stuff you wouldn't have mentioned if he were with you."

"Yes, so?"

"That means you were home alone. You went out to dinner with a guy you've been dating for a while, yet you were back at your place, all by yourself, and it wasn't even ten o'clock."

"I had a headache."

I grinned. "Sure you did."

"What are you smiling at? You don't believe me?"

I shook my head. "Not in the slightest. You only went out with him to keep that barrier between us. But in the end, you couldn't even spend the night with him."

"Don't you think a lot of yourself."

I shrugged. "It's okay. You don't have to admit it. I know the truth. And just so you know, I haven't been with anyone else since the night at the police station either. I have patience. I'll wait until you're ready."

She narrowed her eyes at me. "And what if I'm never ready? Are you going to wait around forever?"

I took a half step closer. We were now toe to toe. Autumn made no attempt to back up as she watched me closely. But it was neither the time, nor the place, to see what she'd do if I pushed. Instead, I let my eyes drop to her feet and slowly work their way back up. They grazed appreciatively over the curve of her hip and snagged on her beautiful, full breasts. Her nipples hardened through her T-shirt as I watched, like a flower coming into bloom. When my eyes finally reached her face again, her lips were parted, her eyes hooded.

I leaned in and whispered in her ear. "It definitely won't take forever."

⌒

"Oh my God. And then Lindsey sits right between them and kisses him."

"That girl's nothing but trouble," Bud said.

"I know, right? But apparently our bachelor is into trouble. He likes that Justine, too."

I shook my head. "I can't believe the conversation I'm listening to. I feel like I'm at lunch with Juliette."

Autumn and Bud had been talking about *The Bachelor* for the last twenty minutes. I knew Autumn watched that crap. But Bud? I just kept shaking my head. He'd said his new "lady friend" watched it, and he'd gotten into it, too.

Autumn turned to me. "Who's Juliette?"

"A coworker. Don't worry. She's no threat to you." I winked. "Juliette's not my type."

Autumn rolled her eyes, but I saw the smile as she turned away. "Have you ever even watched it?"

"No, and I'm surprised you do. It's basically a show where a dude gets to date, like, twenty women at the same time while they do over-the-top crap to fight for attention. Women love it, yet the same women lose their shit if a man they're dating wants to date even one other woman."

Autumn shook her head. "There's a difference between what women want in real life and what they want in their reality TV."

"If you say so..."

Storm came in from the garage. He'd been outside cleaning and painting most of the day. "I'm starving."

"I'm serving hot, open-face sandwiches for dinner tonight," Bud said. "And you can help yourself to the fridge."

I shook my head. "Why don't I order us a pizza? Your hot open faces are always a big hit, with no leftovers."

Bud smiled. "That's because I toast the bread on the grill and melt the cheese before I pour the brown gravy on top. It was Donovan over there's favorite as a kid. I'd have to hide three if he didn't show for dinner early."

Storm scratched at his temple. "You used to eat with the poor people?"

"No, I used to *be* the poor people."

"But now you're rolling in it. You're a lawyer with a fancy car, and your shoes are always shiny."

"Yeah, and?"

He shrugged. "Most of the time poor stays poor."

I'd been fixing a cabinet door, but I stopped and gave Storm my full attention. "If you think like that, that usually is what happens. You have to be able to see yourself successful to have a shot at finding success. And you need to work harder than someone who has things handed to them." I felt Autumn's eyes on me, so I looked over. "No offense."

She smiled. "None taken."

"You ever run track at school?" I asked Storm.

"Yeah."

"You know why the runners don't all start from the same line?"

"Because the inside track is shorter."

"That's right. They make it fair for everyone. But in real life, that crap doesn't happen. Some people start from behind—and for reasons other than just being poor." I paused, making sure he was following. He gave the smallest of nods. "So learn to run faster, and never forget there are people starting even farther back than you."

I finished repairing the cabinet and then helped Autumn, who had been painting the trim in Bud's kitchen while I worked. I could've given Storm a hand, but Bud had gone out there to help, and I thought a little one-on-one time with him might do the kid some good. Besides, I couldn't resist the opportunity to work close to Autumn. I stole glances every chance I got—when she stretched above her head to paint the top moldings and her top rode up, exposing her creamy, smooth skin, when she bent over to dip her brush into the paint, giving me a straight-line view of her phenomenal ass.

I was pretty damn obvious. And Autumn caught me red-handed on more than one occasion, but each time she'd smile, rather than call me out. I knew she had an idea of what was going through my head, but I wondered if she could read my mind as well as I could sometimes read hers. Since I hadn't gotten smacked, I'd say we probably only had one mind reader in the room.

After we'd polished off an entire pizza pie, Bud needed to get ready to head out for dinner service, and Autumn had to get Storm back to Park House, so I drove them over to the body shop to see if they'd been able to repair Autumn's car enough to get it to a drivable state. Unfortunately, it turned out not to be just a simple crack in the rim, and it needed to be sent out for welding. So we left her car there, and Autumn and I dropped off Storm together. Right before he got out, she asked him if he had any plans for the night, and he responded that he was going to study.

"Do you really think he's going to study tonight?" she asked me once we were alone in the car.

"Definitely not."

"Maybe he actually listened to you say you had to work twice as hard?"

I glanced from the road to her, flashing a face that said *not a chance.*

"Well, I'm going to think positive and assume he was being truthful."

I smirked. "You do that. But he wasn't."

"How can you be so sure?"

"I'm good at telling when people are lying. It's my superpower. I'm a human lie detector."

"Is that so?"

"It is."

She tapped her finger to her lips. Even while driving, I could see the wheels in her head turning.

"I love pineapples on my pizza. It's my favorite food."

I raised a brow. "Am I supposed to tell if you're lying?"

"Yup. Go ahead, Human Lie Detector. Let's see how good your superpowers are."

We were about to pass a Wendy's, so I put my blinker on and turned into the parking lot.

Autumn's forehead wrinkled. "Are you hungry?"

"No. But I need to look at you for my superpower to work." I pulled into the first available parking spot and put the car in park. Then I shifted in my seat to look at her.

I definitely like this game. With this view, we should play more often. "Go ahead," I said. "Talk about your favorite pizza again."

Autumn turned to face me and straightened in her seat. Her amused smile was freaking adorable.

"I love pineapples on my pizza. It's my favorite food."

I actually couldn't tell whether she was lying or not, but I figured I had a fifty-fifty shot, so I bluffed. "Lie."

Her eyes sparkled. "How did you know?"

"Told you. I have a bullshit-arometer."

She laughed. "That could have been just luck. Let me try again."

"Have at it."

She gazed out the window a moment and then turned back. "When I was twelve, I ran away from home."

Her presentation was pretty different from the way she'd spoken about the pizza, so I figured this wasn't a lie. "Truth."

Her jaw dropped, but she did her best not to look impressed. "Another lucky guess."

I folded my arms across my chest. "How many is it going to take for you to believe in my skills?"

"I don't know. Five in a row?"

"Well, then, let's go. Actually, hang on a second. I'm curious. Why did you run away from home?"

She frowned. "My mom had died six months earlier, and my dad came home with a woman I'd never met and told me he was getting married."

"Shit. Sorry."

Autumn shrugged. "It's okay. I only went a few doors down to my friend Jane's house, and her mother made me cookies, so I wasn't exactly roughing it with a bandana tied to a stick slung over my shoulder. Plus, that marriage only lasted eight months."

"That marriage? How many have there been?"

"A lot. He just got engaged again recently."

That bit of truth made me wonder if her dear old dad was part of the reason she was so sour on relationships.

"Okay...I have another one," she said. Only this time, as she spoke, she reached up and adjusted her earring. "I once had an affair with my college professor."

"Lie."

"How did you know that? I could've. I had one hit on me a few times."

"Bullshit-arometer. Told you." I reached up and fingered her earring. "Plus, you play with this when you lie."

Her eyes widened. "I do?"

"You do."

"Wow. I've never noticed that. Are you just super perceptive? Do you notice things like that on everyone?"

"I don't notice it on everyone." My eyes searched hers. "Just people I'm interested in."

Autumn's eyes softened, and I completely forgot we were in a busy parking lot in the middle of Brooklyn. Cars pulled in and out of the drive-thru line behind us, a random car blared its horn somewhere in the not-too-distant vicinity, yet the moment felt oddly intimate and romantic—and I'd definitely been accused of *not* being romantic over the years by more than one woman.

"How about you?" I whispered. "Think you can tell if I'm lying?"

She stayed so still. It made me wonder if she felt the same thing I did—like we were in a little bubble, one I didn't want to burst with movement.

"I don't know," she said quietly.

"Let's try it out." I moved an inch or two closer and lowered my head so we were exactly eye to eye. "I think you are absolutely incredible."

She swallowed. "I don't know."

"Truth. Let's try again." I moved another inch closer. "I haven't been able to stop thinking about you since I saw you standing there with my luggage."

Autumn bit on her bottom lip. "Lie."

I shook my head back and forth slowly. "Truth. One more. I want to kiss you so badly it fucking hurts."

She swallowed again and whispered, "Truth?"

A smile spread across my face. "Abso-fucking-lutely."

Autumn smiled back. And for a few seconds, I thought we were making progress, that she might actually give me the green light to suck on her beautiful lips like I'd been dying to since the moment she'd walked back into my life. But then I saw it happen. Whatever it is that holds her back hit like a flash of lightning. Her smile wilted to a frown, and she cleared her throat as she leaned back into her seat.

"That must be useful in your profession. Having— what did you call it? A bullshit-arometer?"

I kept watching her, even though she turned her head and stared out the window.

"Yeah, it's helpful."

"That's good."

She said nothing more. Apparently, our little game was over.

So I put the car in reverse and drove her the rest of the way home. The remainder of the drive was limited to meaningless small talk.

Autumn was quiet as I walked her to the door.

"By the way, I never thanked you," I said.

"For what?"

"You saved my ass."

"Oh?"

"After we hung up last night, I was able to call the client I'd fired and smooth things over. It was physically painful to kiss his ass, but I managed it, so I didn't blow my shot at partner...yet."

Autumn smiled as we arrived at her door. "I'm glad I was able to help, because I owe you quite a few favors. Thank you for everything you did today, Donovan. I feel like I say that to you often. I'm always thanking you for something—helping Storm, helping me find him when he runs away, helping me deal with my car today. You're very..."

I raised a brow when she trailed off. "Helpful?"

She chuckled. "I was going to say you're a very good friend. But yeah. You're helpful."

I tugged a piece of her hair. "Is that how you think of me? As a good friend?"

"Yeah." She looked down, but nodded. "You're a good friend."

I reached out and touched the wrist of her hand currently fiddling with her earring. At first she was confused, but then she realized what I was pointing out.

Autumn covered her mouth. "Oh my God."

I smiled and winked. "I can't wait to make you say those words again soon, *liar*."

13

Autumn

Eight years ago

"**O**ne more." Nick held the bottle of tequila out to me.

I shook my head. "No way. I've already hit my limit."

My friend Felicia thumbed toward me. "Her limit is one. Give me that."

Nick rolled his eyes. "I thought we were celebrating you kicking all our asses on the calc test."

"We are. But I celebrate responsibly. You get blackout drunk and strip naked while standing at the drive-thru ordering Taco Bell, then get belligerent when the woman at the pickup window won't give you your food."

Nick grinned. "That was once, and that woman really needed to loosen up."

Felicia and I laughed. "I think we've discovered the reason we're celebrating my perfect score on the test and not your sixty."

Nick took the bottle from Felicia and knocked back another long swig before handing it to one of his frat brothers. "Dance with me, ladies."

I looked around. No one else at the party was dancing, but that never stopped Nick, and man, could he dance. I shrugged. "Sure. Why not?"

Nick made a big commotion about needing more space in the living room and then yelled to his buddy to turn up the music. By the time we were halfway through the song, most of the party had joined in. Nick stood in front of me and stuck his ass out, and I pretended to smack it. Felicia and I sandwiched him between us and gyrated our hips as we moved up and down. It was harmless— the three of us had been goofing around since we met at freshman orientation last year. Plus, Nick was more into our Calc TA, Ian, than he was Felicia or me.

We danced a few more songs and then sang along to a new Ariana Grande ballad while acting it out. At one point, I turned, pretending to be the girl in the song who walks away, and I happened to look across the room. My eyes met Braden's. I blinked a few times. I'd had a couple of drinks, but *that couldn't be him.* Though it looked *exactly* like him... Anyway, whoever it was did *not* look very happy. The guy stood in the corner of the room and made no effort to come toward me, even though he was very clearly staring. I motioned to my friends that I'd be back and headed toward the guy, wiping sweat from my forehead.

"Oh my God, it's really you. I thought I was seeing things." I smiled. "What are you doing here? I had no idea you were coming up this weekend."

"Obviously. I came to visit my girlfriend and find her grinding on some guy. So I guess that makes two of us surprised."

I waved toward my friend. "That's just Nick. I've mentioned him."

"Pretty sure you said you study together, not dry hump."

"Nick's *gay.* He's not interested in me. We're just having fun."

"Having fun making me look like an idiot?"

"How am I making you look like an idiot?"

Someone turned the music up even higher. Braden frowned. He had to lean forward and yell just so I could hear him. "This isn't my scene. I'm going to go. I'll see you whenever the next time you come home is."

"Go? What? *No.* Don't be ridiculous. Let me just tell my friends I'm leaving. I'll be right back."

I squeezed through the crowd to make my way back to Nick and Felicia. I could barely hear myself as I yelled to them over the music. But I pointed to Braden and waved goodbye, and they seemed to get what I was trying to tell them.

I walked back to Braden, and we headed outside together. When I stepped outside onto the porch, my friend Jason didn't see the guy behind me and engulfed me in a bear hug.

"There she is. Be my beer-pong partner, gorgeous?"

I could feel the tension radiating off the man behind me before I even turned around. Disentangling myself from Jason, I said, "Umm...I'm just heading out. This is my boyfriend, Braden."

Jason held out his hand. "Braden, you lucky bastard."

Braden looked down at his hand and back up at him without saying a word, then folded his arms across his chest.

Jason might've been drinking for a few hours, but there was no way he could miss the cold shoulder. He took the hint and pulled back his hand. "Alrighty then." He caught my eye. "You good, Autumn?"

I smiled, appreciative of his concern, however misplaced it was. "Yeah, I'm good. Thanks, Jason."

Braden and I walked down the stairs and crossed over the lawn. He veered right at the sidewalk, so I followed his lead, even though my dorm was to the left. We passed a few more fraternity houses as we walked down the block in silence. When we came upon a BMW, Braden walked toward it.

"Is this what you're driving? Whose car is it?"

He walked around the passenger side and opened the door for me. "It's mine."

"Yours? What happened to the Toyota?"

"I got rid of it. I figured I needed a nicer car to take clients out, now that I have a job."

My eyes widened. "You got the job? Which one?"

"I got offers from three. But I took the job at Andrews and Wilde."

"You took the job at our dads' firm? I thought you didn't want to do that?"

"I thought it over. It was the best offer. Plus, I'll get to try cases a lot sooner than I would at other places."

"Wow. Congratulations!" I threw my arms around his neck and squeezed. Braden didn't hug me back, but he also didn't stop me. "I'm so proud of you."

"Thanks." He nodded toward the open car door. "Why don't you get in?"

Once we were both inside and buckled, I decided to clear the air. While I was surprised to see Braden, I really was happy he was here. "Listen, I didn't mean to upset you by my dancing with Nick. I guess I just see him as harmless since he doesn't like girls, and we were just dancing."

"Grinding isn't dancing. It's simulating sex. Even if the guy isn't interested, you're putting a show on for a damn frat house, Autumn."

I'd never thought of it like that. In fact, I'd never actually given dancing any thought at all. We'd just have a few drinks and burn off some stress. "I'm sorry. I didn't look at it that way. But I guess you're right."

Braden kept shaking his head and staring at the road, even though we were still parked. "Is this what you do every weekend? Go to fraternity houses and get drunk? Play beer pong and act like a whore?"

My head snapped back. "Whore? I don't act like a whore. I might've been dancing with my friends, but don't call me a whore."

"Then maybe try not acting like one."

"I apologized. I said I wasn't thinking about how my dancing might appear to others. But don't call me a whore. In fact, don't call me any names." I unbuckled and grabbed for the door handle. As I went to open it, Braden caught my other wrist. His grip was really tight.

"Owww. You're hurting me. Let go."

Braden's jaw flexed. He stared right at me, but I felt like he wasn't actually seeing me. "Braden, *let go*. That hurts."

After a few more heartbeats, he released my hand. "Stay. Don't get out."

I rubbed my wrist. "That hurt, Braden."

"Sorry. I didn't mean it. I just wanted to stop you from leaving."

Something about the incident didn't sit right, and my gut told me to get out.

But Braden stroked my hair. "I'm sorry, babe. Sorry about it all—for calling you a name and for squeezing you too hard." He lifted my wrist to his mouth and kissed the inside. "I just drove all the way up after work to surprise you and tell you the good news, and when I found you, you were all over another guy, and then some other guy grabbed you." He shook his head. "I overreacted. I love you. Forgive me?"

I felt bad. He'd driven five hours up to Boston only to find me rubbing myself all over another guy. "It's okay. Just please don't let it happen again."

He smiled. "It won't." Leaning across the center console, he brushed hair from my face. "I missed you. I'm glad I found you."

I softened. "I missed you, too."

As he started the car, it dawned on me for the first time that he *had* found me. "How did you know where I was tonight?"

"Your iPhone. Location tracker."

"Oh." I thought a minute. "I didn't realize I had that on. Don't I have to grant you access or something?"

Braden shrugged and held out his hand. "I guess you did at some point."

Again, I had a fleeting funny feeling. But this was my boyfriend of two years... I'd probably shared my location with him at some point and just didn't remember. So I pushed it aside and laced my fingers with his.

Yet for the rest of the weekend, I couldn't shake this niggling feeling. I kept trying to remember exactly when I'd shared my location with Braden. I had a pretty good memory, yet no matter how long and hard I thought, I couldn't ever recall doing it.

14

Donovan

"Come on, Elliott. Work with me on this."

Elliott Silver tossed a file from his desk over to a folding table set up on the right. The file hit a giant pile and knocked two other folders to the floor. He frowned.

I definitely didn't miss my days at the DA's office.

"He's got two priors and he's twelve, Decker. He also broke two bones in the guy's nose—the violence is escalating. This is *exactly* the type of case I *shouldn't* cut a deal on."

"What if we give you a dealer?"

Elliott waved his hands around his office. "Do I look like I need another case?"

"This wouldn't be *another* case. It would be a *better* case. You can get rid of this nickel-and-dime shit on a minor *and* put away a guy whose been polluting the streets with drugs for years."

He shook his head. "No offense, Decker, but all I gotta do is drive my car over to just about any corner in that neighborhood, roll down my window, and flash some green—I can pick up a drug dealer. Why am I going to let some punk off when I don't need whatever he's got?"

This was turning out to be harder than I'd thought. "Storm isn't a punk. He's a good kid with good grades who just got screwed over in life. He's a victim of his surroundings. Putting him in juvey is only going to compound that, not make it better."

Elliott squinted at me before chuckling. "Damn. You've gotten even better over the years. I almost believe you think this kid's got a chance."

I blew out a deep breath. *This kid does have a chance.* I know it because I *was* this damn kid. I'm generally not the kind of guy to lord shit over people, but I felt pretty desperate right now.

I leaned forward in my seat. "Listen. Didn't you ever make a mistake?"

"Did I ever break another person's nose? No, I haven't."

"Okay, but you have to have made *some* mistake." I hesitated, because it's really not my style to threaten someone—at least not since I grew up. But *fuck.* I needed this, for more reasons than one. "Maybe here at work once even? Didn't you ever make a mistake that could have screwed you somehow, and someone somewhere gave you a second chance?"

Elliott had started packing up his briefcase, but he stopped in his tracks and looked up at me. During our first year in the DA's office, he'd royally screwed up a case— broke confidentiality to a woman he was sleeping with, who it turned out was the drug dealer's sister setting him up. I'd taken the case over and buried it for him, cutting a deal the guy didn't deserve.

He held my eyes as he shook his head. "You're a motherfucker, you know that?"

I bowed my head and nodded, too ashamed to look the guy in the eye. "I need this one, Elliott."

He resumed shoving files into his briefcase and spoke between gritted teeth. "Fine. But I'm not dropping the charges right away. He's going into a pre-trial diversion program. He goes to a psychologist weekly for a year, enrolls in an anger-management program, and does fifty hours of community service." He held up a finger in warning. "If and when he completes everything, and provided he gets into no further trouble, then I'll drop the charges."

I inwardly fist pumped. "Deal."

Elliott looked me straight in the eye. "And we're even after this. I'm not fucking around, Decker. Don't pull this shit on me again."

I nodded. "Understood."

He motioned to the door behind me. "Now get the hell out of my office."

―――――

"Why are you so late?" Juliette wiped her mouth, crumpled up her napkin, and tossed it into her empty food container on the table.

I reached for the bag and pulled out my lunch. They'd phoned in our usual Wednesday order while I was on my way back from the DA's office.

"I was downtown on a case."

"Oh yeah? What undeserving billionaire did you save today?"

I sat down and opened my Szechuan shrimp and broccoli. "Today I used my superpowers for the good of a child, if you must know."

Trent and Juliette looked at each other. "Have you figured out a game plan for how you're going to handle things?" she asked.

I picked up a shrimp with my chopsticks and popped it into my mouth. "No game plan needed. Worked out a deal."

Juliette shook her head. "I wasn't referring to the kid. I meant his social worker."

My forehead wrinkled, and I shrugged. "I haven't told her yet. But I'm sure she'll be happy about it."

"I meant how are you going to handle things once you're sleeping with her again? Or has that already happened? We haven't seen you in a few days..."

"I'm not sleeping with Autumn, *Mom and Dad*. But if I was, why would I need a game plan? It's pretty simple... sort of like doing the vertical hokey pokey. You put your penis in, you pull your penis out, you put your penis in, and you shake it all about. I can write down directions, if you want. I know it's been a while for both of you."

Juliette had been nibbling on the end of her chopstick, but she now used it to jab into my arm. "Seriously, dumbass. What are you going to do about Dickson?"

"Well, I'm *not* going to do the vertical hokey pokey with him."

"Stop being a jerk, and be serious for a minute," she said. "You *need* Dickson's vote. Do you really think that when he finds out you're banging the woman he's been seeing, he's going to vote for you?"

"First of all, I'm not sleeping with Autumn, and second of all, if I was, it wouldn't be any of his business."

Juliette frowned. "So that's your plan? You don't have one."

I looked at Trent as the voice of reason. "What am I missing here? What plans should I have?"

Trent sucked on the straw in his soda until it made an empty slurping sound. "Your plan should be to retreat, at least until after the partner vote."

"How can I retreat from a case?"

Juliette rolled her eyes. "You just said yourself that you settled the case she's involved with. You call her and give her the good news, and then you don't speak with her again for a month or so."

I'd been thinking more along the lines of telling her in person and suggesting we have a drink to celebrate. But I didn't mention that. "You're worrying about nothing."

We ate our lunch in a conference room with glass walls, basically a fish bowl. Just as I lifted another piece of shrimp to my mouth, none other than Dickson himself walked by. He glanced inside, saw me, and opened the door.

"Decker, what's going on with the Stone case?"

What an idiot. I knew what he meant, but why let him off easy? "Stone? Did it just come in? I'm not familiar with it."

His lips pursed. "You don't even remember the damn kid's name? The pro bono I assigned you…"

"Oh! Storm. My client's name is *Storm.*"

"Whatever. Where are you on that?"

No way was I letting him call Autumn with my good news. "I'm in talks with the DA. It's looking promising."

He nodded. "Good. Make it happen. This case is important to me. Keep me updated."

I gritted my teeth and plastered on a politician's smile. "Sure thing."

Just as he turned to go, he said, "I don't think I have to remind you that you have a lot riding on how things go the next month. Make sure you give every case your all—even the ones we don't get paid for. Don't just skim the surface because there's no billable hours involved."

As if he actually gave a flying shit about pro bono cases. Last year when my freebie case was for a nursing-home resident, he'd told me the time I put in should be in proportion to how long the woman was going to last.

My jaw flexed. "Of course. I won't skim. I'll penetrate as deep as possible."

From the corner of my eye, I saw Juliette's eyes widen. She quickly looked away. If Dickson noticed, he didn't show it. He looked between the three of us and nodded. "Good. Keep me updated."

As soon as the door closed and he was out in the hallway, Juliette's eyes bulged. "Are you nuts?"

I smirked. "Just doing what the boss wants."

"You are *such* an idiot. Forget the dumb, deep-penetration remark. Luckily that seemed to fly right over his head. But he asked you if you settled the case—which you did—and yet you said you were working on it because you want to be the one to tell Autumn."

"So?" I shrugged. "Why shouldn't I get to tell my client the good news?"

"Autumn is not your client. The kid is. Besides, he asked you to keep him apprised of the status of the case. Don't you think he'll be annoyed when he finds out from the woman he's seeing that you settled it?"

She had a point, but I wasn't about to let that bozo take credit for the strings I'd had to pull. I shook my head. "Stop worrying so much. It'll work out."

"You know what you need?"

I nodded. "I do. In fact, I'm the only person who knows what I need."

Juliette ignored me. "You need a distraction."

Being here in the office had felt like a distraction lately. "I'm fine."

"I'm going to set you up with my friend. She's a yoga instructor—bends like a pretzel and gorgeous."

"I'm good, but thanks."

Trent had been quiet, but he looked at me and shook his head. "Juliette's right. It's a little over a month until the partner vote. Dickson's riding you about how that case is going for a reason. He's obviously really into Autumn. I'm not saying you back off forever. But maybe put what you want on the back burner for a while. A month isn't that long to wait."

It had been less than a *week* since I saw Autumn, and it was already too long. I was sure my friends were overreacting. But it wouldn't take long to realize maybe their perspective had some merit...

15

Autumn

I did *not* feel like going to a party.

My insides churned as we drove out to the Hamptons for the barbecue. I couldn't seem to shake the feeling that I was doing something wrong—like I was guilty, even though I hadn't committed a crime. Well, no physical crime anyway. Now, emotional strangulation? That was an entirely different story.

Blake glanced over to where I sat staring out the window. "You feeling okay today?"

"Yeah. I just have a lot on my mind with work."

He nodded. "Is Stone giving you trouble again?"

I frowned. "Storm. And no, he's actually been a little better lately."

"Blake Jr., my eight year old, goes through phases where he acts out, too. Usually it's just because he wants a little extra attention."

Ummm...I think Storm might be more upset that his mother is an addict who ditched him, and he's stuck living in a group home filled with troubled kids no one wants. "Most of my kids act out because they're angry, rather than wanting attention. They don't know how to handle their emotions, and they've been taught on the street that any display of feelings is a weakness."

Blake smiled. "Listen to you—you sound like Dr. Wilde already."

I attempted a smile and went back to staring out the window.

Rupert Kravitz's home was in the tiny village of Sagaponack, which was part of the Hamptons. If Blake hadn't told me it was the most expensive zip code on the East Coast, I might've actually liked the quaint little town as we drove through. But as soon as he started to rattle off the names of famous people who lived here and how many Goldman Sachs brokers owned houses on the water, I got the same bad taste in my mouth as I did going home to good ol' Greenwich and my father's uppity cronies.

To be honest, I regretted coming today.

Inside the Kravitz compound, I felt like I'd walked into a retirement party. Men with white hair, khaki pants, and navy blazers stood around drinking out of crystal tumblers, while their frozen-faced wives wore big hats to keep their Botox shielded from sun damage. I smiled as Blake made introductions, putting on the same plastic smile I'd used at my father's parties for years. Outside, there were some younger guys, but Blake definitely seemed to be one of the youngest, if not the youngest. I also noticed I'd met a lot of partners named Rupert, Michael, and Larry, and while there was at least some diversity among the men, there wasn't a single Susan, Michelle, or Christine.

"Does your firm not like women partners?" I asked discreetly on our way over to an outdoor bar set up by the pool.

Blake smiled. "We have one. We had two, but one left."

"How many partners are there in total?"

"There are nine senior partners who manage the firm, and twenty-eight additional partners who share in equity."

"Thirty-seven partners and you have one woman— and of course the one who left. Could she have left because she felt out of place?"

He chuckled. "Elaina left because she moved to Greece, actually. That's where she was originally from. Her mom got sick, so she took a leave to go take care of her, and while she was there, she decided she wanted the simpler life back home."

"Why are there so few women partners?"

"I guess because it's not easy to make partner at the firm. The average attorney works seventy to eighty hours a week for more than ten years before they make it. You graduate law school around twenty-four, and a lot of women want a less-demanding job because they get married and have kids, or they plan to."

"That sounds incredibly archaic."

"Maybe." He shrugged. "But it's a work-life-balance decision. If you're married to your job, it's difficult to be married to anyone else. Just ask my ex-wife." We stepped up to the bar. "You want wine?"

"Sure. White, please."

While we waited for our drinks, I gazed around. "You introduced me to a lot of wives, so how do these guys make it work?"

"They don't. Not with their first wives anyway." Blake surveyed the room. "Not a single woman I can see at the moment is an original. When you marry the first time, you usually marry for love, and that person expects your love and time in return. After that doesn't work out, you marry for companionship and convenience. All your cards are on the table, so both of you know what you're getting yourselves into."

"That sounds...sad."

"Maybe. But it's also realistic. Many women lose out on partnerships because they want a family, but just as many men lose out on a family because they want a partnership."

I wasn't sure if it was my mood before we arrived, or the conversation we'd just had, but a feeling of melancholy settled in. Blake's description of a second wife made me realize that was basically what I was searching for—a companion to spend time with but never really love. It made me sad that I'd never have passion, not the kind that consumes your heart, body, and soul, anyway. Sure, there was sexual passion—that I could have. And over the last few years that had been enough. I might've even forgotten anything more than that could exist. But it seemed impossible to put out of my mind these days.

"Will you be okay for a few minutes?" Blake asked. "I need to hit the men's room after the long drive."

"Oh...yeah, sure."

He kissed my cheek, and I actually felt relieved when he walked away. I needed to be alone for a few minutes. My stupid emotions were getting the best of me today. Yet as I stood staring into the clear, blue pool water, I couldn't help but think about Donovan. What I felt around him was so different than what I felt when I spent time with Blake. Donovan made me *want*—want more, to take more risks, to trust again, to believe the world could change and be a good place. It physically hurt to keep trying to stomp all of those feelings down. I sighed and sipped my wine.

Too soon, Blake returned. "Did you miss me?" he said.

"Of course," I lied.

A light breeze blew, prickling my skin. I had on a sundress, and I rubbed my arm from the chill.

"You're cold?" Blake's brows furrowed.

"I wasn't until just now. The breeze gave me a little chill."

Blake had a napkin wrapped around the drink in his hand. He took it from the glass and used it to wipe perspiration from his forehead. "I must've missed that breeze you got. If it comes again, send it my way. It's hot as hell over here by the pool."

I figured it was because he had a long-sleeve dress shirt on, while I was wearing a sundress. "Why don't we go stand under the awning? I'm not really cold. It was just that little breeze that gave me goose bumps."

"That'd be great, if you don't mind."

We started to walk toward the house, me in front of Blake. I'd been looking down, careful not to get my heel stuck in the lawn, but when we reached the patio, I looked up and froze. Blake bumped into my back, spilling some of his drink over my exposed skin. He apologized, but I was too busy staring straight ahead to pay attention to whatever he said.

Those goose bumps hadn't been from a breeze after all.

I blinked a few times to make sure my mind wasn't playing tricks on me. But the blue eyes boring into me were as real as could be.

What is Donovan doing here?

⟋

Now I was the one sweating.

I stood next to Blake, doing my best to pretend to be part of the conversation he was having with one of his partners, but my eyes kept going back to the man standing on the other side of the patio. Every thirty seconds or so, I glanced over at him, and each and every time I'd find him staring right back at me. I'd grown nervous that Blake was going to catch him and think he was checking me out, and it would hurt his chances of making partner. Blake had already said he wasn't a big Donovan Decker fan. I stood rod straight, feeling like I was waiting for a car accident to happen. I could see it coming, barreling down the road at ninety miles per hour, yet I couldn't do a damn thing to stop it.

I'd been lost in my head as the people around me talked, until the conversation finally caught my attention.

"I see that Mills and Decker have arrived. What're your thoughts on the two of them?"

"I like Mills," Blake said. "He's got a good head on his shoulders, makes solid decisions, and has put in his time. Decker's a better lawyer, but he's also a hothead. He acts on emotions, and that signals he's probably not ready for partnership."

"That's true." The other guy tilted his drink at Blake. "But Decker also runs circles around Mills's billing. And he brings in a nice chunk of new business. He's made a name for himself among the Wall Street rainmakers as one to go to when the shit hits the fan. I wouldn't want him to jump ship and take that business with him. We need to give him a reason to stick around."

Blake shrugged. "I haven't decided for sure yet." He looked over at me and winked. "I'm seeing how a few things pan out."

I cleared my throat. "I thought today was a barbecue just for the partners?"

"It is. Well, sort of. The partners all come, but the final candidates up for partner are always invited, too. It's a way to get to know them outside the office. A lot of the partners have had very little interaction with guys from different divisions, yet they get to vote. So it's tradition that the candidates are invited."

The other guy smirked. "It's their final opportunity to grovel."

A few minutes later, the partner who owned the house called Blake inside. He excused himself and kissed my cheek. "I'll be back in a few minutes."

The minute he stepped from the deck through the archway, Donovan made his way over. My heart was beating out of my chest by the time he stood next to me.

"Didn't expect to see you here." His voice was steady, but his eyes were swimming with emotion.

I frowned. "I had no idea you would be here either. Blake said it was a partners' barbecue, and you never mentioned you were coming."

Donovan drank from a beer bottle. It wasn't lost on me that he was probably the only one *not* drinking from a crystal glass at this swanky party. He eyed me over the top of the bottle as he swallowed. "I called you yesterday. You didn't return my call."

"Sorry. I...I was busy."

"Busy avoiding me..."

"Donovan, I..." Over his shoulder, I saw Blake step out of the house and back onto the deck. Donovan must've noticed the change in my face, and he turned to follow my line of sight.

Blake was only a few feet away when Donovan turned back around. He looked back and forth between my eyes before leaning forward to whisper, "It's fucking killing me to see his hands on you—even just your back. Do you like the way it feels when he touches you?"

His words might've sounded angry, but there was so much hurt in his voice. My chest tightened, and I had to swallow to clear the lump in my throat. Donovan pulled back and straightened, chugging the rest of his beer without taking his eyes from me.

"Decker," Blake said with a curt nod. His hand snaked around my waist and Donovan's eyes shifted to stare at the fingers visible from the front. My eyes closed as I silently prayed he wouldn't do something stupid.

"Dickson." Donovan returned the brisk greeting.

"What's going on with Autumn's case? I thought passing it to you would be a smart decision. But I'm starting to second-guess myself. I was counting on you to at least get the charges knocked down to a misdemeanor."

Donovan's jaw tightened. "Actually, I was able to get Storm into a pre-trial diversion program. The charges will be completely dropped if he does a few minor things and keeps his nose out of trouble for a year."

I blinked. "You were?"

Donovan nodded. "I called you to discuss the details yesterday—went right to voicemail after one ring. You must've been on the phone...or pushed ignore."

I laughed nervously. "I must've been on the phone. I guess I haven't checked my messages, but that's such great news. How did you manage to make that happen? It was his third strike, so I thought he was really in trouble."

Donovan's lips curved to what resembled a smile, yet there was nothing happy about it. "Sold my soul to the devil. But I figured this was an important case and worth it."

Blake took his hand from my waist and extended it toward Donovan. "Nice job. I'll remember this. You've really surprised me lately. I thought for sure you'd dump old man Bentley after the crap he pulled last week."

Donovan's eyes flashed to mine. He put his hand in Blake's waiting one, but his words were clearly directed my way. "I wanted to, but I realized it probably wasn't the best idea."

The woman whom I'd been introduced to earlier as the hostess of the party, the wife of the partner whose house we were at, walked over and wrapped her hands around Donovan's bicep. "There you are. It's nice to see you, Donovan."

"You, too, Monica."

"My husband refused to ask if you were single, so I thought I'd come over and do the honors."

Again Donovan's eyes met mine. "I am."

"Good." She tilted her head toward the pool where a gorgeous woman stood.

She was probably in her mid-twenties and wore a short, white dress that showcased tanned legs a mile long. "I'd like to introduce you to my niece. She just moved here from California and starts law school in the fall. I thought maybe you two could be friends."

Jealousy coursed through my veins. I knew it was absolutely ridiculous, considering I was standing with another man's arm wrapped around me. But logic didn't change what I felt.

Donovan smiled graciously. "Of course." He nodded once more to Blake and followed the hostess over to the woman at the pool without another glance my way.

For the rest of the afternoon, I attempted to focus on whatever conversation I was supposed to be part of while trying not to watch a certain two people across the yard. I failed miserably. Every time the blonde tossed her hair, I felt like a bull eyeing a red cape—and Lord, did she whip her tresses around. I was grateful it was a hot day, so the reddening of my face would be less conspicuous. At one point, she pressed her hands to Donovan's chest as she laughed, and I just really wanted to go home.

"Excuse me for a minute, please," I said to Blake and whatever partner we were now talking to. Honestly, they all looked the same. "Could you direct me to the bathroom?"

"Of course." He pointed toward the house. "Straight up the stairs and make a left or right. There's one in either direction."

At the top of the stairs, I turned left. But someone was in that bathroom, so I went in search of the other. Finding it free, I shut myself inside, tossed my purse on top of the toilet tank, and gripped the sides of the sink, exhaling deeply. It felt like the first time I could breathe in hours. I wanted to splash some cold water on my face, but I didn't have makeup to fix the mess I'd make. So instead, I dropped my head, closed my eyes, and took a few deep breaths. After a minute or two, I started to feel a little better—until the knock came.

I have no idea why, but I just stared at the door without saying a word. After thirty or so seconds of silence, the handle jiggled back and forth, but I'd locked it behind me. When a little more time passed, I thought maybe the person had taken the hint, but then another knock came. And this time, it was followed by a voice.

"It's me."

Donovan.

I walked over to the door and leaned my head against it, speaking quietly. "Go away."

"I'm not going anywhere. Open the door, Autumn."

I debated arguing with him, but I had a feeling he wouldn't back down, and I didn't want anyone to notice him standing around talking through the bathroom door. So I unlocked it.

Donovan opened it hesitantly. When I didn't say or do anything, he stepped inside and clicked the lock shut behind him.

"You better not stay too long," I said. "Your new friend will wonder where you are."

The corner of Donovan's lip twitched. "Jealous?"

I frowned. "No."

His twitchy lip gave way to a full-blown, smug smile. "*Right.*"

I sighed. "What do you want, Donovan? You're going to get caught in here. You should go back downstairs."

"I don't give a shit about getting caught. And what do I want? I thought you'd figured that out by now." He moved closer. "I want *you*, Autumn."

I looked down, shaking my head. "Just go with the blonde." Even saying the words caused a sharp pain inside my chest.

"I don't want the blonde. I want what's right in front of me." He slipped two fingers under my chin and nudged my head up so our eyes met. "I'm goddamn crazy about you, Autumn. And I know you feel the same way about me. What's it going to take for you to finally admit it?"

I tasted salt in my throat and swallowed hard to fight the tears I knew were on their way. "I can't, Donovan."

He stepped closer. "You can. I don't know what's got you so afraid, but whatever it is, I'll help you get through it."

I could handle being jealous. I could handle him being jealous and angry, but I couldn't handle him being so damn amazing and caring. Tears brimmed my eyes.

"Donovan..."

He took another step closer and cupped my cheeks. A warm tear spilled over and started to roll down my face, but his thumb caught it. "I don't know what else to say to convince you. So I want to show you." He looked back and forth between my eyes. "Stop me now if you're not okay with that."

My heart pounded in my chest. My head was a damn mess of conflicting emotions, but my body wasn't. It wanted what was on the verge of happening more than I could ever remember wanting anything—so much so that my lips parted, and my tongue slid along my mouth to wet them before I could even catch up to think about what they were preparing for. Donovan watched intently. Even though my body had basically just rolled out the red carpet and invited him to kiss me, he still gave me time to change my mind.

He leaned closer, inch by painstaking inch, until we were nose to nose, and my inhales became his exhales. One of his big hands slipped from my cheek to trail its way around to the back of my neck. Donovan looked into my eyes one last time, and even though he'd said I'd need to stop him, I saw a hint of hesitation. In that moment, the panic I'd been feeling about him kissing me suddenly turned into panic that he wouldn't. So I nodded.

The biggest smile crossed his face, just before he crushed his lips to mine. Our tongues eagerly collided. It had been close to a year since we'd kissed, yet our bodies needed no time to get reacquainted. Donovan's hand at my neck slid down to my ass, and with one quick hitch, he hoisted me into the air. My legs wrapped around his waist, and he turned and walked us until my back hit the wall. Donovan grinded between my parted legs, and a hand wound into my hair and yanked my head back, exposing my neck. He groaned as he kissed his way from my lips to my chin and sucked along my neck.

"Fuck," he growled. "Do you feel it? You must. It's clawing from the inside trying to get out." He took my mouth again.

Nothing had ever tasted so good or felt so right. Absolutely nothing. It was impossible to deny the physical connection, even if I kept denying the emotional one.

I wasn't sure how long we stayed like that—kissing and grabbing, groping and grinding—but I never wanted it to end. Everything felt so very right, so perfect. Though you know what they say about all good things...

They get interrupted by a knock at the door.

"*Donovan...*"

16

Autumn

"**D**onovan..." I nudged at his chest. "Did you hear that?" He mumbled through our joined lips. "Say my name again. I fucking love it."

"No...Donovan..." I pulled back. "Someone knocked."

He cupped my neck firmly and tried to bring me closer again. "That's just my heart pounding against my ribs."

Could I have been imagining it? I didn't think so. But I'd been so engrossed in the moment, anything was possible. I listened carefully for a few heartbeats, but the only sound was our heavy breathing.

"See?" Donovan said. He nudged my neck closer to him once more. "Now give me that mouth."

But just as our lips met, another knock came, this time louder. "Is someone in there?"

I gasped at the sound of the man's voice. Donovan quickly covered my mouth with one hand and held his pointer up to his lips with the other. My eyes were wide as he leaned his head toward the door and spoke. "Occupied. I'll be out in a minute."

"Sorry. No rush."

143

Donovan's eyes returned to mine. He again made the *shhh* sign with his finger. I nodded, and he removed his hand and set me down on my feet before guiding me to the far side of the bathroom and turning on the faucet.

He leaned in and whispered in my ear. "Kyle Andrews. He's a partner—decent guy. But eats lunch every day with Dickson."

I felt the color drain from my face. "What are we going to do?"

"I'll go out first and try to talk him up so you can slip out."

"Oh my God! We're going to get caught."

"I won't let anything happen to you."

"I'm not worried about me, Donovan. Yes, it's a shitty thing to do when I'm here with another man, and I'll be mortified. But things with Blake are casual. *You* will lose your job, though."

"Don't worry about me."

I shook my head. "Let's just stay in here."

Donovan frowned. "The guy's waiting. Plus, eventually people will notice we're missing. Dickson certainly will if he's got half a damn brain."

"Why don't we just say I wasn't feeling well and you came in to help me?"

Donovan's eyes dropped to my mouth, and he ran his finger over my swollen bottom lip. "He's not an idiot."

I blew out a nervous rush of hot air and nodded. "Okay."

"Listen at the door. When I say it's hot out today, that means it's clear for you to slip out."

I nodded.

Donovan turned off the water and walked to the door. I followed close behind so I wouldn't miss hearing anything. Just as he reached for the knob, he stopped and turned back. Cupping my cheeks, he leaned in and dropped one last gentle kiss on my lips. *Ready?* he mouthed.

I wasn't, but I nodded nonetheless.

I felt physically sick as he opened the door enough to slip out. Rather than shut it behind him, he left it open a crack for me to listen.

"Took you long enough," the man's voice said.

"Sorry. Hey, where's your wife, by the way? Cheryl, right?"

"Yeah. She didn't come. She's home with what she calls the 'never-ending pregnancy'. God forbid I remind her she still has two months to go."

Donovan chuckled. "She's a designer, right?"

How the hell is he staying so calm and sounding so damn normal?

"Mostly she spends a fortune redecorating rooms she just did a year or two ago at our place, but yeah—she was an interior designer."

"Did you see the painting down at the end of the hall?"

"No, why?"

"Would you mind taking a picture of it and asking her if she knows who the artist is?"

"Why don't you just ask Kravitz?"

"He doesn't remember."

"Oh...yeah, sure."

I listened as footsteps moved away from the door. When they stopped, Donovan said, "This is the one. I guess it's probably for the best your wife didn't come, seeing as *it's hot as hell out there today.*"

Oh God. That was my cue. I thought I might throw up, but I cracked open the door enough to peer down the hall. The partner's back was to me while he faced the painting and fidgeted with his phone. Donovan leaned back and glanced in my direction before motioning with his hand for me to leave. So I took a deep breath, hitched my purse up on my shoulder as I slipped out the door, and darted for the stairs as quietly as I could.

I had no idea if anyone saw me, because I didn't stop to look back. Blood rushed through my veins as I sprinted down to the main level. It wasn't until my feet left the very last step that I even noticed I'd been holding my breath. And apparently, I also wasn't paying attention to where I was going, because I ran right into a solid chest.

"Whoa. Where's the fire?" Blake smiled. But he took one look at my face and his upturned lips wilted. "Are you okay?"

My hands were shaking. The tips of my fingers felt numb, and I couldn't even try to hide that I had no blood left in my face. A sheath of sweat also broke out across my forehead.

When I didn't answer right away, Blake put his hands on my shoulders. "Are you sick?"

Oh, thank God. I needed someone to give me a solid lie. I nodded. "Yeah. I'm sorry. I'm not sure if I'm coming down with something or maybe I ate something that didn't agree with me, but I just got sick."

"I was wondering what was taking you so long in the bathroom. Do you want me to get you anything? Some soda or a water or something?"

"No." I shook my head. "I'm sorry. I think I'm just going to call an Uber and go home."

"An Uber? Don't be silly. I'll drive you."

"No. It's your work party, and we haven't been here very long. You should stay. I don't want to ruin your afternoon."

Blake smiled warmly. "You aren't ruining anything. I hate these things, anyway. I put in some face time. That's all I needed to do."

I *really, really* just wanted to slink out the door, jump into an Uber, and hightail it back to the city, but I also didn't want to raise any suspicions. So I nodded, though the thought of spending two hours driving back from the Hamptons in a car with Blake after what had just happened in the bathroom made me feel like I might break out in hives.

Blake leaned forward and kissed my forehead. "There's a library right down that hall—last door on your left. Why don't you go sit down in there. I'll do a quick round of goodbyes, and we'll get out of here."

I needed to get my head screwed on straight, so I thanked him and walked down the hall. Ten minutes later, Blake came into the library.

"Sorry that took so long," he said. "You ready to go?"

I stood and attempted one last-ditch effort. "It's really no trouble to take an Uber. Are you sure you wouldn't rather stay than spend two hours in the car with someone who doesn't feel well?"

Blake wrapped his arms around me and brought me to his chest. "Two hours with a sick you is better than an afternoon with all these clowns, anyway." He kissed the top of my head.

God, why did he have to be so damn nice? As if I didn't already feel like shit.

"Come on." He released me and gestured toward the door. "Let's get you out of here."

I thought we'd gotten out of the party unscathed until Blake opened the front door for me. Donovan was standing outside on the porch by himself.

He looked at me, then Blake, then me again, without saying a word.

"What are you doing out here, Decker?" Blake pulled the door closed behind him. "You're not trying to escape the party, are you?"

Donovan's face remained impassive. "Nope. Just needed some fresh air."

"Are you feeling sick? Autumn thinks something she ate might not have agreed with her. I hope the whole place doesn't come down with food poisoning."

Donovan looked straight at me. "Pretty sure it's not food poisoning."

"Good. Alright then, enjoy the party." Completely oblivious, Blake put his hand on my back. "And Decker, this is a good opportunity for you today. So don't do something stupid and screw it up."

I shut my eyes. God, where was that advice half an hour ago? I felt Donovan's eyes on me, but I didn't want to make matters worse, so I kept my head down when I said goodbye and walked to the car, slumped in a walk of shame.

The ride home was long, and I spent it lost in my head. I answered when Blake asked me a direct question, but otherwise I didn't talk much. Thankfully, both the physical symptoms I'd displayed and the mental distance could be blamed on not feeling well. When we pulled up to my apartment, Blake started to look for a place to park, but I really needed to be alone.

"I'm so sorry I caused you to leave the party early, but if you don't mind, I'm not really up for company right now."

"Oh. Yeah, of course. I get it. I like to be left alone when I don't feel well, too."

I forced a smile. "Thanks."

"I'll park and walk you to the door."

I shook my head. "It's fine. You don't need to walk me."

"You sure?"

I nodded.

"At least let me double park and open your door."

"Okay."

Blake walked around to my side and opened the passenger door. Extending a hand, he helped me from the car and kept my hand in his. "I'll text you later to see how you're feeling."

I was pretty sure I'd still be feeling the same—like a giant piece of shit. Yet I smiled again. "Thank you."

He leaned in for a kiss, and a wave of panic washed over me. Without thinking, I put my hand on his chest and stopped him. Blake's face wrinkled.

"I...I don't want to get you sick."

He smiled. "I'll risk it."

I covered my mouth. "No...really."

Blake gave me a conciliatory smile and lifted my hand to his mouth, brushing his lips over my knuckles. "Feel better. I'll see you soon."

17

Donovan

I'm not going to call. The ball is in her court here. If she wants to keep seeing that assface, that's fine with me. Nothing I can do about it.

I sucked back my third vodka tonic since I'd walked in the door not even an hour ago, grabbed the spray bottle off the kitchen counter, and proceeded to angry-water my plants as I ranted.

"It's bullshit. There's no fucking way she feels the same with Dickson."

Spray. Spray.

"I just need to get laid. That's all this shit is."

Spray. Spray.

"I'm not calling her. Screw that. You know what? *Screw her.*"

Spray. Spray.

But then I remembered what she'd looked like in that bathroom—red cheeks, lips swollen, hair that looked like it had just been fisted—because it had, by me. Fucking gorgeous.

And then what she'd looked like as she walked out of the house—pale, nervous, as sickly as she pretended to be.

Maybe I should just check on her...

I looked over at my cell phone on the counter and shook my head.

"No. You're not calling her. She's fine."

Spray. Spray.

But what if...

"No." *Spray. Spray.* "Just no."

Ten minutes later, my plants were drowning, so I figured I'd join them and poured another vodka tonic. I was more of a couple-of-beers guy, or a glass of wine with dinner, so liquor hit me like a ton of bricks.

I downed half the fourth glass and stared at my cell phone.

"Stop looking at me, or I'll spray you, too."

That last comment, for some ridiculous reason, made me laugh maniacally. I felt a little insane standing in the middle of my apartment bent over in hysterics, but when I was done, my anger had dissipated. Apparently, I needed a good laugh...*or a fourth vodka.*

No longer angry, I swiped my phone from the counter and headed to the living room with the rest of my drink in hand. I kicked my feet up and alternated between lolling my head back and staring up at the ceiling and sipping my vodka tonic, lost in thought.

That fucking kiss. As corny as it sounded, I was a kiss guy. It didn't happen very often, but when you slipped your tongue into a woman's mouth and her taste consumed you—it was better than most sex. Yes, it's true. I'm a dude, and I think a kiss can be better than getting the rest of my rocks off. The thing is, I'm a thirty-year-old guy. Let's face it, my hand gets my rocks off. A hole in the wall would work in a pinch. And not to be a conceited dick, but

I'm pretty lucky with the ladies when I want to be. So sex in itself—coming in a pussy, mouth, hand, or wherever it may be—it's great, but it's generally pretty ordinary. But a kiss with a woman who's under your skin? There's nothing ordinary about that. That shit is unforgettable.

Finishing off my drink, I decided I needed to know if I was the only one who felt that way. So I set my empty glass on the coffee table and called up my contacts. Autumn was first. I didn't even need to waste time scrolling.

She answered on the second ring. "Hey."

At risk of sounding like a bigger pussy than the kiss comment probably already made me, her voice sent a shot of warmth through my veins.

"Do you think a kiss can be better than sex?"

"If you'd asked me that a year ago, I probably would have said no."

I let my head fall back against the back of the couch again, enjoying the moment. "And now?"

"Now I think a kiss can feel like oxygen when I'm unable to breathe."

I smiled. "Are you alone?"

"I am."

"Where's The Dick?"

"He dropped me off at my apartment."

"Is that what he wanted?"

She sighed. "It's what I wanted."

"And why is that?"

"Because I'm not in the habit of sticking my tongue down the throat of two men in one day."

We were both quiet for a while. Eventually, I said, "That was some damn kiss." When she didn't respond, I prodded, "Wasn't it?"

"Yes, but it was also wrong."

"It didn't feel wrong to me."

"I was there with another man, Donovan."

"Who you have an open relationship with and don't even like very much."

"Who said I don't like Blake very much?"

"I just did. Can you really tell me you're into him?"

She was quiet again for a while. When she spoke, her voice was soft. "It's not that I don't like him. He's very nice, and he's intelligent. We have good conversation."

I snorted. "I had a good chat with my plants earlier. Doesn't mean I want to suck their face."

"Donovan..."

I shook my head. "Autumn."

"I'm sorry about today. I'm giving you mixed signals. The kiss shouldn't have happened."

"Like fuck it shouldn't have."

"I like you, Donovan. I really do."

"And I like you, too. A hell of a lot. So much so that I can't think straight lately. You're all I damn think about. So what's the problem?"

"I told you. I don't want a relationship."

"But you're in one with Dickson..."

"It's a different kind of relationship."

"Well, I'll take what I can get. Whatever the deal you have going with Dickson is, I'll take it."

"I wish it were that easy."

"Why isn't it?"

"Because..."

Down deep I knew the answer, even though I didn't understand it at all. "Because you have feelings for me, and you don't for him."

"I know that sounds ridiculous. But yeah."

"Would it help if I was an asshole to you? Maybe we could plan on going out and I wouldn't show up."

She chuckled softly. "You're a good guy, Donovan."

I could tell this conversation was coming to an end. So I pushed one more time. "Tell me why you won't go out with a guy you like. At least give me that so I can accept it and move on."

"I just...I want to stay focused on my job and finishing school."

I knew that was bullshit, but short of being an asshole, I had nowhere to go from here. This time it was me who let out the big sigh. Neither of us said anything for a solid five minutes after that. But I heard her breathing and wasn't about to hang up. In negotiations, the first one to break a standoff almost always loses.

"I'm sorry, Donovan," she eventually said. "But I think we need some distance between us at this point."

I had to clear my throat and sit up. "Fine. Do you want me to have Storm's case transferred to someone else?"

"No. He trusts you, and that's not something that happens too often. Plus, you got him a deal, so I'm guessing things are almost wrapped up."

"Yeah. He'll need to appear before the judge to accept the terms, but that should take ten minutes."

"Okay. Thank you."

"Well, I guess there's nothing left to say. I'll have my assistant call you when I get the date of the appearance, so you don't have to talk to me more than necessary."

Autumn's voice sounded as sad as I felt. "Okay."

I wanted to be nice, but I was frustrated, and the alcohol sure as hell didn't help. "Enjoy your emotionless life, Red."

⸺

The following Friday was our work happy hour. I hadn't had any contact with Autumn, not that I'd expected to after our last conversation. But still, the week had sucked. I lost an important summary judgment argument, wasted a full day drawing up motions to stop the bank from seizing more of Mr. Bentley's assets—which they were going to no matter what, but the client had demanded I try—and today I had to fill in for a partner whose wife had lost her mother and second-chair a case for Dickson, of all people.

I wasn't sure what was worse, spending the entire day sitting next to him or the fact that he did a damn good job in oral arguments. At least Autumn never came up. Thank God. All I wanted to do was go home and commiserate to my plants, but Trent and Juliette weren't having it. They'd practically dragged me to happy hour. And now, as I sipped on a beer I didn't want, I realized why Juliette had been so gung ho about me coming tonight.

"Donovan, this is my friend Margo." Juliette smiled. "I mentioned her to you. She's the yoga instructor."

I gave a curt nod. "How you doing, Margo?"

She looked me up and down, not even attempting to hide her interest. "My day just got better."

Shit. The woman was beautiful. Petite with big eyes, full lips, and a tiny waist, but a hell of a lot of tits and ass— exactly the type I'd normally be attracted to, but I had no interest. Juliette, thinking she'd done me a solid, grinned at me and wiggled her fingers. "Tootle-oo. I'll leave you guys to get to know each other better."

Great.

Margo tossed her purse onto the bar next to me and raised her hand to get the bartender's attention. "Can I buy you a drink?" she asked.

I wasn't interested, but I also wasn't an asshole. "No, thanks." When Freddie, the regular bartender, walked over, Margo ordered a baybreeze. I lifted my chin to him. "Put that on my tab, will you, Freddie?"

"Sure, boss." He knocked his knuckles against the bar. "You got it."

"Thank you," Margo said. She turned to face me. "So Juliette tells me you're single?"

"I am."

"And why is that?"

I lifted a brow. "Why am I single?"

She nodded.

"I didn't realize I needed a reason to be single."

Margo smiled. "You're an attorney—a killer one from what Juliette told me. You're obviously handsome. Don't think that's news to you since there's a mirror right over there. And my friend says you're a genuinely good guy. Men like that aren't single for long."

I smirked and rubbed my lip. "Juliette said I'm a killer lawyer and a good guy, huh?"

Margo shrugged. "She did. But don't let it go to your head. She also said you could be a giant dick sometimes."

I laughed. "Alright. Now that sounds more like the Juliette I know. I was beginning to worry maybe she was dying or something, saying all those nice things about me."

Margo smiled and tilted her head. "So what's your deal? Recent breakup? Manwhore? Commitment phobe?" She squinted at me. "I don't take you for a momma's boy."

"Definitely not a momma's boy. But I also haven't had a recent breakup. I'm not afraid of commitment, and if I'm a manwhore, I'm not very good at it considering it's been about four or five months since I had sex."

Margo sighed and bowed her head dramatically. "Then you're the worst kind of single man."

She was amusing, and I was curious, so I bit. "What's the worst kind of single guy?"

She held her hand over her heart and shook her head. "You have it bad for a woman who isn't interested."

My smile fell.

Margo noticed and rubbed my arm. "Sorry. Didn't mean to bring your head down."

I forced a smile. "It's fine. You didn't."

Freddie walked over and slid Margo's drink across the bar. "One baybreeze for the pretty lady."

"Thanks, Freddie." I nodded.

Margo sipped her drink while studying my face, then set her cocktail on the bar and rubbed her hands together. "Okay, lay it on me."

I shook my head. "Lay what on you?"

"Your woman troubles."

"I can't do that."

"Sure you can. Sometimes it takes a stranger to give you perspective on what's going on—unless you already know what the problem is."

Honestly, I felt pretty desperate. But this woman seemed nice, and she'd clearly come here with different expectations for the night. I didn't want to be a total downer and ruin her evening. "It's fine, but thank you for the offer. I appreciate it."

Margo drank some more of her cocktail, and then as I was finishing off my beer, she said, "I'm in love with a married man."

I coughed the alcohol down the wrong pipe and spoke with a hoarse voice. "Come again?"

She smiled. "You heard me. He owns the gym I work at and two others."

"*Shit*. Does he know?"

Margo wagged her finger back and forth. "Not so fast. If we're not going to go home together and try to make each other forget, we're going to share our secrets fair and square. What's her name, at least?"

"Autumn."

"Pretty name. Does she have red hair?"

I smiled. "She does. And green eyes."

"Nice. Donald has blue eyes." She nodded toward a table. "Wanna go sit and talk? I don't know if it will help either of us, but I don't have anything better to do."

I laughed. "Sure. Why not?"

Margo and I talked for the next two and a half hours. It was a shame I was so consumed with a woman who had no interest in being with me, because I really liked Margo. She was smart and a straight shooter. Plus, *yoga instructor.* Her advice to me was to do the exact opposite of what I'd done with Autumn—not walk away. She suspected the same thing I did—that Autumn had been in a bad relationship and gotten burned or lost someone, which made her lose trust in men. So she suggested I show her I could be trusted by not giving up so easily.

I wasn't entirely sure her approach was correct, but it had been nice to look at things from a woman's perspective. Unfortunately, my advice to her wasn't as thought provoking. I'd told her to find a new job and not look back. Donald liked the attention he was getting from her, but was never going to leave his wife—who was currently pregnant with their second child.

We walked back over to the bar so I could close out the tab. "Let me ask you something... Do you have a type?"

Margo smiled. "Apparently married, balding, and a jerk."

I chuckled. "No, I meant, have you met Trent?"

Her brows shot up. "The short guy who's really young?"

I smirked. "That's the one."

"Juliette introduced me to him earlier. I'll be honest, he's not the type I'd usually go for." She smiled. "You, on the other hand..."

I nodded. "I get it. But give him a shot. He's a great guy. He's also thirty, even though he doesn't look it. Someday that will be a good thing."

She bit her lip in contemplation before smiling. "Okay. What the hell? I will."

"Come on, I'll hook you up talking to him on my way out."

It was still early when I got home, only about ten o'clock. I took a quick shower and watered my plants—this time, without bitching at them. Maybe my talk with Margo had done me some good after all.

The entire week I'd been pissed off, but I suddenly felt a bit more relaxed. So I sat down, took out my phone, and scrolled to my photos, going straight to my favorites file and the one lonely picture in the folder. *Autumn*. I'd had no idea that twenty-four hours after taking it, the picture would be all I had to keep me from thinking the entire weekend had been a figment of my imagination.

And now it was a reminder that fate had brought her back to me.

Maybe Margo was right. Good things don't come to people who walk away. They come to people who fight for what they want. It was what I'd done in school and in my career, and it had served me well, so why was I giving up so damn easily on something I knew in my gut wasn't over?

The answer didn't take long to come to me. *I wasn't. Screw that.*

Throwing in the towel wasn't my style.

I was good for a full twelve rounds in a fight, so we had a long way to go.

With one last glimpse at the photo, I switched over to contacts and brought up the very first name. I'd have to tread lightly—there could be a fine line between letting a woman know you were going to wait her out and harassment. I needed to figure out how to handle it properly, but for now, I'd start with a simple text.

Donovan: I miss you.

18

Autumn

"What do you think of this?" I pulled a green silk dress I'd bought but never worn out of my closet and pressed it against my body before turning to show Skye.

"It looks Gucci with your skin and hair."

My forehead winkled. "Gucci?"

Skye rolled her eyes. "It means it looks hot. Sometimes I can't believe you're in your twenties. Your vocab is the same as my mom's."

"Uhh. Thank you?"

She flipped the page of her magazine while sitting on my bed with a smirk. "It wasn't a compliment."

I chuckled and walked over to the mirror. "Do you think the material is too clingy?"

She flipped another page, lifted the sample flap on a perfume advertisement, and brought it up to her nose for a sniff. "There's no such thing as too clingy. Where are you wearing it? Also..." She wrinkled her nose. "This smells like shit."

"Let me smell." She held out the magazine, and I walked over and smelled the page. "I like it."

She shook her head again and mumbled under her breath. "You really are turning into my mom."

At twenty-two, Skye was only six years younger than me. But sometimes it felt like she could be my child. That's probably because she'd been an actual child when we'd met six years ago.

"What's the dress for?"

"Court tomorrow with one of my kids."

She shut the magazine and wiggled her eyebrows. "Ahh...the hot, rich lawyer who steals shampoo from hotels and has a shitload of plants. What's going on there? I need all the details. Did you see him again?"

I nodded. "Yeah...and things got a little complicated."

"Complicated good or complicated bad?"

"I sort of went to a party with Blake—I told you they work at the same firm. Technically Blake is one of Donovan's bosses. Anyway, at the party, I wound up making out with Donovan in a bathroom."

"Holy crap." She tossed the magazine to the side and clapped her hands together. "I didn't think you had it in you."

I sat down on the bed and sighed. "I don't, Skye."

"So dump the other guy."

"It's not that..."

"So what is it?"

"I'm just... I'm not ready."

"Okay, well...*what are you doing to make yourself ready?*"

I frowned. "You're throwing my own words back at me, aren't you?"

"Nope. I'm just recycling good advice."

I smiled sadly. "I know, I know. I lectured you and pushed you for years. You don't have to remind me what a hypocrite I am. I'm good at talking the talk, but apparently not so good at walking the walk."

Skye took my hand and squeezed. "It's okay. We walk when we're ready to walk. But maybe you need to start taking baby steps."

"I have been. I've been dating the last few years."

"No, you've been having sex with men you see no future with. You only date guys who aren't looking for an emotional connection. The one time you really connected with a guy, you spent a weekend with him and *wouldn't* have sex. Don't you think that's an issue? You'll sleep with a man you're not that into, and won't with the one you are. I'm not sure that counts as taking baby steps. It's more like crawling."

I blew out a deep breath. "Maybe. But I like things the way they are."

"Do you really, though? The thought of hot lawyer banging some other woman doesn't bother you?"

Skye and I had made a pact years ago never to lie to each other about what we were feeling. No matter what. We'd gone through some pretty hard truths, so I wasn't about to lie to her now.

I frowned. "That actually makes me feel like throwing something—like a lamp out the window, without opening it first."

"Oh, honey." She smiled sadly and squeezed my hand again.

Ten minutes ago, I'd felt like Skye was my daughter, and now she felt like the more mature one. In some ways, she had grown more than me. She'd even had a serious boyfriend for almost a year now. And while I dated, I kept things limited to sex. Until last year, I hadn't met a man who interested me enough to want more. Then I lost my luggage and fell hard in only three days. But I'd run the other direction as fast as I could, and eventually stopped thinking about him every day—until life threw me a cruel curveball.

"When was the last time you talked to Lillian?"

Lillian was my and Skye's therapist, and the way we'd met. Usually I never ran into another patient while I waited for my weekly appointment. Lillian's office was super private and discreet—she had two separate waiting rooms so patients never had to see each other. But one day I was early, and Skye came in crying without an appointment. The receptionist mixed up the rooms, so the two of us wound up sitting across from each other. It only took fifteen minutes of talking for us to bond, and the rest is history.

"It's probably been about two years now," I told her.

"Do you think maybe it's time to go back? You're doing amazing—don't get me wrong. But you deserve so much more out of life."

I sighed. I'd stopped going because I didn't feel broken anymore. When I'd started seeing Lillian, I was a mess of shattered glass. She'd helped me put all the pieces back together. It wasn't until now that I realized that my pieces were just taped together, not permanently glued.

"I'll think about it."

"Good." Skye smiled. "Now give me details on the kiss."

"It was..." I shook my head. "Unlike anything I've ever experienced. I completely forgot where we were and felt lost in the moment. It's hard to explain, but Donovan just has this gruffness to the way he touches me that makes me feel like he's losing his mind for me, and it's the sexiest thing ever. It was like that the weekend we spent together, too. He's almost dominant when things get physical, which I'd normally hate, but I know in my heart it's not a control thing for him. It's more of him expressing how much he wants me. If one of the partners hadn't interrupted, I think we might've ended up having sex against the wall."

Skye's eyes bulged. "You got caught?"

I shook my head. "We almost did, though. But I was able to slink out, and then I feigned being sick and Blake drove me home."

"Have you seen him since?"

"Donovan? No. We talked on the phone later that night, and I told him I thought we should keep our distance."

"How long ago was that?"

"About two weeks."

"So you haven't had contact with him in a while, then?"

"Well, that's the odd thing. After we talked on the phone, he didn't contact me for almost a week. But then I got a text one night that just said *I miss you*. I didn't respond, and the next day I got a huge bouquet of flowers with a note that said *Still thinking about you*. And every day since then, he's done something like that, but we haven't seen each other or spoken in two weeks."

"*Huh...*"

"Huh, what?"

"He doesn't know anything about your past, right?"

"No, why?"

"Because he's giving you space, but letting you know he isn't going anywhere. That's exactly how you handle someone like us, yet he doesn't know the history."

"He's very smart and intuitive."

"So then he's probably figured out that you're falling in love with him and are just scared."

I wasn't falling in love, was I?

Skye saw my expression and laughed. "You'll figure it out eventually. Now come on, we have four episodes to watch. I'm dying to know what the story is with that crazy bitch who got taken out of the rose ceremony after fainting."

"Good morning."

Was it possible to be sexy with only two words? I hadn't thought so. But Donovan Decker seemed able to accomplish it—and at only eight forty-five in the morning on a Monday, too. I wasn't sure if it was the three-thousand-dollar, well-fitting suit covering the mass of tattoos I knew were hidden underneath, or the cocky smile that tugged at his lips while his deep voice stayed so steady. *Good morning.* Fuck my life.

I sighed. "Good morning."

Storm looked up from his phone for a half second. "Hey..."

"It's about to open up and pour any minute," Donovan said. "Why don't we go inside, and I'll find us an empty room to talk before we have to see the judge?"

"Okay."

The courthouse had one of those revolving turnstile doors. Donovan held his hand out for Storm to enter first. Once the next compartment came around, he held his hand out for me. But he surprised me by hopping into the tight little area right behind me. And if I wasn't already thrown by the proximity, I felt his hot breath on my neck as he whispered in my ear. "You look beautiful. Green is my second-favorite color on you."

I almost tripped navigating the rotating door, but I made it out the other side, glad to have a little air. Donovan seemed perfectly fine.

"Right this way," he said.

We walked down the long corridor to the last room on the left. Donovan opened the door and peeked inside. Finding it empty, he opened it wider. "Let's go in here to talk."

Storm went first, and then it was my turn. "What's your first favorite?" I asked as I passed.

Donovan's eyes sparkled. "Nude."

This is going to be one long morning.

The playfulness stopped once Donovan put on his lawyer hat and explained the terms of the deal to Storm.

"Do you understand everything I just told you?"

"Yeah. If I don't get in trouble for a year, the charges get dropped."

"Right," Donovan said. "But what happens if you do get in trouble during the next year?"

"Really?" Storm said. "I'm not an idiot."

"Storm..." I warned.

Donovan smiled. "It's fine. I know it seems like I'm asking you a simple question, but the answer isn't as simple as you think. If you get in trouble during the next year, the pending charge is reinstated, along with any new charges brought against you. That means one family court judge sitting on two offenses at the same time. It sounds like semantics, but a judge who has two charges in front of his nose is going to feel obligated to teach you a lesson, so the outcome could be more serious than two different judges presiding over two different charges six months apart. That might not be fair, but that's the truth of the matter."

"So what do I do? Take the hit with this one to have a better shot the next time?" Storm asked.

"No." Donovan leaned forward and made sure he had Storm's attention, then he spoke slowly. "You make sure there isn't a next time. There *can't* be a next time, Storm."

"Fine..." he grumbled.

"I mean it. You will wind up in a bad place you won't come back from." Donovan lifted his arm and pushed up his shirtsleeve, exposing his watch...but he also flashed a glimpse of his tattoos. Storm's eyes snagged on the ink before meeting his lawyer's again, and it made me wonder if Donovan had needed to check the time on his watch at all.

"Fine. I get it," Storm said.

Donovan nodded. "Good."

"Are we done now? I have to take a piss."

"Yeah, we're done," Donovan said. "I'll walk you to the restroom and see if the judge is running on time this morning." He turned to me. "Be back in a few."

A few minutes later, a bailiff opened the door to the room I sat in alone.

"Oh, sorry. I thought Decker was in here."

"He is," I said. "Or he was. He just walked down to the restroom. He should be back any minute."

"Alright. Would you let him know there's a change of plans and Judge Oakley is ready for him now?"

"Oh, okay. Thank you. I'll let him know."

When Donovan didn't come back after a few more minutes, I gathered up my things and decided to go look for him. I spotted him standing outside the men's room, talking to the man I recognized as the prosecutor from the last time we were here. I didn't want to interrupt, so I waited for them to finish from a few feet away, figuring I'd give them privacy. But apparently I hadn't waited far enough away to avoid their conversation.

"So what's the deal with the woman who comes with your client?"

"She's his social worker."

"Any chance you know if she's single?"

Donovan took a minute to respond. "Happily married with six kids. Husband's a pro boxer."

"Shit. Okay. I'll keep my distance."

"Good idea."

Storm came out of the bathroom and walked over to me, rather than Donovan. So Donovan turned to follow him and found me standing maybe six feet away. He studied me, probably trying to figure out if I'd overheard.

I raised an eyebrow and smirked.

He chuckled to himself and turned back to the prosecutor. "I'll see you inside."

When he walked over, the grin was still on his face.

"I think a gun-toting cop would have been more effective than a boxer."

Donovan laughed and put his hand on my back. "You're probably right. But come on, let's go in and get this deal sealed."

As we walked toward the courtroom, Donovan's phone began to buzz. He checked the caller ID and his step faltered.

"Everything okay?" I asked.

"Yeah. It's Bud. He doesn't usually call during the day. He actually rarely picks up the phone at all. But I'll call him back when we're done. They're ready for us." Donovan opened the door to the courtroom.

He settled at the defendant's table with Storm, and I took a seat in the row behind them in the spectator's section. While we were waiting for the judge to take the bench, I noticed Donovan pull his phone out of his pocket again and look at it. His face looked troubled, but the bailiff took his place, and then court was called to order.

The entire process took less than five minutes. It made me sad to see just how routine it was to have a twelve-year-old kid stand in front of the judge so felony charges could be read aloud. Once the prosecutor said he'd agreed to a deal with the defendant, the judge barely even looked up before he banged his gavel and the entire thing was over.

Donovan packed up, and the three of us headed out

of the courtroom. Back in the lobby, he took out his phone again. "Excuse me for a minute."

He took a few steps away, but I overheard his side of the conversation.

"What's up, Bud? Everything okay?"

Pause.

"Shit. Where are you?"

Pause.

"What happened?"

Pause.

"I'll be there in a half hour."

Donovan looked frazzled when he turned back.

"What's going on? Is Bud okay?"

"He…" Donovan looked over at Storm and clearly changed directions. "He's fine." Then he caught my eye and let me know everything was *not* fine.

"We're a done deal here." He turned to Storm. "Keep yourself out of trouble. I don't care if trouble comes looking for you. You run the other way."

Storm rolled his eyes. "Whatever."

Donovan gestured toward the door. "I need to take off. You guys okay getting out of here yourselves?"

"Yeah, of course." I nodded. "Go ahead."

I'd barely gotten the words out, and Donovan was already rushing toward the exit. Luckily, Storm was so busy making up for the whopping eight minutes he couldn't be on his phone that he didn't seem to notice anything strange.

I put my hand on his shoulder. "Come on. Let's get you back to school."

~

I'd been the one to say Donovan and I needed to keep distance, yet I couldn't leave things the way they'd ended today. After I dropped off Storm at school, I went back to my office to dig into a mountain of paperwork. But I couldn't focus. I was worried about Bud and wanted to make sure he was okay. So I shot off a quick text to check in with Donovan.

Autumn: Is Bud okay?

Ten minutes later, my phone chimed with a return text.

Donovan: He was robbed last night. They stole his van. He tried to fight them off, so they beat the hell out of him.

Oh no!

I started to type back, but then decided to call. Donovan answered on the first ring.

"Is he okay?"

"He will be. He's a tough old bastard. He's got a bruised kidney from a boot kicking him in the back, a broken arm, and some stitches in his face. But the doc said he'll make a full recovery, though they want to keep him a night or two for observation. When I got to the hospital, he was trying to take out the IVs himself and sign out against medical advice."

"Why would he do that?"

"Because he didn't have anyone to serve dinner tonight. I'm not even sure how the hell he planned on cooking anything when the van they stole had everything he uses in it."

"Oh my God. That's crazy."

"He only agreed to stay because I promised I'd deal with dinner tonight."

"I can't believe he worries about that more than his own health."

"No shit." Donovan sighed.

"Is there anything I can do?"

"Nah. I already recruited my buddies from the neighborhood to help me serve tonight. I'm just going to pick up twenty buckets of chicken from KFC and mashed potatoes."

"Oh, that's a good idea."

"I just hope he doesn't try to escape again while I'm gone."

"I could go sit with him, if you want. Keep my eye on him."

"That's okay."

"No, really. I'd be happy to visit him, if you don't think he'd mind me stopping by."

"It would probably make his year. Not only are you beautiful, it will give him a chance to tell you more stories about me from when I was a kid that you have no interest in listening to."

"Who says I have no interest in hearing some juicy stories about you?"

Donovan laughed. "Fine. He's at Memorial Hospital. The neighborhood isn't great, so park in the parking lot under a streetlight."

I smiled. "Yes, Dad."

"I'm serious. I don't need the both of you being robbed in twenty-four hours."

"I'll park somewhere safe."

"Thank you."

"Is there any particular time you think I should stop by?"

"I'll stick around until probably five. So anytime after that, he'll be alone."

VI KEELAND

"Okay. I'll go by right after work."

"Thank you."

"No need to thank me. I'm happy to do it. I like Bud a lot."

"Alright. Just be careful."

"You, too. If they're willing to beat up an old man for a van, Lord knows what they'd do for your fancy car."

After we hung up, I sat at my desk for a long time, feeling a rush of emotions I wasn't sure what to do with. I felt terrible about what happened to Bud, but I couldn't stop thinking about how I'd feel if something had happened to Donovan. Some of the things rattling through my head I could deal with—that I'd feel sad, upset, angry, scared. But the one emotion I couldn't seem to accept was *regret*.

I'd spent years regretting things I'd done, or the way I'd handled them, until I'd finally come to forgive myself and accept that what happened was not my fault. I'd used regret as a way to punish myself, and here I was doing it all over again.

So I did something before I changed my mind. I picked up my phone and dialed the therapist I hadn't seen in two years.

"Hi. This is Autumn Wilde. I'd like to make an appointment..."

173

19

Autumn

"It's mud. There's a twenty-four-hour bodega across the street that makes the best dulce de leche coffee in the state."

"Jesus." My hand covered my heart as I turned around. Donovan leaned casually against the visiting room doorway. "You scared the crap out of me. I didn't hear you come in."

He flashed that sexy grin of his. "It's almost eleven thirty. Why are you still here?"

I sighed. "Honestly, I lost track of time until I just came out here to grab a cup of coffee. Bud is so entertaining. He really knows how to tell a story."

Donovan shook his head. "I'm guessing some of those stories made me out to be a little shit."

I smiled. "Did you really get arrested for having sex in a police car?"

Donovan dropped his head. "I wasn't having sex. We were thirteen and making out. That's what we did back in the day for privacy. We'd find a car left open and fool around in the backseat for a little while. It was sort of harmless, usually. In my defense, the cop car was unmarked and parked in an empty parking lot. And the cop who caught us turned out to be the uncle of the boy the girl I was making out with was going out with." He held up his hands. "I also didn't know she had a boyfriend."

I laughed. "The story was much more animated when Bud told it."

"I'm sure it was."

"They just took Bud for a scan. He had a little blood in his urine tonight. The nurse said that happens after a trauma, but they want to make sure there isn't a tear they missed the first time."

"Yeah. I checked in with the nurses' station a few minutes ago. They said it will be an hour or so before he's back in his room. I'm going to stick around. You want me to walk you to your car?"

"If you don't mind, I'd like to wait and make sure everything with his scan turns out okay."

Donovan smiled and tilted his head toward the hallway. "You want to go grab a real cup of coffee, then?"

"Sure. But I'll be the judge of whether it's the best coffee in the state or not. I'm a coffee snob, even though I really can't afford to be."

We walked across the street to a small store that I probably would have passed right by on the way to a Starbucks and not given it a second thought. But Donovan was right; the coffee was incredible.

"I can't believe this big cup was only a dollar fifty. This would be six bucks at Starbucks and not half as delicious."

Donovan sipped his own cup. "Told you it was good. It's a different world here than in Manhattan. Most people in Soho or Chelsea wouldn't step one foot into that place to give a mom-and-pop shop a shot because they don't have fancy signage and leather couches."

I bit my bottom lip. "I know, because *I am* one of those people. Or at least *I was*. This stuff might've changed my mind though."

"Good. You miss out on a lot in life if you only judge a book by its cover."

My eyes caught with Donovan's as he opened the front door of the hospital for me. "That's a good reminder."

Inside the elevator, I pressed number seven to go back up to Bud's floor.

"He's going to be a little while still. It's nice out. You up for getting some fresh air?"

"Yeah, sure."

Donovan lifted his chin to the elevator panel. "Hit ten, then."

My forehead wrinkled. "Ten for fresh air?"

He winked. "It's my secret spot."

On the tenth floor, I followed Donovan down a bunch of mostly empty corridors until we came to a set of double doors with a red sign that read *Employees Only*.

Donovan looked around before he pushed them open. "After you."

"Umm...are we going to get in trouble for going in here?"

He smirked. "Not if we don't get caught."

I shook my head. "Is that what you said to the girl who climbed into the back of the unmarked cop car?"

Donovan grinned. "Come on, live a little. I promise you free legal counsel if you get arrested."

"Uhhh... Can you do that from the cell next to me?"

We laughed, but I walked through the door. After another series of turns, we came to a steel door that led to a set of concrete steps. At the top, Donovan opened yet another door. Turned out that led to the roof.

"How the heck do you know about this?"

Donovan walked over to a bench and dusted it off for us before I sat. "I can pretty much tell you the layout to every hospital in the five boroughs."

"Why?"

He sipped his coffee as he sat down next to me. "My mom spent a lot of time in them when I was a kid. Sometimes a John would rough her up instead of paying; other times she'd overdose. I didn't like to leave her alone, but they don't let an unattended kid stay, so I'd find a place to hang out in the building overnight. Often it was the roof."

"And no one ever noticed you?"

"Sometimes a doctor or nurse would say something if they found me up here alone. But they come up here to hide and smoke cigarettes. So if they said anything, I'd ask them if their chief and patients knew they smoked. That usually made them leave me alone. A few times they called security and had them chase me out."

I laughed. "Oh my God. That's insane."

Donovan shrugged. "That's life."

"Believe it or not, I actually got escorted out of a hospital once."

He raised one brow. "This I gotta hear."

I felt sort of proud of my badassery. "Well, I guess I was about sixteen at the time. I lost my mom at twelve to cancer, and I'd grown close to my dad. One night I was staying over at my friend's house when I got a call that my dad had had a heart attack. I went to the hospital and asked in the emergency room where I could find him. They said they were still working on him, but to have a seat and they'd let me know when I could see him. A woman in the waiting room named *Candy* walked over and introduced herself as my dad's fiancée. My dad had just gotten divorced a few months earlier, and I'd had no idea he was even dating anyone. So I was confused. But honestly, my father lost his mind after my mom died, so I didn't put it past him to get engaged again. A little while later, the doctor came out and spoke to us. He said my dad was stable but needed some surgery and asked if he'd been exerting himself when he started to get chest pain. Candy then proceeded to describe, *in detail*, how my father was a bad boy and had just finished doing fifty pushups after being denied orgasm during sex as part of his punishment."

"Shit." Donovan chuckled. "Did you smack her or something?"

"No. I was kind of shell shocked after hearing that. I smacked her after the doctor walked away because she said she didn't like her engagement ring—it was too small. I looked down and saw she had *my grandmother's* ring on her finger. She acted like I'd stabbed her, making this dramatic scene, so security escorted me out."

"I didn't think you had it in you, Red." He smiled. "There's a badass hiding in there after all."

I bumped my shoulder to his. "Well, I am up here illegally on a roof, you know."

"That's true."

A little breeze blew, and Donovan stood to take off his suit jacket. He offered to wrap it around my shoulders.

"No, that's okay. I'm fine."

"I'm warm. Plus, if you don't take it, I'm going to make us go inside, and I like it out here with you."

Our eyes met. I really liked it out here with him, too. Even though we were outside in the middle of Brooklyn, it felt like our own secret place. So I accepted the jacket. "Thank you."

He sat back down. "So is that why you and your dad don't get along that well? You don't like your stepmother?"

"Oh, Candy isn't my stepmother anymore. She was three or four wives ago. I've honestly lost track."

"Three or four wives ago? Plus he was married to your mom, and you said he had just gotten divorced before he got together with Candy the dom. So that's, what, six or seven marriages?"

"Yep. I actually think it's seven, but he's getting married again in a few weeks, so that would make eight."

"Why does he keep doing it?"

I shook my head. "I don't know. We don't talk much anymore."

"Because of the string of Candys he married?"

"No. There was a time in my life that I really needed him to be there for me, and he wasn't."

Donovan looked into my eyes. "I'm sorry."

"Thanks. I have mixed feelings about distancing myself from him. I know from the little bit I just told you it probably doesn't sound that way, but there was a time he was a great dad and husband. He and my mother were high school sweethearts and really loved each other. When she got sick, it broke both their spirits. I remember in my mom's last days, she was more worried about how my dad would carry on after she was gone than how I would. She made me promise I'd always watch over him for her. So part of me feels guilty that I don't anymore."

"I'm sure you have your reasons." He paused and made sure I was looking at him again. "And I can sit here all night if you want to talk about them."

That made my heart squeeze, yet I wasn't ready to go there. "Thanks. But we should probably go see if Bud's back."

Donovan nodded, a bit of disappointment lurking behind his eyes. "Sure. Let's do that."

Bud was just being wheeled back into his room when Donovan and I returned. He looked between us and frowned. "Am I dying and no one's telling me?"

Donovan shoved his hand into his pockets. "You're too stubborn to kick the bucket, old man."

"Damn straight." Bud adjusted his covers. "How was service tonight? Did everyone get fed who needed to get fed?"

"They did. Dario and Ray helped me, so it was more like dinner and a comedy show, but no one is hungry right now."

Bud nodded. "Good. Thank you."

"Not a problem."

Bud looked at me. "And you should be home sleeping, little lady."

I smiled. "I just wanted to make sure everything came out okay with your scan."

As if on cue, a doctor walked in. "Mr. Yankowski?"

"Name's Bud. Frances Yankowski is only what my mother put down on the birth certificate to ensure I'd learn how to handle myself in the schoolyard."

The doctor smiled. "Alright, Bud it is. I just took a look at your scan. Perhaps your company can wait outside while we talk about the results?"

Bud waved at me. "It's fine. They're family."

The doctor explained that while the kidney seemed to be just bruised, the blood in Bud's urine could be a sign of damage, and they needed to continue to monitor his urine and repeat the scan in twenty-four hours.

Bud shook his head. "I feel fine. I'm going home tomorrow morning. I'll come back if it gets worse."

"I'd prefer if you would give us two nights."

"And I'd prefer to look like him." He pointed at Donovan. "Yet I got stuck with this mug."

Donovan spoke to the doctor. "You have any rules against patients being tied to the bed?"

The doctor smiled. "I'm afraid we do, son."

Donovan raked a hand through his hair. "I'll cover dinner again tomorrow. Dario will take care of your route during the day. We already discussed it."

Bud folded his arms across his chest. "No fast-food crap. These people need a balanced meal."

"I have to be in court all day tomorrow. Will hamburgers and hot dogs do? I can pick up a grill on my way over after work."

"With what side dish?"

Donovan folded his arms across his chest, mimicking Bud's usual stance. "Ketchup. It was once a tomato."

It looked like a standoff was about to ensue, so I interjected. "I make a delicious broccoli salad. It goes great with burgers."

Bud's face softened. "Thank you, sweetheart."

"So we have a deal?" Donovan asked.

"Fine," Bud grumbled. "But get whole wheat buns. All that processed flour isn't healthy."

Donovan mumbled under his breath. "Neither is fighting off carjackers."

The doctor had been watching the negotiation like a tennis match. His brows rose. "So we have a deal, then? Mr. Yankow—I mean, Bud—is staying for at least another night or two?"

Bud held up a finger. "Not *at least* another night. *One* more night. Two, max."

The doctor smiled. "I'll take it. Let's start there."

After the doctor left, Donovan and I stayed a few more minutes before leaving Bud to get some rest. Donovan said he'd be back to check in on him before court, and I left Bud my phone number just in case he needed anything during the day tomorrow. After, Donovan walked me to my car.

He looked up at the streetlight I'd parked under. "Very good."

"Why, thank you."

"You don't really have to make broccoli salad. I can pick up some store-bought sides when I grab the burgers."

"Don't be silly. I told Bud I'd do it, and I want to."

Donovan smiled and nodded. "Okay, then. I can pick the salad up from you after I hit the supermarket to get the burgers after court."

My brows furrowed. "What time do you get out of court?"

"Four thirty, unless we go late."

"Why don't I pick up the burgers when I get the stuff for the broccoli salad? I'm going to be at the store anyway."

"You sure you don't mind? That would actually be helpful because I also need to go pick up a grill to cook on since they stole all of his equipment."

"Of course not. I'm happy to help."

"Alright, then. Thanks."

"I'd like to help serve dinner, too."

"You sure?"

"Positive."

"Okay, then, I'll pick you up after I pick up the grill and other stuff I need, and we can ride over to serve dinner together. You're going to have a lot of stuff to carry to and from the car."

"That sounds like a plan."

"Oh, I almost forgot." Donovan dug into the inside pocket of his suit jacket and pulled out his wallet. "Take this credit card to pay for everything."

I waved him off. "No need. I got it."

"You're not paying for all that food, Autumn."

"You're right. I'm not. I have a black card of my father's that sits in my wallet collecting dust. He always tells me to use it for anything important to me, and this is." I smiled. "I think I'll buy top-of-the-line stuff—maybe Kobe beef burgers."

Donovan laughed as I opened my car door. He held onto the top as I climbed inside.

"Goodnight, Donovan." I smiled.

"Goodnight, Red. Thanks for everything." He paused a moment. "We work well together, don't we?"

I smiled. "We do."

He winked. "Be careful driving home."

20

Donovan

"This is a nice place." I looked around the inner sanctum of Autumn's apartment. It was small, but decorated really cool with a bunch of black-and-white photographs of things in the City taken from odd angles, like the suspension wires of the Brooklyn Bridge shot from standing and Times Square taken while walking up the stairs from the subway. "Did you take the photos yourself?"

"No. I bought them from a street artist years ago. I like how they show iconic parts of the city, but in an atypical way." She lifted a box out of the refrigerator and set it on the counter. "I forgot you've never been here."

"Never been invited."

Autumn smiled. "I hope I didn't go overboard with this broccoli salad. I took a guess at how many people came for dinner the night I went with you. I figured about a hundred."

I nodded. "That's pretty spot on."

"I borrowed two coolers from a neighbor, so the meat is in those. I couldn't fit it all in my refrigerator." She bent to lift another box on the bottom shelf, and I walked over and grabbed it for her.

"Jesus. What's in here? Rocks?"

"I made twenty pounds. I didn't want to run out."

"I think you have the side dish covered."

Autumn's kitchen was a typical New York City galley that barely had room for one, so when I joined her to lift out the container, our bodies were almost touching. At the risk of sounding like a complete wuss, I felt it in my loins. *My loins.* I don't think I've ever had use for that word until now. But fuck if everything from beneath my ribs to the base of my balls wasn't all tingly.

I set the second tray on the counter and made a point of pivoting to speak to her. She looked up at me from under those long, dark lashes with her big green eyes, and it was like the bathroom at the partner barbecue all over again. Except if we got started this time, there would be no one around to interrupt. Sure, we had people to feed, but would they really starve if dinner weren't served for *one night*? I found myself actually debating that thought, until something behind Autumn caught my attention. The kitchen had a small window, which was currently open. A little breeze that I didn't even feel must've blown, because the curtains lifted slightly, revealing a plant on the windowsill.

Was that... *No, it couldn't be.*

But then Autumn looked over her shoulder to see what had caught my attention, and when she turned back, the look on her face told me the crazy thought I'd had was right. She sucked her bottom lip between her teeth, and her eyes sparkled like a kid getting caught with a cookie from the cookie jar.

I nodded to the plant without taking my eyes off her. "That's my plant, isn't it?"

Autumn shook her head with a huge grin. "No."

I skirted her and walked over to the window, lifting the pot. It was bigger, and the container had been changed, but I was pretty certain it was my little plant. I knew because I'd cross-bred two of my existing plants—one had green leaves with a yellow stripe, and the other had little yellowish bumps on its leaves—and this one had green leaves with a yellow stripe *and* bumps. It had barely been a seedling when it disappeared from my apartment. I'd noticed it missing the week after our weekend together, and I'd assumed the kid across the hall I sometimes paid to water the plants had killed it or something.

I studied her face. My bullshit-arometer had zero doubt she was lying. "Really? Where did you get this?"

"At the store."

"Which store?"

She shook her head and looked away. "I don't know. The plant store."

I smirked. "The plant store?"

"I don't remember what it was called."

"I do." I leaned down so we were eye to eye and inched closer. Autumn looked like a deer in the headlights, yet there was still a sparkle in her eye. She was enjoying screwing with me as much as I was screwing with her. "You got it from a place called Donovan's."

"I did not." She smiled from ear to ear.

"Did, too."

"Did not."

"I didn't take you for a thief, Red."

"I'm not a thief. I just...borrowed it, okay?"

My brows jumped up. "You borrowed it?"

She nodded. "That's right."

"Almost a year ago?"

"I guess so."

"So you were planning on giving it back?"

She couldn't contain herself anymore—she cracked. Her hands covered her face, and she burst out laughing. "Alright, alright. I took it from your apartment. I didn't get it from the plant store, and I wasn't planning on giving it back."

Now I was laughing, too. "Do you do that often? Take something from a man's apartment?"

"No! I swear. I've never ever done that before. I've actually only stolen one thing in my entire life—an NSYNC pin when I was ten—and I felt so guilty about it that I went back the next day and snuck it into the store." She still had her face covered with her hands.

I gently peeled back her fingers so I could see her eyes. "You wanted a souvenir from our weekend together?"

"I don't know why I took it. I just did. If you couldn't tell, I'm really embarrassed. I'm sorry."

I brushed a piece of hair behind her ear. "Don't be embarrassed. I'm glad you felt the need to take a souvenir. As long as we're coming clean, I have something of yours, too."

Her eyes grew wide yet again. "You do?"

I nodded. "I didn't steal it. Because, you know, I'm not a thief like you. But I found a folded-up piece of paper under my bed the week after you disappeared on me. It must've come out of your luggage, and I didn't notice it until then."

"What paper?"

I reached into my pocket and took out my wallet. Unfolding the sheet of paper I still carried with me, I showed it to her.

Autumn took it. She closed her eyes after reading the first few lines. "Oh my God. Is there a hole somewhere that I can crawl into? First you realize I stole one of your plants, and now I find out you read an alphabetized list of excuses I wrote." She blushed and shook her head. "Who does these things? Why are you even interested in me? I'm a freaking weirdo."

"Normal is overrated, Red. But I am curious who you use the excuses on."

"My dad. He never forgets anything, so if I gave him the same excuse as the last time I needed to get off the phone, he would remember."

"So you started a list?"

"Right before I met you last year, he'd called me the morning I was leaving for Vegas. I said I was walking into an elevator and needed to hang up. Apparently, I'd said that on our last two calls, and he called me on it. I don't like to fly, so I had a few glasses of wine on the flight and made that list, sort of half as a joke." She sighed. "Can we switch? I'll take this paper back and *burn it*, and you can have your plant back. Then we can pretend this conversation never happened."

I smiled. "The paper is yours. But you can keep the plant, too. I like that you kept something around that reminded you of me."

Autumn was still looking at the ground, so I slipped two fingers under her chin and lifted until our eyes met. "It means while your mind wanted nothing more to do with me, your heart did. I can work with that."

She shook her head with a hint of a smile threatening. "You can work with that?"

"Yep. I'm patient." I tapped the tip of her nose. "The heart always wins in the end."

⸺

Dinner service that evening went smoothly. A few of my old buddies came and helped us, and I made sure one of them stuck by Autumn's side when I got busy. The crowds that came to be fed didn't always have the best manners, especially since some of them were too drunk or high to think straight. On the way home, I mentioned to Autumn that I'd spoken to Bud's doctor who said Bud was doing great and could go home tomorrow or the next day.

"Oh, that's wonderful," she said. "I imagine it won't be easy doing things with that cast on his arm. Maybe I can make him a few meals and bring them over?"

"If the rest of your cooking is anything like that broccoli salad, I'm sure he'd love it. To be honest..." My eyes shifted to Autumn and then back to the road. "When you said broccoli salad, I was thinking that might not go over too well. The crowd that comes in is more meat-and-potatoes than salad, but that stuff was damn good."

"Thank you. It's my mom's recipe." She looked out the window for a moment. "She and my dad didn't tell me Mom's cancer was back until a few months before she died. She had an inoperable brain tumor. She'd undergone chemotherapy and radiation years earlier, which slowed the growth, but a second tumor developed in a place they couldn't even really treat."

"I'm sorry."

"Thanks. They didn't tell me what was going on because I was twelve and busy with my friends, and they wanted my life to continue to be as normal as possible. But my mom decided she would teach me how to cook. I guess it was her way of spending time with me. So most of what I remember about the last months with her is being in the kitchen and laughing. I think it's one of the reasons I love to cook."

"Those are nice memories."

She nodded. "I was angry when she died that they hadn't told me. But in hindsight, it might have been for the best. If I'd known, I wouldn't have been able to relax and enjoy that time with her. I would've been scared."

"Makes sense."

"Anyway." She shrugged. "I'll make Bud some meals to freeze and drop them off after he gets home from the hospital, if you think that's okay."

"I'll let him know." We'd never really spoken about what had happened at the barbecue, or after, so I wondered what the state of her relationship with Blake was. I figured this might be as good a time as any to poke around. "Will it be interrupting plans you have for Friday night?"

She smiled. "No."

I tapped the steering wheel, debating whether I should keep asking questions I might not want the answers to. Eventually, curiosity won. "What about the rest of the weekend? Any interesting plans?"

"Just Sunday night. My friend Skye is coming over. We were supposed to get caught up on *The Bachelor* last time we hung out, but we only got through two episodes and both conked out."

"Shocker," I said. "Since the show is so riveting."

"It was *the wine*, not the show being boring."

"Uh-huh."

"How about you? Any plans this weekend?"

"Work. Bud. Dinner service. That'll pretty much occupy it all."

"I can also help with dinner service. Maybe we can take turns so you don't have to do it every night until Bud is well enough to handle things."

Like hell I'd be letting her drive to an abandoned building to serve people who were too down on their luck to afford a meal. But I knew if I said that, I'd wind up in some sort of an equal-rights argument. So instead, I used the opportunity to poke around some more.

"No *date* Saturday night?"

"Nope."

"Why not?"

"I might ask you the same thing. Why don't *you* have a hot date Saturday night?"

"I'm not the one dating someone."

Autumn's mouth spread to a grim line. She looked out the window and spoke softly. "Neither am I."

"Come again?" I leaned toward her. *Could I have heard that wrong?*

She sighed. "I'm not seeing Blake anymore."

"When did that happen?"

"The day after the barbecue."

A smile spread across my face. "I'm sorry to hear that."

She chuckled. "Yeah, you look really sorry."

"What happened?"

Autumn's head whipped in my direction, and I glanced over at her and back to the road. "What?"

"You don't know what happened?"

I stopped at the light at the corner of her street. "Well, obviously I know what happened at the barbecue, but I meant what made you decide to call it quits."

"*That*, Donovan. Blake was very nice to me, and I wasn't being very nice to him."

The light changed, so I turned the corner and started to look for a spot. Luckily, there was too much for her to carry inside by herself. As we passed her building, Autumn turned her head, studying a car double-parked outside.

"Shoot." She groaned.

"What's the matter?"

"I'm pretty sure that's my father's car."

"The yellow Porsche?"

"It's one of his many midlife-crisis purchases."

"Why would he be here?"

"He's done this on occasion when I don't answer his calls."

"You want me to drive around the block a few times to see if he leaves?"

She frowned. "While I would love that, I probably should just deal with it and get it over with."

There was an open spot a few buildings down, so I parked. "Do you want me to wait here while you talk to him? Then I'll carry up the coolers?"

"No." She shook her head. "If you don't mind, it might make it easier if I have a buffer."

I shrugged. "No problem."

I piled the empty coolers one on top of another and carried them, while Autumn brought the bag of containers and serving utensils. As we neared the double-parked Porsche, the driver's side door opened, and a man I assumed was her father got out. He looked between us.

"It's about time. I've been waiting for almost three hours."

"You wouldn't have had to wait if you'd called me to tell me you were coming. I could've told you I wasn't going to be home."

Her father looked like he was still dressed from work, sans the suit jacket. Did that mean he sat in the car for three hours and never thought to take his damn tie off?

"Well, I need to speak to you." He glanced at me again and then his daughter. "Preferably alone."

I looked at Autumn, and she shook her head. When I turned back to her father, he was looking at me expectantly. "Sorry, sir. If Autumn doesn't want me to leave, I'm staying." I set the coolers on the ground, figuring it best to make peace. I extended my hand, stepping forward. "Donovan Decker. Nice to meet you."

Her father looked at my hand like he was considering not shaking it. But eventually he clasped it and grumbled something.

When I moved back beside Autumn, her shoulders slumped. "What do you want, Dad?"

"I'm getting married in two weeks."

"I'm aware. I received the fancy invitation in the mail."

"Well, then, why didn't you respond?"

"Because I figured if I responded the way I wanted to respond, you'd show up at my door."

"How many years are you going to be upset about me moving on? Your mother would want me to be happy."

"This has nothing to do with Mom. Don't drag her into this. And you've moved on seven times in the last fifteen years." She turned to me and tapped her pointer to her lips. "Or maybe it's eight times. I haven't seen him in a few months. A lot can happen…"

"Don't be disrespectful," her father barked.

Autumn shook her head. "Go home, Dad."

"Will you be at the wedding?" He took a deep breath and reined in the attitude, speaking with a softer, gentler voice. "It would mean a lot to me."

Autumn frowned. "Will Silas be there?"

"Of course not. You know I wouldn't do that to you."

"No, I don't know that."

"Autumn, please come."

She shook her head. "I don't know. I'll think about it, okay?"

Her father pursed his lips, but said nothing more. He walked over to Autumn and kissed her cheek. "Thank you."

"It's late," she said. "I should go in."

Her father nodded. He offered a vague wave in my direction, and then he was back in his flashy yellow car.

I picked up the coolers, and we walked to the entrance to her building in silence. The elevator ride up was quiet, too. When we got to her door, she fished her keys from her purse and turned to me.

"I'm sorry about that."

"Nothing to be sorry about. If you met my mother, you'd understand why I thought that interaction was pretty damn pleasant."

Autumn smiled, but it didn't quite reach her eyes.

"You okay?" I asked.

She nodded. "He just...I don't know. He's got a warped sense of priority sometimes."

"I take it from what you said, you don't like one of your dad's friends...Silas?"

"Silas was his business partner."

"Not a fan?"

"Nope."

"Something happen between you two?"

She shook her head. "Not between me and Silas. I dated his son for four and a half years. Things...ended over Christmas break of my first year in law school."

I waited for her to say more, but she didn't. But then something dawned on me.

"That's right around the time you also started to have career-decision doubts, wasn't it?"

Autumn looked down. "I had a lot of doubts that year." She took a deep breath and blew it out with a forced smile. "I should go in. It's getting late, and I have an appointment early tomorrow. You can just leave the coolers here. I'll bring them inside. I'm going to return them to my neighbor tomorrow anyway."

I hated to leave, especially when she was clearly feeling down, but I thought we'd made a lot of progress the last few days and didn't want to screw things up by not giving her space. So I nodded. "Okay. But open the door and go in before I take off."

She smiled sadly. "You're like a bodyguard."

"Can never be too careful."

Autumn unlocked her door, and I slid the two coolers inside. She held the door open after walking in. "Goodnight, Donovan."

"Goodnight, Red."

I waited until I heard the lock click closed before I left. On the drive home, I thought back through all the unexpected events of the evening. I'd found out the kid I'd hired to water my plants hadn't killed one after all, a certain little redhead had stolen it. Autumn had also dropped a bomb on the car ride home—she wasn't seeing Blake anymore. Then there was her father, who was pretty much what I'd expected from the limited things she'd told me. But even with all that, the thing I couldn't stop wondering about was what the hell had happened during her first year of law school.

21
Autumn

Six years ago

"God, it feels so good to be out with you guys." I leaned my head on my friend Anna's shoulder as we walked from the field to the parking lot. We'd just spent the afternoon watching an outdoor concert with a bunch of friends I hadn't seen since law school started. I'd been accepted at two of my top three choices, but decided to stay home and go to Yale, my Dad's alma mater—and also where Braden had gone.

Anna tugged my hair. "You should try doing it more often. We never see you."

"I'm sorry. Law school has kept me busier than I thought."

"It's fine. I'm just teasing. How are things with you and Braden?"

"Good, I guess."

"*Uh-oh*. Trouble in paradise."

"Not really. Nothing I should complain about anyway. He just... I don't know. He really wants to help me with law school. Braden is smart, so I should probably want all the help he wants to give, but I need to figure it out on my own sometimes. Like, a lot of the people from my cohort study together, and when I've mentioned that I think I'm going to the library to join them, he gets weird about it. I think it offends him that I don't always want his help."

"That's because the man is crazy about you."

I smiled. We'd arrived at the park after the start of the concert, so my car was parked on the grass almost all the way back at the entrance. When I looked around, I spotted a silver car that looked like Braden's BMW. But the sun was blaring overhead, and I couldn't see whether anyone was inside. I shielded my eyes, squinting, but I could only get a glimpse of a man's profile, though it looked like it could be Braden. A few seconds later, the car pulled away. The concert had been packed, and we were in Greenwich, so BMWs were a dime a dozen... Yet something bugged me. It was the second time in the last few days that I'd thought I spotted a car that looked like Braden's, but each time I'd gotten close enough to take a good look, the car had driven away.

"Earth to Autumn."

I looked at my friend, who was staring at me expectantly. "I'm sorry. Did you say something?"

"I *said,* not everyone can have a guy who is crazy about them, but I did meet a guy last weekend who was crazy in bed."

I'd totally zoned out there for a minute. "Oh wow. Tell me everything."

Anna dove into a story about a skinny drummer with a mohawk she'd met at a coffee shop last weekend, who had the thickest penis she'd ever seen. She had me laughing, and within a few minutes, I'd forgotten all about the weird feeling I'd had—at least temporarily.

"Hey, beautiful." Braden sat back in his chair and smiled. "I didn't know you were coming by. This is a nice surprise."

I walked behind Braden's desk, set down one of the two bags in my hand, and leaned in to give him a kiss. "My dad's been working so much lately, I made him a healthy lunch. He forgets to eat when he's on trial. Figured I'd bring you something, too."

He wrapped his fingers around my waist and yanked me down onto his lap.

I giggled. "Your door's open. Anyone can walk by."

"It's Sunday. There're only a few of us here."

Braden brushed his nose with mine. "I've missed you."

"Me too." I smiled. "Are we still on for tonight?"

He brushed a lock of my hair from my face. "We're definitely on. I made a reservation for seven o'clock at that new little Italian place you loved."

"Oh, yum. Will you be here until then?"

"Probably. I didn't get as much done as I thought I would yesterday."

For some reason, the car I'd seen in the parking lot yesterday popped into my head. "How late did you stay last night?"

"I don't know." Braden shrugged. "Probably about nine."

I smiled. "Well, then, I'll let you go so you can get out of here in time for dinner tonight. Plus, I don't want my dad's lunch to get cold. I'm going to run upstairs to his office."

"Alright. I'll pick you up around six thirty."

I kissed him one more time before heading upstairs where my dad had the proverbial corner office.

"Knock, knock," I said. "Delivery for Mr. Workaholic."

My father tossed his pen on his desk and smiled. "What are you doing here, pumpkin?"

I held up the bag of food. "I made you some lunch. I know how you get when you're in the middle of a trial. You either forget to eat or eat crap."

He smiled warmly. "Your mother used to bring me lunch when I worked on the weekends."

"I know. But you didn't work *Sundays* back then."

"I still try not to unless it's absolutely necessary. But I had no choice today. I lost the whole damn afternoon yesterday because of the damn bedbugs."

My nose scrunched up. "Bedbugs?"

He thumbed toward the ceiling. "The insurance company one floor up found bedbugs in a couch in their lobby, so building maintenance inspected the entire place. We had a few in our lobby, too. They bombed the entire building last night. No one could enter for twelve hours."

"I thought I heard you leave the house at six o'clock this morning?"

My dad nodded. "I did."

"What time did they bomb the office yesterday?"

"Five in the evening."

"Five? So no one could be in the building after five o'clock?"

"Not unless they wanted to grow a third arm."

"What if someone was here when they set off the bug bombs?"

My dad shook his head. "No one was here. I had security go office by office to make sure the place was empty before we let the fumigation start."

22

Autumn

"It's nice to see you, Autumn." Dr. Lillian Burke folded her hands on top of the notebook on her lap. "You look really well. You've let your hair grow longer."

I reached up and twirled a strand of my hair. "Yeah, just more that winds up in a bun on the top of my head, I suppose."

"So how are things going? Are you still working for social services?"

"I am, and I still love it." I smiled. "Best decision you ever helped me make."

Lillian smiled. "I'm thrilled to hear that. We spend more time at our jobs than we do with loved ones, so it's important to enjoy what we do."

"I'm actually working toward my PhD now. I don't think I'd started that when we last spoke. I was thinking about how long it's been since I've been here while I was in the waiting room. I thought it was two years, but I think it's been more like three."

"It has. Next month will be three years, actually. I had to look myself earlier. But congratulations on your

200

schooling. We'd talked about you wanting to become a therapist, but you hadn't yet begun a program. That's fantastic."

"I've taken it slow, part time, but I'm getting there. I should graduate after two more semesters. Honestly, I think part of the reason I stopped coming to see you is because I felt like I needed to be able to stand on my own two feet if I was going to be sitting in your chair at some point."

"We've discussed this. Therapists have therapists. It's not only okay, it's encouraged in this profession."

I nodded. "I know. I think I just needed to feel like I could survive without you. Now that I know I can, I don't feel like it's an issue anymore."

"Well, I'm glad to hear you feel like you can survive without me. Although I never had any doubts."

"Thanks."

"So tell me what's going on in your life. How are things with your father?"

"About the same. He's getting married in a few weeks...again. He showed up at my apartment last night because I hadn't sent back the response card, and I'd been avoiding his calls because I didn't want to debate my not wanting to go to the wedding."

Lillian smiled. "Seems like I didn't miss much on that front."

"Definitely not. Married. Divorced. Rinse. Repeat."

"And you? Are you still taking Ambien to help you sleep at night?"

"My regular doctor has been bugging me to try to wean off, like you always did. But, yeah. I still need them to sleep."

She nodded.

"Did you know dolphins sleep with one eye open?"

"Do they?"

"It's called unihemispheric sleeping. The right eye closes when the left side of the brain sleeps, and the left closes when the right sleeps. They can't fully sleep because they need to remember to breathe."

Lillian smiled. "I've missed your random facts. But since you aren't, in fact, a dolphin, I still think weaning off might be a good thing."

I sighed. "Yeah, I know."

"How about your personal life? Is there someone special these days? Dating anyone?"

"I'm not dating anyone. I was, but I ended it recently."

"Why did you end it?"

"I felt bad because I have growing feelings for someone else."

"Oh..." Lillian picked up her pen from the end table and wrote something down in her book. "I'd have to look back in my notes, but I'm pretty sure this is the first time you've mentioned having feelings for someone. Obviously we've talked about men you've dated, but you usually use words like *compatible* or *having fun* to describe your relationships, not *feelings*. I'm excited to hear you're interested in someone you have an emotional connection with. The woman who sat across from me a few years ago would've run the other way if her heart got invested in a man."

I smiled. "Well, I sort of did. It's a long story, but I met Donovan last year. We have the same luggage, and I grabbed his and not mine at the airport. We met to exchange bags, and we hit it off and had coffee. Coffee led to dinner, and dinner led to an amazing weekend."

"That sounds a bit like fate, almost a fairytale."

I nodded. "Except me being me, when the ball was over, I turned into a pumpkin and ran away."

"Did you happen to leave a glass slipper behind?"

I shook my head. "Definitely not—although he says he went back to the coffee shop where we'd met for a few weeks after, hoping to see me. So I guess he was trying to be Prince Charming. But you know I've perfected the art of avoidance, so we didn't run into each other again for almost a year. He wound up being the attorney for one of my kids. I walked into the police station one evening, and there he was."

"Oh, wow." She smiled. "Sounds like fate wasn't accepting what you were doing. Tell me about this man. You said his name is Donovan?"

I nodded. "Well, he's the opposite of most men I've dated. From the outside, you wouldn't think so. He's smart, successful, wears nice suits, and went to an Ivy League school. But underneath the exterior, he's so much more. He grew up with less than nothing, so he's worked extra hard to be where he is, and that makes him much tougher than anyone I've ever dated. The men I date are usually sort of soft on the inside, whereas Donovan is made of steel. I'm extremely attracted to that inner strength."

"He sounds wonderful. Usually when you'd tell me about a man you were dating you'd mention his physical attributes first, then read me his resume. You did neither when you described Donovan. You spoke from your heart."

"Well, he's also ridiculously handsome, so there's that—with a body to die for underneath that crisp dress shirt. He also has lots of tattoos that I find incredibly sexy." I pointed to my arms. "Look. This is why I didn't lead with a description. I have goose bumps just thinking about what he looks like."

Lillian laughed. "Any chance he has an older brother?"

"It's funny. In a lot of ways, Donovan's as protective as I am about letting people see what lies beneath. We just have different reasons."

"But it sounds like he's let you in."

I nodded. "He has."

"Have you shared your past with him?"

I shook my head. "He's a very perceptive person, so he definitely knows there's something lurking. But I haven't spoken to him about...you know."

"What's the status of your relationship with Donovan right now? You said you recently broke things off with someone else, but are you and Donovan dating?"

I frowned. "No."

"Has he asked?"

I smiled sadly. "More than once."

"I'm guessing you won't go out with him because you actually like him?"

I nodded and looked down.

"Don't be ashamed to be afraid, Autumn. Fearing something big is human nature, and we all have fears."

"I hate how weak I am."

"Being afraid is not a weakness. Not in the least. Being afraid is a protective instinct we all have, and it's healthy. Think of it as a home alarm system. Our fears set off a loud warning for people we shouldn't let in, and that's a good thing."

"Yes, but my alarm system wants to keep everyone out."

Lillian shook her head. "It did at one point. But you're here. *You're here today*, Autumn. That means you've already accepted that there's someone you want to let in. You're just not sure how to do it because it's been so long."

I blew out a deep breath. "Yeah, I guess you're right."

"Over the years, your fears have sabotaged your relationships. You went out with men you knew you had no true emotional connection with. And a year ago you sabotaged things with Donovan because you weren't ready to take them on. But you're ready now. You've already taken the first step, just by showing up today. You did all the hard work on your own, so now we need to get you the rest of the way."

"How do I do that?"

"The only way to overcome your fears is to push through the center. You have to embrace what you're afraid of."

"But I've been dating."

"You're not afraid of dating. You're afraid to give someone your trust again."

I sighed. "I guess so. I want to trust Donovan. I really do. But I'm not sure how."

Lillian nodded. "A good place to start might be to tell him about what happened."

23

Donovan

Autumn's car was already parked outside when I arrived.

All afternoon, I'd told myself I wasn't going to leave work early and drop by Bud's. I had a dozen hours I still needed to bill today, clients who needed to be called back, and a trial coming up to prep for. Generally on Saturdays, I'd get to the office by seven. But today Bud had been discharged at ten, so I picked him up and drove him home, then settled him in once we got there.

My usual 7AM start had turned into arriving at the office at almost 1PM, and I had to leave by 4:30 in order to fill in for Bud serving dinner tonight. But I figured there was a lot I could get done in three and a half hours. Unfortunately, I hadn't factored in how distracted I'd be all damn afternoon knowing Autumn was over at Bud's. Eventually, I gave in and called it quits. I wasn't getting jack shit done anyway, so there was no point in sitting at my desk.

The front door was unlocked. I shook my head, thinking I'd have to talk to Bud about that. The man had just spent two days in the hospital after being beaten on the street. He needed to be more careful.

I found Autumn in the kitchen washing dishes. She hadn't heard me come in, so I took a moment to stand in the doorway and watch her. A faint smile graced her beautiful face, and every couple of seconds the corners of her lips twitched slightly—like she was thinking about something that amused her. Damn, she was gorgeous. I'd meant to let her know I'd come in before she saw me so I didn't startle her, but she must've sensed someone watching because her head suddenly whipped up.

"Oh my God." She lifted her wet, sudsy hand and covered her heart. "How long have you been standing there?"

I smiled. "Sorry. Not long."

"Why didn't you say something?"

"I was going to. But I was too busy trying to figure out what you were thinking about that had you smiling."

"I was smiling?"

I nodded. "What was on your mind just now?"

She looked away. "Nothing."

I took a few steps closer and stood on the other side of the kitchen island. "Nothing, huh? You sure about that?"

Autumn cleared her throat. "Bud just finished eating. He fell asleep in his recliner."

I nodded. "They said he didn't sleep well at the hospital. I'm sure he was worried about the house being empty for a few days. People around here see an opportunity and take it."

She frowned. "Why doesn't he move?"

"Because this is his home, and he gets a sense of purpose from helping the community. Plus, he has his garden in the back and workshop in the garage."

"I guess." Autumn shrugged. "Has this type of thing happened before? Where he was attacked?"

"No. People usually look out for Bud because he's a good person and well respected. It's a pretty tight-knit community, for the most part. The problem is it's also easy to score drugs on a half-dozen corners around here, so it attracts outsiders—and not good ones."

Autumn finished rinsing the last dish in the sink and turned off the water. "You want something to eat? I haven't put lunch away yet. It's probably still warm."

"It smells good, but no, that's okay. I'd rather you leave it for Bud. It's not going to be easy for him to do much for a while with that arm in a cast."

"I made a lasagna, pasta fagioli, and chicken Française. So he's got at least a dozen dinners in there to start. I froze some and left a few in the fridge for the next few days."

"Thank you for doing all that for him."

"I figured you'd be at work all afternoon today, since you picked up Bud from the hospital this morning, and you're covering his dinner service."

"I wanted to see how he was doing. I wasn't sure what time you were coming by."

From the other room, Bud's voice boomed. "My ass. He asked this morning if I knew what time you were coming, and I told him you'd called and said you'd be here about now."

I chuckled and hung my head as I yelled back, "Thanks a lot, Bud. You're supposed to be my wingman. Not tell my secrets."

"Can't say I blame you. She cooks damn good."

Now Autumn was laughing. She yelled, "Thanks, Bud!"

"No problem, sweetheart."

I lowered my voice and winked. "I'll go check on him anyway."

Bud was in his beat-up old, leather recliner with his feet up.

"How you feeling, old man?"

"Fine." He pointed to his cast. "If this thing were on the other hand, my life would be a lot easier. I'm shit with my left hand."

"I figured I'd water the plants in the yard so you don't get that cast wet on the first day home."

"Oh, good. Pick the tomatoes that are ready while you're out there, will ya?"

"Sure."

Bud's yard was practically a farm, so watering and picking ripe fruit wasn't a two-minute job. The sun was blazing, and I had on a long-sleeve dress shirt and slacks, so by the time I finished, I was sweaty. I'd tossed a change of clothes into a duffle bag this morning, figuring I'd want to get out of my dress duds before doing dinner service, so I grabbed it out of my car before heading back into the house.

"Mind if I take a quick shower?" Bud and Autumn were sitting together in the living room.

"Use the one in your old room."

After a quick shower, I reached into the cabinet below the sink, the one where the towels had always been kept. Unfortunately, I hadn't thought to check whether Bud still filled the cabinet until after I was dripping wet.

Shit.

I pulled the jeans in my bag up my wet legs and snuck out of the bathroom to grab a towel to dry off before I got fully dressed. But as I went toward the hall bathroom, the door suddenly opened. Autumn came out and blinked a few times before her eyes dropped to my bare chest. I'd come out of the other bathroom grumbling with denim sticking to my legs, but suddenly I wanted to kiss Bud for not filling that towel cabinet.

Autumn didn't even try to hide checking me out. Her eyes took in my chest, slowly worked their way down my abs, and flared when they got down to the top of my jeans. I knew I hadn't buttoned, and I hadn't bothered to throw underwear on to go get a towel, but I hadn't realized that in the haste of pulling up my pants, I'd left the head of my cock pushed up and sticking out. My first instinct was to cover up, not intentionally be a lewd asshole, but when Autumn's lips parted, I forced my hands to stay at their sides.

Jesus Christ. The way she was looking at me, I wanted nothing more than to walk her backwards into the bathroom and shut the door behind us. And in the moment, I thought she might actually let me. But then—

A loud crash sounded from the other room. "Shit!"

Bud might as well have thrown a bucket of ice water on us. Autumn and I both took off running. We found Bud in the kitchen with the refrigerator door open and a mess all over the floor.

"What happened?"

"I tried to get a spoonful of that chocolate pudding pie Autumn brought over, but the stupid cast got in the way."

I closed my eyes and shook my head. The glass pie plate was shattered all over the floor, and Bud had no shoes on. "Go sit. I'll clean it up."

"Why the hell are you half naked?"

"Because apparently you don't keep towels in the guest bathroom anymore."

"Well, go put some clothes on."

Considering the moment he'd ruined, I might as well. I turned to Autumn. "Leave it. I'll suck it up with the shop vac after I get dressed. I don't want you cutting yourself."

I grabbed a towel from the other bathroom and finished getting dried off. For a half second, I considered whacking off to the memory of Autumn staring down at the head of my cock with her lips parted—a memory that would forever be seared into my brain. But you don't do that shit in another man's bathroom, especially one who's kept your head from falling into the toilet bowl in the exact same room on more than one teenage occasion. So instead, I made quick work of getting dressed and then went out to the garage for the shop vac. When I was done cleaning up the kitchen, it was already time to leave to serve dinner.

I walked into the den and found Bud about to fall asleep in his recliner again, watching some old black-and-white western movie on TV.

Autumn's nose was buried in her phone. "Did you know *Gone with the Wind* was the first color movie to win an Academy Award?" she asked, looking up.

I smiled. "I didn't. I'm not sure how I've gotten by without that tidbit of information."

She made a face, and I laughed. "I need to get going to set up for dinner service."

Autumn stood. "Do you want some help tonight?"

"Sure, if you don't mind." As if I'd ever turn down spending time with her, even if it was in an abandoned house with a bunch of questionable people.

We said goodbye to a sleepy Bud, and I told him I'd be back tomorrow to check on him. He wouldn't have been Bud if he hadn't argued with me that he didn't need any help. But I'd be back no matter what he said.

Outside, I told Autumn to hop into my car, and we'd drive together to pick up the food I'd ordered before going to serve dinner. I might've stretched the truth and told her Bud's place was on my way back home, so it would be easy to pick up her car. I mean, it was if I took the completely out-of-my-way route to get home. But I liked her close.

Since I had assumed I'd be working in my office up until the very last minute this afternoon, I'd ordered a few six-foot heroes and some salads for dinner. It made things smoother since we didn't have to worry about keeping food warm. But I was glad Bud hadn't asked what I was serving, because anything other than a hot meal wasn't acceptable to him.

Throughout the evening, I kept close tabs on Autumn. She attracted a lot of attention behind the serving table, most of it friendly, but you can never be too careful. Some of the people who ate here weren't in a stable frame of mind, which is the vibe I got from two guys who stumbled in just as we were about to call it a night and shut down.

"Aww, come on, pretty lady." The taller of the two held his plate out to Autumn. "You can give me more than that, can't you?"

I recognized the shorter one as a local drug dealer—at least he had been back when I'd lived in the neighborhood. He was probably about ten years older than me, and had been in and out of jail, though I didn't keep tabs on people in the neighborhood anymore. Considering my own past, I tried not to judge, but I didn't like the tone his buddy used.

I walked over and stood next to Autumn. "Can I help you guys with something?"

The guy sneered. "Nope. Everything's looking good right here."

The shorter one squinted at me. "You're Decker, right? Used to live two blocks over from here?"

"That's right."

He held up his fist to bump. "How's it going, man? You're a big-time lawyer now or something, aren't you?"

I bumped fists with the guy. "I'm a lawyer, yeah."

"You do criminal?" his buddy asked.

I shook my head. "Not the kind you might be interested in."

The guy pulled his head back. "What's that supposed to mean?"

"I specialize in white-collar crimes—embezzling, corporate fraud, stock rigging, that type of thing."

"Too good for where you came from, huh?"

This conversation was going a direction I didn't like. "Not at all." I shrugged. "It's just what I'm good at. If you're ever in a jam for something like that, I'm your guy."

I could tell from the look on his face he wasn't sure if I was being sincere. He eyed me for a few heartbeats before nodding. "Yeah...okay."

The two of them went to sit down, and Autumn glanced over at me. "I bet you get that a lot—people from here who don't like that you've done well for yourself."

I shrugged. "It is what it is. I get it."

"Storm hides the fact that he gets straight As from his friends."

I smiled. "I used to do the same thing. Most people want to see you do well, but very few want to see you do better than them. It's hard to be a teenager and be different under normal circumstances, but here? It's more than hard. It can be dangerous."

"That's crazy."

"Maybe, but it's the truth. On the street, if people can't relate to you, they don't trust you. And when you don't have much else but your word, trust means everything." I glanced over at the two guys.

The guy I knew from the neighborhood was busy eating, but the other guy was looking at Autumn. His eyes shifted to meet mine, and I held his stare until he looked away.

Fifteen minutes later, my buddy Dario made a surprise visit as we were breaking down the tables I'd brought. We shook.

"How's Bud doing?" he asked.

"Good. Though he's in a cast, so he's gonna need some help for a while."

"That's what I came to talk to you about. The crew and me got the next five days. I know you need to work late, and the old bastard doesn't trust anyone."

I blew out a deep breath. "Thanks, Dario. That would really help."

He pointed at me. "But you're covering next Saturday night. My lady needs some loving on the weekends."

I smirked. "Is that what you're calling your right hand these days. Your lady?"

Dario punched my arm. "Dick."

Over his shoulder, I watched the last two guys leave—the one I knew and the one who gave me a bad vibe. My shoulders relaxed a little. Autumn had stepped away to take a call right before Dario walked in. She came over and smiled.

"Autumn, this is Dario. Whatever he says, he's full of shit."

Autumn laughed. "Donovan has mentioned you before. It's nice to meet you."

Dario lifted Autumn's hand to his lips and kissed the top. "The pleasure is all mine."

I narrowed my eyes. "Take it easy, jackass."

Dario's eyes flickered with amusement. He knew how to get my goat. "Donovan says you're smart. So I figure you probably pick personality..." He patted himself on the chest before thumbing to me with a frown. "...over good looks. This bastard will age, but I'll always be entertaining."

Autumn laughed. "I'm sure you will."

She'd looked upset on the phone a few minutes ago, so I nodded toward the cell in her hand. "Everything okay?"

She sighed. "One of my kids was caught with weed tonight."

"Is he in lockup? Does he need help?"

She smiled and shook her head. "Luckily it was just someone at the group home and not the police. But thank you for the offer. I actually need to make another call about it, though. The service cuts in and out in here, so I'm going to step outside for a minute."

I looked toward the front door. Everyone had gone, but that didn't matter. Congregating was a sport around here. So I gestured toward the back door. "Why don't you try out that way instead?"

"Okay. Let me help you pack everything up first."

"I got it. Go make your call." I motioned to Dario. "This bozo is going to help me anyway."

Since we'd only served sandwiches and salads, it took just five minutes to pack everything up. The only thing left to do was load the car with the tables and chairs and the cooler. I glanced out back. Autumn was still on the phone, so I told Dario to give me a hand carrying everything out. After we packed the trunk and backseat, I noticed the guy I knew from the earlier twosome still hanging around a few houses down. But his friend was missing.

"Hey," I yelled. "Where's your buddy?"

He pointed toward the yard. "He went to take a piss. Dude must've gotten lost."

The hair on the back of my neck stood up, and I didn't waste time shutting the trunk before I took off for the house. I ripped open the front door and ran straight through to the back. The dirtbag was only a few feet from Autumn. He backed up and held his hands up in the air when he saw me fly through the door.

"What the hell are you doing back here?"

The guy kept stepping back. "Just talking to the pretty lady."

I looked over at Autumn. "You okay?"

Dario busted through the back door.

"Yeah, I'm fine." She looked a little nervous as she glanced between the two of us, but she shook her head. "He was just leaving."

"Why don't you get going, Eddie?" Dario gave a curt nod and glared at the guy.

I scowled. "Don't make me ask, too."

Eddie looked pretty pissed off, but that was nothing compared to the anger radiating from me. The vein in my neck bulged and my heart pumped a million miles a minute.

At least the jerk was smart enough to realize walking away was the *only* option he had. He huffed, but walked around the side of the house without another word. I followed to make sure he really left.

As soon as he hit the street, I turned back to Autumn. "You sure you're okay?"

"Yeah, I'm fine. Just a little shook up. He didn't do anything, just caught me off guard because I'd been on the phone, and suddenly he was standing a few feet away in the dark. He asked me if I wanted to party, and I told him I thought it was best if he left."

I rubbed my neck and blew out a jagged breath. "I'm sorry. I shouldn't have left you alone."

"I was only out here a few minutes."

I shook my head. "That's a few minutes too long."

It took until we'd gotten in the car and driven six or eight blocks before my heart started to slow down. Autumn just kept staring at the window, her arms wrapped tightly around her body.

"I'm sorry, Autumn."

"It's fine. It's not your fault, and nothing happened."

"It *is* my fault, and you don't look fine."

She frowned and turned back to stare out the window some more. Bud's house wasn't too far, so a few minutes later, we pulled up outside. I put the car in park. I was never going to be able to relax just letting her drive away. "Would you mind if I followed you home?" I asked. "Or better yet, you can leave your car here, and I'll drop you?"

She looked down for a minute before nodding. "You can follow me. But come inside when we get there. I want to talk to you anyway."

24

Donovan

Autumn was quiet as we settled into her apartment.

"Do you want a glass of wine?" she asked.

"Sure, if you're having some."

She smiled halfheartedly. "I am *definitely* having some. Why don't you get comfortable on the couch, and I'll grab us two glasses."

"Thanks."

Autumn came back a few minutes later. She'd poured the wine and also tied her hair into a messy bun on top of her head and changed into yoga pants and a T-shirt.

She saw me checking her out. "Sorry. I needed to be comfortable."

"Nothing to be sorry about. I actually love your hair tied up like that."

She sipped her wine and smiled. "You do? And here I wasted a half hour blowing it out earlier so I'd look nice. All I had to do was not brush it and twist it up into a knot?"

My eyes roamed over her beautiful face. "Your hair is like that in the picture I took of you during the weekend we spent together. After you ghosted me, I looked at it a lot.

I'd tell you how often, but it might scare you away again, and I think I've fucked up enough for one day."

Autumn set her wine on the table and laid her hand gently on my knee. "You didn't fuck up anything today. In fact, you did just the opposite."

"What do you mean?"

"I'll get to that, but first, what picture did you take of me?"

I smiled. "You were standing at the stove in my kitchen. Your hair was all tied up like it is now, and you had on my T-shirt from the day before."

She shook her head. "I don't even remember that."

I dug my cell from my pants pocket, opened the photo app, and scrolled to the folder I kept it in before turning the phone to show her.

Autumn took the cell from my hand and studied it. "I look like a mess."

"You look beautiful."

She kept staring. Eventually she sighed. "I don't agree, but I will say I look happy."

I took my phone back and glanced at the photo one more time. "I thought you were. I know that weekend I was the happiest I'd been in a long time."

Autumn's eyes moved back and forth between mine. I could see something was troubling her. After a while, she took a deep breath, reached for her wine, chugged the entire remainder of the glass, and lifted one knee up onto the couch to face me directly.

"Summer of my senior year in high school, I met Braden. Well, that's not entirely true. I'd met him a few times over the years, but I didn't really know him. His dad worked for my dad before they became partners. I thought Braden was cute, but he was a few years older, so he never looked my way other than to say hello until that summer when I was eighteen."

Autumn stared down into her empty wine glass. I knew from the very first sentence that this story was not going to have a happy ending. But I also knew I needed to hear it, because it was going to fill in a lot of the missing pieces on the Autumn Wilde puzzle I'd been trying to work out for a long time.

I took her empty glass and swapped it with my three-quarters-full one.

She smiled sadly and took another deep breath before continuing. "Braden was in his first semester of law school and was nothing like the boys I'd gone out with in high school. I had no idea what I wanted to do with the rest of my life, and he was so driven and mature, and he was attracted to me for some reason." She turned her head and stared off for a minute. "When I look back at that first summer, I still don't see the red flags I missed." She frowned. "I think that haunts me almost as much as anything else."

"What happened?"

"Braden and I dated for four and a half years. Things didn't go bad overnight. We grew really close that first summer. I'd dated before, but it was my first serious relationship. Then I went away to college. I only went to Boston, so it was just a few hours' drive. I'd come home often, and sometimes Braden would visit me. Once in a while he'd even surprise me and not tell me he was coming. But sometimes I felt more like he was checking up on me, rather than really wanting to see me."

I definitely didn't like the direction this was heading. It felt like the ominous music of a horror movie had started playing.

"Anyway..." Autumn wrung her hands together. "Over the years, there was never enough to make an alarm go off—not one single thing anyway." She shook her head. "Maybe there was, and I was in denial. I don't know. I'd notice small things—like I'd think his car was following me, but then it would be gone. Sometimes I'd ask him about things I noticed, but his answers were so believable that I just kept chalking it up to my own paranoia. He actually made me feel crazy for thinking he'd have the time or inclination to follow me. Plus, and I know this sounds horrible, but it was an easy relationship. Our fathers were business partners and the best of friends, and I'd made the decision to go to law school, so Braden was able to demystify that entire process." She shrugged. "I just... I was very trusting and naïve back then. *Too* trusting."

I wasn't sure what to say or do. It felt like she needed to get something out by taking the long way, rather than cutting to the chase, but damn, my heart was in agony waiting for that other shoe to drop. Still, I stayed quiet.

Autumn finished off the wine in my glass.

"You want some more?" I asked.

She shook her head. "I shouldn't. I just needed to take the edge off. I promise I'm getting to the end of this story soon."

I took her hand in mine and squeezed. "Take all the time you need. There's no hurry."

She nodded and stared down for a minute again before continuing. "After I was done with college and back home again, more things started to raise red flags. I'd think he was following me, and then I'd catch him in a lie about being at work. He had this way of turning things around and convincing me I felt guilty because I'd been growing distant. I was in law school and meeting new people and wanted some freedom, so he wasn't wrong. We had been growing apart. But he'd waited four long years for me to move back home. So I felt bad even considering breaking things off, especially because while we were together, he was so good to me. Though once I'd caught him in a few lies, I found it hard to believe anything he said. One day I'd noticed some of my emails marked as read, even though I was positive I'd never opened them. Things started to feel really unhealthy, so eventually I told Braden I needed a break."

"How did that go over?"

"Better than I expected, at first. But he was convinced I was just stressed from my first year of law school, and it was only a break and we'd get back together."

"Did you get back together?"

She shook her head. "We kept in touch, but once I'd broken things off, I knew pretty quickly that I'd made the right decision for a lot of reasons."

"Okay..."

"Once he realized it was over, and I was moving on, strange things started to happen."

"Like what?"

"Well, I used to study with a small group. One of the people in my group was this guy Mark. One night, we were the last two of our group to leave the library, and when we walked outside, Braden was there. He said he was going in to do some late-night research, but I suspected he'd been following me again. He was polite when I introduced him to Mark, but I could see how angry he was underneath. A few days later, Mark was attacked."

"By Braden?"

"I was never able to prove it, but that's what I've always suspected. The person attacked him as he walked to his car late one night. But they didn't even try to take his wallet or his car keys. They came at him from behind, so he never got a look at the guy's face, and the guy didn't say a single word during the attack. All Mark was able to tell the police was that the guy had black dress shoes on. Of course, Braden and a few other million men wear dress shoes."

I raked a hand through my hair. "Jesus."

"There were other little things, but at that point, I stopped talking to Braden altogether. I wouldn't answer when he called, and then he'd send me long emails and texts making me feel terrible for the things I was thinking." She took a deep breath and looked me in the eyes. "One night he showed up at my house."

All of the hair on my arms stood up.

Autumn looked down, and when her head came back up, her eyes were filled with tears. "He said he just wanted to talk. He was crying, and I felt bad. So I let him in."

I couldn't breathe waiting for the rest.

Her voice was barely a whisper when she continued. "No one was home. And he...he...raped me."

I froze. I knew the story was heading to an ugly place, but not here. I guess I'd thought he'd smacked her around and scared her maybe. *Not this...* I shut my eyes.

"Autumn..." I shook my head. "*Fuck*. Autumn."

When I opened my eyes, tears were rolling down her cheeks, so I did the only thing that felt right. I pulled her against me and held her so tight that at one point, I worried I might be hurting her. My own tears fell against the back of her shirt. After a while, she pulled back.

"I want to finish." She wiped her tears, and then reached out and dried mine. "I made it this far, and I need to get it all out."

I nodded and swallowed a huge lump in my throat. "You don't have to. Not for me."

She nodded. "Thank you. But I need to do it for me."

God, if I hadn't already been crazy about this woman, I would be now. I bet she had no idea how strong she was.

For the next half hour, Autumn told me the rest of her story. How she hadn't immediately gone to the police, because at first she hadn't seen it for what it was.

They'd had sex for years, and even though she'd told him repeatedly to stop this time, she didn't physically fight him off with more than a shove. Eventually she'd just stilled, too terrified to move, waiting for him to be done. Then when the shock of it all wore off, she felt partially to blame somehow. She'd let him in. She'd accused him of things he might not have done. She'd made him upset—at least that's how she'd seen it at first.

Then to make matters worse, when she'd finally started to move from shocked to angry and decided to talk to someone, that person wasn't supportive.

Her father.

Her fucking father.

The asshole had the balls to question whether she could've been giving Braden *mixed signals*. As if there was any other signal that mattered when a woman said no.

By the time she found the courage to go to the police, of course there was no physical evidence left. So it was her word against his—an upstanding member of the legal community with no prior record. And when they interviewed Braden's friends, he'd either convinced them to lie, or he'd been lying to his buddies all along, because they told the police Autumn had been the one stalking him, that she'd been upset and persistent when he'd broken things off.

The district attorney had said he'd pursue the case, but only after warning her of the likely outcome and how traumatic cases usually were for the victims. I wasn't surprised since I knew firsthand that DAs didn't like to go forward on a losing case. Resources were tight, and let's face it, lawyers didn't like to mar their records.

Autumn blew out a jagged breath and forced a smile. "Now I'd like to have another glass of wine. Would you like another one? Or actually, would you like your first one since I wound up drinking yours?"

I stood. "Definitely. But I'll get them. I need to use the bathroom, anyway."

After I filled two glasses to the brim, I went to splash some water on my face. It felt like I'd just run a marathon, though I'd barely moved from the couch in the last hour. I was physically drained, so I couldn't even imagine how Autumn felt. As I stood there, it hit me for the first time *why* she'd decided to tell me everything tonight. I'd been so consumed with her story, I hadn't taken a moment to realize what might've prompted her sharing it. Tonight in the yard had brought memories of being attacked to the surface.

I felt like banging my head against the wall for what a damn idiot I was. Why the hell did I ever bring her to a place like that to begin with, much less tell her to go stand out back for better cell phone reception? I shut my eyes.

What a dumb fuck I am.

I went back to the living room feeling physically sick. Sitting on the couch, my elbows on my knees and head dropped into my hands, I wanted to kick my own ass. "Listen, Autumn, I'm really sorry for what happened tonight."

"Nothing happened, Donovan."

"That's not the point. I should've never left you outside alone—not even for a minute. I know the type of trouble that comes in."

Autumn reached out and took my hand. "If I had called your name, you would've been back there in two seconds flat."

"Yeah, of course, but—"

She squeezed my hand and waited until I looked at her. "I started seeing my old psychiatrist again. I hadn't been to her in a few years. You know why I went?"

"Why?"

"Because I have trust issues. Big ones. I've spent the last few years dating guys I knew I wouldn't get emotionally invested in because I don't trust myself to see things coming. Honestly, I didn't think I was capable of wanting more with a man."

It wasn't lost on me that she was talking in past tense—I *didn't think* I was capable. Not, I *don't think* I'm capable. But after the last few hours, I was afraid to get my hopes up. I needed shit spelled out.

"But now?" I asked.

She smiled. "I like you, Donovan. I always did. In fact, I liked you *too much,* and that weekend we spent together scared me. They say time heals old wounds. I'm not sure mine will ever fully heal, but I'm tired of letting them control my life. Last year when we met, I wasn't ready. Full disclosure, I'm not sure I'm fully ready now. I still take sleeping pills just to relax enough to fall asleep at night, and I might not be as trusting as I should be. But I'd like to try, if you're still interested."

I smiled. "Is my interest even a question in your mind?"

She bit down on her bottom lip. "Well, I didn't want to assume."

"Let me make it crystal clear." I took both her hands and inched closer on the couch until our knees were touching. "I have never been more interested in a woman in my life. Whether you wanted me or not, you've had me for the last year, Autumn."

She smiled. "We need to take it slow."

"I can do slow."

Autumn chuckled. "I'm not sure I believe that. But I do believe you'll *try* to do slow."

"You don't think I can do slow?"

An hour ago, listening to her story had made my heart

feel broken. Now the smile on her face felt like the glue piecing it all back together.

"I'm not sure either of us is too good at slow when it comes to the other."

"At least we're not alone in the struggle." I lifted her hand and brought her palm to my lips. "It won't be easy, but I'll try to be less charming."

She giggled, and another crack in my heart sealed up. "I'm sure that will be tough for you."

I looked into her eyes. "Thank you for sharing everything with me tonight."

"Thank you for not giving up on me."

"Come here." I tugged her hand, guiding her from the spot next to me on the couch onto my lap. This time when I wrapped her in my arms, it felt different. She wasn't letting me console her; she was letting me hold her because she wanted me to, and it felt fucking incredible. When I pulled back, our faces were close, and I wanted so damn badly to kiss her, but I refrained—and I was pretty proud of myself.

My hands smoothed down the hair on either side of her face. "I think I might need some ground rules for going slow. All I want to do is kiss you right now, and I'm afraid I'll fuck up if I don't have set boundaries."

She smiled. "Okay. That's probably a good idea."

"So lay it on me. How do we do this?"

Autumn tapped her finger to her lips. "I guess we should limit how often we see each other. What about once a week?"

"Three times."

She laughed. "Oh my God. You just jumped into lawyer mode to negotiate. I feel like I need my own attorney now so I don't get trampled."

I smiled. "Sorry. How about two days?"

"I think that's good."

"Okay. What else you got?"

"What about if we try not to get into a routine? I feel like that's what happens when a relationship moves into serious territory. You settle into a day-to-day, familiar predictability. Maybe we could extend what happens at the beginning of dating, where you sort of experiment with where you go and what the other likes."

I shrugged. "That sounds good to me. I like to try new things, and trying them with you is even better."

"And we probably shouldn't make long-term plans. I think keeping things to the immediate future—say, the next few weeks—keeps things lighter."

"Alright. Anything else?"

She bit down on her lip. "Just one more, I think. But I have a feeling you might not like it."

"Lay it on me."

"Well, sex... I didn't have it for a few years after... you know...and then I only had it without an emotional connection. So, it's honestly been a long time since I combined the two, and just contemplating that really scares me."

My face fell, though it had nothing to do with not having sex.

Autumn noticed. "I didn't... No, that came out wrong. I didn't mean to say I didn't have an emotional connection with you the weekend we spent together, if that's what you're thinking. Just the opposite, actually. I felt things for you, and that's why I didn't want to have actual sex that weekend. I thought that would keep things on some sort of a friendlier level. But even without the sex, what I felt made me run as fast as I could. Which is exactly what I'm trying to avoid happening now by going slow."

I dragged a hand through my hair, blew out a deep breath, and nodded. "Yeah, of course. Whatever it takes."

"Thank you. I know I'm asking a lot."

I ran my fingers down her cheek. "It's fair. I'm getting a lot in return. *You*."

She nuzzled her cheek against my hand. "I think that's it for my rules. What about you? Anything you want to add?"

"You didn't mention exclusivity. I don't think I can take knowing you're going out with other men at this point."

She shook her head. "I won't. Even when I was avoiding relationships that might lead to anything, I didn't go out with more than one person at a time. It's just not my thing."

"Good. Then we're on the same page."

"So that's it?" she asked.

The lawyer in me couldn't help but think of things in terms of a contract, and one thing I always liked to negotiate for my clients was an out clause. "I'm going to stick to these rules as best I can," I said. "Because they're important to you. But the ball's in your court, Red. If you get to a point where you're ready to spend more time together, or want to make plans for the future, you just need to let me know."

She smiled. "Does the same go for if I want to have sex? I just have to let you know?"

A wicked grin spread across my face. "No, sweetheart. For that, you have to do more than let me know. After all this time, I'm going to make you beg."

25

Autumn

"Where is he taking you?" Skye laid on her stomach on my bed with her feet swinging in the air like a teenager.

"He won't tell me. That's the problem." I tossed another outfit next to her and walked back into my closet.

"Did you ask him what to wear?"

"He said wear something sexy." I have no idea what that means. "Like, do I wear heels or not?"

Skye grinned. "I don't think I've ever seen you like this."

I popped my head out of the closet. "Like what?"

"A nervous wreck. You really like this guy, huh?"

I sighed. "I do."

"Do you mind if I stay until he gets here? I'm curious to meet him."

I shook my head. "Of course not. But he should be here in about twenty minutes, so help me find something so I'm not naked when he arrives."

Skye got up and joined me in the tiny closet. "Being naked when he arrives might solve your outfit problem. I'm sure he'd love that."

"We're going to try to take it slow."

"Boring." Skye fingered through the hangers in my closet and pulled out a royal blue dress tucked all the way in the back. "You should wear this."

I held it up against me. "You think? It's kind of sexy."

"I thought he said to wear something sexy."

"He did. But I don't want to send the wrong message."

"What do you want the outfit to say?"

"I don't know. That things are casual and I put in effort, but I didn't freak out trying on fifty outfits just for the date."

"Oh, you don't have to worry about this dress saying all that."

"No?"

"Not at all. Because your face is going to say just the opposite anyway."

"Ugh...that's not helpful."

She shrugged. "Maybe not. But it's the truth. So you might as well look smoking hot since you're never going to be able to hide the truth."

I spent fifteen more minutes trying on a half-dozen outfits, but in the end, I wound up wearing the blue dress. When the door buzzed, I opened the app I had on my phone to view who was downstairs and started to feel queasy. "Maybe I should cancel. I don't feel well."

Skye plucked my cell from my hand. "Oooh...he's gorgeous." She pressed the button to talk as she hit the unlock button that opened the lock downstairs. "Come on up, hot stuff."

My mature response when she looked to me was to stick my tongue out.

"Attractive," she smirked. "Maybe he'll suck on it later, if you're lucky."

"I need to pee before I go. Can I trust you to let him in if he's up here before I get done?"

"Of course." She grinned. "What could possibly happen?"

As I fixed my lipstick in the bathroom, I heard Skye speaking from the other room. "So have you ever owned a van?"

"No, I haven't."

"Harmed any animals?"

"Can't say I have."

Oh Lord. I capped the lipstick and yanked the bathroom door open. Just as I approached the living room, Skye said, "Can I see your teeth, please?"

"Skye!" I yelled.

She turned with an innocent face. "What?"

"What are you doing?"

"Trying to figure out if he's dangerous. You need a van to put the puppies in so you can lure children, and I read that most serial killers don't start out hurting people. They work their way up from small animals."

I shook my head. "And his teeth?"

She smirked. "That was for my own purposes. I just like a man who doesn't have a lot of fillings."

Luckily, Donovan was a good sport. I walked over and put my arm around my best friend. "So I see you've already met my friend Skye."

"I did. She's protective. That's a good quality in a friend."

"It is. Though *crazy*...not so much." I squeezed her shoulder. "Skye was just leaving."

She grabbed her purse and kissed me on the cheek before turning to Donovan.

"I have two pieces of advice for you."

"Okay..."

"One, if you can't get her to talk, try Twisted Tea. She guzzles them and relaxes. Then you can't get her to shut up."

Donovan smiled. "Good to know."

"And two, don't hurt her." She reached into her pocket and pulled out a black leather men's wallet, letting it dangle between two fingers. "Because I know where you live now."

Donovan patted his pants. His brows drew together. "Is that my wallet?"

"Don't feel bad." Skye smiled. "I have an angelic face. It fools everyone."

Donovan took his wallet back and scratched his head as she breezed out the door. Once it closed behind her, his eyebrows rose. "Well, that was...interesting. I take it that was her who let me in and called me hot stuff?"

I nodded. "I have an app that connects to the camera downstairs. Depending on which apartment you ring, the tenants can see video of who's at the door. It's one of the reasons I picked the building."

"Nice. Though I think you have a better chance of getting robbed by your friend. Does she steal wallets often?"

I chuckled. "It's one of Skye's many talents. Luckily, she doesn't use that one much these days."

"She used to?"

I nodded. "Back in the day, yeah."

"Was she one of your cases?"

"No. But Skye's very open about her history, so she wouldn't mind me telling you. She gives talks at schools and stuff now. We met at a therapist's office and went to the same victim-support meeting for years."

Donovan's face fell. "So she was..."

I nodded. "Her uncle. It started when she was only nine."

"Jesus Christ."

"Pickpocketing became one of her hobbies, as did cutting and sleeping with grown men when she'd barely hit puberty. But she's come a long way." I shook my head. "Anyway, that's depressing to talk about. Let's not pick up where we left off the other night."

He did his best to smile, but I could see I'd put a damper on the start of our evening. I tried to bring the mood back around by tilting my head. "Why don't we start over? You knock, I'll answer the door, and you can tell me how nice I look?"

The corner of Donovan's mouth twitched. I'd been kidding, but he turned around, opened the door, and walked out, closing it behind him. A few seconds later, there was a knock.

I beamed from ear to ear as I opened it. "Hi. You're a few minutes early."

His eyes dropped to my feet and ever so slowly worked their way up my body. By the time our eyes met, I was tingling all over. "You look phenomenal."

I'd *told him* to go outside, knock, and tell me how nice I looked; yet I still blushed at the comment. "Thank you. You don't look so bad yourself."

Donovan let himself in and shut the door behind him. I felt giddy, a feeling I definitely wasn't used to.

He wrapped one hand around my waist and the other slipped into my hair.

"Kiss me," he growled. "I can't wait any longer."

I leaned forward, but didn't get the chance to pursue the kiss, because Donovan immediately took over. He crushed his lips over mine, swallowing an unexpected gasp. Just like that day in the bathroom, within seconds I had completely forgotten where I was. He smelled incredible, and even though his body was not pushed up against mine, I felt the heat emanating from it, and it set me on fire. I clung to him and my fingernails dug into his back as he tugged his mouth from mine to suck his way down to my neck, teeth scraping over my chin and hot breath sending a shockwave that I felt between my legs. *Lord, can this man kiss.*

By the time it broke, I was panting.

"Is that better?" he growled.

"Oh my God, better than what? I don't even remember what we were talking about."

Donovan smiled. "You told me to make a new entrance." His eyes roamed over my face. "You really do look beautiful."

I had to blink a few times to snap out of my haze. "Thank you."

He stroked my cheek with his thumb. "I could stand right here and do this for hours, but we should probably get going. We have an appointment."

"An appointment? You mean a reservation?"

He shoved his hands into his pockets. "Nope."

"Where are we going that we need an appointment?"

"You'll see."

I didn't usually love surprises, but tonight was an exception. It had been a long time since I'd let my heart lead, and it felt almost freeing. I smiled. "Let me just grab my bag."

―

"Are we here?" I looked around the strip-mall parking lot. There was a barber, a closed-down taco place, a dry cleaner, ballet studio, and a Chinese restaurant.

Donovan unbuckled his seatbelt. "We are."

I glanced at the row of stores again. "Are we going for Chinese food?"

"Nope."

"Picking up your dry cleaning?"

He grinned. "Nope."

"Haircut?"

"You're running out of choices..."

I looked over the stores one more time to make sure I wasn't missing anything. But the only thing left was the ballet studio.

"Oh my God. You're secretly a ballerina, and you're going to perform for me."

"Not quite. But you are getting warmer." He got out of the car and came around to open my door, offering me his hand.

"The ballet studio also teaches couples dance lessons. Last year, during our weekend together, you asked me to describe my idea of the perfect woman. When I asked you about the perfect man, you said he knew how to dance." He shrugged. "I don't. So I figured I need to learn, and you also wanted to avoid day-to-day predictability and take things slow. I thought taking dance lessons would be pretty unpredictable."

My heart fluttered. He'd remembered what I said so long ago and wanted to be my Mr. Perfect. We were twenty minutes into our first date, and I realized *going slow* with this man had nothing to do with anything he could control. I needed to rein in my own heart, or I'd be a goner faster than I could say *two left feet*.

"Umm... I think I should've mentioned something to you."

Donovan's brows pulled together. "What?"

"The reason Mr. Perfect needs to know how to dance is because *I'm terrible at it*."

"I'm sure you're not that bad."

I lifted my elbow and showed him a small scar. "Do you see this?"

"Yeah."

"This is from my one and only dance recital. I was eight and could not get my left and right straight for the life of me. Honestly, I still can't. I have to think about which hand I write with in order to figure it out. Anyway, I went left when I was supposed to go right—*again*. I knocked into a few of the other ballerinas and tumbled off the stage. I landed on my elbow, dislocated it, and had to get nine stitches."

Donovan looked amused. He bent and placed a gentle kiss on my scar. "Poor baby. But don't worry, I promise not to let you fall off the stage today."

"Alright, but don't say I didn't warn you. I have on heels, so your toes are absolutely not safe."

He smiled and looked down at his watch. "I'll take my chances. But the lesson starts in two minutes, so we better get going."

Inside I was surprised to find we were the only ones in the waiting area. A white-haired woman with a ponytail, wearing a bodysuit and a long, flowy skirt walked out from the back to greet us.

"Hello again, Donovan. It's nice to see you." She turned to me and smiled as she held out her hand. "And you must be Autumn."

"I am." We shook.

"I'm Beverly, but everyone just calls me Bev. I'll be your instructor today. Are you ready to get started?"

I took a deep breath. "I guess so."

"Don't worry. We'll stretch out and warm up your ankles to minimize the risk of injury." She opened the door to the back and waved for us to follow. "Right this way." Inside was a typical dance studio, with mirrors on the walls, wood floors, and a ballet barre on both sides of the room. Bev pointed to a wall of cubbies. "You can just put your purse and anything else in one of those. It'll be safe since it's just us."

"It's just...us?"

She looked between Donovan and me. "Your boyfriend booked a private lesson."

"Oh..." I have no idea why, but that freaked me out even more. I guess because all the attention would be on us, and it would be even more apparent that I sucked.

Donovan must've sensed my trepidation. He leaned and whispered in my ear. "We don't have to stay if you don't want to."

I shook my head and managed a smile, sucking it up. "No...no, it'll be fun."

"You sure?"

"Yeah." I nodded. "Let's do it."

Not long into our lesson, it was apparent who the better dancer was.

I squinted at my partner. "Are you sure you've never done this before? Maybe took some lessons as a kid?"

"What are the chances you could get Storm to take dance lessons?"

"Uh, slim to none."

"Not only could we never have afforded dance lessons when I was a kid, but there was no way in hell I would've risked taking them and my friends finding out. They'd either have tortured me for years or beaten the crap out of me. Probably both. Most of the world is changing for the better these days, but nothing changes in the old neighborhood."

Donovan pressed his hand into my back to guide my steps as Bev stood alongside of us counting.

"One-two, one-two. That's it. Two quick to the side and then a slow step forward. You count the slow over two beats of the music and the quick over one."

I was glad he seemed to know what the hell she was talking about. Bev directed us to add in the second step now, something called "Together, Together." But I hadn't even realized we'd been working on two different steps. Though again, Donovan seemed to catch on quickly and took a strong lead. On our third or fourth pass of putting together the two different steps she'd apparently taught us, I started to feel like I was getting the hang of it. Except at one point, I stepped forward when I should've stepped back and wound up stomping right on Donovan's foot.

He winced, but quickly wiped the pain I'd caused from his face.

"I'm sorry."

"No worries." He laughed.

A few minutes later, Bev told us to take a five-minute break and left the room. Donovan bought two waters from the machine in the lobby, and then we went back into the studio.

I was really warm and drank half of the bottle. "I just want to say that it's an old wives' tale that if you can't dance, you're not good in bed. There is no actual correlation."

Donovan smiled. "You have rhythm, you just can't seem to memorize the steps. You definitely still confuse your left and right and sometimes front and back."

"Yeah...that was always my problem when I was little, too."

Donovan chugged the rest of his water and winked. "Plus, I have zero worries about us in bed together. I already know we're a good match."

"How?"

"Eye contact. You give incredible eye contact."

I laughed. "I don't even know what that means."

"You look at me with an intensity. It mimics the way I feel inside when I look at you. Chemistry is all about eye contact."

Our gazes caught, and my heart sped up. I guess he had a point. We'd had that spark from the very first moment we met.

Bev came back in, and Donovan excused himself to go talk to her by the stereo. They exchanged a few words, and she smiled as she glanced over at me, but I couldn't hear what they were saying.

"What was that all about?" I prodded when he came back.

"Nothing." He took one of my hands and wrapped the other around my back as the music started.

Bev was back at our side and counting again before I could interrogate him further. The second half of our lesson went better than the first. I finally started to relax and enjoy myself once I stopped caring what I might look like. To be honest, the way Donovan looked at me, I knew judging me for some missteps was the furthest thing from his mind. At one point, Bev stepped back.

"Alright. There's about ten minutes left to our lesson. I've really enjoyed working with you. If you're interested in continuing, just give me a call."

"Thanks, Bev," we both said.

She walked back over to the music, changed the song, and waved one last time as she walked out of the dance studio and into the lobby.

"I'm confused. Didn't she just say there were ten minutes left?"

Donovan pulled me into his arms. Unlike the way he'd held me during the rhumba lesson, our bodies were pressed close together now.

"I asked her if we could have ten minutes of time to dance alone. Her lesson was nice, but there was too much distance between us. I want you closer."

The instrumental introduction to John Legend's "Slow Dance" ended, and he started to croon. My body melted into Donovan's touch as we swayed back and forth.

"This was a very thoughtful idea. Thank you."

"Let's be real, my motives weren't entirely altruistic. These lessons were also an opportunity to hold you close for the first hour of our date."

I laughed, and Donovan spun us around, burying his nose in my neck and inhaling deeply.

"You know, you ruined a date for me because of how you smell," he said.

I pulled my head back. "How so?"

"You smell like vanilla. A few months after you disappeared, I went out with a woman. After our date, she invited me back to her apartment for a drink. When we got there, she lit a few candles—made the entire room smell like vanilla. I had one glass of wine, told her I had an early morning meeting I'd forgotten about, and called it a night."

I couldn't help but smile.

Donovan shook his head and laughed. "I see you're really broken up about ruining my date."

"Says the man who followed me into the bathroom during one of mine."

He groaned. "Let's not talk about any of that. The thought of you with Blake—or any other guy, for that matter—makes me feel explosive."

"If it makes you feel any better, I feel like punching the woman who lit candles for you."

He smiled. "It does."

"You know so much about my dating history, but you never really told me about yours. I can already tell you're way too good at this dating thing to not have had a lot of girlfriends."

"What do you want to know?"

"Well, have you ever had a serious girlfriend?"

"One, in law school. We went out for about two years. Broke up when we went our separate ways after we graduated."

"So...since then?"

"I've dated, but I've always been upfront that I'm not looking for anything serious and my job is my priority. Turns out, sometimes the best things come when you're not looking at all."

I bit my bottom lip. "You scare the hell out of me, Donovan."

"Right back at ya, Red. But you know what?"

"What?"

"I'm more afraid of what I'll be missing if we don't give this a real shot."

I took a deep breath and nodded. "Okay."

Donovan pulled me against him again and led me around the dance floor a few times. He held me a little tighter, and I had a feeling it had nothing to do with the dance. Normally, any possessiveness from a man sent me running, but not this time. I liked that Donovan felt that way about me, mostly because the feeling was mutual, and somehow it was less scary to me that way.

The song came to an end, but Donovan kept my hand in his.

"You ready for our date?"

"I thought this was our date?"

"Nah. This was just me finding a way to get your tits pushed up against my chest when we're supposed to be going slow."

I laughed, but stood on my tippy toes and brushed my lips with his. "You can't fool me, Mr. Decker. You're thoughtful and sweet and have a very romantic side."

He looked back and forth between my eyes. "Oh yeah? Well, if that's true, you better keep that a secret. I have a reputation of being an asshole that I need to keep intact."

My belly did a little somersault. The way he looked at me turned my insides into warm mush. I still had the urge to flee, but I was learning that I could get past those flare-ups if I just rode it out and took things slow.

Though every minute I spent with this man made the hope inside me bloom a little bigger. I was learning to trust again, and I'd just have to hope that this time, my trust wasn't misplaced.

26

Donovan

"This place is beautiful." Autumn laid her napkin across her lap. "Have you been here before?"

I hesitated before answering that. The lawyer in me always played chess, trying to figure out where the conversation might lead, based on a given response. In this case, if I said yes, that could lead to her asking if I'd taken a date here, and I didn't want her not to feel special.

Autumn lifted a brow. "Earth to Donovan. Are you there?"

I nodded. "Yeah, sorry. I just got stuck in my head. I have been here before once."

"What do you mean, stuck in your head? Is something bothering you?"

Again, I took a minute to debate how this conversation might play out, and Autumn noticed.

"Talk to me," she said. "What's going on?"

I decided to come clean. "I'm overthinking shit because I don't want to screw tonight up."

"But what are you overthinking?"

"You asked me if I'd been here before. I have. But I was trying to figure out whether if I admitted that, you might be put off because I'd been here with someone else."

"I see. Well, you being honest with me is more important than the fact that you brought another woman here."

I raked a hand through my hair. "Yeah, of course. I'm sorry. It's just been a long time since I was nervous on a date."

Autumn smiled. "I changed ten times before you picked me up. So you're not alone."

My eyes dropped to her cleavage. "You picked the right one."

She laughed. "Thank you. But what are we going to do about it?"

"Your dress?"

"No. Our nerves."

I could think of a few ways to work out the nerves— none of which were part of her *go slow* edict. So I kept those thoughts to myself and shrugged. "Wine?"

She nodded. "That sounds perfect."

The waitress came over to take our drink order, and Autumn picked out a bottle.

"You know," she said, "when I first started dating again, my nerves were frayed. I canceled my first two dates because I couldn't take the stress leading up to them. When I told my therapist about it, she suggested I write down a list of all the things I was nervous about and then a list of all the things I'm grateful for. It kind of sounds silly saying it out loud right now, but it worked pretty well for me."

I shook my head. "It doesn't sound silly. It actually makes sense. Acknowledging a problem takes away its power."

She nodded. "Want to try it? Since we're both nervous?"

"Right now?"

"Yeah. We don't have to write them down. Maybe we can just tell each other."

"Alright. Ladies first."

Autumn tapped her finger to her lip. "Okay...well...I'm nervous because I like you. And I'm afraid that if I allow myself to fall, I won't see things I should see."

Fuck. It hurt to hear how much that piece of shit had screwed her up. I reached across the table and took her hand. "A good man doesn't have parts of himself he's hiding, Autumn."

She smiled sadly. "I do know that. But what I logically know and how my emotions handle things don't always reconcile. I'm being honest about the things I'm nervous about."

I nodded. "I get it."

The waitress came over and brought the bottle of wine we'd ordered. She poured a small amount into a glass, and I deferred to Autumn to taste test.

She nodded. "It's delicious. Thank you."

"Would you like me to put an appetizer in for you while you look over the menu? We have homemade burrata today, and our fried calamari is one of our most popular dishes."

I looked at Autumn, and she nodded. "I like both. Either is good with me."

"We'll take one of each, please."

After the waitress disappeared, Autumn said, "So what about you? What are you nervous about? You said you were nervous about screwing up. But is there anything in particular that concerns you?"

I drank some of my wine and debated how honest to be. Realizing I was again filtering my thoughts, even when she had been frank with her answer, I decided to say *screw it* and go with complete honesty.

"I'm nervous because I'm crazy about you, and I'm afraid that if you see the truth about where I am, I'll scare you away."

Autumn smiled. "You're crazy about me?"

"You can't tell?"

She bit her lip. "Can I make another confession about something that makes me nervous?"

"Of course."

"I don't trust my own judgment anymore. So while I did sense how you felt, a part of me has been busy making up other reasons you're interested in me."

My brows drew together. "Like what?"

Autumn sipped her wine. "Well, you're competitive, and sometimes men are attracted to women who don't show an interest in them."

"You think I'm playing a game?"

She shook her head. "I don't... Well, not really. But that's the thing—when you've lost trust in your own judgment, you overanalyze everything until you find something wrong. It's like a compulsive need to find doubt in myself."

I understood the psychology behind that, but I didn't know how to quell the voices in her head. I supposed the only thing I could do would be to talk to them. So I closed my eyes.

"You have a little scar on your right knee. You put cinnamon in your coffee, but if it's not your normal brand, you run your finger over the top of the shaker and taste test it. You also like to rummage through kitchen cabinets that aren't yours when you think no one is watching. When you're thinking about a problem, you tap your pointer to your lip, but when your thoughts are dirty, you bite it instead."

I opened my eyes to find Autumn's wide. "How do you know all that?"

"I saw you rummage through my kitchen cabinets the weekend we spent together. You thought I was sleeping, but the bedroom door was open a crack, and I could see you in the kitchen."

"Why didn't you say anything?"

I shrugged. "Because I wanted you to rummage through my cabinets if it made you happy."

"How did you know about the scar on my knee?"

"You took a nap on the couch while we were watching a movie, and I couldn't stop staring at you. I wanted to memorize every freckle, every curve..."

Autumn's mouth was agape. She swallowed. "I guess I do tap my lip with my finger, too."

I smiled. "I know you do. You know why I know?"

"Why?"

"Because I can't keep my eyes off you, not since the first time we met. And back then, I had no idea you were going to take off. So, no..." I shook my head. "I can't be interested in you because you're the girl I can't have, because I was a damn goner before you even left."

Autumn's face softened. "I don't know what to say, Donovan."

"You don't have to say anything. Just give me the chance to show you..."

She looked me in the eyes for a long time before taking a deep breath and nodding. "Okay."

"Yeah?"

"Yeah." She smiled.

The waitress delivered our appetizers. It felt like we needed the minute that gave us. Since the evening had gotten off to a heavy start, once the waitress left, I rounded our conversation back to what I thought was the safer part of Autumn's therapy exercise.

"So what are we up to? Things we're grateful for?"

"I think so. You want me to go first again?"

"Sure."

She started to tap her finger to her lip, then smiled when she caught herself. "Okay, let's see... I'm grateful for my health, good friends, having a job that's rewarding, good food..." She looked up at me. "And second chances."

"Nice..."

She sipped her wine and lifted her chin. "Your turn. What are you grateful for?"

"Well, Bud would be near the top of that list. I'm grateful for all the things he's done for me over the years, and I'm grateful he wasn't hurt worse than he was when he was attacked."

"I'm grateful for that, too." Autumn cut into her burrata.

"I'm also grateful for a career I like, friends who tolerate me, and having a nest egg in the bank—something I definitely didn't grow up with."

Autumn slipped a piece of burrata into her mouth, and her eyes shut. A look I could only describe as *orgasmic* came over her face. My eyes were glued to her lips. *Damn. I'm jealous of a piece of cheese.* I also started to harden under the table. This woman made me feel like a teenager. We were supposed to be taking things slow, and watching her eat got me worked up? Unfortunately, I sensed *a lot* of whacking off in my future.

She opened her eyes, and I cleared my throat, still staring at her beautiful lips. "Burrata. I'm extremely grateful for burrata."

Autumn looked amused, yet truly innocent. "You're a big fan of burrata?"

"I'm a tremendous fan of the face you make while you eat it."

"What face do I make?"

I leaned forward. "The same one you made when I went down on you."

She covered her mouth and blushed. "Oh my God, really?"

I nodded. "Really."

Luckily the waitress came to check on us and see if we were ready to order dinner. Another minute of this conversation, and the white napkin over my lap would look more like I was trying to wave a flag to surrender.

This time, when we were alone again, I moved the conversation to something way safer.

"So how's Storm doing?"

"He's doing great. Though he keeps asking me when he can go work at Bud's house. He really wants to earn that bicycle Bud promised him. But I wasn't sure if Bud would feel up to it yet."

"I stopped over there this morning, and he was rototilling part of the garden with one hand. He's definitely feeling better."

She smiled. "I'm glad to hear that. He's the type of man you worry about if he sits around watching TV for too long."

"Absolutely."

"Well, if you think he's really up for it, I could probably take him over there Sunday."

"I'll run it by him when I check in again, but I'm sure it will be fine."

The rest of the night went by too fast, even though I stalled and dragged out dessert for so long that the waitress was giving us the evil eye. I just wasn't ready for our first date to be over, and I was certain *going slow* didn't include spending the night.

When we got to Autumn's apartment, I parked.

"Would you want to go for a walk?" I asked. It was a nice enough night.

She pointed down to her shoes. "I normally would, but these aren't really walking shoes."

I'd parked under a streetlight so the inside of the car was pretty well lit. I followed her sexy legs down to the strappy, high-heeled sandals she had on.

"I forgot to mention how grateful I am for your shoes earlier." My eyes trailed their way back up her legs and over the thin material of her dress. "And for that dress. I'm really damn thankful for that dress."

She giggled. "What about my bra and underwear? Aren't you grateful for them?"

"I don't know. Let me see, so I can decide."

Autumn leaned closer to me and took my hand. The beaming smile on her face made my heart swell in my chest.

"I had a really nice time tonight," she said.

"Me, too."

She bit down on her bottom lip. "You could...come up for a little while, if you want."

Of course there was nothing I wanted more, but I wasn't sure that was a good idea. As I inwardly debated her invitation, my eyes dropped down, and that's when I noticed her nipples were hard—sticking out from her dress like the beautiful horns of a devil. There was no way I could go inside and keep my distance. And I couldn't screw up going slow on our first official night. So I cleared my throat and drew on every ounce of willpower I had in me.

"It's probably better if I don't."

Autumn looked a little disappointed, but she nodded. "You're right. Thank you."

We were both quiet as I walked her to the door. Inside the lobby, neither one of us pushed the elevator button. Autumn looked down for a minute before meeting my eyes.

"I think I should clarify that just because I want to take things slow, it doesn't mean the desire to move faster, especially physically, isn't there. Because it is...very much so."

I could seriously get lost in the green of her eyes. I knew when she got worked up they turned almost pale gray, and that's what they were now.

I cupped her cheeks. "I've wanted you since the day we met, even during those months I didn't know if I'd see you again. What I desire is more than just being inside you, I want to consume you."

Her eyes jumped between mine for a few seconds before she caught me completely off guard and launched herself at me. Our lips crashed, and I stumbled back a few steps, fighting to keep my balance. When I steadied myself, I wrapped my arms around her and lifted until her feet came off the ground. Autumn threaded her fingers into my hair and tugged, pulling me closer, even though it was physically impossible to find a fraction of an inch of space between us. I wound my hand into the back of her hair and yanked to gain access to her neck. Then sucked down to her collarbone and back up to her ear.

"You're killing me," I groaned. "I'm going to get us arrested for indecent exposure in a minute."

Autumn mumbled through our joined lips. "I know a good lawyer. Don't worry about it."

I have no damn idea how long we stayed that way—maybe fifteen or twenty minutes. But when we broke for air, Autumn's lips were swollen, her hair had that sexy, *just fucked* look, and both of us were panting.

I used my thumb to wipe away the lipstick smeared beneath her lip. "I'm so hard, I'm not sure I can walk."

She giggled.

God, I love that sound.

"My lady parts are swollen and tingly."

I groaned and shut my eyes. "You're killing me, Red."

We stood in the lobby for a few more minutes. Eventually, it was me who pushed the elevator button. When it came, I brushed my lips with hers one last time.

"I'll text you tomorrow? Is that okay?"

She nodded with a smile. "Definitely."

Autumn stepped into the elevator and said goodnight. As the doors began to slide closed, she put her arm out, causing them to bounce open again.

"Hang on a second..."

She dipped one hand under the hem of her skirt, reached up to her waist, somehow managing not to expose herself, and the next thing I knew she was shimmying panties down her legs.

Fuck me. A black lace thong.

The scrap of material reached the floor, and she stepped out before leaning forward and shoving them in my pocket.

"You said you weren't sure if you were grateful for my panties since you hadn't seen them." Autumn stepped back into the elevator and wiggled her fingers. She had the biggest devilish grin on her face. "Goodnight, Donovan."

I stood speechless as the doors slid closed, then shook my head.

I was wrong. Her smile wasn't devilish—she *was* the devil.

Pulling the lacy thong from my pocket, I looked at it for a minute before closing it into my fist and bolting for the door. Suddenly, I couldn't get out of there fast enough. The minute I got home, I'd be wearing this thing—around my *cock* while my hand had a field day.

27

Donovan

"Where the hell have you been?" Trent sat back in his chair and put his fork down.

"Sorry I'm late. I couldn't get a client off the damn phone."

"I'm not talking about being late for lunch. I came down to your office twice this week to see if you wanted to order in some dinner, and your door was shut and the lights were off."

I grinned. My friends didn't yet know that Autumn and I had gotten together. "I had more important shit to do."

Juliette's brows rose. She covered her full mouth with a napkin and leaned over to feel my forehead. "More important than work? Are you sick?"

"Nope."

"Then what is more important than work right before the upcoming partner vote?"

"My girl."

"Holy shit," Trent said. "Are you smiling over a woman?"

"I am." I'd also had her underwear in my pocket the last three days, but I didn't share that part.

"So there's a woman out there who passed your tests?"

"With flying colors."

"Wow," Juliette said. She turned to Trent while pointing to me. "He's smitten. Our little playboy is growing up so fast."

I pulled the container with my lunch out of the bag. "Poke fun all you want. I don't even care."

Trent wiped his mouth with his napkin. "I never thought I'd see the day. We should double date."

"I don't think she has any sixteen-year-old friends for you," I teased and bit into my sandwich. "But I'll ask."

"I wasn't asking you to fix me up, jackass. If you'd been around lately, you'd know I have my own girl."

I stopped chewing. "Not a blow-up one?"

"Fuck you. A real one—and she's smoking hot, too."

I was glad to see my buddy happy, but that wouldn't stop me from busting his balls. "Not underage, not a blow-up doll, and she's smoking hot? So you're paying her, then?"

Trent threw his napkin at me. "I met her at the bar a few weeks ago. She's Juliette's friend. You actually talked to both of us on your way out. She has excellent taste, so she met you first but came home with me."

I raised an eyebrow. "What's her name?"

"Margo."

Hot damn—the woman I'd sent his way after whining to her about Autumn. I wasn't about to mention that she'd hit on me first. I nodded. "Margo...sounds familiar. Brunette?"

"Yup."

"You two hit it off?"

"Spent almost every night together since then."

I nodded. "Good for you."

Juliette and Trent looked at each other funny.

"What?"

She shook her head. "You're acting weird. Only a few jabs at Trent and...you're smiling too much."

I clasped my hands behind my head. "That's because I'm happy to be alive, ladies and gentlemen."

Trent turned to Juliette. She shrugged. "Don't look at me. I checked his head. No fever."

Trent finished chewing. "Alright. I'll bite. Tell us about this magical creature who seems to have stolen your brain. What does she look like? How big is the unicorn horn on top of her head, and does she let you play with it?"

I might've gotten a little starry-eyed. "She's gorgeous—red hair, green eyes, alabaster skin."

Juliette's face scrunched up. She pointed to me as she looked at Trent. "Did he just use the word *alabaster*?"

My buddy shook his head. "He's definitely lost his mind if this is what I think it is. Red hair and green eyes? Please tell me this isn't Blake's girlfriend."

I smiled. "It's not."

"Thank God."

I grinned. "Because she's not seeing The Dick anymore. She's all mine."

Trent tossed his fork on the table and looked up at the ceiling with a groan. "*Shit*."

"You should be happy for me. I finally met someone. All you ever do is bust my balls because I won't settle."

Trent shook his head. "Let me get this straight. You spent seven years working your ass off to make partner at this firm. And a few weeks before you might actually get there, you start taking half days, slacking on billable hours, and banging the girlfriend of a partner whose vote *you need* in order to get to the finish line."

"Relax, buddy. They were casual, and she called it quits. Blake has no idea we're seeing each other. He doesn't even know we'd met before I picked up that pro bono case he assigned me. And I haven't been slacking. My billable hours are down, but they're down to what normal workaholics trying to make partner bill."

"Uh-huh." Trent nodded. "You're venturing onto some thin ice, my friend. Didn't you ever hear the saying 'what's done in the dark always finds its way to the light'?"

I shrugged. "I could care less if Blake finds out in the long run. Part of me is looking forward to it. It's practically his damn fault, anyway. If he hadn't been too lazy to take the pro bono case he dumped on me, Autumn and I probably would never have seen each other again. Besides, I only need to keep it under wraps for a little longer. Then I'll be a partner, and tough shit on him if he doesn't like it."

Juliette shook her head. "I don't have a good feeling about this. You better be careful."

"Stop worrying. It's fine. There's no way he's going to find out."

Trent puckered his lips and made a loud kissing sound.

I smirked. "No more kisses for you, buddy. I'm a one-woman man now."

"That wasn't me blowing you a kiss, dude." He shook his head. "You said *there's no way he's going to find out.* That was me kissing your luck goodbye as your cocky ass blew it out the door with that rush of hot air."

The following week, my life went from great to phenomenal. If I knew a better word than that, I'd use it, but I hadn't had much reason to bolster my vocabulary of superlatives relating to the state of my life in the last thirty years. Sure, I was successful—and until a few months ago, I thought that was what it took to make me happy. I hadn't even known I was unfulfilled until, well, until I got my fill of Autumn.

On Sunday, we went to Bud's so Storm could do the work he'd agreed to do in exchange for the bike. Autumn and I did some painting inside while we were there, and I managed to sneak her into the garage and cop a cheap feel while we made out like two horny teenagers. At night, I served dinner with Bud. He still had his cast on, but he wanted to help—and by help, I mean he wanted to boss me around like I didn't know what I was doing after fifteen years of doing it with him. But it made him happy, and I was glad he was in good spirits again, so I didn't give a shit.

On Wednesday night, I took Autumn out to dinner—at a bowling alley, where she proceeded to spank my ass and bowl a two hundred and six. Apparently, her father had a bowling team for his law firm, and she'd always joined them growing up. Normally, I was super competitive, and a loss to anyone would have bruised my ego, but this time I didn't give a shit if my girl handed me my ass in a game, because she smiled all night. Also, every time she got a strike she jumped up and down, which I liked *a lot*.

I also somehow managed to bill one of my highest weeks, and old man Kravitz came down from the ivory tower to tell me I'd done a great job for one of his personal VIP clients who'd gotten himself into trouble with the SEC.

Yeah, shit couldn't have been going better.

My phone buzzed on my desk, and the picture I'd taken of Autumn last year flashed on my screen. At the risk of sounding like a complete dorky sap, a little warmth ran through my belly. Actually, if feeling like this made me a dork—I'd been totally missing out by trying to be cool all my life.

Leaning back into my chair, I swiped to answer.

"Hey, gorgeous."

"You answer the phone like that for all women, don't you?" I heard the smile in her voice.

"There is no other woman, sweetheart."

She sighed. "I called to say thank you for the stuff you bought for Storm."

I'd stopped over at Park House this morning and dropped off a bag with a lock for the bicycle Bud had given him, and also a Nike sweatshirt with a reflective stripe down the side for when he inevitably rode in the dark. But he'd already left for school, and I was running late. The woman at the front desk was busy on the phone, so I'd written Storm's name on the bag and motioned that I was leaving. It wasn't until I got to my car that I'd realized I forgot to leave my name.

"How did you know I gave him something?"

"Hmmm... A good guess? When I stopped over at Park House for a meeting earlier, Rochelle at the front desk told me some hot guy dropped off a bag for Storm."

I grinned. "You think I'm hot?"

She laughed. "I can see your gloating, cocky face right now even through a phone call. Let me guess, you're leaning back in your chair, too?"

I sprang forward in my seat. "No, I'm not."

She laughed. "Anyway, I just called to say thank you for doing that. It was very sweet. I don't want to take up too much of your time."

"You're always a welcome break."

"You working late tonight?"

"Yeah. You and Skye watching your show and talking about me?"

"Believe it or not, not everything is about you."

"I definitely don't believe that."

She chuckled. "I'll see you tomorrow night?"

"Can't wait."

"Me too."

An hour later, Blake Dickson appeared at my office door. I was on the phone with a client, but that didn't stop him from coming on inside and taking a seat while I finished my call.

I forced a cheery smile when I hung up. "What's up, boss?"

He picked up a crystal paperweight of the Earth I kept on my desk and tossed it up and down like it was a stress ball. I gritted my teeth—it had been a gift from Bud when I graduated law school, and was the only personal item to be found anywhere in my office.

"I need a favor."

I need one too. Get the fuck out of my office.

"Sure, what's up?"

"I have dinner tomorrow night with Todd Aster. You helped squash an inquiry the feds made about some of his investments a few years back."

"Yeah, I remember him."

"Well, he's going through a messy divorce, and apparently his wife has some documents related to that investment that could be damaging."

"Statute of limitations still open?"

Blake nodded. "Unfortunately."

"Okay...how can I help?"

"Fill in for me at dinner tomorrow."

Shit. "I, uh, have plans."

Blake sat up a little taller. "So do I. And I'm counting on you to handle this for me."

Of course I couldn't say no. So I nodded. "No problem. I'll rearrange my schedule."

Dickson got up and headed to the door without so much as a thank you. He turned back at the last minute.

"The vote's coming up soon. I'll be honest, I was pretty much team Mills when the candidates for partner were announced. But you've proven to be someone I can rely on, someone I can trust to have my back."

The irony wasn't lost on me, though I put on a solid fake smile. "Of course. Happy to help out."

"I'll have my admin send you the details."

After he left, I slumped in my chair. I didn't want to go to a damn dinner; I wanted to spend the evening with Autumn. Her two-nights-a-week rule was already killing me. Going down to one wasn't an option.

When the email from Dickson's assistant came in, I asked if we could possibly move the seven o'clock dinner to six.

The rest of the day got away from me, and it was almost eight before I checked my email and found a response confirming she'd been able to switch the time. Hopefully Autumn wouldn't mind getting together a little later. I knew her friend was over for their *Bachelor* marathon tonight, so I didn't want to call and interrupt. Instead, I shot off a text.

Donovan: Would you mind if we had a late dinner tomorrow night? Something came up at work, and I have to go to a dinner meeting with a client at six. I can probably be done by eight or eight thirty.

Autumn responded right away.

Autumn: Boy, I'm going to start to get a complex. First, Skye cancels on me, now you're changing our date... Just kidding. Sure, that's fine.

Donovan: Did Skye really cancel on you?
Autumn: Yeah. She thinks she has the flu.
Donovan: Sorry to hear that. I know you were looking forward to it.
Autumn: We're down to the last five episodes, and I can't watch TV or go on social media because I don't want to accidentally find out who won! I told her if she tests positive for the flu, I'm watching without her because I need to go online.

I chuckled. I could never understand how so many smart women loved that dumb show.

Donovan: Spoiler alert. He picks the one no one likes.
Autumn: OMG! Are you kidding me? He picks Meghan?

Shit.

Donovan: I was joking. I have no idea how it ends. Or how it begins, for that matter. Though most of that shit ends the same way—whatever is best for ratings.
Autumn: You almost gave me a heart attack. Meghan sucks!

I laughed to myself.

Donovan: I'll text you when I'm on my way tomorrow.
Autumn: OK. Have a good night.

The hearing I had the next afternoon wound up taking two minutes because opposing counsel showed up and asked for a last-minute continuance. Since I was meeting Dickson's client at a restaurant closer to my house than the office, I figured I'd work the rest of the afternoon from home. I had prep work to do for a trial coming up, and home had fewer distractions anyway.

As I walked in, my cell phone rang.

I smiled and swiped to answer. "Hey, beautiful."

"Is that a downgrade from gorgeous? I think I was gorgeous yesterday."

"Definitely not."

"I was just thinking—you asked if we could have a later dinner because you have to meet a client for dinner, right?"

"Yeah."

"Why would we go out to dinner if you've already eaten?"

I shrugged. "You have to eat. Plus, I want to see you."

"I want to see you, too. But we could just hang out here. I'll eat before you come. Skip dessert with your client, and I'll make you the best ice cream sundae you've ever had."

I smiled. "If you're sure you don't mind, that sounds great. Want me to pick up some ice cream on the way over?"

"No need. I have all the supplies from my canceled plans with Skye last night, including fresh, chocolate-dipped waffle cones. They'll go bad before she's able to come over. She tested positive for the flu."

"Sorry to hear that."

"Thanks. I'm going to drop off some soup for her on my way home from work. But I gotta run. I'm about to go into the subway."

"Alright. Be careful. I'll see you later."

I changed out of my work clothes, grabbed my laptop, and settled in on my couch. My office maintained a portal online where I could sign in and download the depositions I needed to re-read. But as I clicked to the web, an ad popped up for the new ABC streaming app. It advertised some of their hit shows available, including *The Bachelor*. I smiled, thinking of Autumn, and clicked to close it. But instead of hitting the X, I must've hit the icon to make it larger because a preview of a bunch of women getting out of limousines popped up, and some doofus handed them each a rose. I went to click off a second time, but then a girl stepped out of a stretch limo wearing a belly dancer's costume.

Hmpf. Maybe I'll watch a few minutes before I dig into my work...

28

Autumn

"**H**ey."

Donovan grinned at me from the other side of the door, and butterflies started to dance in my stomach. *God, he's delicious.* Maybe it wasn't such a good idea to invite him to hang out at my apartment tonight. He noticed my slight hesitation, though he must've misread what was going on in my head.

He lifted a duffle bag I hadn't noticed in his hand. "It's not an overnight bag, I swear. I just threw in a change of clothes so I could get out of this suit I had to wear to dinner."

I stepped aside to let him in, and he stopped in front of me, toe to toe.

"I was appreciating the view, not worrying you might overstay your welcome."

The right side of his mouth twitched to a cocky grin. "Oh yeah? Well, you can watch me change if you want the full view." He leaned down and planted a kiss on my lips. With our mouths still attached, he spoke softly, "I've missed you."

Three little words and the walls around my heart were already crumbling. It wasn't because they were sweet—though of course they were—but because I knew he meant it. As a woman who hadn't trusted a man in a very long time, I felt in my bones that he was being honest. And that made me unsettled when it should've made me the exact opposite. So rather than be honest and tell him I'd missed him, too, my sense of self-preservation kicked in, and I backed away from the moment with sarcasm.

"What's your name again?"

He tapped my nose with his finger. "Smartass."

I shut the door with a smile.

"Sorry I'm so late. The client wouldn't shut the hell up."

"It's fine." I pointed to my toes and wiggled them. "They needed to be painted anyway. Skye and I usually do it when she comes over for our binge-watching sessions."

"How's she feeling?"

"Achy with a slight fever. When I went over to drop the soup, her boyfriend was there, and she was letting him take care of her. That's how I know she isn't feeling well. She doesn't let people do things for her. She's very independent."

Donovan tilted his head. "Sounds familiar."

I smiled. "I guess so. I'm sure it has to do with our trust issues."

He nodded. "I get it. Growing up, I never got too close to anyone. If you don't let people in, it doesn't hurt when they take off."

I frowned. "I'm sorry. That's exactly what I did to you last year, too. We had a connection, and I took off."

"It's fine. You had your reasons."

I'd never really considered how it might not be so easy for Donovan to trust me because of what I'd done.

"It's really not fine. I should've at least been upfront about what I was doing and said goodbye."

"That's behind us now."

"But how is it behind you? You've let me in when you keep distance from most people. And I already took off on you once. You make it seem so easy to get over your fear of people you care about taking off."

Donovan stared at me for a moment. "It's not easy, Autumn. But you're worth the chance."

That might've been the single most beautiful thing anyone had ever said to me. "Wow." I shook my head. "I don't even know what to say."

He looked away and then back to me with a boyish grin. "You don't have to say anything. Just don't take off without talking to me again."

I closed the distance between us and wrapped my arms around his neck. "I can do that."

He pulled me flush against him. "Good. Because I know where you live this time, and I'd track your ass down."

"Hopefully that won't be necessary." I laughed. "So did you save room for dessert?"

Donovan's eyes dropped down between us. From this vantage point, he was looking straight down my shirt. "Always room for dessert."

He wiggled his eyebrows, and I laughed.

"So do you prefer toasted coconut chocolate chip, cookies and cream, or chocolate peanut butter?"

"Yes."

"Good choice. I like a taste of each, too. Why don't you go get changed and relax, and I'll make us bowls?"

Donovan disappeared into the bathroom and came back out moments later in jeans and a T-shirt. He tossed his duffle on the side of the couch and settled in.

"I was looking through movies before you got here, but I wasn't sure what kind you liked, so I saved a bunch to my favorites on Netflix, if you want to take a look."

"Actually, I have something in mind I thought you'd enjoy watching," he said. "I'll cue it up."

"Oh...okay." I whipped up two bowls of ice cream with chocolate syrup, whipped cream, and crunchies and headed over to the couch. His bowl was twice as full as mine. "This one is yours. I went a little overboard. I hope you like all the junk I put on."

"There's not much I don't eat—except ketchup. My mother didn't cook much, but when I was about seven or eight, she had this asshole boyfriend of hers move in with us for a while. He used to make us eggs for breakfast and put ketchup all over them. I told him I didn't like ketchup on mine, and after that he put twice as much on my plate. Haven't eaten the stuff since the day he moved out."

"Good to know. I was thinking about adding some ketchup to our sundaes, too."

He chuckled.

I tucked my feet under me on the couch and pulled a blanket over my lap before shoveling a spoonful of ice cream into my mouth. "So what are we watching?"

Donovan grabbed the remote and pressed a button. The TV illuminated with a half-dozen episodes of *The Bachelor*.

"Awww. You're very sweet, but we don't have to watch that. I know you're not a fan."

"How am I going to find out if Kayla's dad really hits Brad during the hometown visit or not, if I don't watch the next episode?"

My eyes flared. "You watched *The Bachelor*?"

"You said you were going to watch the last five episodes if Skye had the flu." He shrugged. "Figured I had some catching up to do. I got out of court early today, so I binge-watched up to where you left off."

My insides melted. "I can't believe you did that."

He swallowed a mouthful of ice cream and pointed his spoon at me. "If you mention it to Bud, I'll deny it."

I pretended to zip my mouth shut over my smile. "Your secret's safe with me."

After I finished my dessert, I snuggled next to Donovan on the couch and covered us both with a blanket. At one point, he took a break from his ice cream and rested his hand on my thigh. It felt like it could burn an imprint into my bare skin. I did my best to ignore it. Halfway through the first episode, my cell phone rang. It was on the end table next to Donovan, so he handed it to me. *Dad* flashed on the screen.

I sighed. "He's been relentless the last few days. His wedding is next weekend, and I still haven't given him an answer. My therapist thinks I should go."

Donovan pushed a button on the TV to pause the show. "But you don't want to?"

I shook my head and silenced my phone. "I don't know. We used to be so close, especially right after my mom died. I don't have much family other than him. My mom was an only child, and both her parents passed away when I was little. But...it's hard for me to forget how he handled things six years ago."

Donovan's eyes roamed my face. "You mentioned he wasn't supportive after, but did he not stand by you when things went down?"

"He insisted I get into therapy, and he did anything I asked. But he was kind of distant during the entire thing. At the police station, when I finally decided to come forward and report what had happened, I cried the whole time, and the policewoman comforted me. My father just kind of sat there, almost detached. And I couldn't understand how he could stay partners with Braden's father after everything he'd heard me say."

"What did he say when you told him that?"

I frowned. "I didn't—not at first, anyway. I let all of my anger toward him build for a long time. About a year after everything happened, my therapist convinced me to talk to him. Unfortunately, I did that after having a little too much to drink one night, and the talk didn't go as it probably should've. I was very emotional and said some horrible things, and then I refused to talk to him once I'd sobered up—not very mature, I know."

"A person who went through what you did handles it however they need to handle it. It sounds to me like you shouldn't even have had to have that discussion, or deal with any of it."

"When I refused to listen to him, he went to talk to my therapist. She wouldn't discuss anything with him, but he asked her to listen to him and talk to me on his behalf. He claimed he'd been in shock for a while, that he saw himself going through the motions with me, but was checked out mentally, sort of like watching a movie about what was going on. That's why he wasn't emotional or sympathetic at the time."

"And you don't believe that?"

"I don't know. My therapist says a lot of the things he described to her are classic symptoms of psychological shock. But I just..." I shook my head. "I felt so alone back then, and it's hard for me to forget. Plus, then there's his string of marriages and the crazy stuff he's done over the years."

"Is he still partners with the father?"

"No, he's not. The week after my drunken tirade, he split from his partner. He claimed he didn't realize how much it upset me because I hadn't said anything, and because they'd fired Braden after I went to the police." I shook my head. "Honestly, he's tried to make it up to me for years. He handled things wrong, but maybe he did have his reasons. I would like to forgive him and forget, but I don't know how."

"Do you have to do both?"

"What do you mean?"

"Forgiving and forgetting—I think they're two different things. When you forgive, you allow yourself to stop harboring resentment so that *you* can be at peace with something. I've forgiven my mother for the shit she did when I was growing up—for disappearing for months at a time and leaving me on the streets to fend for myself. She's not perfect, that's for damn sure. But I needed to let go of the resentment for *me* more than I did for her. Now, I haven't forgotten. Every time she calls to hit me up for cash, I remember. But I ask her how she is and talk to her anyway. Sometimes we even meet for dinner, if she doesn't hang up on me after I tell her I'm not giving her any money so she can put it up her nose."

He stroked my cheek. "I don't think you can forget, and I think that's probably a good thing, because we learn from all the shit in our past. But you can still choose to forgive, if you want." Donovan put his hands up. "To be clear, I'm not taking your father's side. Everything you told me makes me dislike him more than I already did. But I am on *your* side, and if you want to move on, you should. You can't wait until you're able to forgive *and* forget. Because you probably will never forget."

Oh my God. Waves of emotion swept over me. For years, my therapist had been trying to talk me through moving on with my dad, and in five minutes, this man had gotten through to me. He was absolutely right. If I was waiting to have any relationship with my father until all of this was behind me, I'd be waiting forever. It felt like a great weight had been lifted off my shoulders.

"Would you be my date for his wedding if I went?"

Donovan smiled. "Sweetheart, if you asked me to be your date to walk you into hell, I wouldn't say no. Of course I'll go with you. I'd be happy to."

I smiled back. "Okay, well, I'm not sure wedding number eight and a trip to hell are that different, so thank you."

He winked. "No problem."

Donovan scraped the last of his ice cream from the bottom of his bowl like he hadn't just talked me through a monumental breakthrough in my life. The man had no clue how perfect he was. To look the way he did, have the smarts he had, and have such a deep understanding of flawed-human psychology? He was pretty special.

I reached out and pinched his arm.

He glanced down at the spot and looked up with an adorably crooked smile. "What was that for?"

"Just making sure you're real."

He never took his eyes off of me as he set his ice cream bowl on the table and scooped me into his lap.

I giggled as I straddled him.

Donovan dug his fingers into my hair and pulled my lips down to meet his. "Come here. Let me show you real."

His tongue dipped inside, and he tilted my head ever so slightly to deepen the kiss. Lord, could this man do magical things with his mouth. And I remembered from our weekend that he was very generous in showing off this talent in other places. There was something so desperate when the two of us touched. It had been like that from the very start; as if once we collided, we needed each other to survive.

I felt him hardening beneath me as we kissed. With my legs wide open, the denim of his jeans pushed against my clit, and I ground down harder, desperate for friction.

Donovan groaned and gripped my hips. He started to guide me back and forth over his erection, and things built to a frenzy very fast.

Oh my God. I might come dry humping this man.

My body slowed, realizing that was exactly what was about to happen.

"Do you want me to stop?" Donovan mumbled between our sealed lips.

"No, I...I..."

He pulled back so we could see each other. I was a little embarrassed, but I didn't want him to think he'd done anything wrong.

"I almost...you know."

The wickedest grin spread across Donovan's face. "You almost had an orgasm riding me fully dressed?"

"Don't look so smug. I was the one doing all the work."

"Oh yeah?" In one stealth move, he lifted me off his lap, and my back was suddenly against the couch. He climbed and hovered over me. "Well, we can't have that now, can we?" He kissed my nose, then my chin, and lowered his head to kiss my neck before planting a kiss on top of my cleavage. His voice was lower and raspier when he spoke again. "Why should you be the only one doing the work? I think I need to help out here." Donovan raised the hem of my T-shirt and kissed my belly button, then fingered the button of my shorts while looking up at me. His eyes were dark and hooded, but he didn't break contact as he opened my shorts. "I want to bury my face in you and not stop until I feel you come all over my tongue. I crave you, Autumn. *Want* is too tame of a word. What I feel is much greedier than that."

I swallowed.

"Tell me that's okay. I don't ever want to push you too fast and be a regret the next day."

His tone made my heart hurt. He'd been so amazing and steadfast with me, and in return I'd only given him doubts. I'd avoided intimacy with Donovan because another man I'd trusted had taken something from me. Maybe it was time I forgave someone else for the things that had happened—*me*. Like a wise man once told me, moving on didn't have to mean I forgot. I just needed to let go. And looking down at the beautiful man I wanted so badly felt like the first step in the right direction.

I nodded. "I want you, Donovan."

His eyes jumped, looking for reassurance in mine.

"I won't regret it tomorrow, and I won't disappear."

"You sure?"

I nodded.

Yet there was still hesitation in his face. "What's off limits?"

I smiled. "Nothing."

Donovan's blue eyes darkened to almost black. "Nothing? That might be a dangerous edict to give a man who's wanted you for a year now. You might not walk tomorrow."

A shiver ran through me. I relished the thought of being too ravished to get out of bed. But if he thought he was the only one who felt desperate, he was absolutely wrong. I raised a brow. "Or maybe *you* might not be able to walk once I'm done with you."

Donovan's eyes sparkled. "That sounds like a challenge, and I *do not* like to lose."

"Bring it on, Mr. Decker."

He responded by nipping at my navel. Instead of registering as pain, it sent a jolt of electricity straight down between my legs. Donovan yanked my zipper down and tugged off my shorts and panties. He pressed a soft kiss to the top of my pubic bone and looked up at me. "Just for that, you're not going to get to lie there while I make you come."

He sat up on his knees and dragged my body up the couch before flipping onto his back and sliding down into my spot. He guided one of my legs to straddle his chest. "Scooch your ass up, sweetheart. You're riding my face."

My jaw dropped. Donovan reached up and tapped my chin with a cheeky smile. "That's a very generous offer. I'll take you up on it later. Right now, just get your cowgirl hat on."

Before I could fully get my bearings, his fingers were biting into my hips as he lifted me up and guided me onto his face. For a brief second, I felt a little self-conscious, but all that went out the door with one flick of his tongue. My clit was like a lightning rod, and one strike sent electric aftershocks racing through my body. Hunger grew as he traced my opening, teasing me with soft, fluttering licks. He kept a steady pace, building and building, but each time I thought I might fall over the edge, he'd slow, and we'd start the whole cat-and-mouse game over again. After four more go-arounds, each ending with the same result, I grew frustrated and finally started to move my hips.

"There she is," he said. "Ride me, beautiful girl. Ride my face."

Realizing he'd been withholding until I took control, I felt like killing him—but that would have to wait until after. Until then, I'd play his game. Grinding down, I rubbed my wet pussy all over his face and led his tongue to suck exactly where I needed it. That wave built again, faster and more furious, and I moaned as my hips churned shamelessly.

"I'm...I'm...gonna—"

Donovan didn't wait for me to finish the sentence. He latched onto my clit and sucked hard, detonating an explosion inside of me. I heard the muzzled sounds of him groaning as I came undone, my body convulsing so hard that tears stung the corners of my eyes. Long after the wave crested, he still lapped at me like a man who hadn't been fed in days and I was his last meal. I could barely hold my body upright by the time he finally slowed. Sensing my spiral down was about to crash land, he lifted me and guided me to lie on top of him with my head against his chest.

"That was..." I paused and tried to find the right adjective, but *amazing* didn't seem to do justice to what had transpired.

Donovan kissed the top of my head. "The beginning. It was just the beginning."

29

Autumn

Sex without an emotional connection could be physically fulfilling, but truly having feelings for someone brought things to a whole new level—a place I'd forgotten even existed, or maybe I'd never actually ever known.

After Donovan went down on me, we laid on the couch talking for a long time. I traced the outline of one of the smaller, black-and-white tattoos on his arm.

"Is there a reason all your tattoos are black and white?"

He shrugged. "I got the first few that way, and I guess I just haven't felt like any new ones needed to stand out more than the others."

"Does this one have any special meaning?"

It was a small bird closed into a birdcage.

"I got it when I was sixteen. It pretty much summed up the way I was feeling back then. I felt like that bird."

"I didn't realize you could get tattoos that young."

"You can get anything in the old neighborhood. Might not be in a shop that has a license, but a lot of guys tattoo out of their houses."

"Oh."

Donovan smiled and stroked my hair. "Not how it's done in Old Greenwich, Connecticut?"

I chuckled. "Probably not." I rubbed my finger over the lonely little bird. "I think I can relate to this guy, too. Except you felt like you were locked in by your environment. I locked myself in voluntarily the last six years. To be honest, I even struggled with sex. I thought I was broken," I said.

Donovan tilted my chin to look up at him. "What do you mean?"

"I couldn't have an orgasm the way I just did. I only had them during actual sex, and only if I was on top."

Donovan frowned. "You needed to keep control. That's understandable."

"But I don't want that with you. Will you promise me something?"

"Anything."

"Don't treat me like glass."

His brows furrowed. "Is that what you think I just did? Having you ride my face was treating you like you're fragile?"

I smiled. "No, definitely not. But you were hesitant at the beginning, and we had a conversation where you asked what was off limits."

"You'd made some rules, Autumn. I've been tiptoeing around, trying not to break them."

"Exactly—exactly what you just said. Tiptoeing. I don't want you to feel like you need to do that. It took me a while to get here because I was scared, but I'm here now, and I don't want you to hold anything back anymore."

He studied my face. "Are we talking emotionally or sexually?"

"Both."

His thumb caressed my cheek. "So it's okay to tell you I'm head over heels for you? That I think about you all day long, and that my entire life lacked purpose until the day I met you? That you give me a purpose in life, and that's to make you happy?"

I almost couldn't breathe. Donovan flashed a boyish grin. "Too much?"

I shook my head. "No, it's not too much. You just caught me by surprise is all."

He smiled. "Okay."

"And sexually, too. Don't hold back. I mean it. I want the edge you had with me that weekend we were together, before you knew what had happened to me. It's hard for me to admit, but you can be sort of bossy when we fool around, and I actually really love it."

A wicked grin spread across his face. "Oh yeah? You like me bossy in bed?"

I rolled my eyes. "Don't let it go to your head. Lord knows your ego is big enough."

Donovan shifted us on the couch so I was now on my back, and he lay on his side. He helped slip the rest of my clothing off before tracing an imaginary line from my collarbone to my breast, up and over my nipple, and down to my navel before following the same path back up to my mouth. He tapped my bottom lip. "So...no limits, then?"

Our eyes met, and I shook my head.

I watched as the light blue of his eyes darkened again. "So putting you down on your knees with your hair wrapped in my hands and fucking your face? That's okay?"

I swallowed. *Jesus.* I was getting turned on just thinking about it, so I nodded.

"*Nice.*"

His hand again traveled down to my breasts, and he pinched my nipple hard before rubbing between my cleavage. "And sitting on your chest while I slide my cock in and out of here and coming on your neck? That's okay, too?"

I swallowed again, but nodded.

"*Beautiful.*" Donovan's hand dipped down to between my legs. I was already wet, but he ran his fingers up and down, spreading the moisture before gently slipping a finger inside.

I gasped and arched my back.

"Fingers? So no limit on how many inside of you?"

I shut my eyes as he started to move in and out. After a few wet pumps, he added a second finger.

"Two fits nice and snug, but I think at least another one will feel good, maybe even a vibrator sometimes. You do have one of those, don't you, sweetheart?"

I opened my eyes and nodded.

He smiled and sped up the pump of his hand. "Good. I can't wait to use it on you. Maybe when I take you from behind. Is your ass off limits?"

My eyes widened, and Donovan smiled and withdrew his fingers. "Just clarifying if you really mean no limits."

I shook my head. "I've never...done that."

"Opposed to trying?"

"I don't think so."

Donovan leaned forward and brushed his lips with mine before sliding his mouth over to my ear. "I'm in no rush, but I am looking forward to making that mine now that I know it will be your first time." He looked into my eyes with so much intensity. "Anything else we need to discuss?"

My chest was rising and falling so fast. "I don't think so."

He grinned. "Good."

The next thing I knew, he was standing, and he scooped me up off the couch and tossed me over his shoulder.

I giggled. "What are you doing?"

He swatted my bare ass as he headed toward my bedroom. "Taking you to bed so I can have my wicked way with you, now that you just took the cuffs off."

I kicked my feet, but loved every minute of it. "Owww."

"No limits, sweetheart. Get used to a little pain. This ass is going to have many handprints on it."

Inside the bedroom, I expected him to fling me on the bed. But he didn't. Donovan set me down gently, tossed his wallet on the nightstand, and straddled me sitting up as I lay in the center of the bed. We were both smiling so big.

He tugged his shirt over his head and leaned down to press his lips to mine. "I love this smile. It does things to me."

Getting a look at all the ripples on his eight-pack abs, I ran my fingers up and down, over the peaks and valleys of his muscles. "*This* does things to me."

Donovan caught my hand and brought it to his mouth, kissing my palm. The way he looked at me, with so much reverence in his eyes, made me feel warm all over, even though I was completely naked.

He lowered his body on top of me and took my mouth in a kiss while he pushed his pants down his legs. The warmth and hardness of his erection against my stomach made me desperate. God, I wanted him so badly, and my body was wet and aching for him. When our kiss broke, he reached over to the nightstand and pulled a condom out of his wallet, tossing everything else to the floor.

My body tingled with anticipation as I watched him use his teeth to rip open the wrapper. He sheathed himself and settled between my legs once more, looking deep into my eyes as he pushed inside me.

"Fuck," he groaned. "It's heaven in here."

He rocked in and out gently, taking his time to make sure I was ready. Even though I'd touched him before, I'd forgotten just how long and thick he was, and my body needed some gentle encouragement to accept all of him. When he was finally deep inside, his arms shook, and he stilled as he looked into my eyes.

"You're so beautiful."

I felt a rush of emotion. "So are you."

He kissed me softly. But before long, the gentle thrusts turned hard, and the strain became evident in his face. Sweat bathed our skin, and everything except for our wet bodies slapping each other faded into the distance. The sound was utterly erotic, and my body was barreling toward climax. Veins bulged in Donovan's neck as he grinded down, creating friction against my clit, and I lost my battle of self-control.

"Donovan..." I yanked at his hair. "Don't stop..."

He bit down on my shoulder, and my body flew over the edge. Orgasms were normally something I chased, but not today. Today, I struggled to not let it run me over. My muscles pulsated, and my eyes closed while wave after wave of ecstasy wracked through my body.

"Open," he rasped. "I want to watch you."

It was a struggle, but I kept my eyes locked with his. Finally, as the waves started to crest, Donovan quickened his pace, moving toward his own finish until he groaned and buried himself within my body one last time. Even through the condom, I could feel the heat seeping out of him and spilling into me.

Most men I'd been with over the years would roll over onto the bed or get up and go to the bathroom after. And if they didn't, I did. We hadn't made love, and I'd never wanted those intimate moments after, but I craved them with Donovan almost as much as the actual act.

He wiped a sweaty strand of hair from my face. "How big of a wuss would you think I was if I said that felt almost...holy?"

I laughed. "I might think I went to the wrong church growing up."

He brushed his lips with mine. "I wish I didn't have to get up and deal with this condom. I want to stay right where I am...maybe tie you up and keep you underneath me for a few days."

I cupped his cheek. "You don't have to tie me up. I'm not going anywhere this time."

Donovan smiled. "I like the sound of that."

He climbed out of the bed, and I propped myself onto my elbow to watch him walk to the bathroom naked.

"Hey, tight ass," I yelled as he reached the doorway.

He turned around with a grin. "Yes?"

"You might not have to tie me up to keep me anymore, but that doesn't mean I wouldn't enjoy you doing it anyway."

He chuckled and mumbled as he left the room. "You're going to be the death of me. I just know it."

I woke to blinding light shining in my eyes. A ray of sunshine had streaked in from between two wayward blind slats and landed right on my face. I shielded my eyes with my hand and looked over at the end table to the clock.

11:33? Could that be right? I grabbed for my cell to double-check. It had been years since I slept this late. But sure enough, it was indeed almost noon.

I couldn't help the smile that crept onto my lips as I recalled the reasons I'd slept in—the many, many reasons. Donovan and I had had marathon sex. I wasn't even sure how many times we'd done it, but the last time had been with the most gorgeous light. Dawn had just broken, and that yellowish-gold morning sun had streamed in through the blinds like it was doing now. Only then, the streak had landed on Donovan's handsome face while I was on top of him, rocking myself to yet another blissful orgasm. His jaw was peppered with stubble, and his eyes blazed the most incredible blue. The gold from the sun had made them seem almost translucent. But it was his smile that took my breath away. He seemed so truly happy watching me, and it made the moment that much more intimate.

My body ached in the most delicious way right now, and between my legs was swollen. But just thinking about the way he'd looked made my body not care how sore it was. So I rolled over to see how deep of a sleep the sexy man next to me was in, only to find he wasn't sleeping at all. Patting the sheets, my hand met cold. Apparently I was the only one who'd slept in. Tugging the sheet from the bed, I wrapped it around my body and went in search of Donovan.

My apartment was quiet, and he was nowhere to be found, but the smell of coffee wafted through the air. I followed my nose to the kitchen and found a fresh pot of coffee with an orchid sitting next to it. Beneath the plant was a note.

Had to run to the office to pick up a file. When I was eight or nine, I asked Bud about sex. He wouldn't give me any of the gritty details, but he told me the most important part of being with a woman was making sure she was fed the next morning. So there's a yogurt and fruit parfait in the fridge and a buttered bagel on the counter. I wasn't sure what you would be in the mood for. I set the coffee for eleven, taking a guess you'd sleep at least four hours. Be back by noon with lunch.

X
Donovan

P.S. Your place needs more plants, and this one reminded me of you. Most people don't understand orchids and think they're fragile, but they're actually not. The truth is, they're far tougher than anyone realizes, and of course beautiful.

I held the note to my chest like a schoolgirl. Seriously? This man was too good to be real. He was gorgeous and tough on the outside, but inside he was soft and almost vulnerable. I sighed and set the note down to pour myself a much-needed coffee.

A little before twelve, I decided to jump in the shower before Donovan returned. I left the door open to the bathroom, so I could hear if he knocked before I got out. But I was just wrapping myself in a towel when he did.

"Hey," I opened the door.

Donovan's eyes swooped down and back up again. "Damn." He thumbed down the hall and held up a box. "The Amazon delivery guy was just about to knock to deliver this when I told him I'd take it. You would've made that kid's day."

I smiled coyly. "Just the kid's day, not yours?"

He stepped inside and wrapped an arm around my waist, dragging me close to brush his lips with mine. "You made my day a few times before the sun rose."

The way he looked at my lips when he spoke gave me butterflies.

"I think we made each other's day."

Inside my apartment, Donovan set the box down on the kitchen counter. "What time did you finally wake up, sleepyhead?"

"Oh my God. Not until eleven thirty."

"Is that from the Ambien on your nightstand? I didn't see you take one."

I blinked a few times. *Holy shit.* I *hadn't* taken a sleeping pill last night. That was the first time I'd fallen asleep in almost six years without some sort of chemical assistance. "I...I didn't take one."

Donovan grinned. "Does that mean my dick is better than drugs?"

He was of course being cheeky, but he didn't understand how significant not taking anything was for me.

"I haven't slept a single night without a pill in nearly six years, Donovan."

His smile fell away. "Really?"

I nodded.

"Never even after..." He shook his head. "I'm sorry, it might be the Neanderthal in me but I can't finish that sentence. Just the thought of you with another man..."

"No, never. Not once. I keep a bottle in my bag and a bottle at my bedside. A few years back, I was really into running. I did a half marathon and then went to an after party. I was exhausted when I got home and thought it might be the night I could do it. But it's not a physical thing; it's mental. No matter how tired my body is, my brain won't turn off."

"I guess we found the tipping point for flipping that switch. It might be hard to keep up with what we did last night, but I'm game to try. I'll happily replace your pills."

"That's very noble of you, but I don't think it was the exertion as much as something else."

Donovan's brows drew together. "What, then?"

"I felt safe."

I watched as he swallowed what I'd said. *I felt safe.* Something so simple, yet it meant everything to me.

Donovan closed the gap between us and brushed a lock of hair behind my ear. "I want to give you the world, but you just gave it to me by saying that, Red."

30

Donovan

"When do you find out if you make partner at your firm?" Autumn slipped off her shoes and lifted her folded legs up on the seat. "It should be soon, right?"

I looked over my shoulder before changing lanes. "The Tuesday after Labor Day, so a little more than a week."

We were on our way up to Connecticut for the weekend for her father's wedding.

"Do you think you'll get it?"

"Your buddy Dickson has been pretty friendly lately. The client he schlubbed off on me to take to dinner was really happy with the advice I gave him. He even referred a friend of his, which Dickson gave me a half pat on the back for. Although the guy is a dirtbag, and I'm not looking forward to working with him."

"Not to be a jerk, but aren't all your clients dirtbags? I mean, they come to see you because they got caught doing something underhanded and illegal."

She had a point. But I didn't think they all were. I shrugged. "Some really aren't bad people. They just get lost along the way in their climb to the top. Believe it or not, a lot of times these people don't even see what they're doing as wrong at the time they're doing it. I had a new client charged with insider trading last week. He's a trader and found out some non-public information about a company a friend works for. The company was on the verge of getting a new drug approved by the FDA that would make their stock go nuts. His wife told her sister, and her sister mentioned it to her new boyfriend who hedged and bought a shit ton of stock. He made a fortune, but also caught the attention of the regulators who traced it back to my client. Guy shouldn't have told his wife, but he did. Doesn't necessarily make him a bad person."

"Yeah, definitely not in that case. But it's got to be hard to represent some of them."

"It's not always easy. But some people can learn from lessons, especially hard ones. I try to think about it that way. Look at me—I did some pretty dumb shit and was on a path to a bad place. I'd been arrested three times before I was sixteen—mostly minor stuff, but that's how most people in prison started, too. If someone wouldn't have helped me out, I have no doubt that I'd be where a few of my friends are today: serving time."

"You're talking about Bud?"

"He risked a lot for me. The last time I got in any real trouble, the judge wanted to teach me a lesson. Bud put his house up for bail and took out a loan for a lawyer. The one the court appointed was about twenty-three, and I was going to be his first real case."

"Oh wow."

"Bud gambled. We got a lawyer who wore custom-made shirts, and he got me off on a technicality, even though I didn't deserve it. I learned three things from that last arrest: One, I'd gotten lucky, and chances were that wouldn't happen again. Two, Bud believed in me, and it was time I started believing in myself. And three..." I grinned. "I really wanted to wear custom-made shirts."

Autumn laughed. "So that's why you became a lawyer? So you could afford custom shirts?"

I glanced over to her and back to the road. "I should probably say it's because I wanted to help others or fight for justice or some other noble shit. But knowing I'd never have to hit up a soup kitchen or a guy like Bud for a meal? That had a lot to do with it. Plus, like I told you, I'm good at reading people and arguing, and that's half the battle in my job."

"Oh, that's right," she teased. "I forgot you think you're so good at knowing what people are thinking."

"I don't think I'm good at it; I know I am."

Autumn grinned and shut her eyes. "What am I thinking right now?"

I chuckled. "We've had this discussion. There's a difference between reading people and being a mind reader. I can't study your face while I'm driving."

Autumn bit down on her bottom lip. "You could pull over..."

Now *that* tone I could read. We were only about a half hour from the hotel we were staying at, but who the hell cared?

I caught her eye for a second and put my blinker on to get off at the upcoming exit. After pulling into the empty parking lot of a construction site, I made sure to park away from the streetlights before cutting the engine and turning to face Autumn.

She hadn't said a word, and it made me wonder if she'd been teasing, and I'd taken it too far by getting off the road. Though the wicked smile on her face when she'd spoken had me hopeful.

Autumn lifted to her knees on the seat and turned her entire body to face me. "Is this better?" She tilted her head. "Are you able to read what I'm thinking now?"

I glanced down. Her nipples were practically piercing through her shirt. "You're thinking about sitting on my lap and riding me..."

She scanned the quiet parking lot and reached for the button of my pants. With a quick flick, she popped it open. "Wrong, counselor. I was actually not thinking about riding you."

Well, that was a damn shame, because my cock was already pretty hard. But I played along. "Your nipples have my mouth salivating, and the dirty look on your face says you're gearing up for something."

She pulled the zipper of my pants down slowly. The sound of the teeth separating was better foreplay than any porn I'd ever watched.

Autumn looked up at me from under her thick lashes, her eyes glinting devilishly. "Oh I'm gearing up for something alright." She ran her tongue along her top lip. "I want to suck your *cock*."

"Jesus Christ, Red." My head fell back, hitting against the headrest. "Say that again..."

She leaned over to my side, her nose touching my ear, and whispered in the sexiest damn voice. "I want to suck your cock."

I groaned. "That is the sexiest thing I've ever heard."

She bit down on my earlobe. "I want you to show me how you like it. Wrap your fingers in my hair and show me."

I was panting like a dog, and she hadn't even touched me yet. "This is going to be embarrassing. I'm so fucking turned on already."

"Slide your pants down for me?" she whispered.

I shimmied those fuckers to the floor in two seconds flat.

Autumn bent her head and licked the moisture that had already formed at the tip of my dick. I'd thought she was going to torture me for a little while with more teasing, but she surprised the shit out of me when she opened her jaw wide and took almost my entire cock down her throat.

"Jesus Christ." I bucked, and my ass lifted from the seat as she sucked the length of me back almost to the tip. My cock basically had a mind of its own and followed her. She stilled at the tip, so I dug my hands into her hair and pushed her back down. Autumn moaned. *Fuck, yeah.* So I pulled her back up and pushed her down a second time. Again she moaned.

Fuck me. I wasn't going to make it more than another minute. I shut my eyes and rested my head against the seat as I pulled her hair again, guiding her head back up. My cock was soaked with her saliva, and the slurping sound she made as she bobbed up and down drove me wild. I couldn't get enough, and suddenly I couldn't get it fast enough. My grip on her hair tightened to a fist, and I sped up the motion—pushing her down and then tugging her back, pushing her down and...*oh, the gurgling sound* she made when I pushed her a little farther.

Best. Damn. Sound. In. The. World.

That was it. I was done. My orgasm was barreling like a runaway freight train, so I loosened my grip on her hair. "Autumn...babe...I'm gonna come."

She kept going, keeping the pace I'd set even though I wasn't guiding her anymore.

"Autumn...you got five seconds..." I groaned, trying to hold back so she could move before I shot my load. But she did just the opposite. She sucked me even deeper, until I felt myself hit the back of her throat. There was no holding back then.

"Fuck..." My body convulsed as I let out a long stream of cum. "Fuck...fuck...*fuuuuuuuck,*" I groaned.

I panted like I'd been sprinting, trying to catch my breath. Autumn just kept gliding up and down as I sat there with my skull lolling against the headrest. Eventually, after a minute or two, she wiped her mouth with the back of her hand and sat up.

"That was..." I shook my head. "I think you might have to drive the rest of the way. I can't see straight."

She giggled.

"And here I thought this was going to be a tense weekend going to your dad's wedding."

"Oh, trust me. It will be. I'm going to be uptight and ruin your weekend. That was just my way of saying thank you for coming." She smiled. "I guess that sort of has two meanings right now."

"I'm happy to come...anytime, anywhere, with you. And I definitely mean that in two ways." I took her hand, threaded it with mine, and brought her knuckles to my lips for a kiss. "I'll do my best to make sure you have a good weekend."

We smiled at each other, and I meant what I'd said. I wanted to help her stay relaxed and enjoy the time in Connecticut. Of course, I had no idea it wouldn't be her ruining the weekend...it would be me.

"Shit. I forgot to pack dress socks."

The next morning, I'd gone into my bag to grab my running gear and realized I'd only packed white socks to wear with my sneakers. Autumn and I had woken up early, had sex, and ordered room service. After, I'd asked her if she wanted to come out for a run, but she seemed content to stay in bed for the few hours we had before we needed to get ready for her father's wedding.

"We're only about a block off the main shopping strip. I can walk over while you go for your run and pick some up." She sat up in bed, and the sheet slipped down, giving me a beautiful view of her perfect tits. I guess my eyes lingered a little longer than I thought.

"We just had sex an hour or two ago, and yet you're looking at me like I'm your lunch." She smiled and lifted the sheet to cover herself.

I walked over and sat on the edge of the bed next to her. Tugging the sheet back down, I said, "I absolutely would like to eat you for lunch."

She blushed.

"My heart's not really into a run, anyway. Why don't we walk over to get the socks together when you feel like getting up, and we'll get another coffee, too. When we get back, I'll do some pushups for exercise...with you beneath me."

She grinned. "That sounds good. Although you sweaty from a run also sounds pretty yummy."

"I'll tell you what, I'll run around the hotel when we get back, just enough to get sweaty before I hit the pushups."

She laughed, though I wasn't really kidding. If she liked me sweaty, sweaty I'd be.

A little while later, we were walking down Greenwich Avenue. A woman turned the corner and walked straight into Autumn. She stumbled, but I had her hand so I was able to stop her from falling.

"I'm so sorry!" The woman held her hands up. "I wasn't paying any attention to where I was going. Are you okay?"

"Yeah, I'm fine."

The woman squinted. "Autumn? Autumn Wilde?"

Autumn's brows dipped. "I'm sorry. Do we know each other?"

"I'm Cara Fritz. We used to be good friends when we were kids. We were in Mr. Fleming's fourth-grade class together."

Autumn cocked her head, and then a look of recognition washed over her face. "Oh my gosh. Of course! How could I not recognize you...Cara Fritz. God, it's been a long time."

Cara looked over at me. "My parents got divorced in sixth grade. I moved to the next town over, and that meant a new school, so Autumn and I eventually lost touch. Four miles might as well be four hundred when you're that age."

Autumn nodded. "That's very true. It's really nice to see you, though." She put her hand on my forearm. "I'm sorry. I'm being rude. This is my...boyfriend, Donovan."

Cara nodded. "Nice to meet you, Donovan." She smiled at Autumn. "So do you still live here in Greenwich?"

"No, actually, I'm just in town for a wedding. I live in Manhattan now."

"Oh, a wedding!" Her face lit up, and she held out her hand and wiggled her fingers, displaying a sparkly ring. "That's why I wasn't paying attention to where I was going. I just got engaged last night, and I can't stop staring at my hand."

"Oh, wow. Congratulations."

"You know, I still live over in Rock Ridge, but my boyfriend..." She smiled. "I mean my *fiancé*, lives here in Greenwich. He's somewhere parking the car because it's so impossible to find a spot here on the Avenue. But he was born and raised here. You might know each other. You two went to the same high school, though he was a few years older than us."

"Maybe," Autumn said. "What's his name?"

Just then a guy who looked like he definitely belonged in Greenwich walked across the street and headed toward us. He wore khaki shorts, a long-sleeve button up, and had a pink sweater tied around his shoulders.

"Oh, here he is now," Cara said. She gazed at the douchey-looking guy like he was some sort of celebrity and snuggled onto his arm. "Honey, do you know Autumn Wilde? You guys went to the same high school."

Mr. Pink Sweater smiled. If I wasn't mistaken, that glowing white mouth definitely had a few extra teeth.

"I do. Hello, Autumn. It's great to see you."

I waited a few seconds, but Autumn didn't respond. So I turned to check on her, and it looked like she was about to pass out. All the color was gone from her face. I grabbed her. "Autumn? Are you okay?"

Her entire body was shaking. Was she having a seizure?

"Oh my gosh." Cara's face fell. "I'm a nurse. Does she have low blood sugar or something?"

I had no idea what the hell was happening. "I don't think so." I squeezed her arm, but Autumn just stared forward. "*Autumn*, are you okay?"

When she didn't answer, but also didn't pass out or anything, a sickening feeling washed over me. I followed her line of sight to Mr. Pink Sweater. Unlike his fiancée, he didn't look concerned at all. In fact, he still had that big, toothy smile on his face. *What the fuck?* He actually looked pretty fucking pleased about Autumn not feeling well.

Then it hit me, like driving a motorcycle a hundred miles an hour straight into a brick wall. The hair on the back of my neck stood up, and I knew. *I just fucking knew.*

"Your name?" I lifted my chin, still holding Autumn. "What the hell is *your name*?"

The guy's face finally fell. I'm guessing it might've been because he saw the murderous look on mine. He also didn't answer my question.

Cara looked back and forth between her fiancé and me a few times. She looked as confused as I'd been a minute ago. "What's going on?"

The standoff between us continued while he ignored her. It felt like smoke was billowing from my nose and ears.

Cara grew louder. "*Braden*, what's going on?"

31

Donovan

I held my head in my hands, pulling at the hair on both sides, as I kept replaying yesterday over and over in my head. Eventually, I stood and walked to the cell door. Hanging on to the bars, I yelled to the cop sitting at his desk twenty feet away. "Can I make another phone call, please?"

The cop kept looking down at his paperwork and completely ignored me.

"I get three phone calls. I only used two."

He sighed, and his pen stopped writing, but he still didn't look up. "We know you know your rights, counselor. You don't need to flex. You think you're special because you're a lawyer—you all think you're special. But today, you're not a lawyer, you're a perp. I'll get to it when I get to it."

I paced back and forth in the holding cell. I'd called Autumn twice since everything went down. Both times it went straight to voicemail. Arraignment was going to be in the next few hours, so if I called her and she didn't answer again, there was a good chance no one would be there for my hearing, and I wouldn't be able to make whatever bail they set. At this point, I should probably call Trent or Juliette—someone who could at least maneuver through the system from the outside. But I'd rather sit in lockup for another day than not try to reach Autumn. I needed to apologize... I needed to see if she was okay.

I paced for another twenty minutes before the cop finally walked over and unlocked the cell. He held his hand out for me to exit, and we walked to his desk again.

"Number?"

I rattled off Autumn's cell, and he handed me the receiver.

It rang once.

Come on. Come on...not voicemail again.

I was relieved when it didn't go directly to a recording after the first ring like it had last night.

It rang a second time.

Pick up, Autumn. Pick up.

Nothing. My heart raced as the third ring came.

Fuck. Fuck. Fuck.

Mid-fourth ring, it cut to the same voicemail. I closed my eyes as I listened to her voice and then cleared my throat.

"Autumn...I'm so sorry. I just need to know you're okay. If you don't want to talk to me, that's fine. Please just answer so I know you're okay."

The cop held his hand out and put the old phone receiver back on its base.

"If you're calling the redhead," he said, "she was physically fine. Said she just fell on her ass when you and the victim were tussling. My partner took her statement at the scene after we put you in the squad car."

"He's not a fucking *victim*. He's a rapist."

"Maybe so. But he's got a fractured eye socket, broken nose, and a concussion. So today he's the victim. And he's *your* victim. If what you claim is true, you should know better than anyone that taking things into your hands isn't the right way to go."

I looked at the cop's finger. He had a wedding band on. So I looked straight into his eyes. "Is that how you'd handle it if you stumbled onto the guy who raped your wife and got away with it?"

The cop's face softened. "We leave for arraignment in an hour. You look like shit. I'll take you to the men's room and let you wash up."

Two hours later, I was sitting in the private hall on the side of the courtroom, the place they parked the criminals waiting for their names to be called. I'd denied court-appointed counsel in favor of representing myself at the hearing.

"Decker!"

I stood. The minute I stepped through the courtroom door, I scanned for Autumn. I found her sitting in the first row, with a very angry-looking man beside her.

She brought her father.

Fuck.

Her dad stepped forward to the small wooden door that separated the players from the spectators. "Gerald Wilde for the defendant, your honor."

My first reaction was to say *thanks, but no thanks.* This was my field, and I knew how to play the game better than most. But I hesitated because it was her father. And I was glad I had once the judge spoke again.

"Gerry...shouldn't you be on your honeymoon?"

Her father's eyes flashed to me before looking at the judge. "Had to push it back a day."

I glanced back at Autumn a few times. She finally made eye contact, but quickly looked away.

The hearing was pretty standard, and Autumn's father did a good job. Bail was set at ten grand, which wasn't a problem. After the judge banged his gavel, Autumn's father grumbled at me. "I'm not putting up your bail. I'm assuming you can cover it?"

"Yes, sir. Could I trouble you to make a call to someone at my firm who can handle it from here?"

He closed his briefcase and lifted it. "I don't think that's necessary. Someone from your firm is already here."

"They are?"

"Apparently one of the court officers in this building used to be a paralegal in your office. She saw your name on the docket and made a call for you. If I'd have known, I wouldn't have had to postpone leaving for my honeymoon."

"I'm sorry about that, sir." I shook my head. "I'm sorry about the mess I caused on your wedding day. I just...I lost it seeing that guy even look at Autumn after what he did."

Autumn's father bowed his head. He put one hand on my shoulder and patted it twice. "Good luck."

As the court officer led me out of the courtroom, I glanced around to see if Trent or Juliette was inside. I'd been so focused on Autumn, I hadn't even noticed if anyone else was here.

But sure enough, someone was. Someone from my firm, alright.

Icy daggers shot at me from the last row in the courtroom. I shut my eyes and blew out a jagged breath.

Just when I thought the last twenty-four hours couldn't get any worse.

God, was I wrong.

Because Blake Dickson was currently glaring at me.

It took until late afternoon to get processed out. After I collected my personal belongings from the cashier and signed the bail paperwork, I walked out onto the courtroom steps and took a deep breath. My phone must've cracked during the altercation, and I wasn't sure if it was dead from not being charged or just dead altogether. I'd hoped Autumn would be waiting for me, but there was no sign of her. Though leaning against one of the tall pillars nearby, someone was definitely waiting to speak to me.

Shit.

Dickson.

I took a deep breath and walked over. He'd clearly been stewing since this morning, and it was best to get it over with.

"Hey. Sorry about everything," I said.

Dickson's face was steely. "Define *everything*. Would you be referring to getting arrested for assault, making me drag my ass out of bed bright and early on a Sunday to come bail you out, or fucking a client who not too long ago was my girlfriend?"

I shut my eyes and shook my head. "It's not what it looks like."

"No? So you're not fucking a client?"

"Technically Autumn isn't a client. Storm is."

I knew the minute the words left my mouth it was the absolute *wrong* thing to say, even if it was the truth.

Dickson's eyes narrowed. "When I asked you to make sure you took good care of the client, I didn't think I needed to explain that didn't include sticking your dick in her."

I raked a hand through my hair. "It's not that simple. Autumn and I have a history. When you assigned me to help Storm, I had no idea she would be there. We hadn't seen each other in a long time. There were a lot of unresolved feelings."

Dickson stared at me for a solid minute in silence before pushing off the pillar he'd been resting against. "And to think I was actually leaning toward voting for you."

He shook his head and started down the courthouse steps. Halfway, he turned. "Your arrest is something the partners need to be aware of, as it has an effect on the firm. It's my responsibility to inform them, regardless of the personal breach of trust."

"I understand."

With only the look of disgust for a goodbye, he turned back around and kept walking. I stayed rooted in the same spot until he left, the weight of everything suddenly sinking in. My career, my license, my freedom, a probable civil lawsuit... I'd really fucked up this time. But the worst was what was missing as I stood here alone on the steps: *Autumn.*

"Hi. I was in room fifteen-ten. We checked in on Friday and were due to check out today. But something came up, and since it's past checkout time, my key isn't working. Would you happen to know if the other guest who was with me already left?"

The woman punched a few keys into the computer and smiled. "Mr. Decker?"

"That's me."

"It says there's something in the back the other guest left for you. Hang on a second, and I'll grab it."

She came back wheeling my luggage, with an envelope in her hand. "Can I just see some ID, please?"

"Of course." I dug my license out of my wallet and showed it to her before she brought my luggage out from behind the counter. The woman offered me the envelope. "Here you go. Anything else I can do for you?"

"I don't think so. Thank you very much."

I only made it a few steps from the counter before I ripped the envelope open. Inside was a note in Autumn's handwriting.

Donovan,

I'm sorry about everything that happened. I promised I wouldn't run away without saying anything ever again, but I need some time and space. I hope you understand.

—Autumn

32

Donovan

The entire office was buzzing when I walked in on Monday morning. No one said anything to me, but voices quieted as I passed, and there was a sort of awkwardness to the smiles and greetings I received. So I assumed Dickson had opened his mouth to more than just the partners. I wasn't surprised. To him, it wasn't just a professional blow. It was personal, and I couldn't say I blamed him.

Trent and Juliette marched into my office two minutes after I did, both carrying legal pads. They shut the door behind them.

I sighed and sat down behind my desk. "I take it you already heard."

"What the fuck, man?" Trent shook his head as he took a seat in a guest chair.

"I *knew* this was going to blow up in your face." Juliette frowned.

"How much do you know?"

"Dickson told his assistant you got picked up for felony

assault and were also screwing a client. He also insinuated
that you have a drug and alcohol problem."

"Great." I shook my head. Dickson's assistant has
a giant mouth. She was like the pipeline to all gossip. I
rubbed my temples. "I guess the good news is I don't have
a drinking or drug problem. I was perfectly sober when I
beat the crap out of the guy."

"Who the hell was he?"

I slumped into my chair. "It's a long story, and not
mine to tell." I held Trent's eyes. "Just trust me when I say
he's had it coming for a long time, and he deserved every
bit of it. He hurt Autumn, and I'm not talking about her
feelings."

Trent nodded. "Okay. Okay. So where do we go from
here? I'm licensed in Connecticut. Did you use a court-
appointed attorney at arraignment or represent yourself?"

"Neither. Autumn's father came. He's an attorney in
Connecticut. I think it actually may have helped me. He
was friendly with the judge."

"Does he do criminal?"

I shook my head. "Estate planning, I think. He owns
a decent-size firm. I'm sure they have a criminal section."

"You want them involved?"

"Definitely not."

"Alright. Well, I'll file a notice of change of counsel
today to get on record that I'll be your attorney."

"I appreciate the offer, but I can handle it."

Trent frowned. "The assault is related to something
that went down between the guy and Autumn, correct?"

I nodded.

"Was this incident the first time you came in contact
with the guy?"

"Yeah."

"Did he say or do anything to provoke you?"

"He smiled."

Trent shook his head. "You beat the crap out of a guy for smiling. You don't think maybe it's not a good idea to represent yourself? Do I really need to remind you of the old adage? 'A lawyer who represents himself in a criminal trial has a fool for a client.' What are you going to do when the guy smiles at you from across the aisle in the courtroom? Even if you manage not to lunge over to his table, how good will your decisions be when they're all emotional?"

I raked a hand through my hair and blew out a big breath. "Alright...yeah, you're right. But you don't do criminal."

"It's okay. You'll teach me. There's no better criminal attorney than you. You just need a mouthpiece with a calm demeanor to deliver your case."

I nodded. "Okay. Thank you."

Juliette had been quiet until now. "Are you and Autumn okay?"

My chest tightened. The legal and criminal implications of what I'd done didn't worry me half as much as what I might've done to my relationship with Autumn. She had some major trust issues, not to mention she hated violence, and I'd showed her firsthand that you can take the boy out of the rough neighborhood, but you can't take the rough neighborhood out of the boy.

I shook my head. "I haven't talked to her since Saturday. She was at my arraignment with her father and posted a bond for my bail, but she left town before I got released and asked me to give her some time and space. I figured I'd call her tonight."

Juliette winced.

I sighed. "I know. I definitely know. I've told women I needed a little space on more than one occasion. You know what I really meant? 'You're a little too fragile to dump all in one fell swoop, so we're going to do this with baby steps.' Trust me, I get that it's not good."

"Maybe it's not so bad," she said after a moment. "I obviously don't know the details, but I know you had a damn good reason for what you did. She knows the man you are and probably just needs a little time to work through some things."

I hoped Juliette was right, but I had a sickening feeling in the pit of my gut. Autumn's biggest struggle in getting over what happened to her was coming to terms with not having seen who Braden was before he attacked her. Now she might be feeling the same way about me— and doubting herself all over again.

Voicemail. Again.

I hadn't left a message the two other times I'd tried today, not wanting to leave the ball in her court. But the message was coming through loud and clear now, and if Autumn wasn't going to pick up the phone to listen to me, I'd have to hope she at least listened to my voicemail.

I tried to get my thoughts in order as I listened to the short recording, but it wasn't easy.

"Hey," I began. "I know you asked me for some space, but I just want to make sure you're doing okay." I paused, looking for the right words, but there weren't any. So I spoke from my heart. "I know what I did was wrong. I messed up, and I let you down. When I was a kid, Bud used to always tell me a moment of patience when you're angry can save years of regret." I dug my fingers into my hair and yanked. "I just... He *smiled* at you. He doesn't deserve to breathe the same air you breathe, and I lost it.

I'm sorry, Autumn. I'm so very sorry. I know how you feel about violence, and I don't know how to show you that the person you saw that day isn't me. I would never hurt you."

I squeezed my eyes shut to keep the tears back and shook my head. "*Fuck*. I'm in love with you, Autumn. This is not the way I wanted to tell you, but it's the truth, and I need you to know it. You might feel like it's too soon, but I think I have been from the moment you walked into the coffee shop last year." I blew out a deep breath. "Anyway. I get that you need some time. Please call me when you feel up to it."

I swiped my phone to off and sat at my desk. It was nine o'clock at night, and a few people were still milling around the office, but I didn't give a fuck. I cried like a baby.

33
Autumn

Just a week ago, I felt like a butterfly that had spent years inside some sort of cocoon. I'd been so afraid to venture out into the world on my own. But I flapped my wings a few times, and once I started to fly, the isolated darkness I'd been in for so long seemed more like a punishment than a place of protection. Now I desperately wanted to crawl back into that cocoon, yet it seemed I could no longer fit.

Over the last few days, I'd kept replaying this silly little moment Donovan and I had shared. We were at the hotel the night before my dad's wedding. Because even crossing the state line from New York into Connecticut made me feel tense, I'd decided to take a hot shower. After, I'd sat at the desk diagonally across from the bed where Donovan was watching some baseball game on TV.

I'd been lost in my head, thinking about how long it had been since I'd been to my dad's house, while drying the back of my hair. At one point, my eyes caught Donovan's in the mirror. He smiled, apparently no longer watching the game, so I turned off the drier and asked what he was looking at. He'd shrugged and said he was just enjoying watching me. I went back to doing what I was doing—which was a pain in the ass since my hair had gotten pretty long. Donovan walked over and took the dryer and my brush from my hands. He looked completely out of his element, almost as if he didn't even know how to angle the dryer with one hand and work the hairbrush with the other. But he stood there—still wearing a custom-made dress shirt from work that day, one that covered all of his badass tattoos—for ten minutes and finished drying the back of my hair.

And that's when I knew. I knew that no matter how hard I tried, no matter how hard I fought it, I couldn't stop myself from falling for him. And that's why today, after spending days curled in a ball on my bed, I got up, looked up the address of a certain lawyer whose name I never thought I'd type into Google, and took the train to Hartford.

"Hi, I'm here to see..." I took a deep breath. "Braden Erlich."

The receptionist smiled. "Of course." She hit a few keys and then looked up. "Hmmm... I don't have an appointment down for Mr. Erlich this afternoon. He must've forgotten to put it in the master calendar."

"Actually, I don't have an appointment."

"Oh."

"But we have some business that needs to be finalized. Could you just let him know I'm here?"

"Sure. What's your name, please?"

"Autumn Wilde."

I watched her face as she called back to Braden. "Hi. I have Autumn Wilde here to see you. She's not on the calendar but said—"

The man on the other end had clearly cut her off. She listened before covering the phone and whispering, "Did I get your name right?"

I smiled. "You did."

She uncovered the phone. "Yes, the name is definitely Autumn Wilde."

The receptionist looked confused as she set down the phone. "Umm... He must be on the other line or something. I'm sure he'll call back when he's off."

No sooner than she'd finished speaking, Braden came marching down the hall behind her. He had two black eyes, a bandaged nose, and one eye was swollen shut even though almost a week had passed. His face was hard as he stared at me, and I thought I might throw up. He walked directly around the reception desk and took my elbow.

I yanked it away and hissed, "Don't touch me."

Braden's eyes jumped to the receptionist and back to me, and he held up his hands. "What do you want?"

"To speak to you."

His jaw flexed. "Not here. Come into my office."

"That is usually how it works," I murmured.

Somehow I managed to put one foot in front of the other as I made my way into the inner sanctum of his fancy law office. When we arrived at his door, he extended a hand for me to enter first. I did, but stopped in front of him.

"The door stays open."

"I would prefer privacy."

"And I would prefer not to have to take drugs at night in order to sleep because I'm afraid an animal might come into my apartment and rape me. I guess neither one of us gets our preference, huh?"

Braden rubbed his face with his hand as he stared at me. "Fine. Keep your voice down."

I took a seat on the opposite side of his desk. My hands shook, so I gripped the arms of the chairs with all my might so he wouldn't see it.

He folded his arms across his chest. "If you're here to try to get me to drop the charges against your hoodlum boyfriend, you wasted a trip."

When I'd thought about coming here, I thought it would be difficult to look at Braden, but in the moment, it was just the opposite. Maybe it was that he was beaten and bruised, but staring at him made me feel stronger, not like the cowering weakling I'd thought it would. My heart still ricocheted inside my chest, my skin was clammy, and my posture was most definitely rigid, but I thought there might be some exhilaration mixed in with my terror.

I tilted my head. "Do you think about what you did to me?"

He flinched, but tried to hide it. "Nice try. Are you wearing a wire or attempting to record me on your phone?"

I held eye contact as I lifted my purse, dug out my phone, and placed it on the desk. I swiped it on and turned the cell to face him as I pressed the button to power it down. He said nothing, but still didn't look convinced. So I stood and held out my arms.

After a minute-long stare-off he motioned to my seat. "What do you want, Autumn?"

"I want answers."

He looked back and forth between my eyes. "To what?"

"You've moved on. I want to know how."

He flashed a maniacal smile. "Did you think I'd stay celibate after we broke up?"

I shook my head. "No, but I want to know how you sleep at night knowing you raped me."

His eyes jumped to the door behind me. "Lower your voice."

"Or what?" I smiled sardonically. "*Oh*...of course. No one here knows what you were accused of—what you *did*.

If they knew, they'd look at you a little differently. Most of them would say they didn't believe it. But in the back of their minds...there would always be just..." I held my thumb and forefinger up, displaying a quarter inch of space. "*That much*—that much doubt that you might've done it. Even the people who like you would never feel the same way about you. I bet a few of the ladies would make sure they were never the last ones alone in the office with you at night, too."

Braden's jaw flexed. "Cut to the chase, Autumn. I'm not an idiot, so I'm not answering any of your questions. If that's all you came to do..." He motioned a circle with his hand. "Don't let the door hit you in the ass on the way out."

"I didn't expect you would answer my questions, and honestly, I'm not sure there's anything you could say that has any value to me. But you *are* going to listen to what I have to say." I took a deep breath.

"For a year after you raped me, I used to watch old videos of us together. I spent countless hours studying them—watching the way you looked at me, watching your eyes to see what I'd missed. I mean, the devil doesn't just come out of someone one day. He seeps into your soul and little by little sucks the good out of you. It's like a cancer left untreated. It festers and grows and takes all the good from your body until you're a rundown shell of who you once were. So I didn't understand how I hadn't seen it happening." I tapped my chest. "I *couldn't* accept that I'd spent four years with a person who was capable of doing such a heinous thing all along. So it had to be that *I* missed something. The alternative was so much worse. If I didn't see it in you, how would I see it in someone else? That meant no one could be trusted."

I paused and shook my head. "Did you know that when you're looking for something, you always look from left to right? You never start scanning a room on the right side. And when another man comes near you, even a guy passing by who isn't paying you one bit of attention, you square your shoulders. You should've been a peacock, at least you'd have pretty feathers to show off. Oh, and when you're having a drink? You always hold it up to examine how much is left before you take the next sip. We spent four years together, and I never noticed any of that. But watch a few videos—*oh, I don't know*, ten, maybe twenty-thousand times—and you notice things."

I picked imaginary lint from my pants. "Do you know how hard it is to see the face of the man who raped you on video over and over again? Especially when he's laughing and having a good time in them, and you realize he's probably laughing and having a good time right now, too. While I, I'd just thrown up my dinner...again."

I took another deep breath and studied Braden's face. What I saw made me smile. I was certain the smile came off as insane, but I didn't give a shit.

I tapped the skin at the corner of my left eye. "You just twitched. It was very slight, because I assume you've gotten better at hiding your tells over the years, but I saw it. I forgot to mention that while studying those videos, I also learned that you felt extremely threatened by my father and your own father." I pointed to the corner of his eye. "It's a little hard to see today, surrounded by all that black and blue and bruising, but it was there. You're feeling threatened right now."

Braden spoke through gritted teeth. "Don't flatter yourself. The muscle in my eye is probably damaged, which causes involuntary twitching. I'll make sure to note that in my civil suit against the thug you're dating—*after* I make sure he's locked up."

"Sure, that's it." I smiled and looked at my nails. "Anyway, I just wanted to let you know a few things more.

First, you ruined my life for six years. I blamed myself for not seeing things in you, and because of that I kept my distance from anyone I might've had a real connection with. I was afraid having feelings again would make me blind to seeing the truth about a person, like it did with you. I trusted you. Even when I knew you were following me and lying about it, I still trusted you enough to open the door to my home and let you in that night to talk. I *felt bad* for hurting you, even though I'd done nothing wrong in our relationship. When you refused to stop, it did more than break my trust in you. It broke my trust in all men—hell, it broke my trust in humanity. *You were my first, Braden.* My first serious boyfriend, my first sexual experience, my first everything. Firsts are where we learn things for our second and third. And I learned things no woman should ever have to learn. *You ruined my life.*"

I'd been on an adrenaline high since I walked in, but now I felt the inevitable crash starting to take root. So I knew it was time to go. Standing, I smoothed out my pants and looked up at the face that haunted my dreams for so many years. It was fitting that it was beaten and bruised.

"Goodbye, Braden."

I made it almost to the door when he yelled after me. "That's it? You're not even going to beg for leniency for your boyfriend?"

I turned back. "I begged you to stop once, so I already know how that goes. I'll save my breath to pray for the other survivors. Because I'm sure I'm not the only one you did this to."

The corner of his eye twitched, and his jaw tightened.

"I thought so," I said. "Rot in hell, rapist."

34

Donovan

Ten days had passed since I last saw Autumn. She'd texted once and said she was okay but needed to work through some things by herself. But it was quickly becoming clear that one of the things she needed to work through was *me*.

It was the Tuesday after Labor Day—the day I'd been looking forward to for months, and now dreaded.

"You coming?" Trent poked his head in my office door.

"Do I have to?"

He smiled sadly. "Nope. But if you're ever going to make it through this, you need to start holding your head up high and taking your lumps."

I sighed and tossed my pen onto my desk. "Fine."

We rode the elevator together up to the executive floor. The "announcement" of the names of the new partners was always done in the conference room before popping the champagne. But the people about to be named had been informed before Labor Day, because they had to write a big fat check to formally buy into the partnership. Needless to say, my phone hadn't rung over the weekend.

Trent punched my arm as the elevator halted. "Chin up, buddy."

I shoved my hands in my pockets. "Sure thing."

The fourteenth floor conference room was crammed with people, so we had to stand out in the hall, which I was relieved about. Juliette was packed in near the door, along with the other sardines. When she saw us, she squeezed her way out to us. She took one look at my face and frowned.

"You still haven't heard from her?"

I shook my head. It was pretty funny that we were standing and waiting for the announcement that someone other than me had made partner, and Juliette knew that wasn't the reason for my long face.

She rubbed my arm. "She'll come around."

I could tell from Juliette's face that she didn't even believe what she was saying. But she was a good friend, and I didn't have the energy to argue anyway.

"Thanks."

For the next twenty minutes, I stood while they announced the names of the new partners. I kept my eyes straight ahead, even though I felt others watching to see how I'd react. When it was finally over and the first bottles of champagne had been opened, I leaned over to Trent. "I'm gonna get out of here."

He slapped my shoulder. "Yeah, of course. You did what you had to do. No reason to prolong the torture. Order dinner at seven?"

I shook my head. "Actually, I'm just going to call it a day." I smiled halfheartedly. "One of the benefits of derailing from the partner track—doesn't matter if I put in fourteen hours every day."

Trent nodded. "Take it easy, buddy."

Outside on the street, I took a deep breath and loosened my tie. The air had been stifling up there, but I knew if I went home at this early hour, I'd wind up drinking to numb my thoughts. So I decided to head over to Bud's house. I'd spoken to him a few times, but hadn't been to see him since the weekend in Connecticut.

I found him in the garage with a three-foot ruler hanging out of his cast and a saw next to him on the table.

"What the hell are you doing?"

"Got this goddamn thing stuck. I need to saw it off because I keep whacking shit as I walk."

I chuckled and walked over to examine what the heck was going on. "Why is it in there to begin with?"

"I had an itch. I'm sweating in this thing, and it's making my skin itchy as hell."

"Did you try pulling it out?"

"Oh, that's a great idea. Wish I would've thought of it." He rolled his eyes. "Whatta you think, I'm a dumbass? Of course I tried to pull it out—it's stuck."

"Let me give it a try before we saw it off."

It took about ten minutes and some olive oil for lube, but I got the thing out.

Bud shook his arm. "Don't know that I'll be able to make the eight weeks they want me to keep this thing on."

"Take it day by day, and do the best you can."

Bud smirked. "I believe that was my line to you for half your life."

I nodded. "True."

We went into the house, and Bud pointed to the watering can he'd had since I was a kid. "Help me do the inside ones, will ya? If I use my other hand, I spill half the water on the floor. If I use the hand with the cast, it drips down my arm and makes me itchy."

"Why don't you sit down and relax. I'll hit them all."

Bud pulled out a stool on the other side of the counter while I filled the can. "Anything new on the charges in Connecticut?"

I shook my head. "Nah. We filed some paperwork and requested a conference. But I don't expect to hear anything for a few weeks at least."

He nodded. "Things with Autumn smooth over?"

I frowned. "She doesn't even want to talk to me."

My eyes caught with Bud's before I started to water his million houseplants. He was quiet for a while, which didn't surprise me. Bud wasn't a man who talked for the sake of filling silence.

"I bet she's hurting."

As if I didn't feel enough like shit. "Of course she's hurting. And that's my fault."

"Maybe." He shrugged. "But let me ask you something. Don't you think she'd probably be hurting just running into the guy? Even if you hadn't swung?"

"Yeah. You should've seen the way she looked when he walked up—like she'd seen a ghost. What happened might've been six years ago, but it was two seconds ago in that moment."

"Okay...so let's say you'd handled things differently. She'd probably still be a bit on edge for a while. What would you do about that?"

"What do you mean, what would I do about it? I'd talk to her, listen to whatever she wanted to get out. I wouldn't fucking leave her side, if that made her feel better."

"Okay... And yet you're here and not at her place tonight."

I finished watering a fern that was probably as old as I was and set the can down. "She doesn't believe violence is ever justified. She doesn't want to talk to me."

"And what do you believe?"

"I believe the guy deserves a hell of a lot worse than I gave him. But that's beside the point. It wasn't my choice to make. I made a mistake."

Bud smiled. "Damn. Why couldn't it be this easy to get you to admit stuff when you were a teenager?"

I sighed. "I thought I'd grown past this shit. I really did."

"I'm not so sure I would've done anything different in your shoes, son. This isn't a case of you getting into a fight over the dumb shit you used to brawl over. A man hurt your woman—a man who never got what he had coming to him—and you wanted to change that. Violence might never be justified, but sometimes it feels a hell of a lot like justice." Bud's eyes met mine. "I take it you're in love with Autumn?"

I nodded. "I was never sure if I was in love before. But now I realize when you are, you damn well know it."

"Do you remember in eighth grade when you got in trouble for cutting some advanced math class they had you in, and the guidance counselor told you to just drop the class because you wouldn't be able to handle the work anyway?"

"Mr. Schultz. Guy had the worst breath."

"Did you drop the class?"

"No, I got a hundred on every test."

"And what did you do with those tests when you got them back?"

"I slid every single one of them under Schultz's door. I wouldn't be able to handle the work, my ass."

"And when you were disappointed that you only beat ninety-nine-point-five percent of all people taking that test you had to take to get into law school, and I suggested maybe you should apply to some other law schools besides Harvard, just to be safe?"

I shrugged. "I retook the LSAT and got a perfect score. Then I got into Harvard."

"Are you sensing a pattern here, son?"

"That I don't listen?"

Bud grinned. "Well, yeah. That's definitely true. But that isn't my point this time. You don't give up when you want something. All your life, you've encountered obstacles, and you've found a way around them all."

"Okay..."

Bud shook his head. "Jesus, sometimes you can be such a knucklehead. You're in love with this girl. You made a mistake. Don't let the mistake make you. Fix it. Find a way around it. Don't sit on your ass and hope it will work itself out."

The entire way back to Manhattan, I kept thinking about what Bud had said. There was a difference between giving Autumn space and sitting on the sidelines. I'd screwed up, and I needed to own it, but I also needed to make sure she knew I wasn't going anywhere, and the way to do that was sure as hell not over text and voicemail. So when I got off the bridge, I turned downtown toward her place instead of uptown toward mine.

By the time I found a parking spot, it was close to nine. I still had no idea if I was doing the right thing, but how much worse could I make it at this point? So I took a deep breath, walked to the door, and hit the buzzer for her apartment.

I knew she had an app where she could see and hear who was at the door before allowing them entrance, so as I stood there and waited to hear the sound of the door lock clanking open, I looked up at the corner and stared at the camera.

Come on, Red. Buzz me in.

A minute passed, and my chest started to feel heavy. She could be sleeping or maybe even out, but she could also be pretending she wasn't home to avoid me. Since I'd come this far, I buzzed a second time, and I looked up at the camera.

"Autumn, I just want to talk. Will you let me up? Or come down if you don't want me inside. I won't stay long, I promise. I just need to say a few things and I'll get out of your hair."

Again I waited. The minutes that ticked by were grueling. At first, I'd decided I'd wait five minutes since I'd asked her to come down, and she might have to wait for the elevator or something. But after five minutes passed, I justified why that might not be long enough.

Maybe she was sleeping and had to get dressed?

Or she needed to go to the bathroom and then get dressed?

Ten.

I'll wait ten minutes. Five was too hasty.

But after six-hundred seconds, I still wasn't ready to give up.

Her elevator is pretty damn slow.

Better make it fifteen.

Yeah, fifteen.

Fifteen turned into twenty, and twenty turned into a half hour. It felt like I had a knot in my throat as I turned to leave. I made it a few steps, then stopped and turned around.

Fuck it. If this was the only way she would listen to me, I needed to take the opportunity. So I hit the buzzer once more and looked up at the camera.

"Autumn, I know you've read my apologies. And I'm sorry for what I did. But I don't know how long this thing records, so I'm going to dive into the things that I haven't said." I raked a hand through my hair, trying to come up with a way to express how I felt. "Ever since I was a kid, I've wanted more than I had—more money, more respect, more clothes, more recognition, more family, just more. Until you walked into my life. Now none of those things seem important. I don't need more money, more recognition, more anything. All I need is you. Looking back, a year ago I thought I knew everything, but the truth is, I had no idea what love was. But I finally figured it out. Love is...enough. None of the other things are important when you find the right person. You're in my heart, Autumn—hell, you *own* my heart. Please don't forget that." Tears welled in my eyes, and I suddenly felt really damn exhausted. I looked up at the camera one last time. "I hope you're okay."

I decided to take a walk to clear my head a little before getting behind the wheel. Two blocks into it, I passed a bar and decided to go in. It was dark and sad inside, so it felt like I'd found the right place. I took a seat at the bar next to an older man, who was hunched over his drink.

He looked over, so I lifted my chin. "Hey."

"Hey, yourself," he grumbled, not very welcoming.

When the bartender came by, I ordered a beer at first. "Actually, I need something stronger."

"What do you want?"

I shook my head. "I don't care. Something strong."

The old guy next to me frowned. "Bourbon—make it two, one for me."

I smiled at the bartender. "Two bourbons, please."

The amber liquid burned going down, though the guy next to me didn't seem to notice. He gulped three fingers back like it was nothing.

"Your generation's soft," he sneered.

I chuckled to myself. He wasn't wrong. About most people, anyway. Though I liked to think I was a little different than most of the people born the same year. I nodded. "It's the trophies."

The old man's face wrinkled. "What's a trophy?"

"You know, metal statues, or these days they're mostly plastic I'm sure. Kids get 'em when they play sports and stuff."

"Oh, a trophy."

"That's what I said."

"I figured there was some new meaning I didn't know about. What's a trophy got to do with why you people are soft?"

"Well, in your generation, there was only one trophy. It went to the winning team. Nowadays, kids get trophies when they finish a season—just for finishing. Even the last-place team gets a trophy."

The old man thought it over and nodded. "That's just stupid."

I finished off the liquid in my glass. The third gulp went down as hard as the first. I shook the ice, rattling it around. "How do you drink this? It tastes terrible and burns going down."

He smiled. "I never had a fucking trophy."

I laughed and lifted my chin to the bartender. "Another round for me and..." I looked to the old man.

"Fred."

I nodded. "Me and Fred."

For the next few hours, I sat next to my new friend and drank too many bourbons. Turned out Fred was down on millennials because he had a grandson about my age who had disinvited him to a party he was having this weekend and wouldn't take his calls. "He wanted me to go to a *gender reveal* party. Who the hell throws a party and has a cake baked to find out the sex of the baby?"

"Actually, a lot of people do that these days."

Fred frowned and shook his head. "Like I said, *soft*."

I smiled and sucked back my third bourbon on the rocks. It was starting to hit me now, which was just fine.

"In my day, men didn't even wait at the hospital to find out what they were having. We just dropped the woman off and went home to get some sleep. If you married a nice girl, she wouldn't call you until the morning to tell you what she'd had, so you'd get your rest."

I laughed. "Pretty sure that wouldn't fly with women today."

He waved me off, grumbling.

A little while later, I stood to go to the bathroom and stumbled. *Shit.* I was drunker than I thought. I went to relieve myself and intended to close out my tab. But when I returned, Fred had bought me a round for a change.

He tilted his glass toward me. "You're not so bad for one of those alphabet kids. I can never remember what ages are for generation X, Y, or Z."

I smiled. "Thanks."

"So why are you sitting in this depressing place trying to outdrink an old pro like me?"

"Woman problems."

Fred held his glass toward me to clink. "Fucking women. Gotta watch out for them. They're dangerous. You know any other animal that can get juice from a nut without cracking it?"

I laughed so hard, I fell off my seat. Fred offered a hand to help me up from the floor. His grip was pretty strong for a guy who had to be pushing eighty.

Once I was standing, I put a hand on his shoulder. "Thanks a lot, buddy. This was just what I needed."

"To fall on the damn floor?"

"Nah. To not be able to stand."

I said I was going to head out, but Fred convinced me to have one more. That last drink totally did me in. I went from happy drunk to feeling pretty miserable about Autumn again. There was no way I was driving home in my condition, so I started toward the train, figuring I'd get my car tomorrow. But at some point, I veered and walked back to Autumn's place.

I had no idea what time it was, but it had to be after midnight when I buzzed.

"Autumn...it's me." I looked up at the camera and pointed to my face. "Please let me in."

When a few minutes went by, and she didn't answer, I went from feeling down to feeling angry. What I should've done was go the hell home. But instead, I buzzed again.

"Autumn, are you going to talk to me?"

No response.

I was hurt and sad and so damn frustrated. So I buzzed again and looked up at the camera. "You know what your problem is? You got a damn trophy. No one has to work hard when you get a damn trophy just for showing up. But life is hard, Autumn." I leaned my head against the door and mumbled. "Life is fucking hard." I shut my eyes, and I think I might've started to fall asleep standing there. After a minute, I forced my eyes open and pushed off the door. I was drunk and emotionally drained and filled with so much pent-up anger that beating that douchebag didn't even begin to take the edge off. My anger was not directed at Autumn, though in my drunken haze, I lashed out at anyone. I held up my middle finger to the camera. "*Fuck everything!*"

35

Donovan

I woke to the shake of a subway car at six in the morning. *Shit.* I lifted my head. Where the hell was I? The woman across from me gave me a dirty look and put her arm around her kid.

"Sorry."

She looked away.

What the hell happened last night? I remembered the partner announcements at the office, and going to visit Bud. But everything after that was a bit blurry.

Oh, wait. I'd gone over to Autumn's place, but she hadn't been home. Then I'd wandered into some bar.

The train pulled into a station. It wasn't mine, but I needed some fresh air, so I hopped off and walked up the stairs about half a mile from my apartment. As I reached the top, a homeless guy was sitting next to the entrance. That jogged my memory some more.

Fred. I'd downed disgusting bourbon with a guy named Fred at the bar for a few hours. Then there was a belligerent stop back at Autumn's apartment, which ended with me giving the finger to the security camera. After that,

329

on my way to the train station, a homeless person had asked me for money. He'd been sitting outside a liquor store, so I went in and bought a bunch of those small bottles they serve on planes and proceeded to take a seat next to the guy. We drank every single one of the bottles together. *No wonder I feel like shit.* I couldn't be sure, but I think I might've cried at one point. *Great.* Just great. You're really pulling your shit together when Autumn needs you, Decker.

On my walk home, I stopped at a deli and picked up some orange juice and Motrin. By the time I made it to my apartment, I was ready to crash for a few hours. I had no idea how long I'd slept on the train, only that it wasn't enough. It felt like I could pass out and not wake up for days. I even leaned against the elevator wall as I rode the car up to my floor.

Happy to be close to crash landing on my bed, I stepped out of the elevator with my head down and my mind in a thick fog. But a few steps down the hall and it felt like someone had put the paddles on my chest and jolted me awake.

Had I fallen asleep in the elevator and I was dreaming?

My stride, which had been lumbering at best, suddenly picked up as I made my way down the hall. And my heart followed right along.

Autumn sat on the floor next to my door looking down at her phone, but she stood once she saw me.

"Hey, sorry for stopping by without calling," she said.

"You never need to call first."

She looked me up and down. My clothes were a wrinkled mess, and I'm sure my face was covered in stubble. "Were you...out all night?"

I nodded. "I went by your place. You weren't home, so I stopped at a bar a few blocks away and had a little too much to drink. I woke up on the subway."

"That doesn't sound like you."

I blew out a deep breath. "Apparently I haven't been acting like myself a lot lately."

Autumn nodded. "I stayed at Skye's last night."

She looked tired, even though she was still absolutely gorgeous. Her green eyes were puffy and had small streaks of red in them, and under her eyes was dark and hollow.

"You okay?" I asked.

"Yeah. Do you think we can talk?"

"Of course." I unlocked my apartment door and opened it for her to walk through first. She went straight to the living room.

I tossed my keys on the adjoining kitchen counter. "You want coffee?"

"I'd love some."

I took the grounds from the cabinet and grabbed the pot to fill with water. But I had to wipe my palms on my pants in order to open the canister because I was such a clammy mess from nerves. Once I pushed the button to start brewing, I told Autumn I'd be right back and went to the bathroom to wash up and brush my teeth before returning to fill two mugs.

"Here you go."

She'd sat on the chair, not the couch, which I overanalyzed in my head as a bad sign. In law, the seat a client or attorney selects often tells you a lot about the person or their power position. Autumn sitting to keep distance between us troubled me.

We were both silent as I sat. She stared down at the floor, while I watched her intently. Eventually, I couldn't take it and spoke. "Are you sleeping? You look tired."

Her eyes lifted to meet mine. "Off and on. I stopped taking the Ambien completely a few days ago. I looked it up, and insomnia is common after you stop. My body is basically going through withdrawal after years of use."

"You slept pretty good the night I stayed over and you forgot to take it."

She smiled sadly. "I think that was because you were in my bed."

I smiled back. "Well, if I can be of any assistance... Sleep is important, you know."

Her smile was more genuine this time. She sipped her coffee and set it down on the table. "I want to tell you some things about what happened six years ago. I told you the parts I thought you needed to know, but I wasn't exactly open about how I handled things afterward."

My brows furrowed. "Okay..."

She took a deep breath. "I didn't actually go to the police two weeks after Braden raped me. I mean, I did speak to them, but it didn't happen the way I might've led you to believe. They actually came to me." Autumn looked up and met my eyes. The pain swimming in hers caused a stabbing pain in my chest. "They came because I'd attempted suicide. My father found me unconscious and called 9-1-1. After they got the drug out of my system and my vitals stable, a policewoman coaxed me into telling her what happened."

I tasted salt in my throat and swallowed. Reaching out, I took her hand and squeezed and didn't let go.

She tried to force a smile before continuing. "I'd gone to my regular doctor and told her I had trouble sleeping, and she gave me a prescription for Ambien. I'd researched that it would take a lot of pills to overdose—more than I had, unless I chewed them and forced them into my bloodstream all at once." She took another deep breath. "So I put the contents of the bottle into my Magic Bullet and then snorted the powder." She laughed, but not in a funny way. "I'd never done cocaine in my life. My first white lines were Ambien."

Jesus Christ. I just wanted to wrap her in my arms and hold her, but her body language told me that was not the right thing to do. I also suspected this revelation wasn't the only thing she wanted to share...

I shook my head. "It doesn't matter how you reported it. What matters is that you're healthy and you made it through."

"I thought I'd made it through, too. I was honestly beginning to feel like I was moving on and the past was behind me. But it wasn't. A few days after we ran into Braden, I started to spiral again. That animal was walking around like nothing had happened, and here I was unable to sleep and eat again, and you'd been arrested. I felt really low. One night I took the bottle of Ambien into my hand and sat with it for an hour, staring at it." Autumn looked down. "I never really contemplated taking them again, but it hit me that I had a lot to deal with. Not fully dealing with things last time had only made things worse. I needed to get myself in the right headspace. I didn't want to wind up in a bad place again. So I went to my therapist a few times. We talked a lot about closure, and then..." She took another deep breath and looked into my eyes. "I went to see Braden."

When my eyes grew wide, she shook her head and her hands.

"No—don't panic. I went to see him in his very full office and made him leave the door open. I was always safe."

While I was relieved, I still couldn't breathe very well. "What happened?"

"He was snide and thought I was wearing a wire trying to record him admitting to something—pretty much what I expected. But I didn't go there to get anything from him. I went for myself, because I needed to say some things

333

to him." She shook her head. "I don't even remember everything I said, but I wanted him to know he'd ruined many years of my life and made me not trust anyone or myself, how much damage he had done—not that I think he cares. But I needed to look him in the eyes and call him a rapist." She smiled. "I also told him to rot in hell, which, surprisingly, felt more cathartic than the rest of the stuff I said."

I smiled. She'd been carrying the weight of other people's choices on her shoulders for too long, and I was damn proud of her for unloading it. "Good for you."

"His face was a mess. You fucked him up good." The corners of her lips twitched up, but she quickly looked down again. "I hate violence. Not only because of what happened to me, but also because of all the kids I work with. It never solves anything. It just makes new problems."

"I know. And I made a shitload of new ones. I'm sorry, Autumn. I really am."

She leaned closer and lowered her voice. "Can I tell you another secret?"

I nodded. "Of course."

"I'm not that sorry, so you shouldn't be either."

My heart leaped, but I was still afraid to get my hopes up. "Really?"

She nodded. This time, it was her who squeezed my hand. "I'm sorry I pushed you away. I just needed some time to work through things. Actually, that sounds like I'm saying I've finished working through them. I'm sure I haven't, but I think I've finally started. I can't promise you that getting closer won't scare me, or that I won't do something stupid like run away again. But if you'll have me, I'd like to try."

"*If* I'll have you?" I reached over and yanked her out of her seat and onto my lap. "Sweetheart, just try to get rid of me."

She smiled. "Did you mean what you said in your voicemail?"

"What did I say?"

Autumn bit down on her lip. "That you love me."

"Would it freak you out if I did?"

"No." She leaned closer so we were nose to nose. "You know why?"

"Why?"

"Because I love you, too."

The biggest, dumbest smile took over my face. "I fucking love you."

She giggled. "Fucking love, huh? Is that equivalent to a lot?"

I took her cheeks into my hands and smashed my lips with hers. When we came up for air, I smiled. "Totally enough."

Her brows dipped. "Enough? You don't want more kisses?"

I grinned. "Oh no, I want more kisses. Does your doorbell, by chance, keep the videos it records when someone rings it?"

She nodded. "For a month or until I delete them, why?"

"You can watch it later and figure out what I meant by enough."

I went to kiss her again, and then it hit me that I hadn't just professed my love to her on that doorbell video and told her she was enough. I'd come back drunk and belligerent. *Shit.* "Actually, can I borrow your phone a second? I need to see that app..."

⸻

That afternoon I'd run out to get us some dinner and made an unexpected pit stop. I'd texted Autumn so she wouldn't worry when I was gone longer than the fifteen minutes it should've taken me to grab Chinese food two blocks over.

"I was getting concerned." Autumn looked up from her laptop when I finally returned. She was sitting bare legged with her feet up on the couch. "You've been gone almost two and a half hours."

I set the takeout bag on the kitchen counter and walked over to kiss her. "Sorry."

She closed her laptop. "I thought talking to plants was an old wives' tale. It's an actual thing."

I smiled. "Deep dive on talking to plants while I was gone?"

She shrugged. "I thought you were making it up."

I walked back to the kitchen and unpacked the cardboard containers of food. "Nope. But I admit, when Bud first told me he talked to them, I thought he was nuts. I looked it up myself."

Autumn came into the kitchen. She took a seat at the island across from me. "I watched an entire episode of *Mythbusters* about it. They set up a bunch of greenhouses next to each other. The silent greenhouses actually showed the least amount of plant growth."

"Oh yeah?"

She nodded and took an eggroll out of a bag. "I'm starving."

I laughed. "I could tell. You didn't even wait for me to get plates or utensils."

She grinned and covered her mouth. "Sorry."

"I'm teasing. Let's just eat out of the cartons and share."

"Okay." She finished chewing and extended the eggroll to me. "So what took you so long, anyway?"

I shrugged. "Had to get something fixed."

Her brows drew together. "Vague much? And take a bite and give me back that eggroll."

"Wow, you're bossy when you're hungry."

She held out her hand. "Bite or give it back."

I took a bite and handed it off.

"What did you get fixed?"

I pointed to my left arm. "A tattoo."

She laughed. "You're kidding, right?"

I pushed up my sleeve and showed her the bandage. A piece of gauze was stretched over the area, followed by a clear plastic covering. "Nope."

"You just randomly decided to get a tattoo fixed on the way to pick up our Chinese food? What tattoo?"

"The bird."

"The one in the cage that you got when you were sixteen? I love that one. It was so meaningful, and I could relate to what you were feeling at the time you got it."

"I could, too. But things change."

"I don't understand."

I slowly peeled the plastic back from my forearm, then lifted the gauze. The original tattoo was a single, small, black bird alone in its cage. Jimmy at Dark Ink had done a few of my tattoos over the years, so I knew what I wanted would be an easy fix. He'd modified one of the bars and turned it into a door, and now the cage was open. I'd also had him add a second bird just outside the door.

"It's in color!" Autumn smiled. "I thought you said you didn't think anything was important enough to put in color."

"It wasn't. Until now."

"Wow. Well, it's beautiful. Before it was so lonely, one bird locked in a cage. But now it almost looks like the little red bird is leading the other one out."

I smiled. "She is."

"She? The red bird is a she?"

I nodded. "She's you, Red."

I watched Autumn's face as she stared down at my arm. She'd been smiling and teasing, and her face suddenly fell. I wondered if maybe it was too soon and I'd freaked her out. When her eyes filled with tears, I thought I might've really fucked up. But then she got up and walked around the counter.

Autumn leaned down and kissed just above the top of the bandage that was still partially in place. "I love it." She looked into my eyes. "And I love you, Donovan."

My head dropped as I let out a loud rush of air. "Jesus. Thank God. I thought I'd upset you."

"Upset me? God, no." She placed her hand over her heart. "I just got a little overwhelmed with emotion, that's all. I love it, and I love what it represents to you, though I think you have it backwards, Donovan. You're the red bird who helped open my cage and set me free, not the other way around."

I leaned my forehead against hers. "This was meant to be, Red. You know what else I realized earlier?"

"What?"

"You have to sign a release form when you get a tattoo—at least in the legal places I go to now. I had no idea what the date was, so I asked the guy behind the desk. Today is September thirtieth. It was one year ago today that you stole my luggage."

"Really?"

I nodded.

"Are you sure? I know the bachelorette party was after Labor Day, but I don't remember exactly when."

"I checked the date on the picture I took of you. It was the morning after we'd stayed up all night. The date was October first."

"Wow. So a year ago today. That seems like a lifetime ago." She smirked and wrapped her arms around my neck. "You've been crushing on me a long time, then."

I smiled. "Damn straight. You might've disappeared on me, but I couldn't stop thinking about you. For a long time I couldn't understand why that was. But it all makes sense now. I couldn't let you go, because I wasn't supposed to. We were meant to be."

EPILOGUE

Autumn

One year later

We arrived at the restaurant a few minutes early. Donovan had driven us, even though we typically walked or took the subway to a place this close. But the sky-high heels I had on for our celebratory dinner weren't exactly concrete friendly.

"Hi," I said to the host. "We have a reservation for six people at eight."

"Last name, please."

"It's probably under Decker."

Donovan walked up as I waited. He wrapped a hand around my waist and leaned to kiss my bare shoulder.

"I'm sorry." The maître d' shook his head. "I don't see a reservation under Decker for eight PM."

I looked over at Donovan. "It was for eight o'clock, right?"

"It's under your name." He winked at me before speaking to the maître d'. "The reservation is under Wilde. *Doctor* Wilde."

The man scanned his book again. "Ah yes, here we are. Dr. Autumn Wilde."

340

I rolled my eyes at Donovan, but I also hadn't been able to get the smile off my face since they'd called *Dr. Autumn Wilde* at the graduation ceremony earlier today.

Donovan whispered in my ear. "I can't wait to get home later. I've never fucked a doctor before. And those heels stay on when I rip that dress off of you, doc."

Just like that fateful day we'd met at a coffee shop to exchange luggage two years ago now, butterflies fluttered in my stomach. Things never dulled with this man, and certainly not over the last twelve months. So much had happened, but all of it had made us stronger.

In the weeks that passed after I'd gone to see Braden, I couldn't stop thinking about the face he'd made when I'd mentioned praying for his other victims. The countless hours I'd spent torturing myself by watching videos of us after he'd attacked me had finally paid off. I knew in that moment that I hadn't been the only one he'd hurt. At first, I'd just let it niggle at me. After all, I was trying to lay that part of my life to rest and move on. But eventually I realized that was impossible. If there were others, there might be more in the future, and I couldn't live with myself if I didn't try to stop that from happening. So I asked Donovan what I could do, and that started a chain of events that would forever change our lives.

Donovan asked a private investigator he used on a lot of his cases at work to poke around in Braden's relationships that had come after me over the years. That's how we came to know about Sarina Emmitt, a woman Braden had dated for a year after me. The investigator had spoken to one of Sarina's previous coworkers and found out that two weeks before she abruptly quit and moved back home to Ohio, she'd shown up to work on a Monday morning with a black eye and told people she'd been mugged. Her friend had wondered if that was actually true, because she'd seemed really rattled, and some of the details of her story didn't quite add up. The investigator checked the story with the police and found no mugging ever reported. So I took a chance and booked a trip to Ohio.

At first, Sarina vehemently denied that anything had happened to her. But I shared my story with her and knew from her face that she was lying. I was disappointed, but I didn't want to push a victim. So I'd left her my cell phone number and flown home the next day. Twenty-three days later, she called. She hadn't been able to sleep since I left and was ready to tell her story. That call changed everything. Unlike me, Sarina had evidence. She'd had a Ring doorbell, the kind that took video of everyone coming and going, and she'd saved the footage from the night Braden attacked her—video that included her answering the door without a black eye, and Braden leaving an hour later with scratch marks all over his face. She even had an image of her walking out the next morning with a black eye, though no one else had entered. Sarina had tried to fight Braden off and lost. She'd been in shock and devastated, but somehow, she'd had the wherewithal to keep her torn clothes, too.

Hand in hand, Sarina and I went to the police together. Braden was arrested three weeks later and charged with two counts of first-degree forcible rape. And unfortunately, while that may have further justified Donovan's actions, his assault case continued moving forward—until Cara, Braden's now ex-fiancée, came forward to tell the police Braden had actually started the fight, and Donovan was only defending himself. Apparently, she'd had a flicker of doubt about her fiancé since she'd seen my face that day. And after hearing Sarina's story, she couldn't deny the truth anymore. We'd been good friends in elementary school, and she wanted to help me, which in her mind meant telling a little white lie.

I don't actually think the prosecutor believed her, but it had given them a reason to drop the charges against Donovan.

"Right this way, please," the maître d' said.

"I wonder if the others are here yet," I mused.

"Guess we'll find out," Donovan said.

We followed the maître d' through the lobby and into a long hallway. I'd been to Tavern on the Green a few times before, but I'd always been seated in the main dining room. We turned left and then right, and at the end of that hall was a set of double doors.

Rather than opening them, the maître d' stopped and smiled at Donovan. "I'll let you seat Dr. Wilde."

"Thank you."

My forehead wrinkled as he walked away. "He's letting us pick any table we want?"

Donovan brushed a lock of hair behind my ear. "I guess you can say that. Before we go inside, I just want to say one more time how proud I am of you. Not just for graduating, but also for everything you've gone through over the last year. I know it wasn't easy."

"I couldn't have done it without you."

Donovan smiled. "That's nice of you to say, but total bullshit. You can do anything. I'm just lucky to be along for the ride, Red." He brushed his lips against mine before holding out his elbow to me. "You ready to celebrate, Dr. Wilde?"

I laughed and took his arm. "You're acting weird, but yes, I'm ready."

Donovan opened the double doors, and we walked inside. Skye and her boyfriend, and my dad and his new girlfriend (Yes, he got divorced *again*.) were already seated.

"Hey, guys!"

Skye stood. "I hope you don't think I'm paying you to listen to my shit now that you're a big, fancy doctor."

I laughed. "Never."

We hugged. But as I went to say hello to her boyfriend, I noticed a familiar face over Skye's shoulder. My eyes widened. "Oh my God. Is that Storm?"

He smiled. He looked adorable in a shirt and tie. But who was he here with? I scanned the table and got even more confused. Half the staff I worked with at Park House was here, too. I glanced over at Donovan, and he leaned in.

"I wouldn't let them yell surprise because I didn't want to scare the shit out of you," he whispered. "But keep looking..."

I scanned the room, and there had to be a hundred people—friends of mine, friends of Donovan's, people from my work and school, Bud and his lady friend, Donovan's new partners Juliette and Trent (They'd all left Kravitz, Polk and Hastings three months ago and started their own firm together.), and Trent's new fiancée, Margo, was smiling, too.

I clutched my chest and turned to Donovan. "Oh my God. You did all this for me? How did you even contact everyone?"

"I had a lot of help from Storm and Skye. You deserved a graduation party."

"This is crazy. But thank you so much!" I threw my arms around his neck and crushed my lips to his. "I love you."

"Right back atcha, Red."

I rubbed my nose with Donovan's. "Did you know some of the topiary Edward trimmed in *Edward Scissorhands* used to be on display here before the restaurant closed for a few years?"

Donovan laughed and kissed my forehead. "You're just a plethora of useless information, Dr. Wilde. It's one of the things I love about you."

For the next half hour, I made my way around the room to greet people. Donovan stayed dutifully by my side, only disappearing occasionally to refill my wine glass. And people were handing me presents! I was completely overwhelmed. By the time we'd visited the last table, both our hands were full again. There was a long buffet table off to one side of the room where we'd been piling up gift bags and boxes. We walked over and set the last batch down, and I looked around one more time.

"I still can't believe you did all this. And all of these people came to celebrate with me." I pointed to the gifts and shook my head. "All of these are just over the top."

Donovan wrapped his arms around my waist. "Well, I still didn't give you my present."

"You mean there's more than just a giant party at a fancy restaurant in the middle of Central Park? Pretty sure you can't top all of this."

Donovan smirked. "You know I love a challenge." He kissed my forehead. "Stay right here for a minute."

I watched as he walked over to Skye and came back with two glasses of champagne. Handing one to me, I thought we were going to have a quiet little celebration drink. But instead, he cleared his throat and yelled, "Can I have everyone's attention, please?"

The room had been rumbling with voices but settled down.

"Thank you." He smiled. "I just wanted to make a toast, and then I promise I'll let you all eat."

"Talk fast," Storm yelled, and everyone laughed.

"First off, I want to thank you all for coming to help celebrate Dr. Wilde's big day. Anyone who is in this room knows how passionate she is about helping people." He pointed at Storm. "Even the ones who are a pain in the ass."

Everyone laughed.

"A minute ago, Autumn told me she was overwhelmed by all this." He motioned to the present table. "And I reminded her that I hadn't given her my present yet. She told me it would be hard to top this perfect night, but you know me—I'm nothing if not an overachiever."

Donovan set his champagne glass on the gift table, and everything began to play out in slow motion. He got down on one knee and took my hand. His was cold and clammy, and when I looked down, I could see how nervous he was. It made the moment that much more surreal, because my arrogant man had nerves of steel.

Donovan lifted my hand to his mouth and kissed my knuckles. "Autumn Renee Wilde, two years ago you walked into my life and knocked me on my ass. I thought I had everything I wanted, but you very quickly showed me I didn't even know what I was missing yet. You're the toughest person I've ever met, yet somehow you also manage to be the kindest. Before I met you, I lived for the next challenge at work. But now, the only challenge that seems important is being the man you deserve."

Donovan paused and looked down. When his eyes met mine again, they were brimming with tears. "Red, I was so damn proud watching you walk across that stage today. The only thing that could possibly make me any prouder would be to tell people Dr. Wilde is my wife." He reached into his pocket, pulled out a ring box, and opened it. The most gorgeous princess-cut stone sparkled from inside. "Marry me, Autumn...please?"

I practically knocked Donovan over as I crashed into him, wrapping my arms around his neck. "Yes! Yes! Of course I'll marry you."

He gripped me in a bear hug and stood, lifting me off the floor as he crushed his lips to mine.

The entire room broke out in applause, cheers, and whistles.

I couldn't stop smiling as our kiss broke. "Well, you did it. Just like you said, your present topped everything."

"Sweetheart, that wasn't the present I was referring to." He winked. "I'll give you that one when we get home later."

ACKNOWLEDGEMENTS

To you—the *readers*. Thank you so much for your enthusiasm and loyalty. I hope Donovan and Stella's story allowed you to escape for a short while, and you'll come back soon to see who you might meet next!

To Penelope – Writing is a lot like riding a rollercoaster— it's so much better when you have a friend sitting next to you who reminds you to throw your hands up and enjoy the ride. Thank you for always buckling in with me.

To Cheri – Thank you for your friendship and support. I'm ready for more road adventures!

To Julie – Thank you for your friendship and wisdom.

To Luna –The first person I chat with most mornings. So much has changed over the years, but I can always count on your friendship and encouragement. Thank you for always being there.

To my amazing Facebook reader group, Vi's Violets – 22,000 smart women who love to talk books together in one place? I'm one lucky girl! Each and every one of you is a gift. Thank you for being part of this crazy journey.

To Sommer –Thank you for figuring out what I want, often before I do.

To my agent and friend, Kimberly Brower – Thank you for being there always. Every year brings a unique opportunity from you. I can't wait to see what you dream up next!

To Jessica, Elaine, and Julia – Thank you for smoothing out the all the rough edges and making me shine!

To Kylie and Jo at Give Me Books – I don't even remember how I managed before you, and I hope I never have to figure it out! Thank you for everything you do.

To all of the bloggers – Thank you for inspiring readers to take a chance on me. Without you, there would be no them.

Much love
Vi

OTHER BOOKS BY VI KEELAND

OTHER BOOKS BY VI KEELAND & PENELOPE WARD

ABOUT VI KEELAND

Vi Keeland is a #1 *New York Times*, #1 *Wall Street Journal*, and *USA Today* Bestselling author. With millions of books sold, her titles have appeared in over a hundred Bestseller lists and are currently translated in twenty-five languages. She resides in New York with her husband and their three children where she is living out her own happily ever after with the boy she met at age six.

CPSIA information can be obtained
at www.ICGtesting.com
Printed in the USA
BVHW031653310721
613344BV00008B/29

9 781951 045500